'**Brilliantly entertaining**. In Matthew Carrey, Ben Kane has created a wonderfully flawed but human hero, a man who, often unwittingly and many times entirely through his own errors of judgement, finds himself caught up in one desperate escapade after another, and which, like the very best historical adventures, see him cross seas and travel continents and, along the way, meet an array of acutely observed characters from villains to femme fatales and to Napoleon himself. Ben Kane's **attention to historical detail is also second-to-none** – in *Napoleon's Spy* he had brought Napoleon's calamitous Russian campaign vividly and compelling to life in **one of the most enjoyable and compelling historical romps** I've read in a very long time'

James Holland, historian, writer and broadcaster

'*Napoleon's Spy* is a **tour de force on an epic scale** that immerses the reader in the scent of cannon smoke and the whistle of grape shot. You can almost taste the fear. The 1812 campaign is a story of immense sacrifice, enormous courage and a man who never knew when to take a step back until it was too late for those who revered him. **Ben Kane is one of our finest historical novelists** and his passion for his subject shines through on every page'

Douglas Jackson, author of *Hero of Rome*

'As soon as I read the first few pages of a Ben Kane novel, I'm all in. It was no different with *Napoleon's Spy*. **Kane's historical detail is as intriguing and fascinating as his characters are compelling. His prose is lively, economical and intimate**, so that this story reads like a first hand account, but with the Kane master storyteller treatment. In fact, *Napoleon's Spy* is an exemplar of a Ben Kane novel; exciting, **immersive, well researched and great fun**. The author's very name has long been a seal of quality, and here he is at the top of his (or anybody's) game. What I love about this book, and his others too, is that it feels nostalgic. It reminds me of those classic, epic Hollywood movies of the 1950s and 1960s, which fired my imagination as a child and, in many ways, shaped me. **We have a flawed hero on a mission, thwarted by colourful villains and beset by every danger, all set against an epic backdrop of nation-defining war. What's not to love? Bravo, Ben Kane, you've done it again**'

Giles Kristian, author of *Lancelot*

'With intrigue, espionage and duels, this is a great adventure story set against the epic background of Napoleon's doomed invasion of Russia'

Adrian Goldsworthy, bestselling historian

'Ben Kane pivots from ancient Rome and medieval England to the Napoleonic Wars, and **delivers up a rip-roaring tale full of both swashbuckling and pathos**. Half-English, half-French Matthieu Carrey battles a weakness for cards and wine which frequently lands him in hot water, finding himself strong-armed into the reluctant position of Imperial messenger for Napoleon and clandestine spy for the English. Matthieu makes an **appealingly flawed hero**, fighting not only illicit duels and Cossack lances on the Grand Armee's campaign through Russia, but his own worst impulses. **It looks like the adventures of *Napoleon's Spy* may continue for future books - I for one will be first in line!**'

Kate Quinn, author of *Blood Sisters*

'**An epic tale** that never loses sight of the raw experience of the hero. **I loved *Napoleon's Spy***'

Simon Scarrow, author of the *Eagles of the Empire* series

'The first half of *Napoleon's Spy* is fun – a picturesque tale of duels, love affairs and gambling dens. The second is a searing, vivid account of Napoleon's terrible retreat from Moscow'

Antonia Senior, *The Times*

'Richard the Lionheart's name echoes down the centuries as one of history's greatest warriors, and **this book will immortalise him** even more. **A rip-roaring epic**, filled with arrows and spattered with blood. **Gird yourself with mail when you start**'

Paul Finch, author of *Strangers*

'Kane's virtues as a writer of historical adventures – **lively prose, thorough research, colourful action** – are again apparent'

Nick Rennison, *The Sunday Times*

'*Lionheart* has plenty of **betrayal, bloodshed and rich historical detail**'

Martin Chilton, *Independent*

'Plenty of **action, blood, scheming, hatred, stealth and politics** here, if that's what you want in your read – **and you know it is!**'

Sunday Sport

'To read one of Ben Kane's **astonishingly well-researched**, bestselling novels is to know that you are, historically speaking, in safe hands'

Elizabeth Buchan, *Daily Mail*

'This is a **stunningly visual and powerful** read: Kane's power of description is **second to none** . . . Perfect for anyone who is suffering from *Game of Thrones* withdrawal symptoms'

Helena Gumley-Mason, *The Lady*

'**Fans of battle-heavy historical fiction will, justly, adore *Clash of Empires*.** With its rounded historical characters and **fascinating** historical setting, it deserves a wider audience'

Antonia Senior, *The Times*

'**Grabs you from the start and never lets go.** Thrilling action combines with historical authenticity to summon up a whole world in a sweeping tale of politics and war. **A triumph!**'

Harry Sidebottom, author of the *The Last Hour*

BEN KANE is one of the most hard-working and successful historical writers in the industry. His third book, *The Road to Rome*, was a *Sunday Times* number four bestseller, and almost every title since has been a top ten bestseller. Born in Kenya, Kane moved to Ireland at the age of seven. After qualifying as a veterinarian, he worked in small animal practice and during the terrible Foot and Mouth Disease outbreak in 2001. Despite his veterinary career, he retained a deep love of history; this led him to begin writing.

His first novel, *The Forgotten Legion*, was published in 2008; since then he has written five series of Roman novels, a trilogy about Richard the Lionheart, and a collection of short stories. Kane lives in Somerset with his two children.

Also by Ben Kane

The Forgotten Legion Chronicles
The Forgotten Legion
The Silver Eagle
The Road to Rome

Hannibal
Enemy of Rome
Fields of Blood
Clouds of War

Eagles of Rome
Eagles at War
Hunting the Eagles
Eagles in the Storm

Clash of Empires
Clash of Empires
The Falling Sword

Spartacus
The Gladiator
Rebellion

Lionheart
Lionheart
Crusader
King

Short Story Collections
Sands of the Arena

NAPOLEON'S
SPY

BEN KANE

ORION

First published in Great Britain in 2023 by Orion Fiction,
This paperback edition published in 2024 by Orion Fiction
an imprint of The Orion Publishing Group Ltd,
Carmelite House, 50 Victoria Embankment
London EC4Y 0DZ

An Hachette UK company

1 3 5 7 9 10 8 6 4 2

A CIP catalogue record for this book
is available from the British Library.

ISBN (Paperback) 978 1 4091 9791 1
ISBN (eBook) 978 1 4091 9792 8

Typeset by Input Data Services Ltd, Bridgwater, Somerset

Printed and bound in Great Britain by Clays Ltd, Elcograf S.p.A.

MIX
Paper from
responsible sources
FSC® C104740

www.orionbooks.co.uk

For Stephen, most loyal of brothers

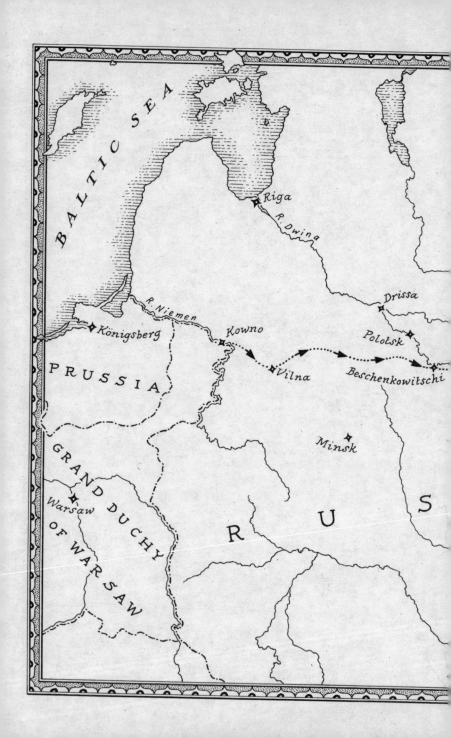

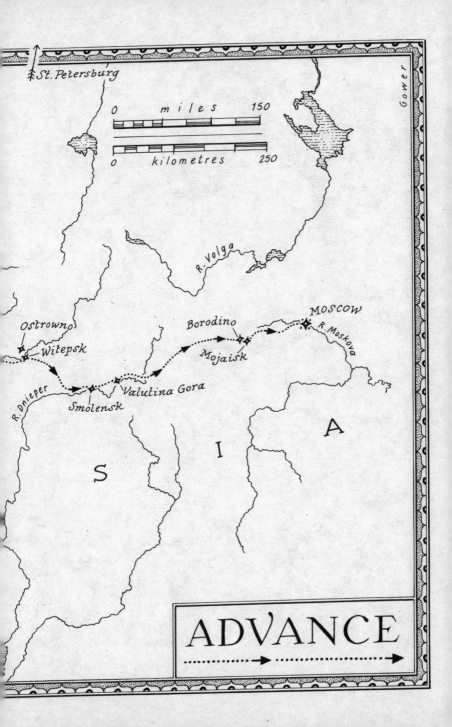

St. Petersburg

Gower

0   m i l e s   150

0   k i l o m e t r e s   250

R. Volga

Ostrowno

Borodino

MOSCOW

R. Moskova

Witepsk

Mojaïsk

R. Dnieper

Valutina Gora

Smolensk

S   I   A

ADVANCE

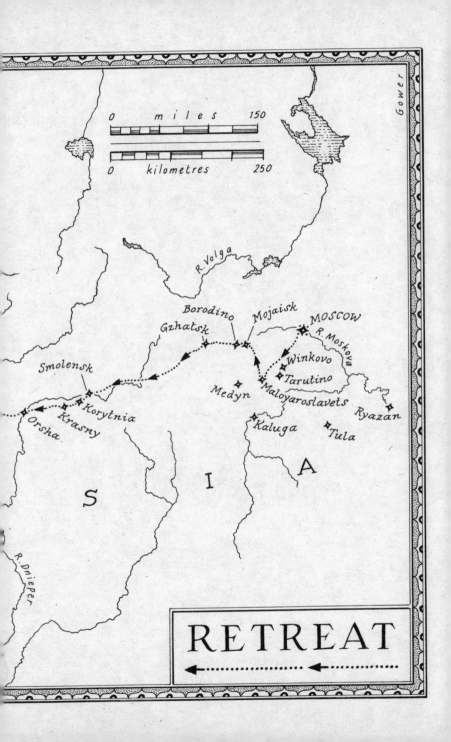

Gower

0   m i l e s   150

0   kilometres   250

R. Volga

Borodino   Mojaisk   MOSCOW

Gzhatsk   *R. Moskova*

Smolensk   Winkovo

Tarutino

Korytnia   Medyn   Maloyaroslavets

Krasny   Ryazan

Orsha   Kaluga   Tula

S   I   A

R. Dnieper

RETREAT

It is a little odd to put an historical note at the start of a novel, but I felt moved to do so with *Napoleon's Spy*. The simple reason is the number of duels fought by the hero, Mathieu Carrey. From the moment I wrote his third or fourth clash with the same opponent, I could see the emails of complaint, the negative Amazon reviews. *No one would fight that many duels, over literally nothing,* they read.

Oh yes, they would.

Duelling was nothing more than a massive exercise in (almost exclusively) male ego. It will come as no surprise that many duels were associated with the consumption of alcohol, or that men often tended to call each other out over perceived insults to women. Duels also came about for even more farcical reasons. Examples include a disagreement over the interpretation of the translation of a Greek word, and two British army officers who duelled after their dogs had got into a fight.

And the historical basis for Carrey's duelling?

Pierre Dupont de l'Étang and François Fournier-Sarlovèze, two officers in Napoleon's Grande Armée, are recorded as having fought more than thirty (30!) duels over a nineteen-year period from 1794. Joseph Conrad wrote about them in his short story *The Duel*; Ridley Scott used that tale as a basis for his first film, *The Duellists*. I recommend both.

CHAPTER I

From the west came the plaintive *weoo* of a curlew. A faint breeze rippled the dew-laden grass around me. I pulled my woollen cloak tighter and settled down into the sand. Atop a seaward-facing dune, my attention was fixed, as it had been since my arrival two hours before, on the water. There was insufficient light to discern any craft, but the flash from a tinder box – the signal I expected – would be visible. My ears were pricked; sound carried long distances. In my current line of business, avoiding the attention of revenue or naval vessels had a strong link to my chances of discovery or capture.

I heard the Frenchies muttering to each other. Instantly anxious – a far greater danger than His Majesty's navy was the local militia, hunting escaped prisoners of war – I twisted around and whispered, '*Calmez! Le bateau arrive bientôt.*'

Reassured that the boat would come soon, they settled.

My conscience needled me. Rather than slumber peacefully in my blankets like most, here I was, engineering the escape of some of Napoleon's soldiers: enemies of Britain. I was a traitor, I told myself. At once the rebellious part of my character – that is to say, the French part – bridled. Britain might have been at war with France for most of the previous nineteen years, but I wanted no part of it.

My inner conflict was familiar. Born to an English mother and French father, my whole life had been spent not quite knowing who or what I was. Like many Royalists, my father had fled France not long after the Revolution. He had met and married my mother in Kent, where I had been raised. I spoke English like a local, and my surname, Carrey, did not scream 'Frenchman' either. That helped somewhat, but for reasons I could not explain, and quite unlike my brother and sister, I had never felt at home in England.

Bitterness tugged at me. Shame gnawed my insides. Lacking my usual daily cushion against these feelings – copious quantities of wine – and with time on my hands, I was unable to stop my mind from picking at the detail. I quickly reached a damning conclusion. Not feeling wholly English was not reasonable grounds to commit treason. It was my own fault that I was in this predicament.

I squirmed mentally, but I could not avoid the bald, ugly truth.

My love of gambling had brought me to this.

Keen to unhook myself from my own barb, I thought of the charismatic Frenchman I had met five days since. He had a lot to do with my being here. But for him, I might still have been in the gutter in London. Credit exhausted, unable to make even a small payment towards the debts I had run up at my favoured betting salon, I had been roughed up by the owner's hired thugs. Unwilling to fight back because of what I had done to my brother years before, I had simply taken the beating.

Cowed, bruised, drunk, I had lain there for an hour or more before the Frenchman came to my aid. He had helped me up, and taken me to a nearby tavern, where he had seen to my cuts and bruises. Half won over by this unexpected kindness, I had gratefully accepted his offer of 'a sup of wine'. As I drank, he made polite conversation. He was an émigré, living with his family in London these past twenty years. His children were grown, two daughters married and with children of their own, one son, the youngest, working with him in the family company. He was in the cloth trade, the Frenchman said, and was on his way home when he had chanced upon me.

Taken in by his apparent candour, tongue loosened by the drink, I had laid out my own life story. How I had been well educated, and reaching manhood, brought like my brother into my father's importing business, where I had thought to die of boredom. How I had discovered wine, and then card games, dice and horse racing. Beginner's luck had seen me win large amounts – at least at first. My luck had turned, naturally, and I had taken to 'borrowing' funds from the family business's safe. 'I would have paid it back,' I had told the Frenchman, almost convinced I was telling the truth.

'Bien sûr,' he had murmured, refilling my cup. 'What happened after that?'

'My father paid my debts, and threw me onto the street,' I said, my shame too great to admit the tragic truth of it. My crime revealed when it came time for the end-of-year accounts, I had endured the humiliation of my father's disappointment and then that of his easily granted forgiveness. He had written off the monies I had taken from the business, and honoured my debts in full. All I had had to do in exchange was hang my head and promise never to gamble again as long as I lived.

I did not admit that less than a week had gone by before I fell back into my old ways. Nor did I relate how, arrogant, sure of my father's love, I had made no attempt to see if I was being followed. I remembered my welcome back into the salon, the toothy smiles and fresh credit. To the Frenchman, I mentioned only a pleasant, wine-fuelled evening losing money, and how when I emerged, late on in the day, my father had been waiting.

Mortally fuddled as I was that night with the Frenchman, even I had been unable to miss the whine in my voice as I complained about being disowned. Was it any surprise, I continued, that I had fallen further into debt? And as for the rates of interest charged on my debts, they were extortionate. A man had no chance of making good; it was one step forward and three back.

The Frenchman had nodded and smiled, and commiserated. He no longer spoke of himself, and selfish fool that I was, I had barely noticed. The wine continued to flow, and I, thirsting like a man deprived of it for a year, had thrown back glass after glass. Hours later, my new friend's mention of French prisoners of war, and the vast sums to be made in helping them escape, seemed not just acceptable, but appealing.

The next day, head pounding, body aching, it had been easy to let his generous offer keep my freshly sprung reservations at bay. Twenty pounds per man – with eight Frenchies requiring a boat right now – would provide me with a princely sum, and more than half what I owed. The landlord of the Shoreditch garret I rented and the salon's heavies would be placated for a time.

Already greedy, envisaging clearing my debts, I had nonetheless taken the Frenchman's assertion of plentiful work with a pinch of salt. Since my journey to Deal to find a boat, however, my opinion had changed. All the locals, it seemed, were either prepared to transport

Frenchies over the Channel, or knew someone who was. Plenty of Englishmen took French gold and thought nothing of it. George Dowall, the ferryman whom I had engaged for tonight, winked and told me he had been at it for years. His casualness had eased the slight qualms I had felt at dealing with men who were regarded by most people as enemies.

I then travelled from Deal to Burntwick Island in the Thames Estuary, where I was to meet the Frenchies. Separated from the shore by mud flats, it was home to a local brandy-smuggling gang, and where escapees from the prison hulks gathered. The Frenchman's intelligence had been accurate; I found eight of his countrymen in a hovel rented from the smugglers. Journeying by night, hiding in hedgerows by day, I had led them the forty-plus miles to the east Kent coast without incident. By the time we reached Deal, I had grown confident, even cocky.

Feeling as if my charges had already made it back to France, and I the proud recipient of one hundred and sixty pounds, I stared out to sea. Miles to the east, where the flat calm water met the sky, there was a suggestion of brightness. I felt a prickle of unease. The cursed guinea boat should have been here by now. It was one thing to make some of the crossing in the daytime, quite another to embark in broad daylight, when anyone could spy us out. The nearest Martello tower was many miles away, but that did not mean it was safe. The primary duty of the local militia, the East Kents, was the defence of the local coastline. No doubt catching escaped Frenchies came a close second.

I thought of my childhood friend William Noble. When I had set off for London and the family business at the age of seventeen, he had joined the East Kents. We had seen each other but rarely since, and for more reasons than our geographical separation. There had been a quarrel over a girl. I shoved away that memory, determined not to dwell on the past. As far as I knew, William was still in the militia. I hoped he was nowhere nearby.

My attention returned to my current predicament. If the guinea boat did not arrive soon, I would have to lead the Frenchies back to the barn where they had spent the previous night and day. A mountain of problems would then face me: keeping their presence secret until I could secure another vessel, finding provisions without arousing suspicion, avoiding militia patrols; the list went on.

The relief that I felt, therefore, when a flash of white light winked at me from a quarter of a mile away, was considerable. It was amazing, I thought, fumbling for my flint and knife, how one spark could be visible from so far away. I struck the flint off the back of the blade, twice, thrice, hoping the men out on the water would see. I peered into the darkness, but still I could not make out the shape of the guinea boat. A moment later, two answering flashes told me my signal *had* been seen. My spirits rose. There was no time to lose. Rowed by a dozen men each side, the boat would soon reach the shallows.

I secreted flint and blade in a pocket and clambered to my feet. Remembering the pistol I had brought for protection, I shoved it back into my belt. '*Maintenant*,' I called to the Frenchies, pitching my voice low. '*Venez, venez!*'

Up they stood, eight of them. Bearded, unkempt, they wore ragtag clothes, part military uniform, part garments that had been begged, borrowed or stolen since their capture. I led the way down to the beach. At once we were in the open, and my belly clenched. Casting my gaze left and right along the strand, I laid a hand to the pistol. If I had hoped for solace from its wooden butt, I got none. I had never used the thing, indeed had not used any firearm since a fowling trip on the Thames Estuary years before.

I would not need it, I told myself, and pressed on. The guinea boat was visible now, the oarsmen slowing their stroke so the craft did not run aground.

'Who goes there?'

My heart lurched in my chest. I stopped. So did the Frenchies.

The shout had come from off to our right. Deal town lay in that direction, perhaps a mile and a half distant. I had expressed my doubts to George Dowall, asking if we should not embark further to the north, but he had laughed, and declared this was the best spot, and that he had not seen the East Kents in years.

'Stand, in the king's name!' The strident voice was perhaps a hundred yards away.

We were within musket range, I decided calmly, but in the darkness, we had little chance of being hit.

'*Que devrions-nous faire?*'

I said nothing.

5

The lead Frenchie grabbed my shoulder and repeated his question – what should we do?

To run back into the dunes risked separation, I decided, and in all likelihood, capture for most of my charges. That would rule out any further business from the Frenchman. Complete penury awaited me in that direction, therefore, and broken limbs – this was what the salon's heavies had promised – along with it.

'*Au bateau!*' I cried. '*Vite! Vite!*'

'Stay where you are!'

'*Courez!*' I shouted, heaving the Frenchie past me. 'Run!'

A musket cracked. I caught its flash from the corner of my eye, heard the ball whistle past in the night. How close it had come, I could not tell, but fear gave me wings. As muzzle flashes lit the night and the peace was shredded by the roaring of muskets, I sprinted for the boat.

'*Courez!*' My bellow would have woken every person in Deal.

Water soaked into my shoes – soon it reached my calves – yet I did not slow. I slammed into the guinea boat, hurting my ribs on the planking. 'George?' I asked the figure in the prow.

'That be you, Master Matthew?' His voice was as calm as a man bidding his neighbour good morn.

'Yes!'

'Brought company, you did. Get they Frenchies onboard if we're not to have a right set-to.'

The lead Frenchman, the one who had asked me what we should do, was already by my side. Willing hands reached out, heaving him aboard. '*Vite!*' I cried, even as a second came hurtling in.

'After them, men!' It was the militia's officer. 'There is the boat!'

I felt a prickle of recognition, but then another Frenchie arrived, and three more. I could see the seventh as well. Stepping away from the prow to try and see the last, and worrying about the militiamen, I pulled out my pistol.

'Best cock that piece, Matthew,' said George drily, 'unless you be planning to use it as a club.'

Grateful that he could not see my flushing cheeks, I drew back the hammer. God and all His saints, I thought, let me not have to shoot a fellow Englishman. There was time to feel the irony of how I had identified myself before the seventh Frenchie reached the boat.

'*Où est le dernier homme?*' I demanded.

'*Je sais pas!*' His fearful tone revealed that he was not about to help me look either. He climbed into the guinea boat even as George and a crewman jumped into the shallows.

The pair set their shoulders to the prow. With a great heave, they pushed the boat several feet back into the water. 'Ready, Master Matthew?' George asked.

Muskets barked. I saw flashes of light, one, two, three in a line perhaps twenty-five yards away. A ball struck the water near me. There was a hollow thump as another struck the boat. The other went I had no idea where. The officer was roaring at his men. I thought I heard him order them to fix bayonets. Again recognition tickled at me.

'We needs to go, master.' Finally, there was urgency in George's voice.

'Wait,' I barked. 'There is one man missing.'

'I will not wait, sir!'

I glanced back, and was relieved to see that he had not got into the boat – yet. I had no more than a few moments, though. Only a fool would stay where he was, and be caught. A lengthy gaol sentence awaited those who smuggled Frenchies over the Channel.

My eyes searching the darkness, my mouth tasting of bile, I went five paces towards the dunes. I held my pistol straight-armed out in front of me, as if I knew what to do with it. '*Venez-ici!*' I called. 'Come here!'

So intent was I on spying out militiamen that I almost tripped over the crouching figure.

'*Aidez-moi,*' he said in a pain-racked, husky voice.

Helping him up, I threw my left arm around his back to grip the far side of his shirt. Together we took a step towards the boat, which thank merciful God, was still there. One of the Frenchies had clambered out, and was coming to our aid. Water splashed behind me, very close. A voice shouted 'Stop!' My flesh crawled. I could almost feel the steel of a bayonet ramming into my back.

We were within touching distance of the boat. The Frenchie reached out for his comrade's hand.

'Look out, master!' George cried.

'Get him in,' I ordered the helpful Frenchie, and relinquished my grip of the injured man.

I twisted *towards* him and kept turning; with the pistol in my right hand, I could aim more quickly that way. Not that I wanted to shoot it – the last thing I had intended this night was to shed another man's blood.

Imagine my utter horror, therefore, to find a militiaman almost upon me. Closer still was the fearful bayonet on the end of his musket. 'Bastard!' He jabbed it forward.

I did well to avoid his lunge, but he was already preparing to go at me again.

Utterly terrified, I did nothing. I could not turn my back on him, or he would gut me like a fish. Nor could I keep avoiding his attack. Judging by the shouts, his fellows would arrive any moment.

'Shoot 'im, master!' George's voice.

Dumbly, I stared down my arm, which was somehow pointing at the militiaman. At its end, in my white-knuckled fist, was the cocked pistol. My gaze went past it, to the fear-clenched militiaman's expression. He had hesitated, presuming I was about to shoot him, but I had not. Now, he was going to stab me – I could see it in his eyes.

Still my finger did not tighten on the trigger.

A belch of orange-yellow flame erupted at the edge of my vision. The thunder of the discharge deafened me, so close was it. The militiaman was punched back by the shot, his face a bloody ruin. He dropped like a marionette with cut strings.

The Frenchie who had fired was already gone, joining his fellows in the boat. '*Vite, monsieur,*' he urged.

I lowered my pistol. Numb with shock and horror, I looked down at the water swirling around what had once been a man. The darkness concealed the blood.

'Master Matthew!'

I took a step backwards, then another.

Another figure appeared out of the darkness. Thick gold cuffs at the ends of his sleeves marked him out as an officer, as did the pistol in his hand.

Fresh anguish filled me. Of all the men it could have been, it was William Noble, my friend. There was no mistaking his angular shape, and his long, straight nose.

Perhaps blinded by the pistol's discharge, William tripped and fell over the corpse, landing face first in the knee-high water.

Voices called out in the night. Fresh flames belched as the militia-men fired in our direction.

I hesitated, torn with wanting to help my friend, who had a great fear of drowning, and aware that I needed to flee.

William came up spluttering, and recognised me. Bewilderment filled his honest face. Shock filled his voice. *'Matthew?'*

I did not answer. I could not.

He raised his pistol, but it was soaking wet. With a curse, he hurled the thing in my direction.

I dodged it and backed away, towards the boat, even as he leaped up and came charging after me.

I was pulled aboard by strong hands. George fended off William with an oar as the crew bent their backs. We scythed forward into the waves. I slumped in the bottom of the boat, my ears ringing with William's accusing cry.

'You are a murderer, Matthew! A murderer!'

CHAPTER II

It was an easy crossing, with light winds and a calm sea. We sighted a Royal Navy vessel close to the French coast, but the speed of the guinea boat was such that it did not even attempt to give chase. The oarsmen cheered as George pronounced with grim satisfaction that it would be 'like setting a cow to race a hare'.

I was brooding, mind filled with images of the militiaman's face as it had been blown apart. The mood among the Frenchies was also muted, thanks to their wounded comrade. Shot in the upper abdomen, he had mercifully lapsed into unconsciousness by daybreak. Perhaps halfway across the Channel, he moaned once or twice, and died. A comrade – a friend, it seemed – set up a great wailing and crying, and had to be quieted by the others. A while after, they closed the dead man's eyes and folded his hands as if in prayer. Then they performed a haunting rendition of *Le Chant du Départ*, the French empire's anthem, several weeping as he sang.

The oarsmen, rough Kentishmen every last one, slowed their stroke to listen. Several bowed their heads in respect. It was a curious moment, the two sets of men – to all intents and purposes enemies – united in reverence for the dead.

I prayed for myself.

I also found my attention drawn to the body. As if to make up for what I had not seen before – I had never been to a public hanging, for example – my eyes were drawn to the pathetic, limp shape on the bottom of the boat. His blood had mixed with the bilge water, turning it the colour of dilute wine. It slopped to and fro against his pale face. At least he had a face, I thought, stomach turning, not like the militiaman back at the beach.

The Frenchie who had shot him, a big, moustachioed officer from Bordeaux, took my fascinated attention for guilt, or sorrow.

'It is not your fault he died, monsieur.' He gave the others a baleful look, but none would meet his gaze. His eyes returned to mine. 'At least you tried to help him, which is more than you can say for this lot.'

I nodded. I would not speak my real mind. That the wretch would have died anyway. That if I had left him to die, the militiaman would still be alive, and better yet, that William would not think me a murderer. Never, I decided, had an attempt to save a man's life been more futile, and borne such bitter fruit. I turned my head to look at the low, rolling coastline of France, thinking, if I go back to England, I will have to live as a fugitive, at constant risk of ending my life dancing at the end of a rope.

I was startled – and disgusted – by a devilish voice in my head. Abandon England, and my debts could be forgotten. The relief I felt from this was brief. Exile meant never seeing my family again. Of more immediate concern, however, was landing in France, where I would be regarded as an enemy. There were aged relations somewhere in Normandy, but I had never met them. My father had spoken of an old friend in Paris from time to time, a Monsieur Dupont, but I had only a vague idea of where he lived.

I laid a surreptitious hand to the money belt hidden under my shirt. It held fifty-five gold guineas. The Frenchman had given me eighty; twenty had gone to George in down payment, and the rest had been spent on food and other sundries. Once I was given the balance of what I was owed, and George was paid off, I would be left with one hundred and fifteen guineas. It was a sizeable sum, and, if I was not robbed and did not lose it gambling, enough to live on for a year, perhaps two. Panic fluttered in my stomach, nonetheless. I had never envisaged living in France for a month, let alone for the rest of my life.

Maybe it would be better to return to England, I thought. Keep my head down for a while, not in Kent, obviously, and let the militiaman's death be forgotten. Mindful of my debts in London, I considered other cities to live in. Bristol was a place I had heard good things about. I imagined opening my own gambling salon there, under an assumed identity. Shame pricked me at the thought of abandoning the Carrey name.

I hardened my heart. This was no time for sentimentality. What was done was done, and I had to make the best of it. And in England at least there would be the possibility of seeing my family again, and making things right with my father. Although we were estranged, I had harboured hopes of a reconciliation.

'What be your intention, Master Matthew?' George asked as if he could read my mind. 'Will you come back with us, or bide in France awhile?'

I gave him a tight smile. He had heard me speaking with the escapees; he had an inkling of my heritage. 'England is my home.'

'Of course, master.' There was a note of apology in his voice. 'We won't linger then. Put these Frenchies ashore, and straight back out to sea. Us will be back in Kent by nightfall, eh lads?'

A chorus of assent came from the oarsmen.

George caught my eye, then whispered, 'Get your money now, master. You don't want to be asking the Frenchies for it with their feet on the beach.' Concealing the movement with his body, he mimed a running man with his fingers.

I nodded, grateful for the advice. Even as we talked, the coast had drawn nearer. It was perhaps three quarters of a mile off. The town of Calais was a dark smudge off to our right. Directly in front of our position, I could see a windmill close to the shore, and beside it, the tiny shape of a wagon. Miniature men heaved sacks of wheat down to other men, who with the heavy loads on their backs, walked towards the mill.

Easing past George, I asked the first Frenchie for his money. The rogue pretended not to understand, but when I told him he could swim the rest of the way, he handed over the coin soon enough. His fellows did the same; I secreted the gold in my waistband. I was in a quandary about the dead man. He would never return home, living at least, but I was entitled to the fee for his passage – and I needed it.

As I reached out to search the corpse, however, the moustachioed Frenchie spoke. 'He should not have to pay.' My protest died in my throat as he continued, 'He has a wife and children. The money should go to them.'

'And who will see to that?' I challenged.

'I will.' This was the man who had set up a great outcry. 'We are from the same village.'

I pretended to look satisfied. 'Very well.'

There was muttering and glowering aplenty from several of the Frenchies – in their eyes, I was now a corpse-robber – but I paid no heed. A well-feathered nest is the most comfortable. The woes of a French widow and her children were not my concern.

We came running into the shore on a gentle swell. The incline was slight, and the water shallow for quite a distance to the beach proper. 'Out you get, *messieurs*,' George ordered, indicating that the Frenchies should disembark. '*Bon voyage* and all that.'

They needed no second telling. When four had jumped into the sea, the rest passed their comrade's corpse over. I flinched as his arm brushed against mine. The moustachioed Frenchie shook my hand; he was the last to climb out. He did not look back. The others, talking excitedly among themselves, did not either.

'Turn, boys,' said George.

With the ease of long practice, the men on the portside dug their oars deep, dragging the prow around. A few strokes, and we were pointing back across the Channel.

Which is when I saw the lean shape of a French cutter, perhaps half a mile away. It was aimed straight at us.

George saw it in the same instant, and swore long and loud. ''Tis a trying voyage, and no mistake. She must have come out of the port right as we came into shore.'

'What will they do?' I asked nervously. This was a civilian craft, one of scores that travelled the smuggling route across the Channel year round. As far as I knew, the French made no great efforts to stop the illegal trade in brandy, gold and escaped prisoners of war. Nonetheless, an encounter with a naval vessel was not a prospect that I welcomed.

'If we do not run, master, they will search us, and take every last coin on the boat. All our effort will have been for naught.'

'Can you outrun it?' I asked, aware of the easterly breeze that was billowing the cutter's sails, and the fact that it was a good way towards blocking our path to the open sea.

'Us will give it our best effort. Won't we, lads?'

The oarsmen looked none too happy, or confident, but they redoubled their efforts, and the boat surged ahead. George bared his teeth, and incredibly, laughed. ''Twill be a close run thing!'

'And if they get within cannon range?'

'We surrender, master. Better to be alive and penniless than blown into smithereens.'

This comment aroused a number of loud 'ayes' from the oarsmen. I was unsurprised. With my gold-heavy money belt, I was the one who stood to be ruined, not they.

I weighed up the odds. If we escaped the cutter, I had only to evade the authorities upon our return to Kent. If we were caught, on the other hand, there was a small likelihood of being sunk, and much more chance of again being reduced to penury. I had another option if we were about to be searched: to try to swim ashore, although my likely fate then was being taken to the bottom by my gold. Let the belt sink to avoid drowning, and I would be seized by the cutter's crew – suspicious that I had fled – and treated as an English spy.

I looked over the side, at the white sand. The water was chest deep, no more. I glanced at the cutter once more, and at the oarsmen's faces, and then at George. I did not like his expression.

It was time to choose. I put figures to the odds, just as I might have with the horses in a race. Six to one against that we got past the cutter. If we reached England unscathed, five to one that I evaded capture. If the cutter blocked our path, eight to one that a shot from a bow chaser hit us.

The chance of being left penniless after the Frenchies had done their search was ten to one, excepting the guinea I had wedged into the toe of each shoe. Those had a good chance of remaining unfound. If I tried to swim for shore and was caught, the odds were similar that I would be interrogated and incarcerated in gaol. I was left with a final option: to jump into the sea now, still shallow enough to put my feet down, and make for the beach, there to decide my own fate.

I tensed. These odds were best. Four to one in favour, maybe more if I could get around Calais without being seen.

'Thank you, George,' I said, and stood up.

'Master, what be you—'

I did not hear the rest of his question, because I had leaped over the side.

The water was shockingly cold. I came up spluttering, my eyes stinging with salt, grateful that my toes reached the bottom. I looked for the guinea boat: it was already thirty yards away and showed no sign of slowing or turning about. I raised a hand, and George saluted back. He wishes me no ill will, I thought, and set my mind to the next task.

14

I would wade ashore and try to get my bearings, then walk several miles inland. Getting away from the coast made the most sense, in case a boat was sent after me from the cutter. My mood brightened. I had a good head start. By nightfall, I would be ensconced by the fire at a local inn, partaking of its finest red wine. Tomorrow I could think about my best plan of action: to go to Normandy in search of my long-lost cousins, or to Paris, to find Monsieur Dupont. It would be best to make the decision from a safe distance, I judged, than to linger here and risk being captured.

I came ashore, chilled and looking forward to the shelter of the dunes. I cast a glance seaward. The guinea boat had lost its race with the cutter, and heaved to before the Frenchies had fired a warning shot. I was pleased; I had gauged the odds well. There was no sign, yet, of a craft being launched to come ashore, but I hastened up the dunes anyway, skirting my way between the gorse bushes and prickly saltwort.

Within a few steps, there was sand in my shoes. A few more, and it had come through my woollen socks. I sighed. Even as a child, I had never been fond of the feeling. Too late I decided that I ought to have shed my footwear first. Cresting the rise, I hurried down into the dune's lee. More dunes rolled away to left and right, and before me, a never-ending succession of dips and hollows were covered in clumpy grass and gorse. There were even a few elder bushes. It was a maze, but if I kept my back to the sea, sooner or later I would come to cultivated land, and a track that led, if not to a village, then a farmhouse where I might ask directions.

I pressed onward, keeping the thoughts of dry clothes and a good meal uppermost in my mind. Too late, I heard voices behind me, and the distinctive rush of men running. Too slowly, I began to turn. Even if my pistol had been dry, I could not have reached it in time.

Something struck the back of my head with immense force. Pain exploded in my brain. My sight darkened, and I was falling, all control of my limbs gone.

As if from the other end of a long tunnel, I heard, 'He would have robbed poor dead Jean. He deserves none of the gold!'

As I slid away into the welcoming darkness, there was time to feel a brief irony. The only odds I had not considered were those of being robbed by the very Frenchies I had helped to escape.

*

The first thing I became aware of was pain – excruciating pain. My head felt as if a band of insane horsemen were riding around it at the gallop. I was cold too, chilled to the bone. Then came the sensation of my shallow, gulping breaths, and the realisation that I was lying on my side. There was a gritty feeling in my mouth. It was sand, I realised with disgust. I did my best to spit it out, which only encouraged the horsemen to greater efforts. Panting with agony, I opened my eyes and saw nothing but blackness. For an instant, I thought I was dead, that the monstrous headache was part of Satan's punishment. Then, as reason returned, I understood that night had fallen.

I managed to get an arm under me. Gingerly, I sat up. The whole world swam; my vision blurred. Almost at once, bile rushed up my throat, and I was sick. That doubled the agony in my head. I sat there, muscles trembling, able to do nothing more than exist.

I had not the strength to move further, but my mind was working, after a fashion. I remembered the voice I had heard, and despair's sharp claws raked me without compassion. Even if I had had the strength to reach down for the money belt, there was no need. The gold was gone, and my pistol too. My shoes were still on my feet, which meant I had two gold coins to my name. It did not seem much in comparison to my woes.

I cried then, sour, self-pitying tears that were witnessed by no one, answered by nobody. Strings of snot ran from my nose, and mixed with the sand on my cheeks. When the sobbing eased at last, I wiped my face with the arm of my coat. I was pathetic, I told myself, a green fool who should have seen what was coming. I knew nothing about smuggling Frenchies over the Channel. Everything I knew about France was second-hand, told to me by my father.

A childish, petulant part of me wanted to lie back down and give up. Appealing as that was – it was still a real effort just to stay upright, and my head was splitting – I knew it would serve me not at all. The night was cold, too cold to remain outdoors until morning came.

I felt around my waist with my left hand, hoping by some miracle to find my money belt. It was not there, and despair threatened to take me again. I beat it back, feebly, and to my surprise, the feeling abated somewhat. I was alive, I thought. The Frenchies could easily have murdered me, yet they had not. I remembered the moustachioed man, whose pistol shot had saved me from being gutted, and wondered if it had been he who stayed his comrades' hands. I would never know.

Unsteady, my world spinning, I got to my feet. I tried to brush away the sand that had mixed with blood and hair at the back of my head, but the stabbing pains that caused put a swift stop to my efforts. The gentle, calming noise of the sea was to my left, so I turned to my right, and began – very slowly – to walk inland. I had no idea where I was going, but the movement would take me away from the beach, and, God willing, warm me up.

Thoughts of the Almighty set me to praying. I had been raised Catholic, following my father's wishes, but I was a poor churchgoer. Gambling and carousing were frowned upon by the Church; it was easier not to attend mass and confession than to have to pretend I would give up my vices. My current predicament was different, however. I needed God's help, desperately, and He, all-forgiving, might be disposed to give it.

Cold, wet, sand-covered, in severe pain, I was in that moment genuinely repentant. I would have sworn on the Holy Bible never to partake of wine as long as I lived, and never again to darken the threshold of a gambling salon, less still to wager money on anything. No bible to hand, I made do with a fervent, silent promise offered up to the heavens, if only God would help. I meant it too, even if deep down, I also knew that despite my willing spirit, my flesh was weak. I buried the knowledge beneath the mind-numbing comfort of an entire rosary.

The fifty Hail Marys and ten Our Fathers – the words coming readily after years of non-utterance – helped to distract me not just from my pain, but from the effort of trudging through the strength-sapping dunes. Hypnotised by the repetitive prayers, I stumbled over a last crest and halfway down the other side before I realised that I had come through the sand.

Flat, open countryside rolled away from me. In the cloud-bound darkness, I could not see if it was farmland. In truth, I had no idea which way to go, and saw little point in blindly taking off. My hope, faint already, began to wither and die. I cast my gaze about, desperate for something, anything, that might help me. Noticing a structure a little way off to my left, I actually shed a few tears.

The building proved to be a rundown fisherman's hut, with not much other than a pile of old nets on the floor. They would serve, I decided. Lying down, my nostrils filled with a strong fishy aroma, I gave in to blessed sleep.

I was woken in the rudest of fashions by the hut's owner, who dragged the nets off me. I cried out in alarm, and he, not having noticed me – my entire body being concealed apart from my head – almost jumped out of his skin.

When we had established that I was no ghost, he was altogether more welcoming. Was I a soldier, he asked. He had come across some of the Frenchies from the guinea boat, I reasoned, and told him that I was. He gave loud thanks to God for returning me to France, unharmed. I managed to convert his gratitude into hard currency: some of the bread, cheese, and rough wine he had brought for his lunch.

My headache's severity had reduced overnight, so the sustenance went a long way towards restoring me. The fisherman was all for acting as a guide to the farm where he said the Frenchies had gone the previous afternoon, a short walk to the west. I managed to dissuade him by filling his ears with profuse thanks and saying that his directions were more than adequate.

The Frenchies were probably gone, but I was in no state for any kind of confrontation. I made my way south instead, and prayed that my good luck held. It did. There was no sign of the prisoners, and at a large stone-built house, I managed to sneak into the scullery unseen and purloin a long-tailed shirt and a pair of breeches.

This success did not remove the stark choices facing me. I could not exist for long with two gold coins to my name. I did not have identity papers either, so I would be detained by the first officials who stopped me. Nor could I remember the exact Normandy village my relatives lived in. It was Saint Martin-something, or perhaps Sainte Marguerite – I was unsure, and that was not enough information to embark on a three-hundred mile journey. The name of every other village in France began with 'Saint' or 'Sainte'. I could spend the rest of my life looking for the right one.

It was considerably less distance to Paris, and racking my brains, I again came up with Monsieur Dupont, an old friend of my father. He lived on the Rue Saint-Honoré, I remembered. As a boy, I had shivered with fear and delight at my father's tales of the noblemen and women taken to the guillotine at the Place de la Concorde, near Dupont's residence. The Revolution was long over, but that did not mean it was wise to journey to Paris. A state of war existed between France and Britain, as it had for most of the previous two decades.

Napoleon had been ruler in Paris for thirteen years now, and emperor since 1804. Since his coronation, he had become de facto ruler of Europe, defeating first Austria, then Prussia and Russia. Only Britain remained undefeated, its navy dominating the seas, and in the last two years, also the brutal war in Portugal and Spain. Napoleon was far from defeated, though; his Grande Armée remained the premier fighting force in Europe. For all these reasons, most Englishmen would not have ventured within a hundred miles of Paris, but I, half-French and desperate, cared nothing for war, even if it was between France and Britain.

I needed help, and badly. If anyone would give it, I decided, it was Dupont. The exact number of his house on the Rue Saint-Honoré eluded me, but it was two hundred and something. That, I decided, was a small obstacle to overcome *if* I could get to the capital.

The odds were against me – perhaps ten to one – but the devil-may-care attitude that flavoured my life had once more come to the fore. I was gambling with my freedom, perhaps even my life, but the potential reward – that Monsieur Dupont would help me – was worth the risk.

CHAPTER III

Paris, France

The cart stopped. Although I had been expecting it to halt, I tensed. Beneath the load of hay, my nose pressed up against the timber side so I could breathe, I was most uncomfortable. Beggars could not be choosers, though, and nor could men without papers.

'Out.' A hand slapped the wood by my head. 'Quickly, before someone comes.'

I sat up, brushing off hay, and found myself regarding the wizened old farmer who, for the extortionate sum of ten francs, had transported me into Paris, thereby avoiding the sentries at the entrance to the city. 'Where are we?'

'Paris, like you wanted.' He took out his stubby clay pipe and spat his opinion of the city, before replacing it in his mouth. 'Come on, move.'

I clambered out of the cart onto the muddy street surface. A *diligence* went by, its postillion walking alongside, conversing with the passengers. 'No, it is not far to the centre, monsieur,' he said to someone inside the carriage.

The farmer gave me an 'I told you so' glance, and hauled himself up behind his pair of oxen. Clicking his tongue, he urged them onward.

'The Rue Saint-Honoré?' I called after him.

He did not turn. A grimy forefinger pointed straight ahead.

I swallowed a curse, and moved into an alleyway to gain some privacy. There I spent a few minutes picking hay from my coat. Thus far I had avoided all contact with the gendarmerie. To be stopped because of my appearance now, so close to my destination, would be not only disastrous, but foolish. Finally satisfied that I did not look as if I had slept the night in a barn, I set off down the street.

I drank in the scene with sidelong glances. The houses were stone built, with fine front doors decorated with carved knockers. Many had businesses on the ground floor. There were shoe shops, print sellers, chandlers, furniture makers and upholsterers, just as one might find in an English town. The buildings were between three and five storeys tall, with chimneys adding to the impression of great height. I spied a maid leaning out of a dormer window and beating a bedside carpet off the grey slate roof.

I soon realised that the best way to avoid the constant stream of wagons, carts and diligences was to stay to the right of the street with everyone else. The surface was unpaved and muddy, but a central gutter allowed drainage. There was no familiar stench of human waste, a welcome change from London, and the pedestrians, of which there were many, seemed polite and courteous. Men lifted their hats in greeting, and bid each other good day. The path before a pair of black-clad, wimple-wearing nuns cleared as if by a miracle. Even the carters and wagon drivers seemed respectful of one another. Cautious despite the amicable atmosphere, I kept my responses to nods and muttered 'Bonjours', and tried to catch no one's eye.

I was footsore and bone weary. Apart from a sunny day that I had used to dry out my clothing, I had been walking for a week and a half. My fine shoes had not been made for the almost two-hundred mile journey from Picardy; they were falling apart. Haybarns – sneaked into after dark – had served as my beds. When I could not find those, the middle of a wood had had to suffice. I was not starving, however, because I had exchanged my gold coins for francs. It had been in a village, early on the second day, and I had not wanted to argue, lest the shopkeeper have even more reason to remember the stranger with English guineas. He had been merciless, and his exchange rate outrageous. At least I had had the funds to buy food since, I decided. I could not have walked all the way to Paris on thin air.

I made my way to the Saint-Denis quarter, passing the magnificent basilica, and after asking directions of a stallholder, I continued southward towards the River Seine. Reaching it, I turned right and made my way along the bank. According to a little ragamuffin girl I asked, the magnificent limestone building to my right was the Musée Napoleon. I did not ask, but its splendour and scale – the main part of the structure formed three sides of a great square – told me that it had been a royal palace before the Revolution.

Apparently, the Rue Saint-Honoré was set back from the river, but unsure where to turn, I walked past the fountains and tree-lined avenues of the impressive Jardin des Tuileries, eventually arriving at an enormous square, where I paused. The guillotine was long gone, but I knew the square's name. This was the Place de la Concorde, renamed from Place de la Révolution; it was where King Louis XVI and his wife Queen Marie Antoinette, along with so many others, had been executed in front of the baying Parisian mob. I thought of the *tricoteuses*, the women who had sat knitting as the blood sprayed and the heads dropped into the wicker basket, and I shuddered.

I could not but think of my father, and what he would make of my being here. An ardent monarchist, his plan had been to enlist in the Royalist forces upon his arrival in England, but a French musket ball, which had struck him during his flight to the coast, had put paid to that. Permanently lamed in one leg, and bitter with it, he had done his best to inculcate in me a loathing of first the French Republic, and later, Napoleon.

He had not succeeded. It was partly my resistance to his dominance and overbearing nature; growing up in rural Kent also had a lot to do with it. As a boy, I had had no real grasp of who the French Republicans were, or why I should hate them. Unlike my older brother, I did not like the village boys' war games, nor their insistence that I should always play the part of a despicable Frenchie. The games were what had caused the bitter argument between me and my brother years prior.

We were the same, I had told him. Why should he always be on the British side, and I on the French? He had laughed and called me stupid, as he often did. Then he had shoved past, another habit of his, and a red mist of rage had descended. When my senses returned, it was to find him lying unconscious. After my brother came to, I had tearfully begged his forgiveness. To his credit, he had given it, and even lied so that our parents remained unaware. I had made a vow the very same day. Never again would I lose control. Never again would I let anger dictate my actions.

It was perhaps unsurprising that my lack of interest in war had continued as I grew older. There was no appeal to joining the militia like my friend William Noble, still less to serving in the army. Despite my love of horses, the cavalry did not appeal either. Nor entering the family business. I wondered if my lack of ambition was part of the reason wine and gambling had taken such a hold on me.

I sensed the attention of one of the gendarmes lounging by an entrance to the Jardin des Tuileries, and fear clutched at my guts. Trying not to pace too fast and thereby attract even more attention, I walked north. According to the ragamuffin girl, who had followed me, the first street was the new Rue de Rivoli. The next, she declared without being asked, was the Rue Saint-Honoré. Setting aside my annoyance that she had accompanied me unasked, I nodded my thanks and continued.

She scampered to keep up. 'You're not from Paris,' she pronounced.

'No.' I increased my speed, wishing she would leave me alone.

Instead she began to run alongside, her bare feet slapping off the ground. 'Where are you from?'

'Normandy.'

'Why are you in Paris?'

I glared at her. 'Are you always this nosy?'

'Five sous, and I will go away.'

I laughed. Several days since, at an inn north of the city, the same amount had bought me a large bowl of coffee with as much milk and sugar as I wanted, as well as vast quantities of toasted bread.

She stuck out her bottom lip. 'Three then.'

I tossed her a one sou coin.

She caught it with practised ease, and stood watching as I turned right onto the Rue Saint-Honoré, which was wide and lined with shops. To my good fortune, not a hundred yards further on, I came upon a tailor's premises. This was Dupont's profession. The number on the door was two hundred and thirty six. It was his shop, I decided with delight.

I turned to check that the ragamuffin had not followed me. To my alarm, I saw instead a pair of gendarmes, one of whom was the individual who had stared as I daydreamed on the Place de la Concorde. Panic flooded my veins. Walk on, I decided, and they would continue tailing me. I had nowhere to go, moreover, nowhere in the entire city apart from here – and as yet, it was unclear if I had even found the right premises. I quickly weighed up the odds. It was five to one odds or shorter that I would be caught if I ran, and close to evens that Dupont worked here. Terrifyingly, however, I had no idea of the chances of him hiding me within seconds of our meeting.

I hesitated, and then, hearing the clack of the gendarmes' shoes, threw caution to the wind. I turned the handle and pushed open the door, setting a bell to ringing. I slipped in, closing it quietly. The room I entered was almost entirely filled with rolls of cloth, leaning against each other, filling shelves, stacked on top of each other. The desk at the far end almost seemed out of place. Behind it, in the light of an oil lamp sat a paunchy man of similar age to my father; that is to say, in his late forties. Balding and possessed of a wobbling double chin, he gave me a polite smile.

'How can I help, monsieur?'

My heart was pounding. If the gendarmes came in and demanded my papers, it mattered not that I was innocent. I would be dragged off to gaol. 'Monsieur Dupont?' I croaked.

A surprised nod. 'Do I know you, monsieur?'

It was the right shop, I thought with relief. 'You know my father, Armand Carrey.'

His eyebrows rose further. 'Mon Dieu, I see the resemblance. Are you Mathieu?'

'Even so.' As he got up, smiling, I came forward to meet him. 'Two gendarmes are following me, I think. I have no papers . . .'

He understood in a flash. 'Into the back.'

He led the way, gliding into the empty room beyond, which appeared to be the workshop. Jackets and matching breeches hung on the walls. A large counter was covered with pieces of fabric, shears, measuring sticks. Dupont bent and pulled aside the floor carpet, revealing to my surprise, a trapdoor. Lifting it, he gestured. 'Go on, quickly.'

I hurried down the stone steps. I had an impression of a low-ceilinged cellar, filled with oddments of furniture, and then the trapdoor was closing over my head. Powerless, I sat nervously on the lowest step and listened with all my might.

Perhaps a minute later, the bell at the shop's entrance tinkled. My stomach lurched.

A voice spoke in greeting. Dupont replied.

The voice said something else, but I could not hear what.

Again Dupont answered.

A question followed.

A chair scraped back. I heard the door into the workshop open, and I thought my heart would stop. For all I knew, Dupont had duped me into hiding merely so he could lead the gendarmes straight to my hiding place.

'A young man, you say?'

'Yes. Tall, black-haired, well built. His shoes are falling apart, and there is hay all over the back of his coat.'

'I haven't had a customer for hours, sadly, not even one like that,' said Dupont with a chuckle.

I sagged down with relief, at the same time cursing my naïveté in not taking off my coat to do a proper job.

'Business is not good?' asked the gendarme.

'I have enough commissions to keep me occupied, so I cannot complain. Many others are in a worse situation.' Dupont moved until he was standing right over my head.

'And this door?'

'It leads into the alley behind the building.'

The thunk of a bolt being drawn back. A creak followed. The time the gendarme was outside was only sufficient for a cursory glance.

'See anything?' Dupont sounded solicitous.

'A cat,' said the gendarme with a snort.

'We are sorry to bother you, monsieur,' said the other.

Dupont shifted off the trapdoor. Other feet tramped over it, and the three men disappeared into the front room. The bell tinkled. Then came the sound of the door closing.

I breathed again.

Dupont waited for some time before he came back to release me from the cellar.

'I don't know how to thank you,' I said, clambering up the stairs.

'It is the least I could do for Armand's son.' He waved a hand in dismissal, and then turned his blue eyes on me. 'You look, how can I say . . . harried? My guess is that you do not find yourself in Paris by chance.'

'No,' I said ruefully.

He cleared a corner of the work counter, and from a cupboard, produced a jug of red wine and a pair of clay beakers. He filled them both and handed me one. 'It is a pleasure to make your acquaintance, Mathieu.' He toasted me.

'And yours, Monsieur Dupont.' I returned the gesture, and took a swallow. The wine went down easily, its flavour soft and velvet. 'This is good.'

'It comes from a friend's vineyard in Bordeaux.'

I saluted Dupont, and drained the cup.

He refilled it, and when I had drained that, poured more. 'Am I the only person you know, or know of, in Paris?'

I nodded.

'You did well to remember my address.'

I laughed, and the tension in my shoulders eased.

'How did you come to be here?'

Ashamed, I considered lying, but his plain, direct manner and the way he had saved me, a complete stranger, demanded honesty. I told Dupont everything, from my gambling addiction to the funds I had stolen from my father's business. How he had paid the monies I owed, and how I had promptly fallen from grace a second time, and then, despairing that these new debts could ever be repaid, had let myself be taken in by the charismatic Frenchman. How what had seemed like a simple voyage over the Channel had turned disastrous, thanks first to the East Kent militia, and then the moustachioed Frenchman. I paused, remembering with fresh horror the spray of blood as the militiaman's head was punched back by the force of the pistol ball.

'You did not shoot him?'

I was able to hold Dupont's steady gaze. 'No, monsieur. I could not pull the trigger. If the Frenchman had not killed him, I would not be here – I swear it on my mother's life.'

'I believe you.'

There was a lump in my throat. At least one person knew I was not a murderer. With Dupont's encouragement, I continued the rest of my tale of woe. How I had been robbed by the French escapees, and not knowing what else to do, had somehow made my way to Paris.

'Two hundred miles with no papers, only to end up almost being detained by those gendarmes,' I finished. 'I must thank you again, monsieur, for hiding me.'

'What would Armand say if he found out I had not helped you?'

'My father does not care what happens to me.'

A sad shake of the head. 'Not true. A parent never stops loving their child, no matter what they have done. Your father loves you still, Mathieu, and he would not want you languishing in a Paris gaol.'

As thoughts of both my parents filled my mind, and sadness gnawed at me, I tried to hold on to that thought.

'What is your plan? To return to England and clear your name?'

'No!' I said, horrified. 'My oldest friend thinks I am a murderer. If I went back, it would be his word against mine, and he is an officer in the militia, while I am . . . a bankrupt, and a trafficker of French prisoners of war.'

'And the man who shot the soldier?'

A bitter little laugh escaped me. 'Even if I knew his name or where he is from, I doubt he would return to England to swear that it was not I who slew the militiaman, but he.'

'That is indeed a faint hope. So what will you do?'

I gave him a helpless look. 'I do not know.'

'Without identity papers, you cannot safely leave this shop. That is where we will start.'

'Thank you.' My voice was husky.

'You shall stay with me for the moment.'

'I am very grateful.' I had tears in my eyes. As I realised later, my emotions were running high not just because of Dupont's kindness, but because his words had had the ring of prophecy.

France, it seemed, was to be my new home.

For how long, I had no idea.

CHAPTER IV

Several days passed, during which I did not leave Monsieur Dupont's shop. When closing the window shutters at the day's end, the sharp-eyed tailor had noted a gendarme lurking down the street. It seemed likely that his remit was to see if I emerged from any of the premises on this part of the Rue Saint-Honoré. There might also be eyes watching the alleyway at the rear of the shop, said Dupont, and so the safest thing was for me to remain where I was.

I was well content to obey. Not only were the odds stacked against me, but I had a roof over my head for the first time in days. It was true that I had a straw-filled tick and blankets rather than a bed, but these were more than sufficient. I was warm, safe and well-fed. It was mildly discommoding to always have to use a chamber pot, but this was of small concern compared to the alternative of being arrested and slung into gaol.

Each day, I sat and watched Dupont and his apprentice at work. I had immediate concerns about the latter, a shy lad of eighteen by the name of Joseph. All he had to do was mention my presence to the wrong person, and the gendarmes would return. My worries were soon laid to rest. He was, Dupont told me, one of only two people in his household with a job, and therefore deeply beholden to him. I made sure of Joseph's silence by slipping him ten of my remaining francs.

My evenings were spent alone, immersed in the two novels brought to me by Dupont. It was good exercise, not having read in French since childhood, and the authors de Chateaubriand and Nodier were new to me. I enjoyed both stories, but Nodier's more than the other. His novel *Les Tristes*, a love story haunted by death, struck a real note with me. I had never been in love, not even close, but I longed for the experience. Despite my confident exterior, I was a secret romantic, and the idea of a passion so powerful that it transcended even death seemed noble indeed.

The fourth day saw the arrival of my freedom, that is to say, my papers. Dupont produced them with a flourish when Joseph went out on an errand. I unfolded the square of paper with eager fingers, noting the government stamps and the signature in ink at the bottom, and then, to my amusement, the person named on the document.

I lifted my gaze. 'I am to be Mathieu Dupont?'

'Forgive me.' Dupont cleared his throat. 'Your father's name carries with it, how can I say, some baggage?'

'Because he is a royalist?'

'Even so. My cousins in Picardy, on the other hand, also Duponts, are loyal to France.'

I was a little stung. 'My father would argue that he is too.'

'And I would not argue with him, in private at least. We are in Paris, however, and *l'Empereur, c'est Napoleon*. If you are to move about freely, and to arouse no suspicion, it is better that you fit in. I can think of few better ways than to make you a son of a cousin on my father's side, come to learn my trade. You are a little old to be an apprentice, it is true, but you might have been as a clerk for several years, and not found it your liking.'

I nodded, acknowledging this feasible-sounding story.

'Put them away then.' Dupont pointed at my papers. I stared in confusion, and he indicated the work counter. 'If you are to pretend to be an apprentice, you had best learn something of the trade. Imagine that the gendarmes came in again. You do not want to look a complete fool.'

I had no interest in tailoring, but again my host was right. I had no profession or trade, no way of earning a living. I therefore paid attention to the lesson that followed. Selection of fabric types, measuring a customer, estimate of costs, cutting out the template, needles, thread, stitching, re-measuring, final fitting, it went on and on. Sensing my attention waver, Dupont stopped talking and set me to practising stitching a straight line on a piece of discarded woollen fabric. The task was much harder than it looked, which infuriated me. I was more than capable of such a menial task, I told myself, and redoubled my efforts.

By the day's end, I had pricked my fingers a hundred times, and achieved a dozen definitely-not-straight lines of stitching. My efforts had amused Joseph, although he had done his best to hide it. Dupont was ever patient, and told me that it was a start.

'We will make a tailor of you in the end,' he said, patting my shoulder.

He meant it too. I murmured my thanks, but the idea of settling down to a profession I regarded as even more humdrum than my father's appalled me. I was caught on the horns of a real dilemma. I could remain here in Paris, and suffer Dupont's tutelage, or I could go back to England, and risk my neck.

I liked neither choice, but even to my impatient mind, staying where I was seemed the more sensible of the two. It might be boring, but it was safe.

Months passed. I spent a pleasant Christmas with Dupont and his family. From the start, his wife Hortense, a homely, kind woman, welcomed me as the son she had never had. Anne and Madeleine, their two daughters, who were quite a lot younger than I, also seemed happy to adopt me as a revered big brother. This endearing human contact was balm for my lonely heart, but in consequence, I missed my family terribly, in particular my mother.

I wished with all my being that the letter I had sent to her in secret had been received. Just as with brandy and prisoners of war in the other direction, there were ways and means to see messages carried to England. In it I had begged my parents' forgiveness, and written that whatever I may have been accused of, I had not done. There was no way to know if they had heard of the slaying of the militiaman, and I had not wanted to make reference to it in so many words. Neither had I used Dupont's address, for fear the letter would be intercepted and read by French intelligence officers. I could only hope that if my parents received my letter, they would guess I was in Paris with Dupont, and reply.

The year ended bitterly cold, ushering in 1812 with the avenues and boulevards coated in a thick layer of snow. When the festive season ended, Dupont kept his shop closed for an extra week, declaring there would be no customers worth talking about. Stuck in his house with little to do other than read and pace about my bedroom, I grew bored. I cannot remember who suggested it first, but one afternoon, we began to play cards.

Dupont and his wife had never heard of whist, one of the most popular games in England, so I explained the rules. Anne, sixteen years old and feisty, was keen to act as my partner, and soon caught on to my subtle nudging under the table when I had a good card. During a break for tea, I was able to tell her quietly about other tricks, such as use of the handkerchief, coughing as many times as one had an honour card, and throwing down cards using either one finger and the thumb, or two. She proved adept at learning the signals, and soon we were winning most games. Hortense, bless her, had no idea, but I was less sure about Dupont. Anne's youthful exuberance meant that her signals were easily spotted. Not long after our sixth victory, Dupont sent Anne to her room to read, and asked Hortense to leave us gentlemen to our own company.

I felt a tickle of unease.

Dupont shuffled the pack, the cards sliding between his slender fingers.

'What shall we play now?' I asked brightly.

He made no answer.

'A game of écarté?' I suggested brightly. I knew from my father that the two-person game was as popular in France as it was in England.

'My daughter is young and impressionable, Mathieu. I would prefer if you did not teach her to cheat.' He fixed his watery eyes on me, and I quailed. No doubt he was thinking of my gambling, and how it had led me to where I was now.

'I am sorry. It will not happen again.'

A gentle wave of his hand. 'You spoke of écarté?'

I smiled, relieved to have escaped so lightly. 'You play?'

'I do.'

I set about removing the low-value cards from the pack. I would have liked nothing better than to have begun betting on our game, but I did not wish to test Dupont any further. I selected the highest card, and got to deal. Hearts were trumps. He asked to exchange cards, and I agreed. We did this twice, and then I refused his request to do it again.

With two decent trumps and three court cards in other suits, I hoped to win.

I won the first trick, and the second, but my tactic came unstuck as he took the next three, however, and consequently scored the first point. It was my turn to win a point in the next hand, but he won the following two, giving him three points to my one. In the next hand, he took all five tricks, a *vole*, increasing his tally to four. I won the following hand, but the sixth was Dupont's, and with it, a fifth point, and victory.

He gave me a look. 'As well that we were not betting, eh?'

'Indeed,' I said, but my heart was racing with excitement. I had not fully understood the tactics of playing, but I already had a much better idea. Chalking down my loss to inexperience, I found my appetite to play whetted. I was good at cards, I told myself, with every chance of winning the next game, and more after that.

Sure enough, I beat him four times in quick succession. Only in the sixth game did he come back to snatch victory with a vole. Our playing came to an end then, as Hortense entered, announcing that dinner would soon be served.

Dupont put away the cards, and I went to my room to change. Although I was hungry, I did not wonder what might be served, because my mind was racing with ideas of making my fortune in a gambling salon. I was a fool for not having imagined it before, I thought. There was no need to risk my neck in England when I could enrich myself here. A large city, Paris would have its salons. I just needed to find the right one. The French did not play my favoured game, whist, and I had no partner. So, I decided, écarté it would be.

I positively bounded down the stairs for dinner.

And as for the little warning voice in my head, I listened to it not at all.

In the coming days, I played écarté with Dupont as often as I thought it politic. It was never enough. What I wanted was to be playing for money, in a gambling salon, but wary of his disapproval, I found a previously unknown patience inside myself, and bided my time. I concentrated on my tailoring lessons with Dupont, and walking the streets of the neighbourhood at lunchtimes, often with Joseph as my guide, and when the days gradually began to lengthen, after the shop closed. The little ragamuffin girl – Marie, her name was – sometimes walked with me too. I could not make her leave; more truthfully, I had not the heart to be unkind to the child.

I had a new pair of well-made shoes, bought with my wages – my host insisted on paying me – and even better clothing, made by Dupont himself. Clad in such finery, I was delighted to catch the eye of more than one young lady when walking the avenues of the Jardin des Tuileries, although I dared talk to none. I told myself it was because of their fierce-looking chaperones, but it had more to do with my bashfulness towards the gentler sex.

On the way back to Dupont's shop one day, I plucked up the courage to ask Joseph, in the most casual manner possible, if he knew of any local gambling establishments. He gave me a curious look. 'Do you like to wager?'

'From time to time,' I said, my tone offhand. 'It can be a pleasant way to spend an evening.'

'Provided you do not lose all your money!'

His reply, the opinion of so many, did not surprise me, and I could not enquire of Dupont, for obvious reasons. I would have to wait, I decided, fighting back disappointment.

'Some of my apprentice friends go to a place near where I live. It is rough and ready; they tend to go in twos and threes.'

'Oh,' I said, masking my excitement. 'Where?'

He mentioned a street name. I nodded, as if uninterested, but silently repeated it several times to be sure I did not forget it. Immediately, I began planning a visit. My next payday was Friday, in two days' time. Once the shop closed, I decided, I would tell Dupont that I was going for a walk, and find my way to the gambling den. The fact that Joseph's friends went together should have dissuaded me, but it did not. In my eagerness, and my desire that my plans should remain secret, I did not ask him to accompany me either.

Friday came none too soon, and the day dragged by as if time itself had slowed. I received my pay – ten francs – from Dupont, and stowed it in an inside pocket with my remaining money, some twenty francs. It was not a huge sum, thirty francs, about a pound sterling and five shillings, but it would suffice.

Dupont's only comment when I announced my intention was to advise me not to be late for dinner that evening, because Hortense was serving roast pork. I promised to return in good time, and left. Fortunately, Joseph had to stay behind to finish a pair of trousers, which meant I did not have to try to avoid him as I walked towards his neighbourhood of Faubourg Saint-Antoine, about a mile to the east. Marie followed me, however, despite my ordering her not to.

'Why can't I come with you?' Her tone was petulant.

'I want to be alone.' The truth was that I did not want anyone knowing I was gambling.

This did not put Marie off. She skipped along a few paces ahead of me, loudly commenting on everything of interest she saw: a water-carrier with two buckets in each hand and another pair dangling from his yoke, a butcher splitting a pig carcass outside his shop. Her prattle never stopped.

It was time to be firm, I decided. 'Marie.'

'Yes, Mathieu?' Her expression managed to be angelic and cocky at the same time.

I suspected I knew the reason for her confidence. Her father was dead, and her mother worked every hour of the day and night to provide for Marie and her four siblings. The child was on her own from dawn to dusk, living on her wits. I liked her because she was bright and funny, and reminded me of my sister Philippa. It also explained why I tolerated her disrespect. Philippa could always get the better of me.

'Marie, stop this.'

'Why?'

I cursed inside. I had sharpened her interest, not lessened it. 'My business is private.'

'I will not tell a soul.' A grimy forefinger touched her lips.

I stopped. 'No, Marie, I mean it.'

She pouted. 'I am a free citizen. I can walk wherever I want.'

I proffered a five sou coin. 'This, if you go back to Dupont's.'

She snatched the copper as if it were a louis d'or, while still complaining.

I said nothing, instead pointing back whence we had come.

A flick of her hair, worthy of a court beauty, but she obeyed. Not quite trusting her, I watched until Marie was swallowed up by the crowd, and then waited for a few moments lest she reappear. She did not, and I continued my journey, more relaxed.

The gambling den was close to the Place de la Bastille, where the infamous prison had stood. Towering sometimes six and seven storeys tall, the ramshackle buildings looked as if they might fall into the street. The houses and businesses here were one and the same thing, with workshops at the front and workers and their families crammed into the room at the rear. The passers-by and the loitering children were also noticeably poorer than in the area around the Rue Saint-Honoré. It was perhaps no surprise then, that my fine clothing attracted more attention than I liked. I avoided men's gaze, and although I wanted to check that my coins were safe, kept my hands by my sides. I strode along with confidence, as if I knew where I was going.

The den was simple enough to find; before long, a stallholder selling pots and pans had directed me to a narrow, unpaved street. I hurried down it, taking care not to walk in the muddier sections. To my relief, I saw someone of my own age knocking on a solid-looking door and being admitted. For all I knew, the house was a private residence, and the man an expected visitor, but my hopes had risen.

There were no *décrotteurs* in this neighbourhood, so I used the wall to scrape the worst of the mud off my shoes. Licking suddenly dry lips, I stepped up to the door and rapped with my knuckles. After a short pause, it opened a crack, and I found myself regarding a craggy, unfriendly face. I was delighted. Twenty to one this was the right place, I thought.

'Yes?'

'I wish to play cards.'

The doorman's eyes went up and down me, assessing my wealth.

I held my breath.

He pulled open the door. 'Enter.'

CHAPTER V

I walked in, wishing I had been able to bet my francs on the business run here. The doorman was perhaps thirty-five, broad-shouldered, and held himself in an upright manner. It seemed that as in England, the proprietors of gambling dens favoured ex-soldiers as their security. He gave me a final, cold stare, as if to be sure his opinion had been correct, and then, answering my enquiring look, jerked his slab-like chin down the gloomy hallway. 'At the end.'

The threadbare carpet was sticky underfoot, and the paint on the walls was cracked and mouldy. This was a low-class establishment, I thought, Joseph's words echoing in my mind. The chances of being cheated of my money, or robbed as I left, were high. I did not let myself consider the danger. Reaching the door at the corridor's end, from beyond which came the noise of conversation, laughter and song, I hesitated. It was not too late. I could still leave. I glanced over my shoulder. The doorman pointed and leered, managing to convey encouragement and threat in one look.

If I tried to leave now, I thought, it was ten to one that he would extort money from me, calling it an 'entrance fee'. This sharp practice was commonplace with unsure customers in London. Refusing to admit that I felt intimidated, telling myself this was indeed what I wanted, I turned the door handle, and pushed. I was met by a fug of tobacco smoke, sweat and cheap wine. The room within was better lit than the hallway, but not by much. A pair of candles burned at each table, of which there were five. A bar of sorts – barrels with planks laid on top – ran along one sidewall; several more candles guttered there, silhouetting those drowning their sorrows, or less likely, celebrating their winnings.

Every table was occupied by players; behind them stood groups of spectators, many drinking wine and smoking pipes. There were workmen in roughly spun clothing and leather work aprons and off-duty soldiers aplenty, but there was also a smattering of better-dressed customers, a mixture of clerks, merchants' assistants and lowly government employees. A handful of whores, all bosoms and rouged cheeks, were draped across men's laps, or murmuring sweet nothings in the onlookers' ears. A couple of women were playing cards, something quite rare in London salons.

My eyes roved about. There was the proprietor, a youngish man with oiled hair and a long-tailed coat. He was talking to a man who was waiting on the gaming tables, but whom I soon saw was also spying on players' cards. The croupiers, or 'crow-pees' as they were called in England, were obvious at the green-baized faro tables. There were two large men at the bar, who made no pretence of drinking, instead watching the customers and by turns, glancing at the proprietor in case of a summons. They were more muscle, and would be armed with coshes and knives, perhaps even a pistol each.

The puffs, who were given money to decoy others into playing, would only be spotted once I began to play. The same applied to the blacklegs, or gripes, cardsharps like myself. I felt a thrill of excitement. Spotting puffs and blacklegs was part of the sport.

'Monsieur?' The proprietor had materialised. I could sense his keen interest; my well-cut clothes had been noted. 'Welcome. This is your first time here?'

'It is.'

'A drink?' He clicked his fingers, and the spy-waiter came over.

'Wine,' I said. 'Red.'

The waiter made for the bar, and the proprietor asked, 'What is your fancy, monsieur? Dice, maybe, or cards?'

'Cards.'

'I thought so, monsieur. Do you prefer faro, piquet, or quadrille?'

'Have you any écarté tables?'

An unctuous smile. 'But of course. The fee to play is half a franc, and the house takes a fifth of any winnings.'

There was no point in protesting about the large cut. His gambling den, his rules, I thought, and smiling, handed over the silver coin.

'This way, monsieur.' He led me to one of the furthest tables, where six men were playing, and murmured, 'As soon as there is space, monsieur, you can join in.' He vanished, circulating around the room like a wolf watching a flock of sheep.

I was content. There was time to study my potential opponents, and those standing around the table. One at least would be in the proprietor's employ, to keep a tally of the monies wagered. Now with a cup of wine in my hand – it was strong and sour – I sipped and watched. I also eavesdropped on the nearby conversations. As was often the case these days, they were of war.

Napoleon was intent on invading Russia, and everyone knew it. No one, least of all the drunk soldier who was expounding on the theme, seemed that interested in why he wanted to take the Grande Armée east. No lover of war, I found it strange, but when I had said so to Dupont, his explanation made sense. The emperor had been leading French armies with enormous success for more than a decade. Austria had been humiliated; so too Prussia, Spain and Portugal. Russia's and Britain's noses had also been bloodied more than once. It was true that the conflict on the Iberian peninsula had been going badly for the last couple of years, but Napoleon was still loved and adored up and down the land.

As the soldier owlishly declared, if the emperor wanted to defeat Tsar Alexander again, then he for one would be happy to follow. His remark was met with loud encouragement. I had no interest, however, so I returned my attention to the table.

Five of the half-dozen players were ordinary working men. They had cheap clothing, and dirty nails. The sixth was a clerk, better dressed, and fastidious with it, despite the ink stains on the fingers of his right hand. The six were playing écarté in three pairs. I quickly decided the workers were no gripes. About the clerk, I wasn't so sure. He was certainly a good player, and it was not long before his opponent lost yet another game, and with it, the last of his money. He thumped the table in frustration, gave the clerk a filthy look, and left.

The proprietor, aware of the total monies due thanks to one of the onlookers – his employee – swooped in and took his cut.

I glanced around. 'Is anyone . . .?'

Some of the spectators had been betting between themselves, but none seemed keen to take on the clerk.

I caught his eye. 'May I, monsieur?'

'Please.' He indicated I should take the stool vacated by the angry workman.

I reached into the inner pocket of my coat, and feeling the shape of the coins there, carefully drew out ten francs. It was several days' wages for an ordinary worker, but not too much to reveal. Despite my caution, I caught greedy eyes on my hand.

'Ten francs, monsieur.' The proprietor had already seen and counted it.

'Yes.' I glanced at the clerk. 'What stake shall we play for?'

'Five sou per hand.'

I nodded my acceptance. 'And per bet?'

'Half a franc maximum.'

'Good,' I said, pushing a five sou coin so that it lay between us, and thinking, I was not going to get rich today. That was all right. This was my first foray into card playing in Paris. It was not the place to win large quantities of money, unless one had friends to walk home with, or a pistol. Catching a particularly unsavoury character's eye, I decided that having both might be preferable. The odds of leaving here without being robbed began to spin around my mind, but my rising sense of anticipation meant I was able to shove them away. It was all about the game now.

Some time later, after a to-and-fro exchange that could have seen either of us come out on top, I emerged the victor. The proprietor's cut was a fifth, but I would still walk away with almost half again what I had come with. It was time to stop, I thought. Play for longer, and the clerk could easily turn the tables. If I kept winning, I would draw down even more hungry stares and attention.

'Thank you, monsieur,' I said to the clerk. 'I have had enough.'

He looked disappointed.

I gestured towards the bar. 'It would be a pleasure to buy you a drink.'

He joined me as I left the table. Two fresh players took our places at once, and the spectators' attention left us, which had been my hope. Reaching the counter, I cast a casual glance whence we had come. I was troubled to see that one man, an unshaven, scruffily dressed fellow with a pipe clamped between his teeth was staring in my direction. The instant he saw me look, he turned his head away.

I felt my belly twist. Gripped by the thrill of playing, I had not considered the risk of betting two francs per game, as I had towards the end. What were the chances, I wondered, of making it back to

Dupont's without being robbed. The little devil in my head, the one that liked to consider the odds on the most dreadful things, now threw in his unasked opinion. The likelihood of making it back to my bene-factor's uninjured was poor. The chance of bleeding out in a gutter was also quite high. Cursing my rash behaviour, I took a big mouthful of wine.

'Does someone like your winnings?' asked the clerk quietly.

'I think so.'

He let his eyes slide over the room. 'Are you on your own?'

'No,' I lied. I had no idea if the clerk was trustworthy. The barman arrived, and I ordered a small jug of good red. 'And you?'

'My friend Pierre was rather taken with one of the whores. I think he is still engaged upstairs.'

The proprietor arrived, and relieved me of his take. 'Would you care for a game of quadrille, monsieur, or piquet?'

'Perhaps, in a while.' I raised my cup. 'I will have a drink first.'

'Of course, monsieur.' He gave me the obsequious smile I was grow-ing used to, and moved on.

'What is your name?' asked the clerk.

I tensed. He has no reason to be suspicious, I told myself. 'Mathieu. Mathieu Dupont. And yours?'

'Guillaume Bardin.'

We shook hands. I decided I liked Guillaume, who had an open, kindly face. Wine was drunk; conversation flowed. Our favourite card games were similar, and both of us loathed faro, because of the impos-sibility of ever winning meaningful amounts. Of all the entertainment available in gambling dens and salons, it was the most rigged.

Guillaume asked where I was from, and seemed to accept that I originated in Picardy, and had come to train, late, as a tailor with my uncle. A clerk at the Ministry of War, he was from Montbard, a town some hundred and fifty miles south-east of the capital. His uncle was Jean Bardin, a famous painter, or so he said. I had never heard of the man.

'You did not follow in his footsteps?' I asked.

A chuckle. 'I can paint a wall, but that is about the limit of it.'

'You have no interest in serving in the army?'

A look. 'I have more sense.' As I chuckled, he asked, 'And you, what made you want to become a tailor?'

I wondered if it was better to lie, or not. Guillaume was also a card-player, I thought. He would understand my motivations, and the odds of not being found out if I told the truth, or part of it at least, were better than lying.

'I am more of a failed merchant, to be honest. My father gave up on me, and I was sent to Paris. Tailoring will give me a trade here, but it is at cards I wish to make my fortune.'

His eyes gleamed. 'We are kindred spirits then!'

'Do you and Pierre play together?'

A dismissive shake of his head. 'Only a little. He is not a natural. Like you, I would venture to say.'

Complimented, I toasted him. 'My thanks. You are also a fine player.'

He dipped his chin in acknowledgment. 'And your friends, do they like cards also?'

I considered my options. I had caught the pipe-smoking, unshaven man staring at me again. He had a companion too, another hard-faced type I liked the look of not at all. I decided that when I left, the odds really *were* stacked against me. I did not know what they were with Guillaume, but he seemed honest.

I took a deep breath and said, 'I am here alone.'

'I did wonder.' At my look, he went on, 'You did not mention your friends by name, or indicate who they were, and a man who has got up from the table with winnings in his pocket must be careful.' He smiled. 'How do you know I can be trusted?'

I gave him a rueful look. 'I don't.'

'If I were to take your money, Mathieu, I would do it at the table.'

Grateful, I said, 'I would give you another chance, but it will be dark soon. If I am to get away from that rogue and his friend, I had best leave.'

'Have you a plan?'

'Other than to run? No.'

'Listen, then.'

Hope flared in my breast to hear his suggestion. It was risky, but less so than mine, and appealed more than simply running away. I did not know Paris well. I was reasonably sure of my ability to outstrip the thugs – I was possessed of a fleet pair of heels – but if I took a wrong turn, or tripped and fell, I would be undone.

'And your price for aiding me?' I asked, suddenly wary again.

'When the opportunity arises, we shall go to a better class of gambling establishment, you and I, and work as a team.' He offered me his hand.

I seized it fiercely. 'That is no price at all!'

They say the simplest plans work best. So it was that night. While Guillaume stayed at the bar, I ventured up to the first floor with one of the whores. The pipe-smoker and his friend watched me go, content that I would soon come back down. Thanks to Guillaume's information, however, I was after more than sating my lust. Paying the bemused whore an extra half franc to use a room at the back, I refused her breathy invitation to join her in the bed, instead clambering out of the window and dropping into a muddy alley at the rear of the building.

Following Guillaume's directions, I made my way back to the Place de la Bastille by a different route to that which I had taken earlier. Within moments of my arrival, he had joined me. Of the two rogues, there was no sign.

We laughed most of the way back to Dupont's house.

I had, I realised, made a real friend.

Several weeks went by. Guillaume and I took to meeting for a drink after work. Dupont, who had accepted my lie that we had got talking in the Jardin des Tuileries, seemed happy for me to have a friend of my own age. Little did he realise that our primary activities consisted of talking about gambling, and engaging in it on Fridays and Saturdays. These were the busiest evenings, and also when my absence from the Dupont household would go uncommented upon.

Neither of us had wanted to return to the place where we had met, judging it too dangerous. Instead, a hefty bribe paid to the head doorman of a higher-class establishment in the former Palais Royal granted us regular entry. This ate up much of our combined monies, but we judged the gamble worthwhile. To make our fortunes, we needed to frequent illustrious establishments, not miserable dens down dark alleyways.

Guillaume suggested a cautious approach to start. My imagination already laden with massive winnings, I did not want to listen, but it was sound advice. Far poorer than the other customers, a mixture of merchants, top government officials, army officers and a smattering of nobility, we could not afford to lose our hard-earned francs. Better, said Guillaume, to win small amounts, thereby building up our funds. I agreed. We also made a pact not to cheat, at least for now. Once we had become regulars, our thinking went, any initial suspicion would be dulled, and allow us to engage in a little illegal activity.

One Thursday in March, my day's work completed, I was waiting for Guillaume at one of our customary drinking holes, Bar de l'Entracte, a tavern at the back of the Palais Royal. A tiny place, it was frequented by workers from the nearby Comédie-Française theatre, and with the city full of Napoleon's soldiers, the military as well. Nursing my cup of red wine – I had grown fond of Burgundy – I kept playing myself at écarté. Still relatively new to the game, I wanted to improve my skill.

Guillaume arrived in a state of high excitement, flourishing two small, rectangular pieces of paper. 'Look!'

I barely glanced up. I had the king of trumps, and was about to beat my 'opponent' with a vole. 'What are they?'

He slapped them down on the table, obscuring the cards. 'Tickets for the theatre.'

I moved them aside, and played my first card. 'For the Comédie-Française?' It was only a few minutes' walk away, not that I had any interest. Better, I thought, to call in to the gambling salon for a few quick games.

'No, for the Gaîté.'

'Where is that?'

'Boulevard du Temple, about a mile away. Let's go. The show starts in an hour!'

CHAPTER VI

Finally, he had my attention. I peered at the tickets, and then at Guillaume. 'Why would we go to the theatre?'

'It is the last night of a fantastic play, *Le Pied de Mouton* by Martainville.'

'The Mutton Foot? It sounds dreadful.' I gave him a jaundiced look, and played for my 'opponent'. To my annoyance, he won the trick.

Guillaume sat down on the stool I had kept for him, and taking a great slurp of my wine, made an appreciative noise. 'Burgundy, eh?'

I rolled my eyes and poured him some more, which he threw back.

'We *are* going to this play,' he said.

I stuck out my jaw. 'I want to play écarté, not watch some dreadful acting about a leg of lamb.'

'Foot of Mutton! It is marvellous, you philistine, and the leading lady, well, she's a real beauty. This will be the last chance you get to see her, because she's off to Moscow.'

'Is that not foolish? Even the dogs in the street know Napoleon's plan.' This was to invade Russia the moment summer began.

An expressive shrug. 'I imagine that those who tread the boards do not concern themselves with talk of war. Besides' – he bent towards me – 'it is not as if the Grande Armée will march to Moscow, is it?'

Guillaume had lowered his voice because almost every second customer was a soldier. Nobody seemed to think that the emperor would have to go as far as the Russian capital, but it was not prudent to say so in case someone overheard and took offence. The common consensus was that the Russians would defend their territory, resulting in a set-piece battle soon after the invasion. A conclusive French victory would follow, after which Tsar Alexander would agree to Napoleon's terms. The Grande Armée would march triumphantly back to France by mid-autumn, leaving the emperor as undisputed leader of all Europe.

'Good luck to her,' I said, playing my next card.

Guillaume laid his hand over the cards of my 'opponent'. 'Please, Mathieu, come. You will enjoy it, I promise.'

When he put it like that, I could not refuse without looking like a churl, so I relented. The odds were considerable that I would not enjoy myself, but sometimes one did things for one's friends. I divided what was left in the jug between us, and we drank a toast. I paid the waiter and walked onto the street with an impatient Guillaume. He set off at great pace.

'It's, what, a mile to the Gaîté?' I said. 'Why the hurry?'

'The doors open an hour before the performance, and the pit fills quickly. We want to be as close to the stage as possible.'

We strode on, Guillaume filling my ears with chatter. Tonight was the final show in a booked-out season. The Pied de Mouton was the original and first-staged version of a much-loved style of play in France, the *féerie*. It was a fairy-tale and love story combined with ballet, duels and music. The sets were fantastic, and changed frequently; there were acrobatics and even flying actors. The leading lady, known on stage as Mademoiselle Préville, was one of the finest actresses in theatre.

Despite myself, I was being drawn in. When we reached the Gaîté, and I saw the queue stretching down the street, my sense of anticipation grew further. The crowd was made up of ordinary folk, laughing and talking excitedly, but there were plenty of soldiers too, including a red-faced one whose wife, a stout woman with shoulder-length, wavy brown hair, was loudly declaring what she thought of him drinking a month's pay in three days. His comrades in the 21st Regiment of the Line would eat well on the march east, she told him to the onlookers' amusement, but he could expect short rations. Guillaume explained that she was a *cantinière*, who cooked and provided for soldiers on campaign.

Boys selling roasted apples from trays did a brisk trade; there was a housewife offering hot bouillon for those with a real appetite. Those who could not afford the tickets offered by touts at eyewatering prices walked up and down, seeking a bargain from members of the queue. Few were successful. As more than one soldier told the ticket-hunters, this was perhaps their last chance to go to the theatre before going to war with the emperor.

'See?' Guillaume said to me. 'This is the place to be!'

Before long, the line began to move, and the crowd's excitement soared. Amid more banter and laughter, and not a little good-natured pushing, we shuffled forward.

We had just reached the door when I heard a loud, 'Make way! Make way there!' I had had no more than a moment to react when I was unceremoniously shoved aside, into Guillaume. Those around me moved back, fear and resentment in their faces.

'Make way!' The voice belonged to a tall, moustached man in an immaculately cut black coat. It was he who had pushed me.

An anger such as I had not allowed myself to feel in years surged through my veins. My older brother had been fond of shoving me aside, even when I was not in his way. Breathing deeply, I kept my tone neutral. 'Sir, that was most discourteous.'

It was as if the interloper had not heard. 'Let us go in, madame.' He was speaking to his companion, a lady in a deep blue silk dress with an incredible, ornate hat perched on her coiffured hair. She caught my eye, and her perfect top lip curled.

Blood rushed to my head. Despite my rage, I was not prepared to insult a lady, but her companion was another matter. I took a sideways step, back to where I had been.

The man's mouth became a tight white line. 'You are blocking our way.'

I heard mutters from those nearby. Guillaume plucked at my sleeve. 'Let them in. It's not worth the trouble.'

I caught the man's eye, noting it was an unusual shade of grey. Loudly, I said, 'I was before you in the line, sir. I am sure you did not mean to push me. Apologise, and we can easily put the matter behind us.'

'Are you stupid? It is you who should be begging my lady's pardon.'

Again, my brother's taunts rang in my ears. 'But you pushed me, sir,' I said, my tone rising. 'And everyone close by saw it.'

'The foolish pup whines,' he said, and his lady friend tittered. His gaze bore down on me, and there was a coldness in it that set my heart to pounding. 'Out of my way, if you do not want your hide tanned.'

Consumed by fury, forgetting the oath I had taken after beating my brother unconscious, I slapped him across the cheek.

Gasps erupted. The lady's hand rose to her mouth in shock.

The man's cheeks turned puce. 'You would challenge me to a duel?'

46

'Mathieu,' said Guillaume, pleading.

I was beyond reason. 'I would, if you are not too much of a coward.' My first action, slapping him, was a common cause of duels, and this insult poured fresh fuel on the fire.

'I, sir, am Daniel Féraud, captain of hussars, and you are . . . who?' His voice quivered with reined-in anger and contempt.

Content that every person for fifty paces was watching, I said in my broadest peasant accent, 'Mathieu Dupont. A tailor's apprentice, I am, and a loyal citizen. Think you're better than me, do you?'

He did, and so did his lady friend, but as his eyes darted around the onlookers, who were hissing and clicking their tongues in disapproval, it was clear which way the wind blew. This was France, where since the Revolution, all men were equal. To declare oneself superior to another risked a massive loss of face, not to mention social opprobrium.

His stare came back to meet mine. 'Very well. I prefer the sword. Is that acceptable?'

Only now did the madness – the insurmountable odds – of what I had done hit home. I had fenced a little as a youth, but not since. This was not a time to lie. 'I am no swordsman,' I said.

'Pistols then.' There was so much mockery in his words.

I nodded, thinking how I had not been able to shoot the militiaman, even when he would have gutted me.

'The Bois de Boulogne, tomorrow morning at eight.'

'That is too soon!' To me, Guillaume whispered 'You do not have to accept. Tell him you will meet him in a week, say, or even two.'

I considered this for the briefest of moments. I had no wish to live in anticipation any longer than was necessary. 'No,' I said to a horrified Guillaume, before demanding of Féraud, 'Where in the Bois de Boulogne?' West of the city centre, the woods were enormous.

'I know the place,' said Guillaume.

'Is this your second?' demanded Féraud, conveying yet more disdain.

Before I could say no, Guillaume, his eyes glinting, said, 'I am. And yours?'

'He will be with me tomorrow: Lieutenant Bachasson.' Done with me, his expression already convivial, Féraud offered his arm to his lady.

Quickly, I pulled Guillaume through the doorway, thereby entering the theatre before Féraud.

The onlookers cheered to see it, and someone who saw clapped me on the back.

Guillaume shook his head. 'You are a dark horse, Mathieu Dupont.'

I was surprised at myself. Until that moment, I could never have envisaged challenging a man to a duel, let alone fighting one. Not since that dark day when I had beaten my brother had I acted so. Mind spinning with what might happen the following morning, I followed Guillaume into the foyer.

A grand, candle-lit chandelier hung from the ceiling, illuminating the packed room. The crowd ebbed and flowed. Ladies preened and eyed other women. Voices called out in recognition as friends met. Queues formed in front of the beer and cider vendors.

We aimed for the pit, securing ourselves places on a wooden bench only a few rows from the stage. The space filled rapidly. We were soon packed in like fish in a barrel, but there was a great sense of camaraderie. Men were telling jokes, and singing. Watching other members of the audience, especially the wealthy in their boxes, was a major source of amusement. Loud comments rang out about such and such a lady, and how soon it would be before the gentleman to whom she was talking tried to kiss her. When a baby began to cry, there were good-natured shouts of 'Give it the breast!' and 'Sit on it!'

These diversions did not hold my attention for long. My anger had dissipated, leaving behind an odd, hollow sensation. Catching sight of Féraud and his lady companion in one of the smaller boxes, the gravity of my situation became clear. In a little over twelve hours, I would face him in the Bois de Boulogne, where we would try to kill each other. He was a trained army officer, and I had never fired a pistol. The only odds any bookmaker would give on me would be ludicrous.

I had been a fool to let my anger blaze out of control, I thought. The memory of what I had done to my brother stirred. With it came the shame. I shoved both away.

'I do not even own a pistol,' I said to Guillaume.

'You can borrow one from a friend of mine.' He saw my concern. 'There is a way out, you know. Send Féraud an apology, and he will be honour bound to accept.'

I pictured the hussar officer gloating to receive such a letter, and my cheeks warmed. 'He pushed me!'

'I know, but he is the soldier, and you are not. No one you care about will ever know if you do not go through with it.'

His suggestion was appealing. Better, surely, crowed the little devil in my head, than dying, or being grievously wounded. Both were common sequelae. 'Maybe you are right,' I said, sighing.

He squeezed my arm. 'Not everyone is made for duelling, Mathieu, or war. I know I am not.'

His sympathy stung, although he had not meant it to. I had never thought of myself as a coward, but then, I decided, my courage had never really been tested. Tomorrow it would be, if I chose to go ahead with the bout. I imagined the black-ended muzzle of Féraud's pistol aimed at me from twenty paces away, and behind it, his cold grey eyes. My gorge rose, and I almost brought up the wine I had consumed.

Loud knocking, a signal that the performance was about to start, took me from my misery. A partial hush fell, although many in the audience – drunks, late arrivals to boxes, those who did not care – continued to talk in loud voices. Even when the *trois coups*, the three blows, came, they did not quieten. As the curtain began to lift, however, they finally succumbed to the spell, as did I.

We were introduced immediately to Guzman, the hero, played by Michel Baron, an actor blessed with Casanova-like good looks. Tanned, muscular, with a glossy mane of black hair, he was joined on stage by Leonora, his true love, played by Mademoiselle Préville. The first sight of her set many in the pit to whistling and catcalling. She paid no heed whatsoever, stalking about with Guzman trailing after, begging for kisses.

I could not take my eyes off her. Blonde-haired, slim, she was not tall, but she had a presence such as I had never seen on the stage. Her face was heart-shaped, her cheekbones high, and her lips, which were thinner than most, were mesmerising. So too was her long, straight nose. The audience was similarly entranced.

When she spoke, answering Guzman's plea that he woo her, total quiet descended. She would accept his courtship, she said, but on her own terms. Before we heard what they were, Guzman's arch-enemy abducted Leonora. Smoke covered the stage, and when it cleared, she had vanished. I booed and hissed with the rest.

The remainder of the play was frenetic, with poor Guzman undergoing ordeal after ordeal to try to save Leonora. The music, ballet and theatrical effects put the playhalls of London to shame. Actors flew, and transformed into musicians; portraits moved, food disappeared from plates. Thanks to his lucky mutton foot and the help of a good fairy, Guzman ultimately triumphed over his enemy. Reunited with Leonora, the couple declared their undying love for each other to rapturous applause. It continued long after the curtain fell, with those in the pit stamping their feet until the floor shook.

Guzman and Leonora came out to take a bow. Flowers were brought up to both; as Guzman gallantly gave his to Leonora, the audience's cheers increased even further.

Guillaume had to lean close to be heard above the din. 'Glad you came?'

I nodded, without taking my eyes off Leonora.

'Quite smitten, aren't you?' I did not respond, so he dug an elbow into my ribs. 'Mathieu!'

I shot a glance at him. 'What?'

'Would you like to meet her?'

'How could we do that?' I asked, even as I thought, *she would have nothing to do with me*.

'It is the last night; well-wishers are allowed to wait outside the actors' dressing rooms. Those who get there first have the greatest chance of being allowed in.' Guillaume studied my face, which showed a mixture of desire and embarrassment. 'Well?'

I thought suddenly of Féraud, and sickening reality crashed home. 'No.'

'This might be your only chance.'

'What does it matter? In the unlikely event that I survive tomorrow, she is going to Moscow.'

'You could still apologise.'

Until that moment, I had given it serious consideration. Faced with what seemed certain death the next morning – fifteen to one that I would be injured, at the least – I made up my mind. Duelling protocol meant that an apology was only acceptable if sent before the injured parties met.

'You're right. I will write it within the hour.'

'Good. I will find him before he leaves, and ask for his address. Let us meet outside.' Guillaume joined the throng making their way to the exit.

My eyes rose to the box where I had seen Féraud and his lady companion. They were still there, he bent close to her, speaking, she listening and nodding. Then, to my horror, her eyes moved, the glittering, chandelier-cast light allowing her to somehow find mine down in the pit. Her pretty face twisted in contempt, and she said something to Féraud. I could have looked away, lost myself in the crowd, but was prevented from doing so by the shreds of my pride. Seeing me, Féraud smiled. His right hand came up, fingers shaping a pistol.

Before he could mime firing it, I looked away. The anger came bubbling up again, and for the second time that evening, I forgot my oath.

'Guillaume!' I shouted.

Almost at the exit, he turned. 'Yes?'

'Come back. I have changed my mind.' It might be rash, I thought, but there was only so much battering my pride could take. I would face Féraud tomorrow, no matter the consequences.

CHAPTER VII

Irritable, tired and scared, I barely slept a wink that night. What rest I had involved unpleasant dreams of Féraud. With no desire to have any more, I got up when the grandfather clock in the hall struck half past six. There was no need to write a will, as I had no offspring, and my only possessions were my clothes. I wrote a short letter to my mother and father, asking forgiveness for all my misdeeds, and assuring them of my love. I penned a note to Dupont, thanking him for all he had done, and asking that the letter be sent to England in the event I did not return later in the day.

Dressing again in my fine clothes – if I was to die, I wanted to look my best – I crept downstairs in my stockinged feet. Anna's cat, a delightful tabby of which I was fond, twined itself around my legs, purring. The Dupont's maid, a stout motherly type, however, was more startled by my appearance. Pulling on my shoes, I muttered something about having to go the shop early, to finish a gentleman's coat. Before she had time to ask questions, I had grabbed my cloak and slipped out of the front door into the cool spring air.

What Dupont would make of my lie, I had no idea. *You need not worry about it,* the little devil in my head declared. I had not the energy to shout him down, nor to stop the fearful odds spinning around my mind. Ten to one I would die. Fifteen to one that I was maimed. Fifty to one that I hit Féraud, but did not badly injure him. One hundred to one that I killed him.

I brooded over my rash behaviour. Until Féraud, I had been successful in controlling my temper. Triggered by him calling me stupid and then shoving me, however, I had completely lost control of myself. Perhaps he was to be the instrument of my punishment for the breaking of my vow, I thought. It seemed apt. Deep in gloom, I made my way towards Jardin des Tuileries. Passing a bakery, my nostrils filled with the delicious aroma of fresh bread. My stomach heaved, and I hurried past.

We had arranged to meet at a quarter past seven, but Guillaume was already waiting at the entrance to the gardens. My heart lifted a little. I was able to return his smile with a weak one of my own. As we began walking westward, I noted the cloth-wrapped bundle in his hands.

'The pistol?' I asked.

'Yes.'

I said nothing else. I did not want to see it, until I had to.

We took the most direct route to the Bois de Boulogne, along the Champs-Élysées. In normal circumstances, I would have stared at the unfinished, magnificent Arc de Triomphe, Napoleon's monument to celebrate his victory at Austerlitz. Today I walked by without even looking at it.

I had visited the Bois de Boulogne several times with the Duponts. A former royal park, it was popular with Parisians for Sunday walks. Drawing close to the edge of the forest, I wished that were my purpose now. Trees spread out to our left and right, as if we were in the middle of the countryside. There were early blossoms on the cherry trees. In the distance, between the beeches and oaks, I could see the former hunting lodge of Pavillon d'Armenonville. Birds were singing, welcoming the new day. More peaceful a scene I could not have pictured.

'This way,' said Guillaume, taking a path that went left among the trees.

'Have you been to a duel before?' I asked nervously.

'Mon Dieu, no, but everyone knows where they are fought.'

It made sense. I had never been to the spot in Hyde Park where men duelled, and bled, and died, but I knew its location.

Guillaume sensed my mood, and made no attempt to draw me into conversation. At length, we came to an enormous grassy clearing. Perhaps a hundred and fifty paces away, two figures were visible.

'What time is it?' I asked.

Guillaume consulted his pocket watch. 'Ten minutes to eight.'

There was no point in delay, I thought, my nerves tightening. 'Show me the pistol.'

He knelt and unwrapped the cloth, revealing a duelling pistol with a plain wooden butt and brass-plated barrel, a small leather bag and a powder flask. There were also several tiny squares of cloth, wadding to go around the ball. 'It is not expensive, but it's a good quality weapon,' he said.

'I will load it. That is your job, I know, but I must do it. I have to.' I had done it once before, with the pistol I had had at the beach.

Guillaume nodded.

Aiming the barrel end at the sky, I pulled the tip off the end of the powder flask. 'How many grains?'

'About thirty.'

I made a rough count as they fell, then set down the flask. Guillaume had already taken a ball from the leather bag. I wrapped it in a cloth square, then shoved the lot into the end of the barrel. Pulling the ramrod out, I pushed ball and wadding down as far as they would go.

I glanced at Guillaume, flask at the ready. 'And in the pan?'

A shrug. 'Half cover it,' he said.

Pan filled, I gently brought the steel back down to protect it. 'Happy?'

'As I can be.' Guillaume's kindly face was troubled. 'Perhaps it is not too late. You could try apologising to Féraud.'

'I could,' I admitted. The truth was, I regretted my behaviour the previous day. If I had just taken the humiliation, I would still be in my bed, rather than facing death in the Bois de Boulogne. 'Let us see what mood he is in. If it seems possible, you can ask.'

To look less confrontational, I gave the pistol back to Guillaume, who held it balanced it in the crook of his left elbow. We walked at a measured pace towards Féraud and his second, leaving a trail of shoe-shaped impressions in the dewy grass. My mouth was dry, fear mounting, but I kept my face impassive. Whatever Féraud might think of my apology, he must not see that I was afraid.

Féraud's second came forward. He was a thin-faced type with bad teeth. As was the custom, Guillaume went to meet him.

'I am Bachasson,' he said politely enough. 'That is Dupont and you are . . .?'

'Bardin.'

'What distance is agreeable – twenty paces?' This was standard.

'I – my friend was wondering if Captain Féraud would accept an apology?'

A surprised sniff. A glance at Féraud, who was staring off in the opposite direction, as if he had no interest in the proceedings. 'I can ask.' He did not sound hopeful. Off he went, and Guillaume shot me a look. He did not think Bachasson would be successful either. Twenty-five to one, I thought, at the least.

A few moments later, Bachasson returned. 'Captain Féraud refuses. Any such attempt should have been made before this morning's meetings, as Monsieur Dupont ought to know.'

'He *is* aware.'

'I see.' Another sniff, one that intimated Bachasson thought I was stupid, or a coward, or both. 'As I say, Captain Féraud will not consider an apology. Shots must be fired for honour to be restored.'

My stomach did a neat and unpleasant roll.

'Very well,' said Guillaume. 'Twenty paces it is. First blood will be sufficient for my principal.' This meant the duel could end if a man was wounded, rather than have to continue until one participant was dead.

'That is also acceptable.'

'How many shots each?'

Two was the norm. I felt sick to think of having to stand not just once, but twice while my enemy took aim and fired at me.

'Captain Féraud says he only needs one,' Bachasson declared.

Guillaume agreed, and I tried to wipe my sweaty palms on my trousers without being obvious. I had no idea if I would even be able to shoot at Féraud, vile human being though he was. He, on the other hand, seemed fully prepared to kill me.

'Can the participants advance before they shoot?' asked Bachasson.

We had talked of this. 'No,' said Guillaume.

He and Bachasson walked to Féraud, who had taken off his coat and armed himself from a wooden box that was lying close by on the grass. He took up a position side on to me, pistol held down by his right side. Guillaume and Bachasson paced in my direction, both counting out loud. Reaching twenty a short distance from me, they both beckoned. I walked, the little devil gleefully announcing that these were perhaps the last steps I would ever take. *Shut up*, I snarled at it. To my relief, the voice vanished.

Guillaume proffered the pistol, and said, 'Turn sideways.'

I obeyed.

'When I let my handkerchief fall,' said Bachasson, 'you may both shoot. Understand?'

My 'yes' came out as a croak, so dry was my throat. My heart was racing as if I had drunk half a dozen cups of strong coffee. Breathe, I told myself. Breathe.

Guillaume touched my shoulder, and went with Bachasson to the halfway point between me and Féraud. They stood well back, but near enough that we would be able to see the handkerchief.

'You may raise your pistols and cock.'

Carefully, I drew back the curved metal that held the flint. I lifted my arm and pointed the pistol at Féraud, staring down its barrel at his smug, moustached face.

Bachasson's handkerchief was a little white square on the left side of my vision. Féraud filled its centre. His weapon appeared to be aimed at my heart.

How bad would the pain be, I wondered. Would I feel the lead ball rip into my flesh, tearing blood vessels, shattering bone, or would I just fall to the turf, severely wounded? No surgeon was present: I did not know one, and Féraud had not offered to bring one, probably, I thought, because he expected to emerge unscathed.

'Ready?' called Bachasson.

'Yes,' we chorused.

Guillaume had told me that a duellist's greatest test was from the time the word 'ready' was given until the handkerchief dropped. Until that moment, I had not appreciated the saying's truth. Never had the seconds stretched so long. I felt every beat of my fearful heart, each shallow breath. My right arm stretched out in front of me, elbow locked. My finger was tight on the trigger. Down the barrel, I could see Féraud. His eyes. His pistol.

On the edge of my vision, a flutter of white, heading groundward. Bachasson had dropped his handkerchief.

I did not shoot. I paused, tongue stuck to the roof of my mouth with fear, telling myself that this was all a bad dream.

A puff of smoke rose from Féraud's pistol. The tiniest delay. Then with a sound like thunder, more smoke belched from its end. Air whistled past me, so close, and I was still standing, my weapon yet aimed at Féraud. I blinked, awareness dawning. Christ above, he had missed! My next thought was regret, at not having been able to wager a hundred francs, more, on this improbable outcome.

Féraud had lowered his pistol. He was glaring, but remained in position. 'Take your shot,' he shouted, his voice full of impotent fury.

I stared at him along the length of my barrel, savouring the feeling. My arm was steady. His pistol was empty. I could take my time. I could shoot him in the leg, or if I wished, in the belly, even in the chest. I held the dog's life in my hands. It was surprising how intoxicating the power was.

'Shoot, damn you!' Féraud roared.

Still I waited. I imagined squeezing the trigger. The explosion in the pan, the slight lag. The roar as the charge exploded. Féraud's shock as the ball struck him. His form crumpling. Crimson soaking through his white linen shirt. His bellows of pain.

Do it, urged the little devil. *Kill him.*

'Mathieu?' Guillaume's voice, concerned. 'You must also shoot.'

I did not want to end another man's life, I decided, even that of someone like Féraud. I pointed my pistol at the ground and fired – the delope.

His face, shocked, disbelieving, was a picture.

'There you are, monsieur,' I said with a mocking half bow. 'Honour has been served.'

He gave me a look worthy of the Medusa.

'Gentlemen, please shake hands to signify that your quarrel is over,' said Bachasson. Guillaume was nodding.

We walked towards each other. Smiling, I stretched out my right hand. We shook, but our eyes told a different story. Mine said, you are a boor, and I despise you. His said, you have humiliated me, and this fight is not over.

I did not care. I had survived a duel. I had not injured or killed my opponent. I was also the undisputed moral victor.

Féraud could put that in his pipe and smoke it, I thought, feeling ever so slightly smug.

In high spirits, Guillaume and I found an early morning house, and proceeded to drink ourselves close to insensible. When I considered it afterwards, my behaviour was a reaction to the near-death experience I had been through. For his part, Guillaume was as pleased as I. He had resigned himself to my being maimed or slain, he declared, staring into my eyes in the intensely earnest manner possessed by the inebriated.

By the time I managed to stumble back to the Duponts' house, it was early afternoon. Again the maid was the first person I encountered. Her disapproving sniff said it all. Hoping to reach my room undetected, I set a foot on the staircase.

'Is that you, Mathieu?' Dupont's voice came from his study.

'I – yes.' I did my best to stand up straight.

Emerging, he took one look. 'You are drunk.'

'I am.' There was not much else to say. I swayed, waiting for his next question.

'I read your note.' He stared at me. 'Were you duelling? I can think of no other reason to leave such a message when going out at the crack of dawn.'

I considered lying, but muzzy-headed, could think of nothing plausible. 'I was, yes.'

'And the reason – was it gambling? A debt?'

I shook my head.

'A woman?'

'No.'

Dupont listened as I related my tale. I omitted how I had pushed in front of Féraud after the duel had been agreed, but the whole affair still sounded pathetic, like a school-yard disagreement taken to the point of extreme violence. The exhilaration I had felt to have my opponent at my mercy was long gone. I finished, expecting the full weight of Dupont's wrath, and thinking, I deserved it.

'You were rash to confront him, Mathieu. With the army preparing for war, Paris is full of such men,' said Dupont. He let that sink in, before adding, 'Nonetheless, I am impressed by your courage on the field, and even more so by your restraint during the bout. Duelling is no longer in fashion, yet there are few who would have judged you for shooting the hussar officer, even if he had been slain. To show mercy after he had taken his shot is the mark of a true gentleman.'

I blinked in confusion. This was not what I had expected. 'You are not disappointed in me?'

'Tchhh.' A dismissive noise. 'You are young and impetuous! Believe it or not, I was once like that. I even fought a duel, over a lady.' He chuckled at my stare, and said, 'We both drew blood, and agreed to settle the matter at that.' Now he wagged a finger. 'That was my first and last experience of duelling. Let it be the same for you.'

'Yes, Monsieur Dupont.' I felt quite repentant, like a sinner who has just given his confession.

'And I would stay away from Féraud and his friend Bachasson – those were their names, you said?'

'Yes.'

'Féraud sounds like a nasty piece of work, and Bachasson might well be the Minister of the Interior's son.'

I nodded, determined not to forget Dupont's advice.

CHAPTER VIII

My good fortune in the duel gave me an enormous boost of confidence. Determined to carry this into other parts of my life, on the Monday following the duel I went to the gambling salon Guillaume and I frequented. It was the first time I had gone on my own to the Palais Royal. The head doorman let me in, with the warning that his palm needed greasing again by the night's end. Sure that I would win, I gave him firm assurance of the same.

I started with écarté, the game at which I was most confident. My first opponent, a balding man with the odd habit of rolling his eyes up into his head when he spoke, was shrewd. We played half a dozen games, each winning three, neither winning any money, before he decided to try his luck at piquet. Glad to see the back of him, I stayed at the table, sipping wine and assessing other people in the room with a carefully blank expression. The men who had been watching us moved on to other tables, which suited. Before too long, a fleshy-faced colonel of artillery enquired if the space opposite was free.

'Please, Colonel. It would be a pleasure,' I said, liking the rosy flush of his cheeks. Intoxication was a sure way to lose at cards; if I could also cheat a little, so much the better.

We chose a single card each to see who dealt first. He won, and enquired if twenty-franc bets were acceptable. This would prove uncomfortable if I lost, but I decided that my chances of relieving him of decent amounts of his money were two, perhaps three to one. If I managed to mark some cards without noticing, the odds would improve considerably. I accepted.

I asked if he was to go to Russia, and was told proudly that he was. Feigning interest, I let him wax lyrical about the humiliations Napoleon would heap on Tsar Alexander. I also deliberately lost the first game. My tactics saw the bait swallowed in a single gulp.

Dealing, I asked if we could bet on each trick. 'Five francs, say.'

His protuberant eyes studied me. 'Very well,' he said, slurping his wine. A click of his fingers saw his crystal glass refilled by a waiter. I accepted the same, but each time the colonel drank greedily, I only sipped. A handful of men gathered to watch. The inevitable bets on who would win began.

We played, him badly, while I was blessed with my cards. My winnings began to mount. The colonel was becoming more choleric, and also growing drunker. He was blithely unaware that the onlookers were no longer betting on him, and my suggestion of fifteen-franc wagers per trick was instantly agreed. I decided to mark some high cards with a thumbnail. Beat him in the next two games, and then make my excuses, and I could walk away with four hundred, maybe even five hundred francs.

Over the course of the next game, I managed to score three court cards, including the king of clubs. I managed this by holding my cards against my chest with my left hand, and covering all with the right. This allowed me, if the desired card was in the right place, to gently run a thumbnail over one of the card's corners. It was a delicate operation, performed blind. Too much pressure, and it would be obvious that the card had been marked. Too little, and the card remained indeterminable from the rest.

Sweating more than was comfortable, I took a slow sip of wine, and used the opportunity to let my attention roam beyond the glass, over the spectators. To my complete astonishment, Mademoiselle Préville was standing to the left of the colonel. She had not been there a moment before, and she was watching me. Discomfited, I inhaled some wine. A coughing fit ensued. But for the man who passed a handkerchief over my shoulder, my embarrassment would have been even greater. Gradually the irritation in my throat eased. Eyes streaming, my face puce, I had somehow managed not to reveal my cards.

'Are you well, monsieur?' asked the colonel.

'I am . . .' Another paroxysm. 'Thank you. Some wine went down the wrong way.' My gaze flicked to Mademoiselle Préville, I could not help it, and I saw the corners of her mouth twitch. My cheeks burned afresh. She knew perfectly well the effect she had had on me, I thought.

Despite my discomfiture, the marked cards proved invaluable. I beat the colonel twice more. He had had enough. Glowering, he got up from the table. Pleased that my cheating had gone unnoticed, I gathered up the banknotes that had lain between us, and folded them neatly. Before I could place them in my wallet, a gentle voice asked, 'Do you not wish to continue playing, monsieur?'

Mademoiselle Préville had taken the colonel's seat.

'Mademoiselle,' I said, adding awkwardly, 'it would be my honour to play you.' I was not sure that that was true, but to refuse would seem discourteous, the last thing I wanted her to think. A man using his wits might have wondered why she was not sitting with the senior officers and high-ranking government officials in the room, but her dazzling smile had set me atremble. I gave it no consideration whatsoever.

I began to shuffle the cards, but she called out to one of the croupiers. He came running over like a puppy dog – she was clearly highly regarded, I decided – and with much fawning, gave her a new deck.

'Fresh cards, don't you think, monsieur . . .?'

'As you wish, mademoiselle. As for my name, it is Mathieu Dupont,' I said, wondering if she knew what I had done with my thumbnail. 'And yours?'

One of her delicately plucked eyebrows rose, even as disbelieving guffaws rose around the table. The comments rained down. 'This is Mademoiselle Préville, you buffoon.' 'She is one of the most famous actresses in Paris!' 'Have you never been to the theatre?'

She waved a hand, and the comments stopped, as candles are snuffed out by a gust of wind. 'Perhaps this gentleman is not a theatre-goer. That is not a crime!'

I bowed my head at her grace, and came clean. 'In truth, mademoiselle, I do recognise you, but I only know your stage name.'

'Ooooh,' said someone in a high pitched voice. 'Mark this one!'

I flushed, and my eyes searched for the man who had spoken.

'Ignore them, monsieur,' she said quietly. 'My name is Jeanne Drouin.'

'A name as beautiful as its owner.'

She smiled, ignoring the oohs and ahs, and suggestive comments. 'You are kind, Monsieur Dupont. Shall we play?'

It was soon clear that she was a consummate écarté player. Even if the cards had been with me, which they were not, I was unsure I could have beaten her. Few of the onlookers were betting on me, and as she won yet another game, it was difficult not to suspect that I had been chosen deliberately. I had had the wit to refuse per-trick wagers, though, so my losses were not cataclysmic. I made a decision. Although it was glorious to sit opposite her, free to study her beauty, I had no wish to lose all the gains made against the colonel.

'You have the better of me, mademoiselle,' I said. 'I must call a halt to proceedings.'

Her lips made a moue. 'We are only getting started, monsieur. Your luck will change, I am sure.'

I bowed my head, my only way to resist. 'Another time perhaps, mademoiselle.' I scooped up the notes in front of me, and with another bow as I rose, left her to it.

I circulated the room for a time. It was useful to study other players, as well as to watch the onlookers. If any of the latter were in league with men at the tables, I could avoid such pairings like the plague. Pausing by a game of écarté, I won thirty francs in short time by betting on a middle-aged, richly dressed man, and pleased with this, stayed to watch him play again. He was wearing a wig, nowadays unusual.

Concentrating, I did not pay any attention when someone came to stand by my right side. When an alluring perfume entered my nostrils, I turned my head. Instantly, my pulse increased. It was Mademoiselle Préville.

We exchanged smiles. I wondered if she had been unable to secure another partner, if perhaps many of the clientele were aware of her skill.

'Do you play quadrille, monsieur?' she asked.

'The rules are far too complex,' I said, telling the truth. 'And you?'

'It is my favourite game.'

'I will not play you at that then! I have already learned my lesson at écarté.'

She laughed. 'Fresh cards make quite the difference, do they not?'

I coloured. 'What do you mean?'

'You know perfectly well.'

'But you did not say anything.' If she had told the proprietors, I would have been ejected from the salon. A beating would also have been possible.

'I wanted to see if I could beat you. Also, you are handsome.'

I did not know what to say to that, so I changed the topic. 'I was at the final performance of the *Pied de Mouton*. You were wonderful.'

'That is most kind.'

'You must have heard that thousands of times.'

'It never tires.' A sideways glance. 'Especially if the compliment is genuine.'

'It is. You were correct in your assumption earlier. I am no theatre-goer, but I could have watched you all night.' Another smile, which encouraged me, as did the fact that she had no airs or graces. 'I understand that you are soon going to Moscow?'

'You seem to know a lot about me.' As I began to protest, she touched my arm lightly, and said, 'I jest. That is common knowledge. Yes, I leave in two days.'

'Are the roads into Russia even passable?'

'They are. The journey will be long and arduous, it is true, but I cannot pass up the opportunity.'

I asked her how she had come to be an actress.

She gave me an arch look. 'Rather than be married off with children, you mean?'

Embarrassed, for there was some truth in her question, I said, 'You are the first actress I have ever met; I know nothing about the world of theatre.'

She seemed to accept that. Suggesting that we move to somewhere more private – as she said, 'here the walls have ears' – we moved to the side of the room, not far from where food and drink was served. Her family was from Paris, and theatrical. Both her parents had been actors, and one of her grandfathers before that. Being on stage was all she had ever wanted.

'I am lucky in that regard,' she said. 'Not many people have a profession that they genuinely love.'

'That is true,' I said, thinking of my father's importing business, and my putative apprenticeship with Dupont.

'You do not enjoy your job? What is it that you do?'

'I am learning to be a tailor.'

'You strike me as rather old for an apprentice, as well as, how shall I say, a little too genteel.'

'My uncle took me in a few months ago, after I left my father's employ.'

'You clashed with him?'

I liked Jeanne, and I was already tired of the half lies, the avoidance of the fact that I had grown up in Kent. Yes, war raged between

England and France, but I was no soldier, no spy. Better to tell the truth when I could, I decided.

'I stole from him.'

She looked genuinely surprised. 'It is honest to admit that.'

With an effort I met her gaze. 'I like to gamble, and drink.'

'What did your father do when he found out?'

'He wrote off the monies I had taken, and also paid my debts.'

There was sympathy in her face as she asked, 'But you gambled again?'

Shame swelled in my chest. 'Yes. When he found out, he threw me onto the street.'

'This was not in Paris – I can tell by your accent.'

'No.'

A fresh dilemma presented itself. Reveal my origins, and I would be at her mercy. She likes me, I thought impetuously. The likelihood of her betraying me to the police was negligible.

'Where are you from?'

I took a gamble. 'My father is from Normandy.' Lowering my voice to a whisper, I added, 'and my mother is English. I grew up in England.'

Her dark blue eyes widened. 'Why did you come to France?'

I told her the whole sorry tale. To my alarm, she began to laugh.

'You do not believe me?'

'I am sorry, Mathieu – can I call you Mathieu? Your story is incredible – I would struggle to make it up. It does have the ring of truth, however.' She studied my face closely. 'You are not an English spy?'

'No!' Desperate that she should believe me, my voice had risen.

Heads turned. Men looked. They were not near enough to have heard, but nonetheless, my spine tingled. The inside of a French gaol was not somewhere I wanted to be acquainted with.

'Peace.' Her hand was on my arm again, and this time she did not remove it. 'I believe you.'

Relieved, I nodded.

'So you plan to become a tailor, and to remain here in Paris?'

I shrugged. 'No one in England would believe what happened on the beach. I could live there as a fugitive, I suppose, but the thought does not appeal.'

'And yet that is exactly what you are doing here.'

It was my turn to chuckle. 'I had not thought of it like that.'

'Your dream is to make a fortune at cards, is it not?'

I nodded.

'Mine is the same. With my winnings, I would open my own theatre, put on whichever plays I wished. And you?'

'I had thought about opening my own gambling salon.'

'You also like wine, Mathieu. Therein lies ruin.'

'I do not drink that much,' I said, trying to ignore the little devil's mocking laughter.

'I am glad to hear it.' She gave me a look. 'I am hungry. Shall we eat? I do not mean here, but at Beauvilliers', perhaps.' In another part of the Palais Royal, this was regarded as the best restaurant in Paris.

'Your offer is appealing, mademoiselle, thank you, but we would never get a table.'

She regarded me from beneath half-lowered eyelashes. 'The owner is an admirer. We *will* have a table.'

I nodded in acceptance, scarcely able to believe my good fortune.

I had taken the staircase that led to Beauvilliers' once before, the first time Guillaume and I had been searching for the gambling salon, but I had never been within. Set inside what had been a suite of apartments, it was grander than anywhere I had yet been in Paris. Light from the quinquet lamps bounced from mirror to gilt-edged mirror. There was a profusion of gold scrollwork, and the carpet underfoot was thick and gaily patterned.

To the left of the entrance was a throne-like seat encircled by a waist-high wooden barrier, not unlike the *estrade* in the audience chamber of a Spanish viceroy. Upon it sat a lady of majestic gravity and dignified bulk, attended by a demurely dressed younger woman.

Jeanne saw my curiosity. 'That is Madame Beauvilliers, the proprietress, and her attendant. When the waiters take payment, they bring the cash to her.'

The place looked filled to capacity. Perhaps half the tables were occupied by army officers, enjoying themselves before the invasion of Russia began, and the rest were taken by the rich and well-to-do. There was small chance of dining here tonight, I thought, but my doubts eased with the head waiter's reaction to Jeanne. A trim figure in a close-bodied vest and spotless white apron, he bowed deeply and announced that he was honoured to see her again. There was no enquiry if we had a reservation.

With swift efficiency, our cloaks were taken and we were guided to a quiet corner where a single empty table stood, almost as if it had been waiting for us to arrive. He swept out a chair for Jeanne, and a second waiter did the same for me. Menus were produced, printed on double folio the size of an English newspaper, and when the inevitable enquiry came about drinks, I boldly ordered champagne. This elicited a pleased nod, and then we were alone.

'I have never seen a bill of fare like it,' I said in amazement. 'I will be all night trying to decide. There are thirteen types of soup alone.'

'I have dined here many times. Tell me what you like, and I shall choose for you.'

'Thank you.' Jealousy spiked me as I wondered how many other gentlemen had wined and dined Jeanne in Beauvilliers'. I decided to beard the lion in his den. 'Do you have a particular friend, mademoiselle?'

'That is a bold question to ask of a lady. Since you ask, however, I do not.'

This news felt better than if I had won five thousand francs at the gaming table.

She gave me an appraising look. 'You are pleased.'

'I – well, yes. Very.'

The champagne arrived, affording my embarrassment an opportunity to subside. Crystal glasses filled, we toasted one another.

'To you, Jeanne,' I said. 'May your star rise high above the Moscow stage.'

She liked that, and began to wax lyrical about the theatre where she would work. After a time the food began to arrive, artichoke with pepper for her, cucumber salad with vinaigrette for me, and we continued to talk and laugh with a new ease and familiarity. I made her laugh with details of my walk from the coast to Paris, stealing clothing and begging food from bakeries, and hiding in a hay cart to enter the city.

'I think you might be an English spy after all,' she said again, her tone joking.

I saluted her with my glass, my second or third. The champagne was fizzing through my veins. 'Maybe I am, mademoiselle, but measuring, cutting and stitching cloth will not be of much use to my masters.'

She smiled. 'Nor will the details of theatre life in Paris.'

The main course, an excellent gratinated beef dish that we shared, required a change to red wine. Jeanne ordered an expensive burgundy. A decent amount of my winnings would be going to the venerable Madame Beauvilliers before the night's end, I thought. I did not care. Jeanne's company was worth twice the price.

During the natural break between the main course and dessert, Jeanne went 'to powder her nose', as she quaintly phrased it. I sat back and for the first time since our arrival, cast an eye around the other diners. To my horror, I saw Bachasson, Féraud's second, seated just three tables away. There were three others present, a pair of glamorous women and one man, whose back was to me. The nearest of the women was Féraud's companion from the theatre.

Riveted, I watched sidelong, recognising the hussar officer a moment later, when he turned, revealing his profile. Their conversation was loud and convivial; it seemed unlikely I had been spotted, but I twisted in my seat, eager not to be seen.

'You are as pale as a sheet, Mathieu.' Jeanne had returned. 'Are you feeling unwell?'

'It will pass.' I took a sip of my wine as if to prove the point.

Like all women, she noticed when my attention was not on her. 'You keep glancing to the left,' she said, her eyes roving. 'Who is it?'

'I fought a duel some days ago. My opponent is sitting three tables over.'

One of her hands, with unfashionably short nails that I liked, rose to her mouth. 'A duel? Not the one that resulted from a disagreement at the entrance to the theatre?'

'The same.'

'I have heard a dozen versions of that incident,' she declared. 'I had no idea it was you. Will you tell me about it?'

I laid it out from the start. I had regretted my loss of temper almost from the start, I explained, but Féraud's arrogance had strengthened my resolve to carry through with it. Jeanne's interest grew as I described the duel, and how Féraud had fired first and missed.

'He is sitting here, eating, so you did not even wound him,' she said, curiosity filling her voice. 'You missed as well?'

'No. I chose to use the delope.'

'After the way he treated you, did you not want to shoot him?'

'Honour had been served. Just because a man is an arrogant boor does not mean he should be wounded or killed.'

'*Magnifique!*' Her eyes were shining.

Her smile lit up my heart.

Bill settled a short time later – Jeanne had accepted my paying with a gracious nod of thanks – we began to make our way towards the entrance. It would have been wiser, I thought afterwards, to have taken a path that avoided Féraud, but as the little devil in my head maintained, there was no reason to.

I could also have kept my attention fixed on Jeanne, or on the bustling figure of Monsieur Beauvilliers, busy enquiring of other diners if they were happy with their food. Instead, my dislike of Féraud again coming to the fore, part of me wanting to show off in front of Jeanne and with the little devil egging me on, I watched him as we approached his table, engaged in animated debate. He sensed my gaze, in the way men do, and looked up.

A massive scowl twisted his handsome face.

The little devil was in full control now. 'Mademoiselle, this is Captain Féraud, whom I faced in the Bois de Boulogne,' I said to Jeanne.

'You are fortunate, Captain,' she said. 'But for Mathieu's restraint, you would not be here, enjoying a fine dinner.'

He conjured a convincing, even charming, smile. 'Indeed, mademoiselle.'

We exchanged brief pleasantries with Bachasson and the ladies, while Féraud sat there simmering like a stewpot left too long on the fire, before I took Jeanne's arm again and bid them a good evening. Malevolence oozed from Féraud, but his lady companion said something to him, and he turned away.

'You are a real risktaker, Monsieur Dupont,' Jeanne said in my ear. 'Be careful it does not get you into trouble.'

'Will it get me in trouble with you?' I asked.

'We shall see.' And then, to my surprise and delight, she kissed me full on the lips.

Exhilarated, I did not look back at Féraud. If I had, my joy might have been dampened, because his expression was one of pure and utter hatred.

CHAPTER IX

Begging leave of Dupont, I spent most of the next two days with Jeanne. Not as man and wife, she did not permit that, but she was inventive in ways I had never imagined. Having kissed and only kissed few enough women, I existed in a state of dazed bliss. We rarely left her apartment, a small two-roomed affair close to the Gaîté, unless it was for food and drink, and another time so I could introduce her to Guillaume. It was no surprise, therefore, that our parting on the morning of the third day was bittersweet.

'Come to Moscow,' she urged as we waited at the junction from which she would be picked up.

I took her in my arms. She kissed me, and I wavered. 'What would I do?' I asked.

'You could find a job in the theatre, I am sure of it.'

'Working together, living together – that would not be wise.' I could see by her expression that she thought the same thing, so I kissed her, and said, 'I will see you again when you come back from Moscow.'

'That will be a year!' She pouted. 'By then I might have found a rich Muscovite and settled down.'

'That would be my ill luck and his good fortune,' I said, fighting my jealousy. 'I will wait for you, though.'

At once her expression became serious. 'I would like that.'

The carriage arrived. She exchanged happy greetings with the other actors – six of them were travelling to Moscow – and her bags were loaded. We had time for one last embrace. I held her tight. 'Do not forget me,' I said.

'How could I forget my English spy?' she whispered in my ear, and then, with a playful laugh, she clambered up the step. Ignoring the dirigible's pleas, she hung out the door waving. 'I will write to you,' she called.

'I will reply!'

Then the carriage rounded a corner and was gone.

Gloom settled over me like a heavy winter cloak. When I met Guillaume later, he took one look at me, and announced an immediate trip to the theatre, to a comedy. A convivial dinner with copious quantities of wine followed. A couple of hours at the gambling salon later that night saw us come away with almost two hundred francs profit. By the time Jeanne returned, Guillaume promised, we would both be wealthy men.

I went to bed in fine spirits.

March became April, and with the coming of spring, war clouds gathered over Paris. Units of immaculately turned-out cavalry paraded daily up and down the Champs Élysées. The Imperial Guard, the Young and the Old, marched there too, cheered by the adoring public, with little boys running alongside playing soldiers. One day I saw the band of the Polish Chevau-Légers play, led by a magnificently mounted kettle-drummer with a plumed helmet, and on another my walk home was halted by the passing of two regiments of proud Illyrian infantry.

Off-duty officers filled the restaurants, and packed out the theatres and gambling salons. Rank and filers drank in the ordinary bars, and gamed at dice and cards in dens like the one where I had met Guillaume. I spoke with many, grew familiar with tales of military valour, of Napoleon's successes. Every last man seemed determined to enjoy himself before humbling the imperial Russian bear. So their brave talk went, not just in French, but in Italian, German, Polish and half a dozen other languages besides, the languages of Napoleon's vast empire. The men in the capital were but a tiny fraction of his army.

Hundreds of thousands more awaited his arrival in Germany and Poland. According to Guillaume, the Grande Armée would total more than half a million men. The staggering number almost defied belief, but they explained the loud, confident conversations I overheard in the gambling salons. The Russians could never prevail against such overwhelming force. They would break and run, perhaps not even fight Napoleon, Master of Europe. The moment the Grande Armée crossed onto Russian soil, others said, Tsar Alexander would capitulate. It was commonly accepted that the emperor would be back in Paris by Christmas, if not sooner.

The ebullience passed me by. I had no interest in Napoleon's war; I hoped only that Jeanne would be safe in Moscow. It was too soon for a reply to my letter; even if the letter I had sent had reached her, freshly arrived, she would not have had time to reply. Despite knowing this, I pined. No message had come from my mother either, which exacerbated my low mood. I drank heavily, which made me want to spend more time at the card tables. Dupont soon suspected what I was up to. 'Do not return to your old ways,' he warned. Like a fool, I paid no heed. I took to gambling on my own. Without Guillaume, playing drunk, my fortunes plummeted, and again, I was too blind to see what was in front of my face.

Late one evening in the salon, I was picking at a plate of cold ham and cheese, and trying not to think about the close-to-empty wallet inside my coat. I had either ten francs left, or twenty. Much as I wanted to, I would not take them out. To count in public was the best way to advertise my penury, because the men watching for cheats also took note of those who had lost all their money. I was done, I thought. It was time to go back to Dupont, and ask for his forgiveness. To bury myself in my work.

Oddly enough, I had a natural eye for the way clothing should be cut, and had some time since conceded that I did enjoy the work. Dupont saw it too. Put in the effort, he told me, and I could be a master tailor within two years. I could have my own shop, and build up a list of my own customers, like he had. Broke, much fuddled, painfully aware that a dozen steps away, men were betting hundreds of francs, I decided this was what I would do.

'Is the ham to your liking, monsieur?'

I was disconcerted to find the salon's proprietor standing over me. He rarely bothered with customers like me; I was not rich or influential enough. 'It is tasty enough, I suppose,' I said.

He sat down across the table. 'Can I join you?'

I gave him a jaundiced look. 'Sit where you will.'

'Will you be rejoining the écarté tables after your meal?'

Soused as I was, I knew it was unwise to tell him to mind his business. 'Maybe.'

An awkward silence fell. I attacked my ham and cheese, and hoped he would leave.

'Pardon me for saying so, monsieur, but it has come to my attention that you have had . . . quite a run of bad luck.'

I did not answer. It was no surprise he knew. Between the croupiers, puffs, waiters and dunners, he would have to be deaf and blind not to know about my last four visits to the salon, which had been nothing short of disastrous. I had lost almost a thousand francs, my entire winnings from the previous six months and more. All that remained were the few francs in my wallet.

'Your fortunes will change, monsieur, I have no doubt.'

I grunted. Ten to one he offers me a loan, I thought.

'You have been a good customer these past months.'

Again I grunted.

'You are not going to Russia with the emperor?'

'Do I look like a soldier?' I asked sourly.

An oily smile. 'In that case, monsieur, I would be happy to extend you some funds . . . until your winning streak returns.'

In vain I wished for the strength to refuse and walk out the door. Instead, I said, 'How much?'

'Would five hundred francs suffice?'

I tried not to let my hunger show. 'Five hundred would tide me over.'

'*Eh bien*, it is settled!' He clapped his hands.

All too soon, I was back playing écarté. I lost again, but only fifty-odd francs. I barely noticed. Plied with wine – 'on the house, monsieur,' cried the proprietor – I moved to a table with higher stakes. There I was parted from one hundred francs in the time it took to down a glass of claret. In normal circumstances, I would have been wary of encouragement from strangers. Now, though, egged on by a friendly man of my own age, and sure my luck would change, I continued to play. Loss followed loss. I drank more claret, two bottles at least, sharing it with my new friend. I paid no attention to the onlookers, when normally I would have been watching, making sure that some continued to gamble on me. I wagered one hundred francs on a single game, and lost narrowly, four points to my opponent's five.

Staring blearily at my wallet, which was empty, I muttered something to my new friend about answering nature's call, and rose from the table. When I came weaving out of the room with the earth closet, the proprietor was there, like a terrier waiting by a foxhole.

Rather than scream my fury, I managed a smile of a kind.

'How is your luck, monsieur?'

'Damnable.'

'That is unfortunate,' he said sorrowfully, while somehow conveying the opposite sentiment. 'Do you need more funds?'

I was beyond caring. All I wanted to do was win. 'Yes. A thousand francs!'

The rogue did not blink. 'That may be possible. When would you pay it back, monsieur?'

'If not tonight, then tomorrow. When my luck returns.'

'And the security?' An apologetic gesture. 'For such a considerable sum, I would require a guarantee of some kind.'

I had nothing, other than the clothes I stood up in, and a few knickknacks at the Duponts' house. Inspiration took me. 'You know Dupont's, the tailor on the Rue Saint-Honoré?'

A little frown, then a smile. 'Ah, yes. He is highly thought of.'

'I am his heir.'

'He has only daughters, I believe.'

Cursing the proprietor's local knowledge, I drew myself up to my full height. 'Do you accuse me of being a liar? I am Dupont's nephew, son of his favourite brother. He is training me to be his successor, and to take over the business when the time comes.'

'If it is as you say, monsieur—'

'It is!' I snarled, praying that my feigned outrage was convincing.

He made a placatory gesture with his hands. 'In that case, I can draw up a document, something for the interim. Monsieur Dupont will need to countersign it, of course.'

'Of course.' I could see the thousand francs in my wallet, could picture taking a seat at the high-stakes table. I would double, no, triple my money within the hour. Before dawn, I told myself, it would be as if my debts had never existed. My wallet would be replenished, fuller than before, and Dupont none the wiser.

'Monsieur?'

Staring despondently into my almost empty glass, I did not answer. In the distance, the bells of Notre Dame tolled. It was six in the morning. I had been playing all night. I threw back the dregs, their bitterness mild compared to my disappointment. I was ruined.

74

'Would you care for another game, monsieur?' asked my opponent, a sober-faced cavalry officer of some description. Like everyone in the military, it seemed, he was soon going to Russia.

I was not about to admit that he had just taken the last of my money. I shook my head, and rose on unsteady legs from the table. To my surprise, the proprietor did not materialise. Bleary-eyed, head pounding, but mostly in control of my senses, I studied the room. Half a dozen other players remained, one of which was the friendly, balding young man who had encouraged me earlier. A bored-looking croupier was playing faro against himself, watched by a waiter with a broom. Rather than empty my complaining bladder, I decided to make an unobtrusive exit. I could piss down an alleyway, and make good my escape.

Any respite would be brief, I knew. The proprietor would come to the tailor shop today, seeking either his money, or Dupont's counter signature on the document I had signed however many hours earlier. Shame battered me. Fuelled by wine and arrogance, I had recreated what had happened with my father. There was no reason for Dupont to honour my debts, however, if he even wanted to.

Catching sight of the doorman, my pulse quickened. I had no idea how the proprietor dealt with those who owed him large sums of money, but the beetle-browed, ham-fisted doorman would have a part to play. Pulling a broad smile, and grateful to have given him twenty francs the night before, I strode over as if I had not a care in the world. 'Good night,' I said, before chuckling and adding, 'Or should I say good morning?'

''Tis the morning indeed, monsieur.' Instead of pulling wide the door, however, he moved to stand in front of it.

I was in no state to fight him, man mountain that he was, so I smiled even more, and said in a matter of fact tone, 'I am leaving. Open the door, please.'

'The boss wants a word before you go.' His smile was not nearly as pleasant as mine. He whistled, and caught the croupier's attention. 'Fetch M'sieu!'

Five to one I was about to receive a beating, I thought. Shorter odds that it would involve broken ribs, maybe worse. Evens that Dupont received a visit within the hour, to demand his signature. The last possibility I could do nothing about, but the first two . . . *three to one against you cannot do it*, crowed the little devil. *You are too drunk.*

I walked right up to the doorman. 'It's been a long night. I need to sleep. Open the door.'

'No, monsieur—'

He did not finish his sentence, because I had driven my knee deep into his groin. Mouth open in an 'O' of shock and pain, he went down like a great oak falling to a woodsman's axe. I heaved wide the door and ran for my life.

Although I had my wits about me, there was still a considerable amount of wine flowing through my veins. It was fortunate that there was no immediate pursuit, because a hundred paces from the entrance to the Palais Royal, my much-abused stomach announced that it could take no more. Skidding to a halt, past a surprised-looking man walking his dog, I stumbled into an alleyway and was violently sick. Next I had to empty my bladder.

Feeling a little better, I peeked around the corner towards the Palais. The man and his dog had continued along the street. Coming towards me was a familiar figure. I squinted. Not the doorman, good. Not the proprietor either, also good. Thinning of hair, he was wielding a gilt-topped cane. To my surprise, it was the amicable young fellow who had urged me on during my night of folly. I cursed myself for a dozen kinds of fool. I was a sot not to have seen that his friendly behaviour had had an ulterior motive.

I had no wish to hear whatever he wanted to offer me, so I retreated further down the alley, where I hid like a common thief in the recessed doorway of a large, four-storeyed building.

He found me about a minute later. 'This is a poor place to avoid attention,' he said cheerily.

I brushed past. 'I am going home.'

'To Dupont's? The proprietor will be there not long after you, and if I heard aright, he will come armed.'

I wheeled. 'How do you know where I live?'

'I know a lot of things about you, Matthew Carrey.'

I stared at the young man in amazement. At my request, Dupont had told nobody who I really was, not even his family. 'To say that, you must be English.'

A mocking smile. 'Whereas you, sir, are half only. You are a complete drunkard, however, and a poor gambler. You are also a murderer.'

'I am not!' I cried. 'One of the Frenchmen did it.'

'That is not what Lieutenant Noble says.'

'He did not see! I had a pistol, it is true, but I could not use it.'

He cocked an ear. 'Hark. We had best be out of here, else you will be taken. I do not think the doorman will treat you kindly either. His stones will be black and blue for a month.'

He led me down the alley, away from the street, and I began to think he was intent on murder. Then a tiny opening, just a slender gap between two buildings opened up. Entering, he vanished.

'Come on, Mr Carrey.'

As I hesitated, loud, angry voices carried in from the street. What were the odds I was caught before I made it past the mouth of the alley? Fifteen to one, I decided. Odds not worth taking. It was the young Englishman's way or nothing.

Spiderwebs tugged at my hair and pottery crunched underfoot as I followed him through the gloom. Thoughts of murder began to fill my head again.

'If I wanted to kill you, Mr Carrey, I could have simply shot you back there.'

I felt rather foolish. 'Where are you taking me?'

'To a safe house.'

We emerged into an alleyway I did not recognise, but my guide strode off with purpose. Aware that I had no real idea of how to deal with my dire situation, I followed meekly. Whatever he had in store could not be worse than the brutal treatment I could expect from the salon's doorman, nor the shame I would feel when Dupont – who had treated me like family – discovered I was both a charlatan and rogue.

The streets were coming alive, but no one paid us any heed. At length we came to a nondescript house. My guide threw a casual glance to left and right before letting us in. The long hallway beyond smelt of cooking and damp. We took the stairs to the third floor, where the poorest rooms would be. Rapping on the second door, my guide said, 'It is I.'

'Enter.'

We did so. The bare-floored chamber was furnished with two beds, a table, stools, and a dresser. Light entered from a small casement window. I did not recognise the sharp-featured man who was laying a pistol back down on the table.

'Mr Carrey,' he said.

'You have the advantage of me, sir. I do not know your name, or this gentleman's.' I indicated the friendly, balding man, who was also divesting himself of a pistol. I eyed the weapons, and wondered what the odds were of making it out the door unharmed. 'Do I need to be concerned?'

'Not in the slightest, Mr Carrey. We are all friends here.'

'Are we indeed?' My tone was sharp. 'Maybe you will tell me your names then, and what in the name of damnation is going on.'

'I am Mr Bellamy,' said the young man, rearranging the mat of longer hair he used to cover his bald spot. 'This is Mr Wilson.'

'You are Crown agents.'

His mouth twitched. 'We are.'

'How do you know who I am?' Maybe Dupont had betrayed me, I thought.

'You sent a letter to your mother some time ago. It was intercepted. So was its reply, which was sent to Monsieur Dupont's address here in Paris.'

'I never received a letter from my mother,' I said, my heart aching.

'That was nothing to do with us.'

I set that concern aside. 'So you have been watching me?'

'For a while.'

'Are you here to arrest me for the death of the militiaman?' I was astonished when they both guffawed. 'What?'

'The murder of Private Smith . . . was that his name?' Bellamy glanced at Wilson, who shrugged, then he returned his gaze to me. 'Whatever he was called, it was tragic and unnecessary, but there are far more important matters at play. Napoleon is about to invade Russia, or have you been too busy playing écarté to notice?'

'Of course I know Napoleon's intentions, but what have they to do with me?' I did not like the look they gave each other. 'Well?'

They laid it out. Their initial plan had been to bring me to this room, much as Bellamy had done just now, and to threaten me with being taken in secret to England, there to face trial for the killing of the militiaman. Unconvinced that that would be enough, for I seemed settled in Paris, they had waited for a better opportunity. When the duel with Féraud happened, said Bellamy, they had thought their hopes had all been in vain.

'But you survived, only to borrow a ruinous amount of money last night. All of which you lost.'

Beginning to sense his purpose, I glowered.

'How do you intend to deal with the proprietor of the salon, Mr Carrey? What will Monsieur Dupont say when he hears how you used his business as a guarantee against your loan?' Bellamy cocked his head at me.

'I do not know,' I said sourly. 'But I wager that you have a solution for both.'

'Wager? You have not a sou to your name!' Bellamy laughed at his own joke. So did Wilson.

'Are you done?' I demanded. 'I have business to deal with.'

'And bones to be broken, Mr Carrey, if I am not mistaken. Go, if you wish.' Bellamy waved at the door.

My bluff called, I sighed. 'Very well. Speak.'

'Do you know of the Marquis de Caulaincourt?'

'I have heard the name.' I had tended to ignore the chatter in the gambling salon, and Guillaume rarely talked about work. 'He is Napoleon's Grand Écuyer, his Master of Horse, whatever that is.'

'He is one of the emperor's most trusted aides, who will accompany him to Russia.' Bellamy's smile was broad. 'You are to join Caulaincourt's staff as a messenger.'

'What? How would that even be possible?'

'Fortunately, we have agents in the Ministry of War who can engineer the paperwork for such appointments. There is great need for men in the Grande Armée at the moment: no one will question why you are there.'

It was not that surprising an assertion. Young noblemen in the gambling salon often boasted about how their connections had secured a post in this unit of hussars, or that of dragoons. 'I see.'

'Your task will be to gather information and pass it on, wherever possible, to the Russians and our own agents in Russia.'

'What possible use could I be?'

'You will not be the only Crown agent in Napoleon's army. Every snippet, every little detail could be of use in helping the Russians defeat old Boney, and if that happens, Good King George and Britain benefit.'

'Your offer sounds insane. Why would I even think of agreeing?'

'Let me remind you, Mr Carrey, that the gambling salon's proprietor is out for your blood. After his heavies have broken a few of your bones, he will require immediate payment, or some kind of guarantee that the monies will be forthcoming. I suppose you could flee Paris, but goodness knows what he would do to poor Dupont.'

I threw him a hate-filled look, but what he had said echoed my own thoughts.

'And if I accept?'

'We will immediately honour your debts, thereby allowing Dupont to remain in the dark.'

Bellamy had me in a corner, and he knew it, the dog. 'And I would join Caulaincourt's staff how, exactly?' I demanded, fully aware my challenge would be futile. Bellamy and Wilson did not come as across as the type of men without a plan.

'Leave that to us.'

It did not take long to make my decision.

CHAPTER X

Dresden, Germany, May 1812

'M essage!'
    The man in front – François, one of my new comrades –
hurried inside, leaving me in the courtyard. Glad not to have been
chosen yet – although it would be my turn next – I glanced around
the great courtyard. A skewed rectangle, it was the hollow centre of
the royal palace, Napoleon's choice of residence since we had arrived
almost a week before. The Emperor of Austria and every king and
prince in Germany, summoned to pay homage to Napoleon before his
great invasion began, were lodging elsewhere in the city.

The space was busy. Servants hurried to and fro, carrying tables,
chairs and candelabras, and pursued by their chivvying seniors. A
dozen of the mounts used by us messengers stood quietly nearby, loose-
tethered to a rail, munching on hay laid on the ground. A pair of
grooms were working along the line, currying manes and tails, checking tack, tightening girths. An off-duty sergeant of the Imperial Guard
lounged in the sunshine, puffing on his pipe, and alternately eyeing the
maids and the sentries outside the door where I waited.

Just as I would have with Guillaume, sadly left behind in Paris,
I had bet a franc with François that the sergeant would strike up a
conversation with one of the women before I was summoned. Ever the
practical joker, François had wanted a side bet, that one of the maids,
scandalised, would empty a chamber pot over the sergeant. I had refused, even though the odds were with me in that regard. For my part,
betting was a serious business.

Caulaincourt was not within – as always, he was with Napoleon,
at the daily *lever* – but that did not stop a stream of orders arriving at
the room commandeered for the aides-de-camp and staff officers, and
afterwards, dispatches for the messengers. It would not be long before
I too was sent off to one or another part of the army.

My unit was made up of men from all over France; upon arrival I and the other new messengers had spent a few days being the butt of every joke, and were then accepted into the ranks. After several weeks with the Imperial Household, I was used to the routine. Standing around waiting for orders formed a large part of it, which was agreeable enough, if boring. My real purpose, feeding intelligence to the Russians, was something I had avoided thinking about. So too was Bellamy's chilling warning that there would be eyes on me. If I deserted, Dupont would be denounced as an English spy. The thought of that was unconscionable.

The man behind me spoke. 'D'you think they are attending Marie-Louise at her toilette yet?'

Glancing at my pocket watch, which read a quarter past nine, I chuckled. 'It is happening now, I reckon.'

At nine each morning, the Emperor of Austria and King of Saxony and a score of other princelings had to present themselves to Napoleon in the palace's monumental hall, where the entire court and diplomatic corps were gathered. Immediately afterwards, the emperor led the most important nobles to his wife's boudoir, where they watched her going through an astonishing quantity of jewellery, and assisted her in selecting what would grace the royal neck that day.

'It is so clever. So humiliating,' said my companion. 'The King of Saxony and the Grand Duke of Würzburg, helping her choose necklaces or bracelets. Imagine how it is for the Austrian Empress.' Twenty-five years old, Maria Ludovica was a mere four years older than Marie-Louise, and thanks to the poor condition of Austrian finances, her jewels were paltry in comparison to those of the French Empress.

'Short of wiping either Napoleon's backside or that of his beautiful wife,' I said quietly, 'I cannot think of a better way of driving home his power.'

A snort of laughter. 'Be careful who you say things like that around, friend. Napoleon is God in Dresden, the king among kings.'

'You are right,' I said, knowing I was being cocky. 'From what I hear, he would laugh at the joke, but one of his puffed-up officials might take offence.'

'And there are enough of *them*.' A roll of the eyes indicated a group of self-important looking commissaires crossing the courtyard. Thousands of these administrators followed in the army's wake, part of the unwieldy command structure put in place by Napoleon. 'Not a single one has ever seen combat, or ever will. It is no wonder that they are hated by every soldier and cavalryman in the army.'

'I have never been in a battle.'

'But you will, Mathieu. Like the rest of us, you will ride through musket balls, canister and shot, and entire brigades of Cossacks when the time comes. Anything to see the emperor's messages delivered!' He clapped me on the shoulder.

I nodded and smiled, but inside I was terrified. Perhaps I should have fled Paris, I thought. Guillaume would have helped me. I could even have risked the hangman's noose in England. That way I might have at least seen my mother. I pictured Dupont then, and what might have happened if I had run, and abandoned him to a fate at the hands of the gambling salon's proprietor. The shame would be unbearable, I decided. It was better to accept my fate, the task set me by Bellamy.

The odds of surviving this campaign could not be that bad, I told myself. I was in the midst of the largest army ever assembled, led by one of the finest generals in history. As Napoleon had said only the day before – waiting with a message, I had been privy to his meeting with Caulaincourt – Tsar Alexander would sue for peace within two months. Caulaincourt's suggestion that the terrain might not make this so easy had been brushed aside. Telling the Master of Horse he had turned Russian, and playfully tweaking his ear, Napoleon declared with supreme confidence that he would deliver a shattering blow at the heart of the empire, and that that would deliver victory 'in one instant'.

I did not doubt his confidence, and his mention of Tsar Alexander's capital had made me think of Jeanne. The pleasant thought was soon chased away by the grim recognition that I was not travelling to Moscow to see her. I was a spy, I told myself, charged with feeding information to the Russians. If I was caught, I would be shot. With black amusement, I wondered what odds a betmaker would give to see me return to Paris unharmed.

I had no idea.

Five weeks passed. May became June. Crossing central Germany had been a delight. Its lush landscape was easy to ride through, and there were regular depots in bustling towns, bursting at the seams with supplies. We drank wine and beer each night, accompanying our meat and potatoes. Eastern Prussia and Poland were a different matter altogether. Towns were few and far between, and the villages miserable gatherings of squalid wooden hovels populated by vermin-ridden peasants in filthy rags. Being attached to the Imperial Household, I fortunately avoided the ordinary soldiers' diet, for the most part now buckwheat gruel. To wash it down, there was bad vodka, mead or a foul drink called *kwas*, made from fermented bread.

I managed to procure a horse in East Prussia, an excellent Polish cross-bred mare. Liesje was a dark bay five-year-old, well-built and full of vigour and liveliness. At the time of purchase, her tangled mane had hung down to knee level, and her owner begged me with tears in his eyes not to disentangle it, because her life depended on it. Needless to say, I paid no attention to his pleas. Mane shorn and combed, Liesje was now the favourite of my three horses.

Looting was forbidden by order of the emperor himself, and punishable by death, but as the saying went, 'the good soldier never worries too much about the willingness of his host. When he is not given something, he takes.' Soldiers with empty bellies had few qualms, and most senior officers were sympathetic to their men's deprivations. Riding up and down the army's serpentine-like column, I had grown used to scenes of destruction. Cornfields trampled by units of foraging cavalry, with no regard or consideration for the men following on behind. Villages full of half-demolished houses, in which not a window remained unbroken. It seemed that every fence in the land had been ripped up for firewood. Foundered draught and cavalry horses were simply left where they had gone down, dying of thirst. The heads and skins of slaughtered cattle lay by the roadside, gnawed at by feral dogs and watched over by eager flocks of carrion crows. The locals were not immune either, so terrified of the French soldiers that the mere sight of one would cause panicked flight.

Although I felt no ill will towards the peasantry, I was grateful for their fear. The longer I could go without using the holstered pistols that sat in front of my saddle, the better. I felt the same about the lethally sharp cavalry sabre that hung by my side. Although essential, these were not the most important parts of my equipment. That was my leather satchel, in which official letters were carried.

According to François, the usual lockable dispatch cases had been dispensed with, so we could access and destroy the messages if they were in danger of being captured by the enemy. 'Remember the two methods,' he told me one morning over coffee. 'Keep the letter in your glove so you can quickly eat it before you are taken, or shove it, folded, down the barrel of a pistol. Firing will blow it apart.'

I hoped never to have to do either.

In the third week of June, I was sent north to deliver a message to Count Oudinot, commander of II Corps. The landscape was mostly featureless, with plenty of silver birch forests and the broad, unpaved roads – full of troops every mile of the way – indicated on either side only by a row or two of magnificent trees. Although there were regular *estafettes*, where I could change my horse and refill my water canteen, food was not always available. By the time I reached II Corps on the morning of the second day, my supplies were long finished. My belly thought my throat had been cut. I begged a bread roll from a servant while waiting for Oudinot's reply, but receiving the reply not a quarter of an hour later, had no time to seek out more. By late afternoon, it was all that I had eaten in twenty four hours.

Reaching a Y in the road I did not remember, and between *estafettes*, I stopped to ask directions from a unit of infantry. Part of the Twenty-First Regiment of the Line, they sat by the roadside, dust-covered from the march, pipes clamped between their lips to a man. A thick-waisted soldier, a proper *vieux grognard*, called me over, promising to set me on the right road. As I approached, I spied a plump cantinière beside him; she was tending a pot perched amid the flames of a small fire. Closer, the smell was not that appetising, but starved, I was beyond caring.

Tethering my horse on a long rein so it could graze, I sat down on a log beside the soldier.

He pointed the end of his pipe at my satchel. 'Carrying word to the emperor, monsieur?'

'Yes. It is Oudinot's reply to whatever I carried up north.'

My gaze wandered towards the pot over the fire. I did not get my hopes up, however. Cantinières were fierce, and loyal only to the units they worked.

'Did you take a peep?' The soldier winked.

I gave him an affronted look, although I had done just this – Bellamy's task in mind – several times with previous messages. Only once had the wax seal been badly enough applied for me to take out the sheet of paper within. My hopes had been dashed, for the thing was completely in code, line after line of three- and four-numeral groups. The irony was not lost on me. Most days, I carried information that would be useful to the Russians, but it might as well have been written in Arabic.

Again my attention wandered. I was so hungry that the stew, if that was what it was, smelled like a dish from Beauvilliers', the restaurant where I had eaten with Jeanne, a lifetime before.

'Hungry?' The cantinière's look was knowing.

'Food has been scarce,' I said diffidently.

A snort of amusement. 'You look bloody famished.'

'Is it that obvious?' I asked, wondering if I had seen her before.

'I should say so!' Still chuckling, the cantinière buried a ladle in the pot, then proffered a rough ceramic bowl and a spoon. On her outstretched left arm, a long scar ran from her hand right up her arm. 'Buckwheat stew.'

'My thanks, madame. You are very kind.' I gave her a broad smile, even as I thought her description of the light brown gruel with no vegetables rather generous. My portion did have several lumps of floating meat, however. 'Beef?' I asked, more in hope than expectation.

'Horse,' said the soldier, already slurping at his bowl. 'Dead ones everywhere. We can't eat them fast enough. More's the pity the same can't be said about supplies of flour.'

'Are you running short?'

He snorted. 'Four days' rations each man is supposed to carry, and the regimental wagons are supposed to have another twenty days' worth. That's all fine and dandy when there's flour to be had, and you can find your cursed wagons of an evening! A week it is since any of us had bread.'

Muttering my commiserations, I busied myself with my food. The meat was not cooked through, but I was so hungry I did not care. Slurping down the gruel, I thanked the cantinière again, still unsure if I had recognised her. Lastly, I took a nip of the soldier's vodka, as he said, 'to help me on my way', and climbed into the saddle.

'Keep going that direction,' said the soldier, indicating the left fork. 'Next *estafette* is about five miles away.'

I glanced at the sky, which was clear. It was warm; hours of daylight remained; I would water my mount at the *estafette*, and press on. Mid-summer's eve was either today or tomorrow, and I might easily be able to ride through the night, picking up Liesje from the way station where I had left her at the end of the first day's ride. Letter safely delivered to Napoleon, I decided, I would seek out the corner of a haybarn for a few hours' sleep.

'Come on then,' I said to my horse, a stolid brown with one white sock. At the trot, he could cover more than seven miles per hour, better than most mounts. Raising a hand in farewell to the soldier, I rode off.

Sadly, I had not gone far before my stomach twisted painfully. I soon realised its protest was aimed at the 'stew' served me by the kind-hearted cantinière. I eased my horse to a walk. Thankfully, the discomfort eased, enabling us to resume our previous speed. It was not to be for long. Cramps in my guts tortured me, followed by the most awful wind. Worse was to come. A wave of abdominal pain swamped me, culminating in the most powerful urge.

I immediately aimed my horse off the road and behind a pair of large silver birches. Feet already out of the stirrups, I dropped to the ground. So desperate that I could not even tether my mount, unable to take even a step, or set aside my sabre, I unbuttoned my trousers and crouched down. My satchel slapped off my bare arse cheek, but I barely noticed. A revolting explosion brought instant relief. Momentarily exhausted, I had to place a hand on the earth to steady myself.

Jingle, jingle. The sound of cavalry was so familiar I paid it no heed. Polish or Italian, Prussian or French, it did not matter. They could have been Cossacks and I would not have cared. Another wave of agony struck; more liquid voided from my rear end.

There was more jingling. My horse neighed.

Panicked realisation sank in. I looked up just as the wretched beast cantered towards the road. It paid no heed to my cry. I could only watch in impotent fury as it vanished. My shouts to stop it went unheard amid the general noise. I cursed my luck, and the cantinière as well. Cleaning myself as best I could with a handful of moss, I pulled up my trousers and went in search of my horse.

A unit of artillery was passing, its 6 lb cannon and 24 lb howitzers pulled by teams of horses. They were ribby and unhappy looking, but that was none of my concern. I hailed a mounted officer.

'Ah, yours was the horse that just ran off.' An appraising look. 'Caught short, eh?'

'Yes,' I muttered. 'Which way did it go?' Five to one it has gone the route I came, I thought.

'That way.' His arm pointed south, the direction I wanted to travel.

Pleased to have been wrong, I began to trudge after it. There was no point commandeering one of the nags pulling the cannon. I would walk for a mile, I decided. If I had not caught up by that stage, I would use the letter in my satchel as authority to take a cavalry horse. Thinking then of the cantinière, whose stew had played havoc with my insides, I realised that I *had* seen her before, outside the Gaîté theatre. Rather than tending her cooking pot, she had been castigating her husband for drinking all of his pay.

Coarse but good-natured jokes rang in my ears as the artillerymen walking north poked fun at me, the imperial messenger on foot. I grimaced and threw back insults of my own, and hoped that my insides did not play traitor again.

Shouts and commands carried from the road ahead. A unit of hussars, easily distinguishable by their plumed black shakos and magnificent, gold-braided crimson jackets, was advancing on either side of the artillery, clearly in a hurry to get past.

One of their mounts would do, I decided. I stopped and let them come to me. The front pair of hussars made no attempt to slow down. Thirty paces away, one shouted for me to get out of the way.

Angered by his arrogance, I raised a hand, palm out, in a clear signal to halt. 'I am an imperial messenger,' I cried. 'Stop!'

They reined in, and to my complete astonishment, I recognised Féraud, the hussar with whom I had duelled. I gave him a sardonic smile. 'We meet again, Captain.'

His surprise, even greater than mine, now became disbelief. '*You* are an imperial messenger?'

'I am attached to Caulaincourt's staff, yes, and I am in need of a horse.' I tapped my satchel importantly. 'This must reach the emperor with all speed.'

His mouth twisted, but to refuse was to disobey an order from the emperor himself. Féraud ordered his companion, a gap-toothed corporal, to get down from his horse. 'What happened to your own?' he demanded. 'Was it perchance a fine brown with one sock?'

I had not had the time to come up with a plausible explanation. I hesitated.

And Féraud guessed. 'You stopped to answer a call of nature, didn't tether it, and the beast ran away,' he crowed. 'See, corporal, this fool calls himself an imperial messenger, but he's no better than a first-day-in-the-army new recruit!'

The corporal was wise enough not to laugh in my face, but his lips were twitching.

Enraged by Féraud again calling me stupid, I managed to keep my expression blank as I took the reins from the corporal. To him I said, 'Ask your captain how we come to know each other. Be sure to mention the Bois de Boulogne.' The corporal would never dare question his superior in such a manner, but it did not matter. The reference made it clear a duel was involved.

I took a perverse delight from the hatred in Féraud's eyes. I told them the horse would be left at the next *estafette*, and with a courteous touch of the brim of my hat, began to ease my new mount past.

'Take care of that horse,' Féraud said as I came alongside.

'Of course,' I replied, wondering if I had been wrong in my assessment of him; maybe we could put our vendetta aside.

It was a foolish thought.

He leaned towards me. 'Do not think this is over.'

'I would expect no less from you.' My tone was bold, but I was cursing inside. To meet Féraud in the wilds of Poland was bad, but the rogue now knew how to find me. If we fought a second duel, the odds of another miss were small. My unease did not last long, I am glad to say. Féraud was heading north with his unit. The odds of him having an opportunity to seek me out were infinitesimal.

Despite my nagging guts, I rode on, whistling a happy tune.

CHAPTER XI

The River Niemen, Grand Duchy of Warsaw, 23 June 1812

A day later, grateful that my intestines had returned to normal, I was again attending Caulaincourt and the emperor. François and several other messengers were with me outside Napoleon's immense command tent. Evening had fallen, and the dreadful heat was beginning to abate. I wish the same could be said for the mosquitoes, from which there was no relief. Dense, bloodsucking clouds hung in the sultry air; they fed on man and horse with equal gusto. Slapping them away brought only an instant of relief before they mercilessly descended again. François, always able to find humour in our situation, had challenged me to a five franc bet, the winner being whoever got bitten the most by dawn.

Napoleon had arrived in the middle of the previous night, not long before me, and snatched a few hours' rest. Then, accompanied by a handful of senior officers, among them Caulaincourt, he had spent the day reconnoitring up and down the river, clad in a Polish lancer's cloak and hat, his telescope always to hand. There was higher ground on the west bank – behind this was where the three French army corps were gathering – but the far side of the Niemen was mostly flat and, apart from the little walled town of Kowno, devoid of houses. The only sign of the Russians, Caulaincourt had told me upon his return, was an occasional Cossack patrol. Having ridden the same route several times during the day, as I went hither and thither with messages, I could say the same.

Napoleon's army, on the other hand, filled the landscape. Hidden from the Niemen, the massed battalions of infantry covered vast swathes of ground, looking from a distance like regiments of glinting ants. Lines of artillery and cavalry waited to their rear. Closer to the river, hundreds of sappers and engineers surrounded a mass of pontoons loaded on drays. Although ordered to keep out of the Russians' sight, our presence cannot have gone unnoticed. Any time Napoleon had been spotted, a crescendo rose to the heavens, hundreds of drums and trumpets playing, and men roaring 'Vive l'Empereur!'

Although I felt no animosity towards the Russians, it was impossible not to be drawn into the general excitement and increasing sense of anticipation. Napoleon was in ebullient mood, and that transferred to those around him. Even Caulaincourt and Berthier, the emperor's long-serving chief of staff, both of whom I had heard advising against the proposed advance on Moscow, were in fine fettle.

'Enough of maps,' I heard Napoleon say. 'I want to ride the ground again, and see for myself the disposition of the troops which will cross first.' He emerged from underneath his pine-branch sun shelter with Caulaincourt and Berthier a step behind. The latter was the only senior officer permitted to wear the same hat as the emperor, but it was easy to know Berthier at a distance because both hands were generally in his pockets, and if one was not, it was busy excavating his nostrils.

At first glance, Napoleon was a small, unremarkable figure, perhaps five feet two inches tall, with a middle-aged paunch. His complexion did not have much colour, giving him a full, pale face, but not the kind of wanness that denotes a sick person. His brown hair was cut short all over and lay flat on his round head. His forehead was large and high; his eyes were grey-blue in colour, with a gentle look in them. I had heard men say they were less piercing than earlier in his life. Nonetheless, he had an aura about him, a noticeable charisma. When his grand proclamation launching his 'second Polish war' had been read out to the army, the cheering had gone on for a full quarter of an hour afterwards.

His gaze ran over us messengers. 'You,' he said to me. 'Name?'

'Dupont, sire.'

'Come.'

'Yes, sire.' I was excited to have been chosen. I found myself amused, a gambling, apprentice tailor half-Englishman, willingly serving the French emperor.

Our horses were waiting close by. We mounted, Napoleon helped onto one of his favourites, Friedland, named after his famous victory over the Russians five years prior. I was on Liesje, the faithful creature, and positioned behind the emperor, Caulaincourt and Berthier.

Close up, it was impossible not to notice that Napoleon rode like a butcher. Without moving his legs, holding the reins loosely in his right hand, the left hanging down, he looked as if he'd been hung up in his saddle. At a gallop his torso swayed forwards and sideways with his horse's movements. The emperor's poor horsemanship did not cause him to ride with caution, however, far from it. With only moonlight as a guide, he led the way into a wheatfield at full tilt.

Perhaps halfway across, a hare started up between the legs of Napoleon's horse. To the beast's credit, it only swerved slightly, but this was enough for the emperor to lose his seat and crash to the earth. We came skidding to a stop, but he was on his feet before any of us could reach him. He mounted again without a word, and we resumed our journey, albeit at a safer pace.

'Thank God for the soft ground. He cannot be too hurt.' Caulaincourt's voice was relieved.

I saw Berthier lean over and take his hand. 'We should do better not to cross the Niemen. That fall is a bad sign.'

I was not superstitious by nature, but I felt similarly. Short of Napoleon being badly injured, I could scarce think of a worse omen.

Caulaincourt seemed about to reply, but Napoleon had sensed Berthier's unease. He engaged them both in conversation, making light of his fall, joking and saying he had bruised his hip, nothing more. There was no attempt to blame Friedland either, as one might have expected. Caulaincourt and Berthier responded with enthusiasm, but it was obvious, riding behind the emperor in the darkness, that his performance was bravado, an act, to gloss over something that would trouble even a sceptic.

The rest of our reconnaissance – to see the pontoon bridges, lately placed over the Niemen by the engineers – passed without incident. Upon our return, his mood grown serious, Napoleon sat down to dine with Caulaincourt in his massive tent. They were attended by Roustam Raza, his Mameluke bodyguard.

Not long after, Count Roman Soltyk arrived. A Polish officer, his fluent French had seen him attached to the topographical department in the imperial headquarters. Wild-haired but with a trim moustache, he gave me a friendly nod as he entered the tent.

Noting his excited manner, I gave François a wink and hurried down the side of the tent. None of the Imperial Guard were visible, allowing me to eavesdrop.

'Sire,' Soltyk said by way of greeting to Napoleon.

'You have been across? Did you capture any villagers?'

'I have, sire. It was so dark we didn't know whether we had any enemy in front of us or not. As far as we could see, no patrol, no scout appeared at any point. Only after about one hundred men had established themselves on the right bank did we hear a distant sound of galloping horses, and a strong troop of Muscovite hussars halted about a hundred paces from our weak advance guard. Dark though it was, we recognised them by their white plumes. Coming towards us, the officer in command shouted out in French: "Qui vive?" "France," our men replied quietly. "What are you doing here? Fuck off!" came the response.'

Napoleon laughed. I bit the inside of my cheek not to do the same.

'"You'll soon see!" our men cried, sire, whereupon the Russian officer went back to his hussars and ordered them to fire their carbines. None of ours replied, and the enemy disappeared at a gallop.'

'So you took no prisoners?'

'No, sire. We judged it safest to return over the pontoon, in case the Russians came back with reinforcements.'

'That was well done.'

I had heard enough. I stole back to the messengers' position close to the tent's entrance.

François was waiting to interrogate me. It was something we all did after spending time in the emperor's company. 'Well?' he demanded.

He too was amused by Soltyk's story, but he was more interested in what had happened during the earlier reconnaissance.

His eyes grew wide as I relayed the story of Napoleon's fall. '*Mon Dieu*, that is not a good sign.'

'In ancient Rome,' I said, remembering lessons given by my childhood tutor, 'an omen like this would have caused a general to postpone or even cancel an invasion.'

'It will not stop Napoleon. Nothing will. He is set on his course, and we must all go with him.' The faint note of resignation in his voice was disquieting.

The Grande Armée was vast, I told myself, made up of crack troops who had conquered Europe. The emperor was the finest general of the age, capable of defeating any military commander he came up against. There was no sign of the Russians, moreover – the land on the Niemen's eastern bank lay abandoned. Wherever it was, the Tsar's army was probably in disarray.

And yet I had misgivings, as François did. I wondered which I had more to worry about: the invasion, being revealed as a spy, or Féraud, and which had the worst odds. None of these thoughts made for a good night's sleep.

Nor did my seventy-three mosquito bites.

François, the laughing winner, had almost a hundred.

It was not the Russians that struck the Grande Armée next, but the weather. After days of energy-sapping, burning sun, winter returned. When the main body of the army began to cross the Niemen on the twenty-third of June, thunderclouds gathered as if from nowhere. Lightning streaked down and hit one of the pontoon bridges, knocking several riders and horses into the river. The heavens opened, delivering a deluge of freezing rain such as I had never experienced. While the downpour was brief at the crossing point, it went on for hours as one went east, the same direction we were headed.

The flat landscape provided no shelter, and as I travelled it on roads that were quickly turning to quagmires, it was impossible not to notice that in the fields, the rye and barley being rain-pounded to the earth was green and unripe. This was what horses with the army – more than one hundred and thirty thousand of them – were supposed to eat as the advance continued. The severe shortage of fodder did not bode well.

Napoleon had cast the dice, however. The sense among the staff of the imperial headquarters – I encountered some on the road that day – was that there would be no turning back until a decisive victory had been won. With luck, it would be at Vilna, the Lithuanian capital. This was the city the Grande Armée was heading for, some seventy miles to the south-southeast. Rumour had it that the Tsar was there with General Barclay, commander of one of the Russian imperial armies. Defeating Alexander in battle might end the campaign at one stroke, or so we gossiped. It helped to distract us from the rain, momentarily.

My waxed cloak kept me dry, at least the parts that were not exposed. Hat soaked through, hair caked to my scalp, boots and lower legs covered with thick mud, I endured, as did poor, faithful Liesje. Knowing she was not immune to the brutal conditions, I made occasional stops by peasant cabins. These dwellings were even more dreadful than the hovels in Poland, and all seemed abandoned. In I would go, and drag outside the miserable straw tick that served as the former inhabitants' bed. Cutting the stinking fabric open, I used the straw within to rub down Liesje. A chilled, hungry horse is a horse that will get colic, my father had always said. I was also careful not to let her drink too much from the chilly streams, or the pools in the ruts on the road, and as for the still-green barley and rye, I let her nowhere near it. Hanging from my saddlebow was a waxed leather bag containing good quality German grain, sourced from the imperial quartermasters. I fed Liesje some of its contents twice daily.

Late on in the afternoon of the twenty-fourth after a brief dry spell, I spied a fresh weather front coming across the landscape towards me. I was damp, tired, hungry and thirsty, and at least ten miles remained before I reconnected with Caulaincourt, who was as ever with Napoleon. The drifting, grey curtains of rain dragged my spirits down further. The sight of a largeish cottage, and beside it, a barn, was enough for me to seek shelter. The invasion would not fail if my message went undelivered for another hour, or even two.

I was not alone in making such a decision. Scores of soldiers, many beardless youngsters, were standing at the cottage doorway, angrily demanding to be admitted by those already within. After an exchange of fruity insults, the door was slammed and barred in their faces. I aimed at once for the barn, a poor excuse for one in France or England. Three sides only, open-fronted, with countless holes in its roof, it was nonetheless better than remaining outside. It was already packed with infantrymen of the Twenty-First Regiment of the Line, the same unit I had met some time before. They made space willingly enough when I raised my messenger's satchel as a mark of rank.

Leading Liesje in, I coughed as a thick, unpleasant fug struck the back of my throat. By now, I was well used to the mixture of pipe smoke, sweat, damp wool and onions, but that did not mean I liked it.

'Your letters not urgent?'

I stared at the questioner, a stripling who looked far too young to be holding a musket. 'Shouldn't you be looking for Russians to fight rather than questioning an imperial messenger?'

The men nearby laughed. 'He's right!' cried one. 'Why aren't you out hunting the enemy?'

Instead of directing another jibe at me, the youth made the mistake of challenging his comrades. They needed no further excuse. Insults rained down, demeaning his courage, his ability to shoot, his lack of footwear. Glancing down, I saw he was barefoot, his lower extremities caked in mud. Other men had fared the same. The rest had string tied around the insteps of their shoes, I guessed to prevent their being sucked off by the glutinous sludge on the roads.

'Care to sell your boots, friend?' asked a whiskery sergeant, a vieux grognard who looked as if he had been serving since the Revolution.

I smiled. 'No, sorry.'

A loud cry of alarm caught everyone's attention.

My eyes went to the cottage. A thick column of smoke billowed from the chimney, far more than a stove should emit. It was also pouring from the small apertures that served as windows.

'The fools have set the place on fire,' I cried, tying Liesje's reins to an iron ring on the wall. 'Come on!'

All of us charged from the barn. Some of the men who had been unable to get inside the cottage were hammering on the door with their musket butts. 'Open! Open!'

'We cannot!' came a cry from within. 'The table set against it is burning!'

'Move it then, unless you want to die!' bellowed the sergeant.

He and I ran around the cottage. Other than the main entrance, the only openings were the glassless windows. They might have allowed a small child to escape, but not adult men.

We came back to the front door, which had not splintered beneath the pounding musket butts. Men inside were screaming. Flames began licking out of a nearby window, curling hungrily up to the low thatch roof.

'Unless we do something immediately, they are all dead,' the sergeant pronounced with a certain grim satisfaction, pointing. The rain had not been enough to stop the thatch above a second window bursting into flame. The ominous, hearty crackling sound it made competed with the frantic shouts and cries of the men trapped within.

The little devil in my head began to calculate their odds of survival. Savagely, I shoved the ghoulish calculation away. 'Have you rope?' I demanded.

'I saw some in the barn.'

'Fetch it! I will get my horse.'

A minute later, I was dragging an unwilling Liesje towards the burning cottage. Sensing my purpose, the sergeant had already tied the rope around the middle of a musket, and ordering the men inside to stand back, had worked it butt first through a window. When it was all through, he pulled until the musket was brought up against the inside of the wall and jammed into position.

A soldier ran the other end of the rope some thirty feet away to where I stood, fighting with Liesje. Her ears were back, and the whites of her eyes were showing. Skittering to and fro, she was trying to rear, anything to get away from the burning cottage. 'Come on, girl,' I said to her. 'Steady, steady.' To the soldier, I said, 'Tie the rope to the pommel, quickly!'

Fast-thinking, he had already formed a running knot in it. Before he could slip it over the pommel, however, Liesje ripped her head free of my grasp and went up on her back legs. The soldier backed away, wary of her striking hooves. Rather than do the same, I pulled her back down by the reins, but she was panicked. There was froth on her lips, and she spun her hindquarters this way and that, and kept trying to rear. I could not catch hold of the head collar again.

'The roof is about to collapse!' the sergeant shouted.

I cursed silently, and kept talking to Liesje, but it was no good.

Hooves sounded on the road, galloping closer. It was a unit of hussars, recognisable by the plumes on their black shakos. Their horses were trained for battle, I thought. They would be used to fire. 'Help!' I cried. 'Help!'

I led Liesje towards them, and seeing the other horses, she calmed.

I could not believe my eyes. Féraud was the lead horseman, his corporal beside him. Two by two behind them rode his troop, every man bundled up in his voluminous cape against the weather.

His face blackened when he recognised me.

I set aside my intense dislike of the man. 'There are men trapped in the cottage.' I explained what I had done with the rope and musket, and how Liesje had panicked. 'Will any of your horses do it?'

Féraud was already dismounted, and throwing his cape to the ground. Moving to his horse's head, a magnificent grey, he began to back it towards the soldier with the rope. The well-trained beast did not resist. In no time, the rope had been fastened to the saddle pommel, and Féraud was urging it forward.

I cast an eye at the house. More than half the thatch was ablaze. The heat had forced the soldiers who had been trying to smash down the door to retreat. They stood, distraught, while the anguished cries of the trapped men filled the air.

'Pull,' Féraud said to his mount. 'Come on, *mon coeur*. Pull!'

The grey walked forward a step, then another.

I closed my eyes and prayed.

With a great snap, a section of planking pulled free of the wall. Out came the musket, and with it, any hope of Féraud's horse helping further. But there was movement inside, at the hole, shouts, hands pushing, ripping pieces of timber away.

Next instant, a man emerged. He turned and helped another, who was being bundled through by a comrade within. This third soldier clambered out, and he managed to drag a fourth free, before, with a horrendous crackle, the entire roof collapsed in on itself. Showers of sparks flew up into the air, and a blast of heat hit my face, fifty paces away.

Men rushed to help the four survivors. Féraud gave them not a glance, instead unfastening the rope from his pommel, and caressing the grey's neck. 'Bravo, *mon coeur*,' I heard him say. 'Bravo.'

'That was well done,' I said. 'Thank you.'

A sniff. 'Your mount is untrained?'

'I would not say that,' I replied, temper rising. 'She was terrified of the fire, and the smoke and noise.'

'An imbecile who cannot shoot, riding a pleasure horse,' he said with a snort. 'You must know someone in authority to have been accepted into the imperial messenger service.'

He was correct of course – Bellamy had orchestrated my employment, I was not sure how – but my pride stung, nonetheless. The old barb, being called stupid, jabbed at me also. 'I perform my duties as well as any man,' I said tautly, aware, even if he was not, of the irony of a spy defending himself. 'My business is none of your concern.'

'True enough. I fight. You ride as fast as you can, and avoid trouble.'

'Delivering messages is my job. I am not a soldier.'

'You will still find yourself in the midst of battle, and soon. It is inevitable. There will be musket fire, hundreds of cannons shooting, men screaming and dying everywhere. It is pure chaos.' Féraud's eyes were bright with anticipation. He chuckled. He swung up into the saddle, calling to his corporal, and rode off, his hussars following smartly behind.

'Friendly type, eh?' It was the sergeant.

'We fought a duel in Paris not long ago.'

'Neither of you were injured?'

'He missed, and I used the delope.'

The sergeant blew out his cheeks. 'It is fortunate that you did, my friend, or the men who escaped from the cottage would be as dead as their unfortunate comrades.'

'I suppose so.' I was glad for the sake of the four soldiers, but part of me wished I had been ruthless enough to shoot Féraud. We had had two unpleasant encounters already, and my gut told me there would be more. The man loved horses, it was true, but I was tired of his overweening arrogance, his arrant sense of superiority.

If he challenged me to another duel, I would not back down. I told myself it was not breaking my oath of non-violence. One could shoot to injure rather than kill. Find the right men to wager with, I thought, and I could make a fortune.

If I survived, added the little devil.

I did once, I told him, with a new confidence. *I can do it again.*

CHAPTER XII

After four nights of torrential rain, the twenty-eighth of June dawned sunny and bright. I was riding behind Napoleon's carriage, just in front of the emperor's dragoons. We had spent the night in the hamlet of Owzianiskai, and were now travelling towards Vilna. The road was lined with the carcasses of horses, now a common sight. Since crossing the Niemen, untold numbers of cavalry mounts and draught animals had died of colic. Estimates ranged from three thousand to ten thousand. My prudence with Liesje had been well-founded.

The soldiers could not eat all the meat, and the carrion crows grew so fat that they struggled to fly as we rode past. Ravens and eagles roamed the skies, eager for their portion. I was wearing a scarf across my face, which eased the horrendous stink a little, but my eyes kept being dragged to the bloated corpses. War was more dreadful than I had imagined. Barely a shot had been fired, hardly a Russian seen, and the Grande Armée was suffering massive losses. True, it was horses rather than men, but despair was palpable among the rank and file.

The day before, I had been carrying a message to the cavalry commander Joachim Murat, the King of Naples, whose reckless bravery and outlandish costumes had already endeared him to the Cossacks. Alongside a unit of gaunt-cheeked infantry, a shot rang out. Fifty paces further on, I came upon a group of distraught soldiers, standing around a comrade's body. In despair, they explained, he had simply stepped out of line, and blown out his own brains. Even as we stared at the corpse, a second shot cracked out. Another man further up the column had done the same.

Witnessing the suicides had shocked me to the core, stripped away my grandiose thoughts of seeing Napoleon triumph over the Russian bear. For the first time, thoughts of desertion entered my head.

Travelling west as if on imperial business, changing horses at *estafettes*, there was every likelihood that I could ride unhindered all the way to Paris. Appealing though this was, I did not fancy Bellamy and Wilson discovering that I had reneged on our arrangement. The threat about poor Dupont aside, I had no doubt that they were capable of dark deeds involving blade and gun.

I could always return to England, and a joyful reunion with my mother, if not my father. There, however, I ran the risk of being hanged for the militiaman's killing, and Dupont would still be thrown into prison for supposedly being a spy. Better to stay with the Grande Armée, I decided, and keep my head down. I would have to deliver some intelligence to the Russians, but I would take few risks, and keep it to the minimum. By Christmas, I told myself, I would be back in France with a victorious Napoleon, my task done and debts honoured. There was gambling too; card playing was popular with everyone from the rank and file to the officers. Few would be as sharp a player as I; the potential for winning large sums of money seemed sure.

Cheered by this, I edged Liesje closer to the imperial carriage. Napoleon and Caulaincourt were talking, or rather Napoleon was talking and the Master of Horse listening. Anytime he tried to speak, the emperor took the conversation off in another direction. It was his habit, I had learned, when he did not want to be questioned.

Napoleon had been in a constant state of agitation since the Niemen, demanding that any prisoners were to be brought to him for inter-rogation so he could determine where Barclay's army was, and also Bagration's. The forces of these two Russian commanders formed the barrier to Moscow, and as the emperor said now to Caulaincourt, if a blow could be struck at both, and a wedge driven between them, one of the Tsar's armies might be destroyed. 'Do that,' he cried, 'and the war is half won!'

Caulaincourt, as was so often the case, brought the conversation back to more immediate concerns. 'With the grain stores in Vilna gone, sire, it is imperative that the supply wagons catch up with the army.'

He was right, I thought. The loss was immense, and it was all Murat's fault. Wanting the glory for himself, he had prevented the cavalry of-ficer tasked with riding hell for leather to Vilna two days before. For reasons that were entirely unclear, Murat had moved on the city with no great speed. By the time his cavalry reached it, the stores were ablaze and the main bridge destroyed. Some barley had survived, but it was so smoked that the horses would not eat it.

I found it remarkable how Napoleon had allowed Murat to go unpunished or even reprimanded, but such decisions were far beyond my authority.

'It might be best to wait in Vilna for several days, sire, to let the baggage train catch up,' Caulaincourt went on. 'With the grain those wagons are carrying, there would be fewer casualties in the coming weeks.'

'Tchh,' said Napoleon, sounding peeved. 'We shall see.'

Until that point, I had not considered that to be a successful general, a man had to be largely callous to the suffering of his men. Military success, it seemed, truly came at a price. The emperor seemed at ease with it, but it was not one I ever wished to pay.

Vilna was small and unimpressive, I decided, entering with Napoleon and Caulaincourt. The rough paved streets were mostly deserted. Not a face showed at a window. I could not discern a sign of enthusiasm or even curiosity from the occasional pedestrian. Everything was gloomy. The emperor paid no heed, riding straight through to the burnt bridge, and surveying the terrain beyond, and the still-burning magazines the Russians had set fire to. Ordering the bridge repaired with all haste, he retired to his new headquarters, the palace of the Archbishop of Vilna, and vacated just two days prior by Tsar Alexander. The rooms allocated to the messengers were far from Napoleon's grand chambers, but after our recent hardships, the windowless, drab servants' rooms seemed luxurious indeed. I took great pleasure from snatching a nap on the narrow cot in the chamber I would share with François. Naturally, he had insisted on betting on the number of bites we would each suffer, from bedbugs this time rather than mosquitoes.

Despite its shabbiness, Vilna was of vital importance. It would form a forward base from which Napoleon's main army could strike either at Barclay, now retreating north-eastwards towards the great camp of Drissa, or Bagration, coming up from the south. If the pair met, the Grande Armée could attack both. Thousands of stragglers could be reunited here with the main force, and the river upon which the city stood used to transport much-needed supplies up from the coast.

Two days later, my return to the imperial headquarters coincided with the arrival of a Russian envoy. An excited air hung in the windy palace courtyard; I was not alone in wondering if – hoping that – a peace treaty could be agreed before the invasion pressed deeper into the hinterland. The envoy was expected, having been preceded by a letter from the Tsar two days prior. The delay in his arrival had come about because Napoleon, keen that enemy eyes should not see the appalling wreckage lining the road from Kowno – dead soldiers and horses, equipment – had instructed he be brought to Vilna by a round-about route.

The Russian, Balachof, as I heard him referred to, was hurried off to meet the emperor. A tousle-headed man with a prominent chin, he was nonetheless an imposing figure in his gilt-epauletted uniform.

'What do you think Napoleon will say?' I asked François.

An expressive Gallic shrug. 'I cannot imagine him reacting much differently than he did to the tsar's letter.'

I nodded. Napoleon's response to that was public knowledge. Declaring that Alexander was laughing at him by requesting the Grande Armée to retreat behind the Niemen, pending negotiations, the emperor had declared he would thrust the Russians back into their snow and ice so that civilised Europe would be free of their interference for a quarter of a century at least.

'He will be polite, even welcoming,' François went on. 'But he will accept nothing less than surrender, something I suspect Alexander is not about to offer.'

'No. I heard Caulaincourt mentioning the tsar's advice from his time in St Petersburg,' I said. The Master of Horse had served until 1811 as Napoleon's envoy at the imperial court. '"I would rather retreat as far as Kamchatka than give away provinces and sign in my capital any treaty which only be a truce,"' he said. '"Our climate, our winter will fight for us."'

'God forbid that we should still be here then. They say a man can freeze to death inside a quarter of an hour,' said François with feeling. A droll chuckle. 'We could bet on that, but for the fact that the loser, being dead, would not be able to pay the other!'

Unamused, I shivered. 'We will have long since returned to Paris.' The old refrain came easily, but I had a nasty feeling in my belly.

'Where I will be introduced to your friend Guillaume at the Bar de l'Entracte, before you both drink me under the table.'

I grinned. 'That is my promise.'

'Ten francs says one of you will collapse before I do.'

We reaffirmed the wager with a handshake.

I noticed that a window on the first floor had been blown open by the wind, and was banging to and fro. 'That is in the emperor's quarters.'

As we stood watching, Napoleon himself came and shut it. He looked agitated, with little spots of red marking his pale cheeks. A moment later, the window blew open again. This time, the emperor wrenched the window, frame and all, and lobbed the lot down into the courtyard. But for my warning cry, a passing clerk would have been struck and injured. Glass smashed, wood splintered, and I glanced sourly at François. 'The meeting is not going well.'

Balachof was still there at dinner time, however, along with Marshals Duroc, Berthier and Bessières, as well as Caulaincourt. François and I were again on duty close to the dining room; it was the emperor's habit to order a message sent even at these times. Our position meant that as the servants entered with silver platters of food and bottles of expensive wine, we could overhear the diners. As always, the conversation was dominated by Napoleon, and he gave forth on every subject under the sun.

At one point, Balachof quipped that all roads led to Rome but the road to Moscow was a matter of choice. King Charles XII of Sweden, he went on, had gone via Poltava. This was a sly reference to the Swedish monarch's defeat there a century before. Napoleon's response was that he had no intention of making the same blunder, and then, jokingly, that his 'brother' Alexander had turned Caulaincourt into a proper Russian.

The door closed as Caulaincourt protested his loyalty, and when next I was able to listen in, it seemed that the emperor had taken this into account. A short while after coffee was served, however, Napoleon had grown tired of Balachof's company. Calling Caulaincourt an 'old St Petersburg courtier', he commanded that the Russian be given some of his own mounts, because 'Balachof had a long journey ahead.'

When the envoy had left, Napoleon told Caulaincourt that he was wrong to be incensed at his remarks about having turned Russian. It was only a trick on his part to prove to the tsar that Caulaincourt had not forgotten his tokens of goodwill.

The Master of Horse's response was immediate, and given the discretion I had come to expect of him, unexpected.

'I am a better Frenchman than those who extol this war, sire,' he said. 'I always tell you the truth when others, in the hope of pleasing you, merely tell you tales. When only Frenchmen are present, I take your pleasantries in good part, but it is an outrage to doubt my patriotism and fidelity before a foreigner.'

He then begged Napoleon, voice trembling with emotion, for leave to resign, or be given a commission in Spain, with permission to depart the following day.

I had come to think highly of Caulaincourt, and had noticed his willingness to argue with the emperor when others would not. He spoke his mind, whether or not Napoleon might be angered. His conviction and reasonable opinions were compelling. The emperor, on the other hand, was a high-handed individual who barely listened to his subordinates' opinions. He had received Balachof with courtesy, it was true, but had clearly never had any intention of agreeing to Alexander's request. This was proof that his only intention was all-out war, something the Russians seemed unwilling to grant him.

It was easy to see why. Another month, I decided, and the cavalry will have no horses left. The wagon train will be no different. Heaven knows what state the infantry will be in. Napoleon also had to be aware of this, but it would not divert him from the obvious folly of his course.

This is not my war, I thought. I will ask to go with Caulaincourt. Spain in December compared very favourably to Russia. When Bellamy eventually found out, he would be unable to prove that I had orchestrated the transfer. If it came to it, I could act as a spy there. From Spain I might contrive a return to England and a reunion with my mother; clearing my name might even be possible. Thinking of Jeanne, I felt a pang of regret, but told myself we would never have gone as far as Moscow anyway.

Matters had not come to a conclusion in the dining room. Napoleon must have moved close to the door, because I was able to hear every word. 'Who is doubting your fidelity?' he said quietly to Caulaincourt. 'I know well enough that you are an honest man. I was only joking.

You know perfectly well that I hold you in esteem. Just now you are talking at random, and I shall not reply to what you are saying.'

Caulaincourt was so angry that he gave no answer. I heard two of the others approach and speak with him, and a moment later, the emperor retired to his study. Berthier and Bessières, the pair who joined Caulaincourt, now began to try to placate the Master of Horse, but he was in no mood to listen. With Napoleon gone, he felt free to unleash his temper. He ranted and raved about how the campaign was madness. The losses to the Grande Armée were already catastrophic, and 'that after a few days' rain, without a battle fought,' he said to Berthier. 'Imagine what it will be like when the snows begin to fall. I tell you, the Russians will not even need to fight us. Winter will kill us all.'

Their denials and protests were bluff, but did not sound altogether convincing.

Caulaincourt then departed, telling the others he would settle his affairs at once, and leave in the morning.

'He is right,' I whispered to François. 'Napoleon can defeat the Russian army, but if we never bring it to bay, the enemies we will face instead are hunger and the weather. They cannot be beaten. I will let Caulaincourt calm down, and ask if I can accompany him. Will you also come?'

'I would, but Caulaincourt will not leave. I have twenty francs that say so.'

I thought of the passion in the Master of Horse's voice, and seized François's hand. 'Done!'

Dawn came clear and bright. It promised to be another scorching day. I had not slept well, my mind a jumble of thoughts. The winter climate in Spain might be more pleasant than Russia, but the war there was brutal. François's tales – he had taken part in the invasion and served until the second offensive on Madrid – were hair-raising. The local populace's hatred of the French was such that if a messenger was caught, he was horribly tortured and mutilated before being slain. I vacillated for a time, but seeing Caulaincourt, whose resolve had not changed a whit overnight, decided that to throw my lot in with him offered better odds than remaining. It would also win me twenty of François's francs, and with a bit of luck, see us remain comrades.

My certainty increased when Caulaincourt did not go to Napoleon's bedchamber as usual. Instead, he asked Duroc to take over his duties and receive the emperor's orders. Duroc went to Napoleon with this news, and returned soon after, accompanied by Berthier. They remonstrated with Caulaincourt to no avail. Two messengers came from the emperor, directing him to the imperial presence, but Caulaincourt cleverly absented himself from his room, and so did not receive the order.

I walked with him as he patrolled through the headquarters, issuing commands to clerks and officials. Duroc would be in charge from now on, he told anyone who asked.

I had been waiting for a good time to ask Caulaincourt, but quickly realised there would be no such thing. Nor would it be long before he departed.

'I was wondering, sir . . .' I hesitated, still unable to come up with a plausible reason for my transfer. The truth was, I was scared, but to admit that would see my request denied. The only men in the army who weren't scared, to some degree at least, were fools.

'Yes?' He looked at me down his long, straight nose.

'Might I come with you, to Spain?'

'Why?' Caulaincourt's gaze, as ever, was direct.

'My mother is poorly. According to the doctor, her heart is failing,' I said, thinking of the sad tale another messenger had told one night. 'Before we left Paris, I had word that she is not expected to see the new year. There was no time for me to visit her.'

'And you are from . . . Picardy, isn't it? That is too far from Paris. I will be travelling south with all speed.'

I cursed his good memory. 'I am from Picardy, sir, but she was taken ill visiting her sister in Orléans. If I could see her one last time, I would forever be in your debt.' I bore his stare with fortitude, praying that my story sounded convincing. Orléans was on the main road that led from the capital to the Spanish border.

'You are close to your mother?'

'Yes, sir, and I am her only child. My brother died a few years ago.' He frowned, and thinking I had overegged my story, my stomach twisted.

'Very well. You shall come with me. Ready your things. We leave within the hour.'

'Thank you, sir.' My spirits soared.

They were dashed not long after.

François, who had been with Napoleon, came demanding his twenty francs. 'The emperor sent messengers to look for Caulaincourt through the camp, with express orders to attend him.' The Master of Horse had had no choice but to obey.

'And he is staying now?' I cried. A nod. 'In Heaven's name, what did Napoleon do?'

'Pinched his ear, and asked if Caulaincourt was mad to want to leave him. The emperor said he esteemed Caulaincourt, and had no wish to hurt his feelings. Then he galloped off, and when next they paused, he spoke of everything but the Master of Horse's request. It was as if it had never been made.' François winked. 'I would have bet more, but I thought you might be suspicious.'

'You rogue,' I said, laughing despite my gloom. 'I will get you back for that.'

CHAPTER XIII

Napoleon stayed in Vilna for two weeks, working day and night. We messengers were run ragged carrying his orders all over the region. His ability to deliver a constant stream of commands meant that four secretaries struggled to keep up. Now it was a letter to Davout, Oudinot or Ney, then another to Murat. He was also in frequent communication with his brother Jérôme, and his adopted son Eugène, who commanded parts of the main army. There were letters for the commanders further away: Macdonald on the west flank, and on the eastern, the Austrian corps led by Prince Schwarzenberg. Often the emperor was dictating to all the secretaries at once, and if one was missing, to whoever was present. Once, exhausted, devouring a hunk of bread as I waited outside his office, I heard his voice call for someone, anyone to write down an order.

The office was dominated by a large, central map table, with a chair and table in each corner for the secretaries. Hurrying in, I saw that only three were occupied. With his chief topographer Colonel Bacler d'Albe by his side, the emperor was stalking about the maps, dictating to first one secretary, then another and another. Beginning each letter, his tone was serious, sharply emphatic and with never a pause. As inspiration came to him, it found expression in a livelier tone and jerky movements of his right arm, whose sleeve he kept plucking at. Sometimes the form of his words was incorrect, yet this very lack of correctness set its stamp on his language, which always depicted exactly what he wanted to say.

Apart from Napoleon's voice, the only sound was that of quills scratching furiously on parchment. He waved me to the empty corner table, and continued talking at speed. Scrambling to find a clean sheet of paper amid the pile of documents, I tried to write down everything he said. As he finished, the fourth secretary came back. I handed the letter to him – he would see it was written down in the top secret order book and duplicated – and went back to my station. Sent off moments later with a letter for Murat, I never found out if I had made any errors.

As for my mistakes, I could not help wondering if Napoleon was making some of his own. It seemed he was trying to remain in control of the entire army himself, an impossibility even if the vast force had all been in one place, rather than separated by distances that varied between ten and two hundred miles. I mentioned this to François, who told me that the emperor had always been one for direct command rather than allowing individuals like Davout, Oudinot and Ney to lead their own corps. As I rode to and fro, I often wondered about the odds of success when trying to direct what in effect was six, eight or even ten different armies. The odds never seemed that good.

Although there was no sign of the Russians around Vilna, that did not mean it was safe. With villages few and far between, finding water for my horse was a constant problem. Again I was grateful to François for his experience; we had both purchased leather water bags in Germany. I filled them at every opportunity. Each held about three-quarters of a gallon, which was enough to keep me and my mount alive during the periods when there were no wells or streams to be found.

Another danger, just as great, was the starving soldiers – numbering in the tens of thousands – who were rampaging through the country-side in large gangs. They attacked villages and manor houses with equal abandon, raping and killing. Sometimes they even acted in collusion with rebellious peasants. Napoleon's response was to order the court-martial and execution of any marauders captured and found guilty. Three flying columns, each one hundred men strong, were formed and sent out to capture murderous deserters, but their task was impossible, a light dressing pressed to a wound spurting blood. As I said to François, ten times their number would have struggled to control the men roaming the area.

Mindful of the danger, I travelled in a state of constant vigilance, unable to relax, my eyes never still, and always gripping a pistol butt. I often skirted villages, and if forced by the terrain to ride through a settlement, I made sure there was no sign of any Frenchmen. It was bizarre, having to regard soldiers of the Grande Armée as enemies, but as François said, these were men turned to beasts. Several messengers had been attacked to our knowledge, and at least one shot and wounded, his messages thrown to the wind.

Perhaps ten days into July – I had long since given up trying to remember the exact date – I was riding back towards Vilna from the south-east, where Davout's corps had reached the town of Minsk.

He had got there before Bagration, whose forces were being pursued by the corps commanded by the emperor's brother Jérôme. It had been a grand opportunity to crush one of the Russian armies, but Jérôme's failure to act in time had seen Bagration give both him and Davout the slip. Napoleon had been incandescent. I had heard him ranting about it to Caulaincourt. 'If Jérôme had the most elementary grasp of soldiering, he would have been on the third of July where he was on the sixth, which would have given me a fine campaign!'

Caulaincourt forbore from saying what François whispered in my ear, that Jérôme had no military experience whatsoever, and the emperor knew it. There was more too. Jérôme had clashed with Poniatowski, the commander of one of his three corps, and dismissed his chief of staff. Napoleon could not have been that surprised, François said, because he wasn't.

Nonetheless, there were no Russians for miles around Vilna. That might have been why my guard dropped, but I suspect that the main reason was my extreme weariness. Since arriving in the town, I had spent every minute of daylight in the saddle. Not only that, I knew some roads well enough to ride during the scant period of darkness, which lasted a mere three hours. I had done this during the previous night, and now, according to my pocket watch, it was almost nine in the morning. Liesje was tired too; I would need to marshal her strength if she was to reach Vilna. A slower pace was worth it, I decided. Leaving her at an *estafette* would mean I might not see her again for a couple of days. She was my favourite, and I liked to keep her with me whenever possible.

The sun beat down, welcome warmth after the dawn cool. It would be unbearable within a couple of hours, but for now I was content. Head nodding, Liesje slow-trotting, perhaps fifteen miles remained before Vilna appeared on the horizon. Three hours, I thought fuzzily, and I would deliver the letters in my satchel, and with luck, get to sleep in my cot.

My eyes closed. I began to dream, of Jeanne. Our time together had been brief, but the memories of it were a welcome diversion from the drudgery of endless hours in the saddle. I had no idea if she had written

– not that any letters would have reached me, on campaign with the Grande Armée – and it was impossible to send any communication to Moscow. Instead I imagined surprising her in the theatre where she worked, and her radiant smile of welcome. We embraced. Kissed.

A voice spoke. A man's, not a woman's, and most certainly not Jeanne's.

It was a challenge too, not a friendly greeting or question.

My eyes opened, and cold fear tickled my spine.

Half a dozen barefoot French infantrymen barred the road a short distance in front of me. Unshaven, their uniforms ragged and filthy, they were led by a burly corporal with a single gold ring in his left ear.

'Halt!' cried the corporal – it was his voice which had ended my daydream. His musket was aimed at my chest.

'Do not shoot! I am a loyal Frenchman, like you.' Ten to one they rob me, I thought. Five to one they do worse.

My words got a laugh, and he lowered his musket a fraction, but kept it pointed at me.

'Well met, friend.' I raised my hands in the air, and let Liesje walk towards them.

'Thinks we're his friends, he does,' I heard one of the men say. There was more laughter.

Among the silver birch trees to the left, I spied another score of deserters, for deserters they must be, lounged around a campfire. There was a wagon too, and a few tents, and even a shelter built of interlaced birch branches.

'Come on then.' The corporal beckoned, even as his glance strayed to two freshly-dead men sprawled in the ditch.

My stomach turned. Peasants by their homespun clothing, both had been shot. I decided they were probably the last unfortunates to come down the road. It seemed all too possible that this too would be my fate. My heart fluttered with panic.

'Got any food?' the corporal demanded. 'Money?'

'A piece of cheese. No coin. I bear letters, though, from Marshal Davout to the emperor.'

'Hear that? He's got letters for *l'Empereur*.' There was real contempt in the last two words. 'Give the cheese here.'

Any hope I had of my authority carrying some weight vanished, like mist before a breeze. I would be shot after I handed over the cheese, I decided, and Liesje used, like the ribby nags among the trees, to pull their cursed wagon.

My eyes flicked over the men blocking my path. The corporal and one other had their muskets at the ready, albeit by their waists. The others, cocky, arrogant, were either leaning on their weapons, or had them pointing groundward. The risks of resisting were still enormous – I deliberately avoided considering the odds – but my instincts were screaming that I had to act. Do nothing, and my corpse would soon lie alongside those of the wretched peasants.

'Quickly!' snarled the corporal.

'Sorry.' I pulled an expansive smile and undid the buckle of my satchel. Fishing around inside, I produced first the cheese and then the letters. I tossed the latter towards the corporal, one, two, three.

Holding his musket, he could not catch them, which was my intention entirely. Cursing, he slung it over his shoulder and bent down.

The second man's attention shot to the cheese, as did that of their companions. I lobbed it at him.

I stared at the butts of my pistols for an instant, horrified by the living nightmare I found myself in. One thing was crystal clear: I did not want to die. Not here, not now, not like this, and prayer would not save me. Hoping I could be forgiven for what I was about to do, I tugged the pistols out and drew back the hammers. I aimed at the corporal, who was straightening. He saw me; his mouth opened in surprise. I pulled the trigger. There was a belch of smoke and flame, the pistol kicked in my hand, and he dropped like a sack of potatoes. Without hesitation, I shot the second soldier, and then I was wheeling Liesje and urging her forward as if all the demons in Hell were after us.

Muskets roared. Bullets whizzed by. I crouched low, trying to present a smaller target. Somehow I managed to jam the pistols into their holsters. More shots rang out. They came nowhere close, and Liesje galloped on. I was beginning to think I was safe when a last shot rang out, and a second later, my right calf felt a horrible impact. A stinging pain radiated up my leg. Cursing, I snapped the reins and drove Liesje on. Muskets were not that accurate beyond a hundred paces. Only a sharpshooter stood a chance of hitting his target over two hundred.

After a quarter of a mile, I took a glance over my shoulder. There was no sign of pursuit, which was unsurprising. Like a spider in the corner of its web, all the deserters had to do was wait. Sooner or later, fresh prey would come to them along the road.

I reached down to my right leg, and my fingers came away sticky with blood. Fear gnawed my guts. Even if I only had a 'through and through', as the soldiers called it, infection was a major risk. Gangrene was infection's bedfellow, and the only effective treatment for that was amputation. At once my mind filled with images of the pitiful, one-legged beggars in London, veterans of the war with Napoleon; there had been plenty in Paris too. I sent another fervent prayer heavenward, and savagely stopped myself from calculating the odds of my survival.

Hooves pounded the earth, coming towards me. I straightened, wishing I had had time to reload, but telling myself that the approaching riders would be loyal Frenchmen rather than starving marauders.

A column of hussars came into sight around the bend, and I breathed again.

'Everything all right?' the lead rider called. 'We heard the shots.'

I shook my head in disbelief. They were Fifth Hussars, and I recognised the gap-toothed corporal. It was, I thought with frustration, as if Féraud and I were bound to each other. 'There are deserters a little way up the road,' I said, gesticulating. 'I have been shot in the leg.'

'Why, it's you, sir,' he said as the column reached me and halted.

'Well met,' I said dryly, my eyes searching for Féraud.

Despite their discipline, the hussars were a far cry from the last time I had seen them. Their uniforms were stained and dirty, and their horses in poor condition. A thick bundle of hay had been added to the portmanteau behind each man's saddle; it reached to shoulder height, and looked ridiculous.

'Right leg, is it, sir?' asked the corporal, dropping from the saddle.

'Yes.'

He came around Liesje's head, giving her a stroke, and seeing my bloodied calf, tutted. A pocketknife appeared in his hand, and before I could protest, he was slicing apart my trouser leg.

I winced as his none-too-clean fingers touched my calf, and hypocrite that I was – I only ever prayed in the depths of need – asked God that the injury was not bad.

'Why have you stopped, corporal?' Féraud's voice was imperious. He came cantering up the side of the column. Then he saw me. His expression hardened further.

'We met the messenger, sir, you know the fellow. He has been wounded.'

'And?' Féraud's gaze was full of cool dispassion.

'It's only a scratch, sir.' The corporal grinned up at me, all tobacco-stained gums. 'Shouldn't even stop you from riding once it's been dressed.'

I tried to conceal my overwhelming relief, but Féraud saw it.

He leered. 'Scared, eh?'

'Yes,' I barked. 'Now, are you going to go and deal with the deserters who attacked me, or stay here, exchanging pleasantries?'

Féraud's lips thinned white. 'Questioning my professionalism, eh? Know that I was at Austerlitz and Eylau, Eckmühl and Wagram!'

'I was merely pointing out that those deserters need dealing with.'

'Do you think we were galloping along the road for our own amusement?'

I could see where this was going. 'That is not what I meant—'

He cut me off. 'I will have satisfaction for this, you stupid cur!'

I could have refused his challenge, but Féraud seemed the type to make sure that that information spread far and wide. The thought of being reviled as a coward was odious. Sensing an opportunity, my bravado swooped in. With it, reawakened by his name calling, came my rage, that which had seen me batter my older brother unconscious.

'You know where to find me,' I said hotly. 'Imperial headquarters, although I am not often there for long. Come tonight, if you wish.'

'A contest in the dark?' exclaimed the corporal.

'Why not?' I cried, uncaring. 'By morning, I will have been sent away with fresh messages. Let us not miss our opportunity, Féraud.'

'Pistols or swords?' he asked. As the challenged, the choice this time was mine.

'Pistols,' I said, thinking, I just killed two men. Shooting Féraud will be straightforward.

A curt nod. 'Until tonight.' Then, 'How many deserters?'

'About twenty-four now. A pair are already dead.' I slapped the butt of one my pistols.

Masking his surprise, he barked an order at his waiting men, before asking, 'Do you wish to come?'

'No. The letters in my satchel are important. I must get them to imperial headquarters.'

He sneered, and led the hussars off at a quick trot. The corporal gave me a friendly salute.

I did not immediately ride away. Despite myself, I was curious to see what would happen. Less than a minute later, I got my answer. An order was shouted. Their horses' hooves drumming, the hussars went straight to the charge. Féraud was not interested in prisoners. I heard cries of fear, from the deserters, I guessed, and then came a rolling volley of shots. The hussars were firing their carbines, and the officers their pistols. Next they would draw their fearsome sabres, and close with the enemy.

Pop, pop, pop. A few shots only came in reply. Then the deserters were yelling in panic, and I wagered, running for their miserable lives. There were screams, often choked short, and soon after, the cries of men trying to surrender. These too were abruptly cut off.

I had to see it. I aimed Liesje back down the road, but slowly, so I could reload my pistols. This done, I urged her into a trot.

A scene of utter carnage met me. Bodies lay everywhere, shot, slashed, covered in blood. There was even a man lying in the campfire. The tents hung in flitters, cut apart by sabres. The wagon lay on its side, one wheel idly turning. Laughing and joking among themselves, Féraud's men were gathering again, forming a column. I did a quick headcount. Not a single man appeared to be missing, or even wounded.

The corporal looked surprised to see me. 'Come to make sure we did our job, monsieur?'

'Did-did you take any prisoners?'

A leer. 'An 'andful, monsieur. Three, was it, sir, or four?' he called.

Féraud came riding over from the deserters' rough camp. 'Three.' He added, 'Twenty-odd deserters would have required too many guards. Three captives, on the other hand, two of which are wounded, will require one.' He smiled, as if this explanation was altogether rational.

'You killed the rest?' I asked, horrified.

'Correct.' His puzzled glance seemed genuine. 'These filth would have murdered you.'

'Some, perhaps, but not all.'

He shrugged. 'None are any loss to the Grande Armée.'

'You are not the one who should decide that!'

'Says the man who shot two himself. I checked the muskets of the pair on the road. They were unfired, Dupont. You must have caused a

116

distraction – with the cheese, was it? – and shot them in cold-blood. Why did you do that? At worst, they might have beaten you and taken your horse.'

'They were going to kill me,' I hissed, horrified that he might be correct, that I might have overreacted. 'I had no choice. You did.'

An uncaring shrug. 'If I am questioned about this, which is unlikely, I shall say that the deserters fought back bravely, leaving little option but to cut them down. Now, I need to be on my way. You said something about the urgency of your letters?'

'I shall see you tonight,' I shot back.

'I look forward to it.'

His mocking smile stayed with me all the way back to Vilna.

CHAPTER XIV

'You chose to accept a second duel?' François's voice was incredulous. Twelve hours had passed. I had delivered my messages, seen my wound dressed by Larrey, the emperor's chief surgeon, and then slept through until the evening. Waking with a growling stomach, I had gone in search of food. In the palace kitchens I managed to procure a still-fresh loaf, a hunk of cheese and even a jug of drinkable red wine. It felt as if I were in the finest restaurant in Paris. François, just returned himself, had found me in a quiet corner, and after filching what remained of my repast, listened to my tale. It was clear he thought I was crazy, and I was beginning to think he might be right.

'Will you be my second?' I asked.

'Christ, I suppose so. He is a captain of hussars, you say?'

'Yes.'

'Please say that you asked to use pistols?' I nodded, and François let out a gusty sigh. 'Good. He would have cut you in two.' He knew enough of my childhood to know I was no swordsman. Féraud, a career hussar and veteran of titanic battles such as Austerlitz, would be an expert. 'How is your shooting?' François enquired. He had long recommended that I practise against bales of straw, but telling myself that I would never have to fire my pistols in anger, I had not done it once. 'It must be reasonable enough,' he said. 'Today you slew two men.'

'What if Féraud was right?' I asked. 'Maybe the deserters would not have killed me.'

'They murdered the peasants, you said.'

'Yes, but I am a Frenchman, an imperial messenger—'

'From what you say, the risk was not worth taking, Mathieu, and anyway, Féraud would have dealt with those two the way he did with the rest. Put them from your mind. There are more important things to deal with right now.'

118

It was pointless dwelling on what might have happened if I had not drawn my pistols, I thought, but it brought me to the realisation that I had no wish to shed more blood today. 'I do not want to fight Féraud.'

'Then why did you accept his challenge?'

'I was angry. I did not want to be known as a coward.' I stared down at my hands, which were shaking.

Seeing my anguish, he clasped my shoulder.

'You do not *have* to go through with it. Apologise, and have done!'

I nodded miserably.

'What time is it to take place?'

'Whenever Féraud returns.'

'Tell him then.'

'I will.' This was the best option, but it was deeply unpalatable. I told myself that the vastness of the Grande Armée, spread out over hundreds of square miles, meant that Féraud's ability to spread rumours would be limited. It was not as if I was a career soldier either. I would leave the imperial messenger service the moment the campaign was over. I stifled the sneaking suspicion that Bellamy might have something to say about my doing that.

That was a problem for another day.

It was half-past ten before my enemy put in an appearance at the palace, coming to the room where messengers waited for the emperor's letters. Coated in dust, bags under his eyes, Féraud had come straight from the road. His second was also a hussar, another captain, a serious-looking individual with long sideburns. We went outside, not wanting to attract attention. The courtyard was quiet, and the sentries, tired already, had no interest in us.

Féraud ignored me altogether, but the second inclined his head, and asked to have a word with François. They moved a few steps apart. 'This is a regrettable affair,' he said. 'But my principal's honour has been impugned. He is unwilling to retract his challenge unless an apology can be issued.'

François was ready. 'That is possible.'

Pleased, the second glanced at Féraud. 'Did you hear?'

'Yes.' His cold eyes bore down on me.

I had prepared my words, and even run them by François. 'I am very sorry for insulting you earlier, Captain. I meant to cast no aspersions on your courage or integrity. Please accept my sincere apologies.'

François and the second exchanged smiles. Féraud could accept this without any loss of face.

He had not replied, however.

Nervous, I said, 'Captain?'

'It is not enough.'

The second looked dismayed. 'Daniel, the man has apologised. There is no need for bloodshed.'

'I will accept, but on one condition.'

The second, relieved, asked, 'What is that?'

'He will repeat the same apology at nine o'clock tomorrow morning, in this courtyard.' Féraud's stare was hawk-like.

The place would be thronged at that time with imperial staff and officials, officers and soldiers. I could think of no better public humiliation.

'That is too much,' François protested. 'His words here should be enough.'

'But they are not,' said Féraud in an icy tone. His eyes moved to me. 'Well?'

I ground my teeth, and let the rage in. The thought of him gloating while scores of men listened to my apology was impossible to stomach. 'No. I will not do it.'

'Mathieu,' muttered François, but I brushed him away. 'I will not publicly degrade myself! The duel shall go ahead at once.'

Féraud grinned the grin of a man who had got what he wanted, and I cursed him for it.

'Where?' asked his second.

'There is a cemetery behind a church two streets over,' I answered. Duelling was illegal, so we could not use the more suitable courtyard. It was also close enough to the palace that we could quickly fetch a surgeon afterwards.

The second nodded. 'Two shots each?'

François glanced at me – still furious, I shrugged – and agreed.

Although this was usual, it was a change of direction for Féraud. It was because of his miss the last time we had faced one another, I thought, warring with the unpleasant acid sensation in the pit of my stomach. He really wanted to hurt me.

Féraud's second had a rectangular wooden case under his arm; it would contain a pair of duelling pistols and all the accessories. I had no such thing. François was carrying my army issue pistols in his satchel, the same ones I had used that morning. I would have taken them as they were, but François had insisted on firing the weapons off, and then giving them a good clean before we reloaded both. This, he pronounced, would greatly reduce the risk of misfires. Again I decided that I was lucky to have him as a friend.

We walked in silence from the courtyard. The pain from my wound was bearable, and easier to endure than my freshly returned fear. Overhead, the still-bright sky was clear, and the moon was rising in the east. The streets beyond were dark and quiet. Since the arrival of the Grande Armée, the locals tended to stay indoors at night. There were a few soldiers visible, but they were all drunk, and wrapped up in celebration and song.

The church windows stared at me like accusing eyes. It was probably breaking canon law to fight a duel on sacred ground, François whispered. I ignored him, but could not stop thinking that God, whom I had earlier so earnestly begged for help, just after I had foully slain two men, would now punish my hypocrisy. He would cause Féraud's aim to be true, or mine to miss – or both. It was hard not to think that I deserved it.

The path that ran alongside the eastern side of the church would serve, François declared. Because of the graves, which created a large open space, the light still in the sky and that cast by the moon meant it was reasonably bright. Féraud's second made no argument.

A distance of twenty paces was settled upon. Féraud initially refused to accept that first blood should end the duel, but after forceful protests from his second, he gave his reluctant agreement. I felt sick with relief. Two shots was bad enough, and now, in the eerie quiet of the graveyard, the possibility of death loomed larger than ever before. I did not want to be shot, but more than that, I did not want to die. I wondered grimly what the odds of escaping this waking nightmare with only a wound were.

The thought of firing my own pistols brought back my encounter with the deserters. One of my shots had smashed apart the corporal's jaw and ripped his throat into spraying, bloody ruin. The other had punched a great, bone-shards-visible hole in the second man's chest. The amount of blood had been astonishing.

I had to go through with the duel, I thought, but I had had enough of killing. He could shoot at me, but I would use the delope again. *Twice?* demanded the little devil in my head, and a wave of nausea rose from my stomach.

François dragged a heel in the gravel to make a line, and then he and the other second walked twenty paces along the path. Féraud went to join them. Dumbly, I walked to the first mark. Adding to the physical betrayals, my just emptied bladder somehow felt as if it was about to burst.

Féraud's second opened the case and handed him a pistol. François came and gave me one of mine.

The low call of an owl from a nearby tree could not have been more ominous.

'I have to piss.'

'Can you not wait?' François hissed.

'No! Tell him!' I shoved my pistol at François and hurried around the corner of the church, hearing Féraud's loud protest. François called out in reply. I paid no heed, able to concentrate on only one thing. The relief afterwards was exquisite. Buttoning my trousers, I thought about fleeing the scene, but Féraud would not leave the matter to rest there. He would have his duel, or I would be denounced as a coward the length and breadth of Russia.

'Who's there?' called a muffled voice at the church gate.

I ducked into the shadows, and slipped around the corner. With luck, whoever it was would decide not to follow a stranger into a graveyard.

The others were waiting. 'Done?' asked François.

'Yes.'

'My principal is ready,' he called.

Féraud answered that he was also.

His second was already in place halfway between us. 'Raise your pistols, and cock,' he said.

We obeyed. I could not see Féraud's weapon, just his slim, side-on shape. My throat was dry with tension, my calf wound stung. My arm muscles were trembling just holding the pistol. I could almost feel Féraud's bullet ripping into me.

'God be with you,' François said.

I did not answer.

The second lifted the handkerchief, a white shape in the darkness. 'When I drop this,' he intoned, 'you may both shoot.' Then, 'Ready?'

'Yes,' Féraud and I said.

Silence fell.

For the second time in my life, I faced the duellist's greatest test. My heart banging off my ribs, I stared down the length of my pistol at the figure that was Féraud. *He will try to kill you*, said the little devil. *Do the same to him.*

I hesitated, suddenly unsure what to do.

'In the name of God, what is going on?' cried a loud voice. 'Is this a duel? Lower your weapons at once!'

Concerned that Féraud's second might let his handkerchief fall, and that he himself might fire, I did not obey. Perhaps thinking the same, nor did he.

'Lower your pistols, I say! I am the emperor's Master of Horse!'

Stunned, I obeyed. I half turned to see.

Gravel crunched as Caulaincourt stalked towards us. He reached me first, and scowled in disbelief. 'Dupont?'

'Yes, sir.'

'Have you taken leave of your senses? I go for a breath of fresh air and find you duelling, at night, in a graveyard?'

'My opponent would not accept my apology, sir.'

A *tch* of disgust. 'And so you decided to fight anyway! It is all prideful nonsense, like those fools Dupont de l'Étang and Fournier-Sarlovèze!'

I had no idea who he was talking about.

Caulaincourt beckoned to Féraud. 'You – come here!'

Both of us received a severe dressing down. We were at war, Caulaincourt railed, and our enemies were the Russians, not comrades. Our behaviour was irresponsible, and gave bad example to others. On and on he went, until I realised that his reprimands were to be the limit of our punishment. Although duelling was illegal, it was still acceptable among the officer class.

'Get out of my sight,' he ordered at length. 'And stay away from each other.'

I walked away with François, and allowed myself to feel relieved.

I had reckoned without Féraud. He caught up with us on the street. 'You did this!'

'Did what?' I demanded hotly.

'Told your master about the duel, so he could stop it. And you call *me* a coward?'

'Liar! I did no such thing!' I cried.

He curled his lip, in that way that made me want to batter him senseless.

'You shall have your duel,' I said, my temper bursting its banks. 'At a time and place where no one will intervene.'

'When?' he demanded.

'You have your duties, as do I. Our seconds will have to agree it.'

To his credit, Féraud accepted that.

François did his best to cheer me up on the way back to the palace. 'You did the right thing. No man should have to do what Féraud demanded.'

Cold reason was fast returning. 'Instead I shall have to fight him again, risking death or permanent injury.'

'Look on the bright side: a Russian bullet or blade might get you before that – or a French one.'

It was so awful, and true, that I had to laugh.

'This cloud might have a silver lining,' François said as we entered the courtyard.

I glanced at him.

'Consider the odds of you, a wet-behind-the-ears imperial messenger, in a duel against Féraud, a hussar who has served in all the emperor's great victories.'

'What are you saying – that we bet on Féraud?'

'We could make a fortune!'

'If I survive,' I said drily.

'You will. It's not as if you haven't done it before,' said François, his voice brimming with confidence. 'I will act as the bookmaker. It would seem odd, macabre, for you to wager on your own life.' A laugh. 'Hawking for business yourself might also put off potential customers – we can't have that.'

I chuckled, already wondering how much advance I could get on my pay, because the more I bet, the more I could win. Thoughts of the prospective riches made the prospect of a second duel with Féraud more bearable, for now at least. It would be different, I knew, when we stood facing each other, pistols aimed, waiting for the handkerchief to fall, but that was for another day. In this moment, I decided, it was enough to be alive, and calculating the potential of enormous winnings.

A thought struck me. 'Caulaincourt mentioned two names – Dupont de l'Étang and Fournier-Sarlovèze. Do you know who he meant?'

'Oh yes,' said François with a chuckle. 'They are famous throughout the army. Both are senior officers – generals, in fact. They first fought a duel almost twenty years ago, and continue to do so. Pistols, swords, sabres, they have used them all. I do not know what the count is, but it must be two dozen at least. They will not get to duel on this campaign, however. Fournier-Sarlovèze is in command of a brigade of light cavalry, I believe, but Dupont de l'Étang is still in disgrace, and remained in France.'

'They have fought more than twenty duels?' I asked, incredulous.

'Insane, eh?'

I hoped my encounters with Féraud did not follow that path.

'Monsieur Dupont.' The voice was vaguely familiar.

I peered into the darkness by the palace entrance, where a figure stood. 'Sir?'

He emerged into the light, one hand settling the long, combed-over hair that shielded his pate. 'Well met.'

Utter shock and dismay consumed me. Against all possibility, all likelihood, it was Bellamy. 'What are you doing here?' I croaked.

'That is no way to greet a friend,' he said, smiling at François. 'Carnot, at your service.' They shook hands, and Bellamy explained, 'I often played cards with Mathieu in Paris. I have just arrived.'

'You wear no uniform, monsieur. I assume you are a government official?' François asked.

'Yes. I and a number of colleagues have been seconded from the Ministry of War to the imperial headquarters.'

'Welcome to Vilna! Small and dull though it is, you will be kept busy,' said François.

Meanwhile my heart sank further. I could already feel the pressure Bellamy would put on me. No doubt he would immediately pry for information that would prove useful to the Russians. And I, I would have to start passing it to them, or Bellamy would carry out the threat he had made about Monsieur Dupont.

Bellamy, or Carnot, as he called himself, waved at the entrance to the courtyard. 'Been for a late night stroll?'

'Something like that.' I had no wish for him to know any of my business, still less my quarrel with Féraud.

Bellamy's eyes went to the satchel slung over François's shoulder, but he made no comment. 'Shall we share a jug of wine?' he enquired pleasantly. 'I want to hear how things have been since you crossed the Niemen.'

François, yawning, politely declared that he was for his bed. Bidding us good night, he disappeared in the direction of our room.

'Why are you here?' I hissed the instant he was out of sight.

Bellamy gave me a reproachful look. 'And I thought you would be pleased to see me.'

I said nothing, but pictured him under the barrel of my pistol, as the deserter corporal had been. It gave me great pleasure to imagine pulling the trigger.

'What of my debts?' I demanded. 'Have they been paid?'

'Of course.' His eyes were impenetrable black pools. 'Have you kept your side of the bargain?'

'It has not been possible. There isn't a Russian within twenty miles of here.' He looked surprised, and I went on, 'Having just reached Vilna, you will not know that the enemy is constantly falling back before our advance. The only units to make contact with Russian troops are many miles in front of the main army. I have ridden hundreds of miles since we crossed the Niemen, and I have not seen even a single Cossack. Quite simply, there has been no one for me to pass letters to.'

'That will change.' There was no mistaking the certainty in his voice.

'How do you know?'

'There will be a battle at some point. Tsar Alexander will not continue to simply abandon vast swathes of his territory.' He smiled, and patted my arm, as if to reassure me. 'And then, Monsieur Carrey, you will earn your crust.'

François had taken my pistols, or I would have calmly shot Bellamy dead in that moment.

He saw it too. 'War has changed you. Know that I am not alone. There are other agents on the imperial staff. If anything happened to me, Monsieur Dupont would soon after face charges of treason.'

He had me, the scoundrel, and he knew it.

I made him a stiff, impotent bow and walked away.

CHAPTER XV

I did my best to avoid Bellamy after that. It was not hard, because I was often away from the headquarters at Vilna. When I returned, it was often possible to deliver my letters and immediately take charge of more. With a fresh horse under me, I could depart within a quarter of an hour of arriving. The sacrifice was my bed, and the sleep I needed so dreadfully. After several days, I succumbed, and sneaked to my room. Somehow Bellamy found out. He woke me after only an hour; groggy with tiredness, I meekly accepted the letter he gave me. It was, he ordered, to be handed to the first Russians I met. His tactic saw my planned protest – that I could not give my official communications to the enemy without drawing suspicion – die in my throat. His copy, made in secret, would never be missed.

I tried a different tack. 'I will be shot or run through, surely, by the first Cossacks I meet?' Ranging everywhere, ambushing the Grande Armée at will, the fearsome light skirmishing cavalry were the enemy troops I would encounter.

'I told you before. You must call out *"Bozhe, Tsarya khrani"*,' he said quietly. 'Say it.'

I repeated the words, as I had in Paris, until he was content. 'What does it mean again?'

A look. 'God save the tsar.'

I sighed. 'And that will be enough?'

'I would have thought so.' Bellamy cracked his knuckles, another annoying habit of his. He reiterated the Russian word for 'officer', and several phrases that would identify me as a spy, to be released rather than taken as a prisoner of war.

I shook my head, refusing to believe that every Cossack officer would know this, but all I could say was, 'Very well.'

'Do not think of throwing the letter in the ditch, Monsieur Carrey,' he said as if reading my mind. 'I have other ways of contacting the Russians, and if my messages are not delivered, I will find out. Think of Dupont in Paris.'

'I had no such intention,' I lied.

'Of course not,' he said with a smile.

Another week passed, and the advance continued. I was kept as busy as ever, and to my good fortune, saw little of Bellamy and Féraud not at all. François had made some enquiries about the Fifth Hussars; they were positioned miles in advance of the imperial household. For the moment, organising a duel was impossible, which suited me well.

Promoted by the emperor over Jérôme – who had not been told – Davout took charge of Napoleon's brother's corps. In a fit of pique, Jérôme took his household cavalry and set out for home. The emperor sent Jérôme a reproving letter, and also castigated Davout for his handling of the situation. If he had simply told Jérôme, I said to François, the situation could have been avoided, but as my friend replied, being logical was not always Napoleon's way.

Napoleon moved eastward with Davout's corps, while Prince Eugène was diverted to the north to prevent Bagration's army from joining that of his colleague Barclay. I spent my days riding between the imperial party and Murat's cavalry, which was still hounding Barclay's rear-guard. I now carried several letters written by Bellamy, each updating the last, but to my relief, I saw not so much as a single Cossack. Bellamy fumed and complained, but was powerless to do anything, because the other messengers reported the same.

As Barclay fell back towards the mighty fortified camp at Drissa, I travelled to and fro with messages for Murat, and I saw with my own eyes the price paid for his headlong pursuit. The cavalry's horses were literally being ridden to death. Orders were given never to take off their bridles even during brief rest periods, meaning the poor creatures were unable to feed or drink, sometimes for more than thirty hours at a time. I could often smell a cavalry unit long before I saw it, thanks to the smell of the horrific saddle sores afflicting countless horses. Dehydrated, many succumbed to constipation, forcing their riders to shove their arms up the unfortunate animals' rectums to pull out the bullet-like turds.

They died like flies, from exhaustion, dehydration, colic or, more often than not, a merciful bullet. Hundreds of carcasses lined the roads, a sight which would have turned anyone's stomach. And yet I became inured to it, if not to the horrendous stink of rotting flesh.

A hollow-cheeked cavalry officer I asked for directions one day told me that his men's horses were so weak that after charging the Cossacks, they had to dismount and walk them back. In the event of a counter-attack, the men ran away, abandoning the beasts to their fate.

'That is terrible,' I said with feeling, tearing off a piece of my stale loaf and shoving it into my mouth. I caught his eyes on it. 'Hungry?'

'I have not eaten bread since Germany.' He sounded embarrassed.

I handed him all that was left, and with his thanks ringing in my ears, continued on my journey.

The emperor's great new hope was that Murat could surround Drissa and wipe out one of the tsar's armies. But before Murat could reach him, Bagration slipped away to the east. Hearing that Drissa had been completely abandoned, Napoleon declared himself content, and made instead for the town of Polotsk, from which the tsar himself had only departed a few days before. His plan was to prevent Bagration from rendezvousing with Barclay as well as cutting the supply lines from Moscow.

Again the emperor's two weeks spent at Vilna cost him dear. Barclay reached Polotsk first, and continued along the Dwina River on to-wards Witepsk. Napoleon tracked his path. By the afternoon of the twenty-fifth of July, he had reached the village of Beschenkowitschi and set up his imperial headquarters. I left there in the direction of Witepsk, riding along an unforgettable, splendid wide road, flanked by double avenues of silver birch. I carried back news that Murat, still pursuing Barclay, had encountered the enemy in force at the village of Ostrowno. Bitter fighting had gone on all day, with each side taking turns to advance, only to be driven back by fierce resistance. Murat's cavalry had not fought alone, infantry units and artillery joining them as the Grande Armée caught up. Only at nightfall did the Russians begin to withdraw.

The next morning, fighting resumed some five miles to the east, near the town of Witepsk, where the Russians had made another stand. It seemed set for a major battle, exactly what Napoleon wanted. Advancing from his headquarters on the twenty-sixth, the emperor stayed in the saddle until ten at night, ordering units into position and assessing the lie of the land. He was in fine mood, declaring at one point, 'Tomorrow, at five o'clock. The sun of Austerlitz!' This, François told me later, alluded to the magical moment, remembered by every man who had been there, when the sun had broken through the morning mist on the day of the famous battle.

My own encounter with Napoleon was more mundane; as I delivered my third message of the day to Caulaincourt, he caught my eye and said that I was a fine servant of the empire. I was ridiculously pleased by the compliment.

The twenty-seventh promised more blistering heat and as I rode with François, Caulaincourt and the imperial household, the brutal evidence of the previous day's fighting was everywhere. Through Ostrowno we went, its few poor smoky houses turned into makeshift hospitals. The air resounded with piteous moans and cries. The buildings were all full; blood-soaked, wounded men lay in rows upon rows outside. Bandages were already in short supply; torn-up uniforms seemed to be the only fabric available. The best way to distinguish those treated by a surgeon was to choose the patients with cleanly removed legs or arms. A man-high pile of severed limbs outside one cottage marked the operating theatre.

Far worse horrors awaited on the silver birch-lined road to Witepsk. There were still some dead on the road, but the greater number of those who had been there had been flung into the ditches. Some trees had been damaged or cut down by roundshot. Off the road, where there had been several cavalry charges, the greensward was churned up and men were lying in every posture and mutilated in a variety of ways. There were large numbers of hussars among the fallen. I wished at once that they were from the Fifth, and that Féraud was among them, but an aide-de-camp I knew said they were from the Eighth. I felt instant shame, and found myself unable to take my gaze from the slain.

Some had been burnt quite black by the explosion of an ammunition wagon. Others, who seemed dead, were still breathing. As we approached, I heard them complaining. They lay on their backs, heads sometimes resting on comrades who had been dead for hours, in a state of apathy, in a kind of sleep of pain they were loath to come out of, heeding no one around them. They asked for nothing, doubtless because they knew there was nothing to hope for; nor did they beg for the help already so many times refused.

Scattered among them lay horses, ripped harness, exploded ammunition wagons, twisted sabres, pistols, broken muskets. The debris was on both sides of the road, carrying on into the treeline. A little further on, the uniforms on the corpses changed, and soon we recognised the place where the Russians had attended to their wounded. I had heard estimates of two thousand dead and injured; the French losses, although considerably smaller, were still substantial.

'It is sickening,' I said to François, grateful not to have eaten breakfast.

'They say that war is a vision of Hell on earth. I have never thought to argue with that.' His face was unusually sober. 'This was a small clash, Mathieu. A full scale battle would be ten, twenty times worse.'

I cast a look at Napoleon, who had reined in to survey the scene. There was no visible emotion on his face. 'Does he not care?' I asked, incredulous.

'His sensitivity has passed so many tests,' said François. 'Think of how many battles he has fought, how many times he has witnessed the bloody result.'

I did not want to imagine that, or what was to come as the campaign continued. For continue it would. Despite his professions of friendship towards Tsar Alexander, Napoleon's enthusiasm showed no sign of abatement – if anything, the opposite. If I deserted, I would soon be blackmailed afresh by Bellamy's colleagues in Paris. Short of blowing out my own brains, I decided bitterly, as so many soldiers had done, there was no choice but to endure.

We rode through low hills covered in clumps of birch trees and areas of bog, emerging onto the edge of an undulating plain. Thousands of the emperor's troops were already in position at its edge; Murat's cavalry, lines of tirailleurs and voltigeurs and in reserve, green-coated, bearskin-wearing Italian Guard grenadiers. The sense of excitement was palpable, and the excited soldiers greeted Napoleon with loud cheers.

Awaiting us across the plain, in full view near the town of Witepsk, was Barclay's army. Only a stream – the bridge over it miraculously intact – and the last French outposts lay between us and the enemy.

After studying the disposition of the Russians with his telescope – balanced as usual on the shoulder of a sergeant of the Imperial Guard – the emperor gave orders that his command post be set up to the left of the road, on a hillock crowned by a burnt-out windmill. There, for the first time, I witnessed battle at close quarters. To my astonishment, the fighting took place less than a quarter of a mile away from the hillock. Men fought and bled and screamed and died while we watched, giving the contest a bizarre, amphitheatre-like feel.

Initially, it was all cavalry. As might have been expected, Murat was everywhere, sometimes coming to speak with the emperor, but mostly leading charges at the Russians. He was unmissable in a Renaissance-style hat, adorned with large white plumes that waved in the wind and held in place by a diamond clasp. Around his bare neck was an antique Spanish-style ruff over a sort of light-blue velvet tunic, all bedecked with gold embroidery. It was held in tight at the waist by a silk sash of the same colour as the tunic, tipped at both ends with gold fringes. He wore white worsted breeches and huge deerskin boots of the kind fashionable during the Thirty Years' War, and massive gold spurs. If he had been anyone else, I thought, men would have laughed, but the soldiers of the Grande Armée were used to Murat's idiosyncrasies – indeed they loved him for it.

Despite his heroic efforts and the shooting of the light infantrymen who had crossed the stream, the French cavalry, the 16th Chasseurs, were driven back by Russian lancers. Small groups of the infantry, men of the 9th Regiment of the Line, were then surrounded, and seemingly about to be annihilated. Time and again, however, they drove the enemy cavalry back with concerted musket volleys. Their predicament unfolded as Murat came again to report to Napoleon. When he noticed, he was incensed. Accompanied by only his staff and personal escort – sixty men – Murat charged the Russian lancers, who outnumbered him by at least thirty to one. I would not have wagered a single sou on his chance of success, let alone survival. To my utter astonishment, the lancers turned tail and fled.

I joined in the cheering, yelling until I was hoarse. 'Would you have taken a bet on Murat?' I asked François.

He eyed me askance. 'To succeed or fail?'

'To fail! No one should have been able to do what he did just now.'

'You do not know Murat, my friend. Charges like that are his raison d'être.' He laughed. 'Accepting a wager like that would have been worse than taking sweets from a child.'

I scowled, annoyed with my naïveté. 'Learn the character of someone in battle before you bet on them, just like an opponent in a gambling salon.'

'Exactly. If it had been another cavalry commander, say, the result could have been catastrophic, but Murat is recklessly brave and his men will follow him into the jaws of Hell itself. The Russians esteem him highly as well.'

'I have heard,' I said, shaking my head. 'They say that he rides right up to the Cossack patrols and shares his brandy with them.' I hope they are as friendly to me, I thought, my stomach clenching.

Midday had passed, and the Russians were still in disarray. Thousands more infantry and cavalry had arrived. So too had several units of artillery; lines of cannon were already arrayed along the bank of the stream.

'He will order a full attack now, surely?' I said to François. Our eyes went to a cheerful Napoleon, who was about fifty yards away, deep in conversation with Caulaincourt and other senior officers. He had just returned from reconnoitring some distance along the stream, where Marshal Ney and Count Montbrun were advancing with their cavalry.

'It seems a good moment, certainly,' said François. 'Smash Barclay's army now, and the road to Smolensk and Moscow will lie open. Bagration will also be much easier to defeat.'

A short time later, Napoleon astonished everyone. Instead of ordering an attack, he decided to wait until the following morning to deliver the hammer blow. That evening, perhaps revealing his uncertain frame of mind, he held a rare council of war. It was attended by Caulaincourt, Eugène, Murat, his chief-of-staff General Belliard, and the light cavalry General Lefèbvre-Desnouëttes. Afterwards, they dined on tables outside his tent, the food served on a gold dinner service, and wine in crystal glasses. Delivering a message as the emperor and his commanders dined, I felt a pang of jealousy. My feelings can only have been mild, however, compared to the famished-looking Italian Royal Guards forming the protective cordon around the imperial headquarters. Leaving, I asked the officer who had stopped me on the way in if he and his men had eaten. He gave me a scornful look. 'The only thing to pass their lips today has been a little muddy and unhealthy water, and that after a six-hour march in brutal sunshine, stumbling on the sandy earth, through clouds of dust.' His eyes went to Napoleon, he could not help it.

I spoke to Caulaincourt later, who gave orders that the Italians were to be fed all the leftovers from the emperor's dinner, and more besides. I wished I could have done the same for the rest of the army.

The next day brought a fresh surprise. By the time the first cavalry-men scouted towards Witepsk in the cool before dawn, the town had been abandoned. Yet again, the Russians had slipped away, the wily Barclay leading his troops to safety. Yet again, an empty town greeted the advancing soldiers. It was eerie; not a single inhabitant remained. My skin crawled as I rode along the main street. Murat's cavalry re-ported that the countryside beyond, vast and endless, was also deserted. Unsurprisingly, morale was affected. A deep gloom fell on the army, and Napoleon too.

I was not so affected, content that I had a bed for the night, and that I had not seen Féraud for days.

The day after we entered Witepsk, the twenty-ninth of July, the emperor decided that the troops were to have a much-needed rest. The speed of their advance meant that the supply wagons and herds of cattle belonging to each regiment had fallen behind by several days' travel. Many of the soldiers had barely eaten in days or even weeks. There were rumours of men starving to death, and others so exhausted from marching that they had no energy to butcher and cook the pig or sheep they might have caught.

I was not in quite such dire straits, thankfully, but I too grew used to going without meals from sunrise to sunset. So far, I had shed fifteen pounds or so, a great deal more than the weight I had gained drinking wine and playing cards in Paris. Hungry all the time, often dreaming of my mother's cooking, I was not above pausing on a ride to forage through abandoned houses and farmyards. The inhabitants had often secreted away food before they fled, and searching under floorboards, behind woodpiles and in haystacks often brought rich prizes. What I found did not matter: a supper of pickled onions or stewed cabbage was better than no supper at all. Honey on its own was incomparable, and on one occasion, I even came upon lengths of smoked sausage. They lasted me a day and a half.

Money was currently of no use, so when I had a chance to gamble – usually, this was when I was waiting for a reply to the messages I had delivered – the stakes were for food. A swift game of écarté one day against an aide-de-camp of Murat's – four of my precious sausages against his small half wheel of cheese – saw me come away the victor. That evening, my meal in the saddle seemed like a feast for a king.

Munching happily, paying little attention to my surroundings – I was following the road back to Witepsk – I was caught off guard by the sudden emergence of eight riders from the trees to my left. Astride small, shaggy ponies – known as 'cognats', the corruption of their Russian name – the men wore loose-fitting blue and silver uniforms and were armed with long, deadly-looking lances and sabres. There was no question of them being French; these were Cossacks. At once panic threatened. There was no hope of wheeling my mount to flee. At least a score were spilling onto the road behind.

Sweating, I raised my hands in the universal signal for surrender, and flailed for the words Bellamy had taught me.

One Cossack caught my eye and leered. His expression did not augur well. He shouted something.

I had no idea what he meant. I reined in.

They rode closer, front and back, all aiming their lances at me.

At last I remembered. *'Bozhe, Tsarya khrani!'*

To a man they looked surprised. *'Lyubish'Tsarya?'* asked one.

Apart from *'Tsarya'*, his words were gibberish. *'Bozhe, Tsarya khrani,'* I said again, placing a hand on my heart for effect.

'Franzusky?'

He means 'Frenchman', I thought. *'Da, da,'* I said, asking if he was an officer. He shook his head, but I used the phrase Bellamy had given me anyway.

I was met with a blank look. He gestured at my pistols and sword, indicating I should throw them to the ground.

I tried again, using Bellamy's expression. Nothing. Do not panic, I told myself, but it was hard not to. I was surrounded now by a circle of lances, and behind them, a ring of unfriendly, bearded faces. It was easy to imagine the pain as half a dozen sharp points pierced my flesh, and the agony of the sabre slashes that would come after. Taking my pistols out by their butts, I carefully dropped them onto the dried mud of the road. I did the same with my sword. The irony that I would have received similar treatment from my own side – the deserters – did not escape me.

Something was said. Again, I did not understand, but the Cossack in charge, a ruffian with a squint, was gesturing at my satchel. I handed it over, again using the expressions Bellamy had given me. They made not a bit of difference. I told myself all would be well, but it was hard to stay calm, especially when the ruffian dismounted and coming right up to my horse, indicated I should also get down.

Warily, I obeyed, and after giving my pistols and sword to different men, he began going through my pockets. I protested, and at once lance points were shoved at me, close enough that I had to lean backwards not to be pricked. My wallet was rifled through, and the French banknotes sneered at but stashed away, nonetheless. No doubt he was looking for roubles, I thought, of which I had none. The wallet was not returned. It contained my French identification papers, but thankfully, I had no personal letters to lament. My pocket watch was next, and then my snuff box. That aroused a lot of interest; it was handed around, each man taking a great pinch of the aromatic powder. They sneezed and laughed, and passed it on, which was better than getting angry.

Finding the brandy in my satchel, the ruffian patted me amiably on the cheek. '*Patruschka*.'

I smiled, not understanding, but grateful that he was still being friendly. He drank a slug from the flask, and grinned. There were demands that it be shared, but he snapped back at the others, and kept it for himself.

Next he looked through the letters in the satchel, but did not open them. That was a relief – he would give them to an officer, I decided, someone who would right my situation. All I had to do was remain calm and patient.

I was ordered to mount my horse, and with a Cossack taking the reins, we rode off into the trees. Half a mile away was a circle of tents, hidden in a dell, and shelters made from interwoven branches. Smoke trickled skyward from cooking fires. Hobbled ponies grazed the surrounding sward. I was surprised to see children running to and fro, laughing and playing, until I saw that some of the people were civilians. Local villagers, I thought, who had taken refuge in the woods, and been joined by the Cossacks.

My sympathy towards them rapidly changed.

A woman in a dirty smock saw me, and screeched something in Russian. Heads turned. People came running. Names were called – it is easy to distinguish insults even in a foreign language – and shouts of anger were directed at me. The Cossacks laughed among themselves, and I felt the stirrings of unease.

The peasants swarmed towards us in a tide of unwashed humanity. They were stooping, picking up stones and handfuls of dirt. Their faces were twisted with hate, and it was no surprise. Just a day before, I had overheard a grenadier laughing with a comrade as he recalled the face of a boy spitted on his bayonet and held to the fire, even as his mother screamed. The men of the Grande Armée, I thought grimly, were infinitely worse to the locals than their Russian masters.

'Bozhe, Tsarya khrani!' I said to the ruffian. He nodded, but made no attempt to stop the approaching peasants. Nervous, I once again tried Bellamy's phrases on him, but got no response.

A stone hit the side of my head, and I saw stars. Sensing what was next, I closed my eyes just in time. A shower of dirt and clods of earth landed, and before I knew it, I was being dragged from the saddle. *'Nyet, nyet,'* I cried. *'Bozhe, Tsarya khrani!'*

No one paid any heed. Barely managing to stay upright, I was shoved from one peasant to another. I did not fight back. Slaps rained in, on my face, the back of my head, my arms. Someone with a stone in their fist struck me over one ear. Again I saw stars, and an instant later, felt blood running down my neck.

A snarling face rammed itself into mine. Spittle showered me. *'Sabacki Franzusky!'*

Whatever type of Frenchman I was being called, I thought dazedly, it was not a nice one.

The man punched me in the belly, driving the air from my lungs. I went down, winded, half-stunned. There was no mercy. The peasants began to trample and kick me, all the while shouting and yelling. I did my best to curl into a ball, thinking it was fortunate that they were barefoot, and not wearing hobnailed military shoes.

After what seemed an eternity, I was dragged to my feet, half-conscious. Pawing hands reached in, pulling and tearing at my clothing. Pop, pop, went my buttons, so that my shirt came undone, and my trousers too. The latter half-fell down, but with gnarly hands pinning my arms, I could do nothing about it. If it had not been for the

138

same grip, I would have collapsed. The slaps and punches continued, until I no longer knew where I was.

I did know one thing, however, and had no need to calculate the odds.

I was a dead man.

CHAPTER XVI

A mid the crescendo of sound and blows, a voice broke in, shouting. A fist hit me in the mouth, and my bottom lip split like an overripe plum. There was instant laughter, but surprisingly little pain, perhaps because my head was ringing like a church bell. I longed for complete unconsciousness; then the pain would stop. They could beat me to death, and I would not care.

The voice bellowed again, one word.

The cries of the mob died away. Head lolling, I waited for the next blow, the next slap. None came. For the first time, the tight grip on my upper arms eased. I sagged down, and realising how weak I was, the peasants bore me up into a standing position again. Still no punches landed.

'Atstahvit!'

I looked up, seeing through the crowd a mounted Cossack in the same uniform as the others, but of a more opulent and tasteful cut. A sabre hung by his side. He barked another command, and the peasants gave way before him, until only the two men holding me were left.

I stared at him dully, wondering what new torture awaited me.

'Pardon, camerade,' he said. 'Vous-êtes français?'

'Yes,' I croaked, remembering that the Russian officer class spoke French. I followed this with Bellamy's expression.

A look of sharp interest crossed his face; concern immediately replaced it. 'My apologies, monsieur, for what these fools have done to you.' Changing from French to Russian, he launched into a tirade first against the peasants, who cowered and shuffled away from the horse-whip he brandished, and then at the Cossacks, who had been watching my ordeal from a short distance away.

My identity established, I was treated with the utmost courtesy, although there was no friendliness in it. A spy is looked down on by all, I

140

thought wearily, as two Cossacks half-carried me to the captain's tent. Soon my wounds were being tended by the unit's surgeon. Already thinking of my return to French lines, I had the wit to refuse a bandage for my head. I was given a large measure of good vodka, the officer's own, which I downed in one, and happily accepted a second. New clothing – a silver and blue uniform – was offered. I declined this too.

Soon the ruffian who had taken my belongings was brought in front of me, and lambasted by the captain, presumably for not realising that I was an ally, not an enemy. He scowled, and apologised, although his tone suggested he was being less than genuine. My wallet, pocket watch and satchel were given back, along with my pistols and sword. I got my flask back too, although it was empty. I did not protest about that.

The officer's expression grew more expectant, so I rooted around in the satchel, and feeling like the worst kind of traitor, handed over Bellamy's letters.

He weighed them in his hand, as if assessing their value. 'You have other messages, official ones?' he asked.

'Yes. But if you take them—'

'I understand,' he said with a wry smile. 'It will look bad for you, the same as if you were to wear Cossack uniform.'

'Exactly.' Relieved, I let them fall back into the satchel.

'I would invite you to share our evening meal—'

'I must be on my way.' The Cossacks appeared to have no other prisoners, but the less time I spent in their company, the less chance I might be found out.

The officer looked pleased, which reinforced my feeling that he had only offered out of courtesy. An honourable soldier, no doubt he loathed spies and what they stood for. I hated this. I wanted to tell him about Bellamy, and how he had blackmailed me, but I kept my peace. He would only think I was lying.

My horse was brought back; I was told it had been fed and watered. Although maltreatment did not extend to the enemy's horses, there were plenty of hostile stares as I rode out of the camp, and laughter too. I must have looked a sight. My shirt hung open, and my trousers stayed up only because I was seated. A mass of cuts and bruises covered my face, and judging by the pain, my torso would be black and blue by the morning.

It was a small price to pay, I told myself. I was still breathing, yet the unpleasant experience did not augur well for future contact with the Russians. I would have to bend Bellamy's ear about it, and extract a better way to establish from the outset that I was not to be treated like an ordinary French soldier.

I warily cast my gaze up and down the road before rejoining it. To my considerable relief, there was no one about. I prayed that the Cossacks were the only Russian unit in the area, and that my journey back to the imperial headquarters at Witepsk would be trouble free.

Dusk was falling, but like all the nights before, there was still enough light to ride by. Wishing that I had had more of the officer's vodka, and that Witepsk were a mile away, not ten, I set my horse to an easy trot. The pain was excruciating, but if I let him walk, my journey would take even longer. Suffering greater discomfort for less time was better than the other way around, I decided.

I lasted for perhaps a quarter of an hour before I had to stop. Breath hissing between my teeth, holding the right side of my chest where the pain was worst – several ribs must have been cracked – I let misery consume me. Since that horrific night on the Kentish beach, my life had been completely topsy-turvy. First blamed for the murder of a militiaman, then robbed on the French coast, I had somehow struggled to Paris. True, I had found Dupont, but then I had come up against the gambling salon's owner, and the blackmailer Bellamy, who had forced me to join Napoleon's army. As a consequence of this, I had almost been murdered by Russian peasants. One of the only bright lights in the darkness had been Jeanne, but she was no longer in my life. Moscow seemed as far away as the moon; it was inconceivable that Napoleon would lead us there. My purgatory was never-ending, and over it all loomed the malevolent shadow of Féraud.

I was being disingenuous, and I knew it. If I had not gambled recklessly in London, I would not have resorted to transporting escaped prisoners-of-war over the Channel. If I had not done the same in Paris, I would have had no debts with the salon's owner, denying Bellamy the opportunity to coerce me as he had. I could also have avoided my first duel with Féraud, and with it, our ongoing feud.

I had no one but myself to blame for my situation, but on that miserable, humid evening, hurting all over, lost in the wilds, I gave my self-pity free rein. Tears spilled down my cheeks, unrestrained. My horse whickered, as if in sympathy, and I patted its neck.

'Come on,' I said. 'We had best get on, or we will never get there.'

Witepsk was in sight when I heard a body of horsemen coming up behind me. They were travelling fast, so I pulled to one side, quickly tossing my pistols and sword into the ditch, as far apart from each other as I could. Then I hunched up in the saddle, grateful for the pause. The agony of my injuries had been exacerbated by the ride. The moment I had delivered my letters, I would seek out a surgeon, and beg some tincture of laudanum.

Eyes closed, imagining the painkiller's numbing comfort, I paid no heed to the riders. Seeing me, however, the lead horseman came to a halt, letting the rest of the column go by.

'All well, friend?'

I glanced up. He was a hussar officer, from the Fifth, I saw, but thankfully not Féraud. 'I am just resting until you go by.'

'You look as if you had a wrestling match with a bear and came off second best. What happened?'

I had the story ready. 'I stopped by an abandoned cottage to forage for supplies about ten miles back, and was surprised by some peasants. They beat me within an inch of my life; I would be dead if a patrol of ours hadn't been spotted. In the confusion, I somehow managed to get on my horse and escape. Being on foot, they could not give chase.' I shrugged tiredly. 'Here I am.'

His eyes went to the empty holsters in front of my saddle. 'So you have been travelling unarmed since, and on your own? You have been lucky, my friend. Ride with me the rest of the way.'

My protests were in vain – the hussar was a kindly type – and so, trying desperately to mark the spot so I might recover my weapons, I let him accompany me to Witepsk.

François happened to be in the imperial headquarters when I was delivered by my saviour. He was suitably horrified, and helped me from my horse, demanding to know everything. My story came more easily the second time; François asked no questions, just took my satchel inside so the letters could be dealt with and then brought me to the surgeon. Again my decision to refuse a bandage for my head proved

143

wise; when asked who had cleaned my wounds, I muttered something about using the water from my bottle.

Laudanum administered, eyelids heavy, I was grateful for François, who put me to bed. The temperature in our room was stifling – the day's heat had barely diminished – but that did not stop me from falling into a deep slumber.

I woke the following morning with gummy eyelids and a pounding head, and with my blankets drenched in sweat. Nonetheless, I counted myself fortunate. I had survived when I should not have, and done what Bellamy ordered. Best of all, my treachery remained undetected. I would have to do it again of course, he would see to that, but for now I could recuperate.

My good mood lasted for perhaps an hour, when Bellamy appeared by my bedside with the eagerness of a carrion crow landing by a freshly dead corpse.

'What do you want?' I snarled.

'I have come to see how you are,' he said, solicitous as a dear friend.

'As if you care.'

'But I do, Mr Carrey.'

I closed my eyes.

A few moments went by.

'I am still here.'

I was behaving like a child, and I knew it. He would not go away until we spoke either. I glared at him. 'The expressions, the phrases you told me, they do not work on ordinary Russian soldiers! The Cossacks who took me prisoner did not understand a word, curse you!'

'They did this?' He indicated the bandage on my head.

'No, it was peasants, but the Cossacks did nothing to help me. I could have died!' There was a petulant whine in my voice, which I hated.

'How is it that you are still living?' he asked calmly.

'An officer came upon the scene. He stopped the beating.'

'And you gave him my letters?'

'Yes.'

'Good, Mr Carrey.' Satisfied, he moved to the door. 'What did the surgeon say about your recovery?'

'A week to ten days,' I said sullenly.

'Excellent. I will have more messages for you by then.' He slipped into the corridor, silent as a cat.

I stared after him, wishing that a terrible bout of dysentery would remove him from my life forever. Picking up the little bottle given me by the surgeon, and which François had set on a table, I swallowed down twice the recommended amount of laudanum. I longed for sleep, dreamless sleep, a place where I could not feel every contusion, where it did not hurt to breathe or to turn over. Most of all, I wanted not to think about Bellamy, and what would have to be done for him as soon as I was well.

Thankfully, my brooding did not last, the laudanum tugging me down into oblivion. The next time I came to, I had no idea how much later, it was with the realisation that there was someone by my bed. His shape was familiar. François, I thought fuzzily. He has come to check on me.

It was Féraud.

He smiled at my shock. 'Dupont.'

'Féraud.' I felt most uncomfortable being in bed, and unarmed. He is a gentleman, I told myself. He will not harm me.

'A comrade told me he met you on the road last night.'

'He was very kind,' I said.

'You were set upon by peasants?' Suspicion oozed from his words.

Unwilling to trust my tongue, I nodded.

'A tiro's mistake.' I gave him a blank look, and his lip curled in that way I hated so much. 'In the legions of ancient Rome, a tiro was a new recruit.'

'It is true, I am no career soldier,' I said, thinking, let him have his laugh and he will leave sooner.

'My comrade said that you escaped when a patrol came near.'

'Yes.'

'What type of cavalry was it – cuirassiers, dragoons? Hussars, lancers?'

I could see where this was going. 'I have no idea. I was being battered by a dozen Russian savages. Spying out what type of cavalry was approaching seemed of little importance.'

A sniff. 'How exactly did you retrieve your horse?'

'I do not have to explain myself to you, Féraud,' I said, my anger bubbling over. 'Why don't you go and find some deserters to kill?'

He sneered. 'I suppose you did this so our duel could be postponed, or even forgotten about?'

'When I am well again, you shall have your duel,' I retorted.

'You will need pistols.'

'I am perfectly aware.'

He stooped, picking up a leather bag that I had not seen by his feet. Reaching inside, he produced a pistol. 'I found this in a ditch about a mile from the town.'

It was one of my weapons.

Cold panic swamped me, but I managed to school my features into an expression of complete indifference. 'Really? And what has that to do with me?'

He looked annoyed. 'This is yours!'

'No, it is not.' My voice was light, casual. I wondered if he had found the second pistol, or my sword, and gambled that because they were not with him, he had not.

'It looks like one of the pieces you were to use that night in the graveyard.'

'How can you be sure? It was dark!' I scoffed. 'That pistol could belong to anyone.'

I could not have been more grateful to have owned such an unremarkable weapon. Fashioned perhaps twenty years before, it was ubiquitous among messengers and cavalry officers alike. I was not Féraud, a career soldier with his own pair of specially commissioned, highly individual, duelling pistols. I glared at him, pouring my hatred into the challenge of my gaze.

'I also told you, the peasants took *both* my pistols *and* my sword,' I added.

A few seconds went by.

It was clear that he would have liked nothing better than to beat the truth out of me, but decorum had to be maintained. Without a confession, he could not prove me wrong, and we both knew it.

He seemed to come to a decision, and thrust the pistol forward. 'I have no use for such a cheap thing. Here.'

I accepted it silently, tempted to cock it and shoot him where he stood. Not that it would have fired. After a night in the open, the powder would be damp.

He was poised to go. 'Until the next duel.'

'I will not use the delope again.' It was all I could think of saying.

'Good. Do not expect it from me either!' Féraud performed a mocking little bow, and was gone.

There is not much more to say about Napoleon's stay in Witepsk. I was in bed for the majority of the two weeks, catching a fever that slowed my recovery. François came and went, but like all the messengers, he was constantly busy carrying the emperor's orders all over the region. His company was not the only reason I looked forward to his return. An inveterate scavenger, he often came bearing food, rich finds from abandoned farms and manors. One time it might be biscuits, five different varieties, and almonds, and another, figs, raisins and dried dates, or big, fat local sausages, which he had persuaded one of the emperor's cooks to fry. On one memorable occasion, he even produced two bottles of the finest Bordeaux.

Most of the time, however, I was on my own, overhot, irritable and brooding. I grew so bored of being in my chamber that I took to sitting outside on the street, where I could watch the comings and goings. Officers and men I knew would stop and talk. Over a hand of cards, we would share a cup of *kvass*, the vile local drink. Tasting like weak beer with piss thrown in, *limonade de cochon'*, pig's lemonade, it was all that was to be had unless one had access to the emperor's supplies – or François's occasional booty.

Idling with these comrades, I kept abreast of the general situation. Morale was low, lower than it had been at any point since the crossing of the Niemen. The loss of horses had reached catastrophic proportions: many cavalry units were down to half strength with mounts, and scarcely better than that with men. The human cost was mirrored in the rest of the army: the effectives in the majority of regiments, I was told, were down by a full third. And this, every man would comment, appalled, before we had fought a single major battle against the Russians.

It was all to change soon.

CHAPTER XVII

Smolensk, 17 August 1812

Night was falling. Exhausted, drained, I was standing close to Napoleon's command tent, which was on the low hills that faced the town. Chosen to carry orders to forces nearby, I had been in or close to this position all day. Built on the south bank of the River Dnieper, Smolensk's four-mile long walls and thirty-two towers were still a sight to behold. There had been little noticeable effect, if any, from the hours-long artillery barrage, but mortar shells lobbed over the defences had wreaked a fearful toll, setting much of the city ablaze. I had hoped that darkness would bring an end to the horror, but as the flames continued to lick skywards, a gnawing feeling told me I was mistaken.

The barrage had begun that afternoon, two hundred guns opening up in an attempt to form a breach into the city. I had never witnessed the like. The deafening noise had precluded all normal conversation, shouts into men's ears the new norm. The shock waves had been a surprise, blasts of air emanating from the cannons with each shot to strike me in the face, hundreds of paces away.

It had been quickly apparent that the artillery's 12-pounders had no chance of smashing through the fifteen-foot thick walls. Undeterred, the emperor had ordered the infantry attack to begin anyway. Three entire corps, more than fifty thousand men, had gone marching down the hillslope towards Smolensk. In full dress uniform, accompanied by their regimental bands, they had been a magnificent sight. I had cheered with everyone else.

Across an area of open ground the infantry had slogged, fired on by Russian cannon on the opposite side of the river, and with cavalry of both sides rampaging hither and thither. Shot at by enemy troops in the sprawling suburbs that lay before the walls, the infantry had battled their way into the cemeteries and narrow streets, their distant struggle visible only as clouds of dust, and puffs of smoke from musket and cannon. The cries and screams had carried readily enough, and despite the incredible heat, chilled me to the marrow.

After brutal hand-to-hand fighting, often with the bayonet, Napoleon's brave soldiers had emerged on the far side of the suburbs, to face the deep dry moat that lay in front of the fortifications. Again they had weathered the defenders' musket volleys, scrambling down into the ditch and up the other side. Once there, they had had no ladders to scale the twenty-five-foot high walls. Scrabbling for hand- and footholds, standing on one another's shoulders like so many ants, they were cut down by the Russians in great numbers. Many others were hit by French cannon balls that fell short of their target. One look with François's collapsible telescope had been enough; I had not asked for it again.

After several hours, even Napoleon had been forced to admit that the assault was doomed to fail. The suburbs were taken, but nowhere had Smolensk's defences been breached. Seven thousand soldiers lay dead or wounded, it could be argued, for nothing. The emperor received this news with indifference. He was obsessed with taking the town, and the price did not matter.

The assault was over until the next day, but thanks to the French mortar shells, the Russians had an enemy of a different kind: fire. I could hear screams rising from the streets, and on the ramparts, Russian soldiers were silhouetted in black, like devils in hell. Poor Christian that I was, I nonetheless offered up a prayer for the poor souls who might be trapped in their homes.

The dreadful spectacle was not enough to stop me from dropping off, leaning against the side of the tent. I was woken by the emergence of the emperor. A few hours had passed, I guessed, because the whole town was aflame now, illuminating the entire horizon. A glance at my pocket watch told me it was two a.m. Stifling a yawn, I watched as Napoleon, Caulaincourt and Berthier walked towards the edge of the slope that led down to Smolensk.

'An eruption of Vesuvius!' cried the emperor, clapping Caulaincourt on the shoulder. 'Isn't that a fine sight, my Master of the Horse?'

'Horrible, sire,' said Caulaincourt, shaking his head.

'Bah!' Napoleon riposted. He sat on a stool, and settled down to watch the holocaust. 'Remember what one of the Roman emperors said: "an enemy's corpse always smells good!"'

Slightly ahead of Caulaincourt and Berthier, the emperor did not see, as I did, the meaningful glance that the pair exchanged. It was as if they understood each other without need of words.

What kind of man was Napoleon, I wondered, to remain emotionless as his enemies burned to death? Who could eat off gold plates and drink fine wine while his own soldiers, parched and starving, watched? Taken on their own, these were the actions of a monster, yet in person he was the polar opposite. Often charming, his presence was immense, his charisma remarkable. Although there had been setbacks thus far, his military credentials were unparalleled. He was, I decided, an enigma, and until the campaign was over, my fate was bound up inexorably with his. Although he would emerge victorious, I avoided trying to calculate the odds of my own survival. True enough, the messengers had not yet suffered many casualties, but if the advance continued, and the battles grew bloodier, it seemed inevitable that I would be forced into the dance of death from which so few men emerged unscathed.

My fear was lessening, replaced by a deep sense of resignation. It helped a little to think of England, and my mother, and even a reconciliation with my father.

No more letters came from the emperor, and I dozed fitfully until about four in the morning, when news arrived from the frontline. An NCO of the 107th Regiment had scaled an unrepaired hole in the walls and found the defences abandoned. By five, we knew that the whole town had been given over. The main gate was open, and infantry officers were going in to reconnoitre.

Not until ten a.m. – it was now the eighteenth – did the emperor decide to venture inside Smolensk. With his customary protection of Horse Grenadiers riding fifty paces out in front, he rode initially into the destroyed suburbs. I was at the rear of the imperial party with François, ready to carry any messages.

The stench hit me first, but the incomparable horror, for which I could not have prepared, followed close behind. Everywhere the terrain was ground to dust, encumbered with scattered debris, with twisted or broken weapons, dead men and horses. All were monstrously swollen, something I attributed to decomposition in the extreme heat. Already putrescent, they gave off a fearful odour; I saw more than one man vomit. The corpses had begun to be buried. The French wounded had been taken to the ambulance wagons and disappeared, but the Russians had been left lying in the dirt.

We saw them sitting in the shade of houses, their backs to the walls, calm and impassive, resignedly waiting for someone to come and succour them. Some French surgeons were busy giving first aid. Further on, they were being loaded onto ambulances. Elsewhere artillery wagons were busy picking up abandoned weapons. The suburb's houses, too, all of which had been broken into, abandoned and overthrown, were full of corpses and debris.

Closer to the walls, the Russian dead were literally piled on top of each other. Our horses could hardly take a step without trampling on them. It was the same behind the redoubt in the space separating it from the main gate, where artillery trains had passed over these heaps of human remains, crushing them in a thick sludge of flesh, broken bones and bleeding wreckage. I dry retched, thinking, this could be my fate. Even François, battle-hardened, turned a sickly grey colour.

Napoleon did not look at these dreadful sights, or if he did, made no comment. I heard him as he halted briefly in front of the great earthwork known as the Citadel, however. 'Before the month's out we'll be in Moscow,' he declared. 'In six weeks we'll have peace.'

Moscow, I thought, mostly appalled by the distance, and the bloody battles that would lie between it and us. Incredibly, a little part of me was elated. In the Russian capital, if I were still alive, I might find Jeanne.

It was impossible to ignore the glances that Caulaincourt, Berthier, Ney and the others were exchanging; clearly, the prospect of continuing deep into Russia was not something they thought wise. Yet no one spoke up. Caulaincourt and Berthier would do it, but in private, and as I remembered from Caulaincourt's attempt to be posted to Spain, their comments would make no difference to Napoleon. The course of the Grande Armée was set due east, and nothing short of defeat would stop it.

We rode into the city itself, to be greeted by fresh horrors at every turn. There were countless remains of Russian soldiers who had been fleeing but were asphyxiated instead. Many no longer resembled human beings; they were formless masses of grilled and carbonised matter; it was the metal of a musket, a sabre, or some shreds of accoutrement lying beside them that made them recognisable as corpses.

Almost all the buildings had been destroyed by the fire, killing many more people. These unfortunates, abandoned to a hideous death, lay in heaps, calcinated, shrunken, conserving only just a human form amid the smoking ruins and burning beams. The spaces in between had not been safe either. Between two burnt-out houses, I saw a small orchard whose fruit had been carbonised, underneath the trees of which were five or six men who had been literally grilled. They must have been wounded, I decided, laid out in the shade before the fire started. The flames had not touched them, but the heat had contracted their nerves and pulled up their legs. Their white teeth jutted from between shrivelled lips and two large bloody holes marked the place where their eyes had been.

Revolted, my empty stomach cramping, I turned away, and tried to put the image from my mind. I failed.

Most of the townspeople had fled, but the survivors were everywhere, on their knees, weeping over the ruins of their homes. Cats and dogs wandered about, howling in the most heart-rending way. At the cathedral, one of the stone-built buildings that had remained standing, hundreds of wailing, distressed inhabitants were gathered; a scrawny, bearded priest was doing his best to restore calm. Other churches were full of Russian wounded, abandoned by their own.

In Smolensk that day, death and destruction reigned supreme, and my spirits fell to a new low. At the outset of this campaign, death had seemed unlikely, a mere possibility. Now the odds of living through the maelstrom seemed heavily weighted against all of us: soldiers, cavalrymen, messengers.

'Why did he' – I meant Napoleon – 'not simply march around Smolensk?'

François shook his head wearily. 'I do not know.'

'Did he need to take it?'

'Not really. It is one of Russia's more important cities, but as you can see, it is not big. If we had simply left a besieging force in place and with the rest of the army, skirted around and cut off the road to Moscow, the defenders would have been in an impossible position.' François cast a look at the emperor, who was riding for the eastern gate, and the bridge over the Dnieper.

It was unfathomable, I decided. If the Grande Armée had done as François suggested, we would have crossed the river the day before

– something not possible from Smolensk, because the bridge here had been destroyed by the enemy – and had the Russians at sixes and sevens. Instead, as the roar of cannon and muskets from the north bank made patently clear, the emperor's soldiers would have to build a pontoon, under fire, and then fight their way across the Dnieper.

A fresh bloodbath was about to unfold.

So be it, I thought, resigning myself to whatever happened.

The sun pulled itself hungrily over the horizon the next morning, the nineteenth, its blood-red colour suggesting that today's casualties would be as severe as those of the previous two. Come to deliver a message to Ney, waiting for his response, I took a moment to stand on the new wooden supports projecting out over the water. Working with great determination and humour until late in the night, the engineers had built a new bridge.

And yet again, the Russians had disappeared. Dust clouds to the east marked their retreating columns, which were heading north-east – some said towards St Petersburg. Thousands of Ney's men were already on the north bank, and waiting to march. I noted with amusement how hundreds, unchecked by their officers, were using the delay to cool off in the Dnieper. It lifted my heart, and I have no doubt their battle-scarred ones, to see them cavorting naked in the shallows, splashing and laughing like little children.

Napoleon's plan, as I had heard him tell Caulaincourt, was to have Marshal Ney head straight along the Moscow road, blocking the retreating Russians' access to it. Messages had been sent to Marshal Junot, whose corps was about to start crossing the Dnieper at the village of Prudichevo. If he moved fast, he would strike any Russians already positioned there in the rear, while Ney came marching up to attack them from the front.

The emperor's tactics did not quite go to plan, an eventuality, François commented drolly, which now seemed to be the norm. After only a short distance, Ney's corps was checked by the counterattack of a Russian division. Davout was immediately sent forward with his corps, and together he and Ney drove the enemy back several miles to a hamlet by the name of Valutina Gora. There the Russians took up defensive positions and, bolstered by large numbers of reinforcements, fought like lions. A bloody battle engulfed both sides.

Now was the time, I said to François– I had some understanding of tactics at last – for Junot to strike. His position on the south bank was *beyond* Valutina Gora. Ford the Dnieper, hit the Russians in the rear, and victory would be won. I did not like to consider the odds, the probability, of it happening, however.

An hour ticked by, the baleful sun beating down from the heavens, and of Junot there was no sign. Another hour passed, and a third. By about four in the afternoon, sweltering in his forward command post on the Moscow road, Napoleon was growing tired and impatient. He selected the temperamental but fiercely loyal First Ordnance Officer Gaspard Gourgaud to go and find Murat, whose cavalry was assisting Ney. Napoleon's orders were for Ney, Murat and Junot to co-ordinate their movements, and throw the Russians out of Valutina Gora. François, I and several others were to go also.

We set out at once. The heat was tremendous, perhaps even hotter than the day before. My clothes were stuck to me with sweat, and Liesje's coat was matted with salt. The air danced and shimmered over the dusty landscape, and the Dnieper was a graceful, silver line on our right. It was beautiful, but no bucolic idyll to be peacefully enjoyed. The crescendo of noise coming from Valutina Gora, miles to the east, could not be ignored. Nor could the units of cavalry and infantry marching to join their comrades in the battle.

Gourgaud rode at a fast trot, not talking to anyone. Tall, thin and muscular, he wore a magnificent sky-blue uniform with silver aiguillettes.

'How old is he?' I asked François.

'Twenty-nine, I think.'

'Only a few years older than me and you.' I knew that Gourgaud had been at Austerlitz, though, and at almost every battle of Napoleon's since.

'That is true.' An amused glance. 'Are you wanting to be promoted?'

'I can think of nothing I want less,' I said with feeling.

'Because of Smolensk?'

'That has a lot to do with it,' I said, remembering the horrific sights of the previous day. Of course there was more to it – I was no soldier, I had no lasting interest in Napoleon's desire to vanquish Russia, I was only here because of Bellamy's hold over me – but I was content that François remained unaware of these deeper reasons.

The din of battle grew louder. Enormous dust clouds filled the air, driven up by the thousands of men and horses, and mixed with musket smoke, reducing the visibility. Despite my resignation to my fate, my stomach was in knots as we neared the front line. The screams and musket shots were impossible to ignore.

The rest of the day could have been spent trying to find Murat had it not been for his habit of dressing in wild, theatrical costume. Inside a quarter of an hour, somehow miraculously skirting the fighting, we had spied him out. Today's garb included a square flat cap decorated with innumerable ostrich plumes and diamond brooches.

Murat's expressive brown face grew furious to hear from Gourgaud that there had been no news from Junot. He rattled out orders for his men who were to continue the fight at Gora Valutina, and led us away. Accompanied by a dozen of his gilt-epauletted staff, he took us to the confluence of the Dnieper and a small stream, where a weir allowed a safe crossing.

It was soon apparent that Napoleon's orders had not been followed. The rough track along the south bank was jammed by stationary units of infantry, all part of Junot's corps. Sitting in the dust, their muskets stacked, the soldiers were playing cards, eating, sleeping. Some were even swimming in the river, watched idly by uncaring officers.

Forced to ride parallel to the road by the density of the throng, Murat's fury grew and grew. By the time we found Junot in an area of woodland overlooking the Dnieper and beyond it, Valutina Gora, he was incandescent. Galloping up with such speed that two aides-de-camp fell over one another in their haste to get out of the way, Murat yelled, 'What are you doing here? Why aren't you advancing? You're unworthy to be the last dragoon in Napoleon's army!'

'My cavalry is no use,' said Junot, looking sunburnt and utterly depressed. 'It's no match for the Russian battalions. Besides, I have no definite orders to attack.'

François leaned towards me. 'Want to bet on what Murat does next?'

I snorted. 'No.'

'Then I'll do it instead!' Murat cried. 'I'll put some fire into these Westphalians of yours!'

I watched in awe – we all did – as Murat spurred his horse forward to a light cavalry brigade in the distance. Used to his behaviour, his staff followed as one. His shout, 'Follow me, brave Westphalians!' carried through the muggy air. The Germans did as he ordered, charging at the enemy.

Murat was back before long, face wreathed in smiles. Not a single one of his staff had been injured or killed. To Junot, he said, 'That's the Russian sharpshooters scattered to the wind. Now you can finish it off. Your glory is there, and your marshal's baton.'

'Napoleon has never seen fit to give him one,' François explained from behind his hand. 'As you might expect, it is rather a sore point.'

Junot gave no immediate reply. Murat ranted and raged at him to no avail. After a few minutes, the headstrong King of Naples gave up and rode away, cursing.

Junot watched, expressionless. His aides and staff officers, a cowed-looking lot, muttered between themselves.

Gourgaud tried. 'Sir, what shall I tell the emperor?'

'You'll tell him, monsieur, that I've taken up my position, because night has fallen.'

Like me, Gourgaud glanced in disbelief at the sun, still well above the horizon. 'There are four more hours of daylight at least, sir! You have plenty of time to advance.'

Junot muttered something and turned away.

'You should know that Marshal Ney's corps is suffering badly from the frontal attack it is having to make, sir,' urged Gourgaud. 'I have no doubt that your troops would tip the balance in our favour.'

Junot shook his head in refusal.

'Frenchmen, good soldiers, are dying just over the river,' I hissed furiously to François, 'just because this fool will not follow his orders! I want to give him a good slap, snap him out of his torpor.'

'Fifty francs says you won't,' François replied from the corner of his mouth. 'No, a hundred.'

I glared, for we both knew I would not do it. Gourgaud was a favourite of the emperor's, which was probably why Junot had not reprimanded him. I, on the other hand, was a complete unknown. Even to argue with Junot would be monstrously stupid.

While Gourgaud was still pleading his case, some of Junot's men, encouraged by Murat's charge and expecting the order to advance, took the initiative and moved into the open, towards the Russians. No one followed them. What happened next was inevitable, and awful to watch. First a below-strength unit of voltigeurs, perhaps eighty strong, was cut to pieces by hundreds of lance-wielding Cossacks. Next it was the turn of the Westphalians who had charged with Murat. Drawn by apparently retreating Cossacks into a makeshift ambush, they were cut down by waiting batteries of Russian cannon. Their fire, a wounded officer told Junot a short while later, was as 'precise as on a parade ground exercise'.

Instead of stirring Junot from his despondency, these incidents pushed him deeper. Ignoring Gourgaud's pleas, he gave orders to withdraw half a mile and set up camp.

'We had best get back,' François said to Gourgaud. 'You have done your best.'

'I have not.' Gourgaud's voice was bitter. 'How many men have died needlessly – are still dying – at Valutina Gora while we dilly dally here?'

'That is on Junot's head, not yours,' I said, incensed myself.

My mood, which had improved a little on the ride back, was again badly affected by the discovery that the emperor had left his command post soon after our own departure. Davout had been left in charge. This, in spite of the fact that the battle in Valutina Gora still raged.

'What kind of general leaves his men like that?' I asked François.

He patted my arm. 'Do not take it to heart, my friend. Napoleon, *il est l'Empereur*. It is not for us to question him.'

Even if his grandiose actions border on the insane? I wanted to ask.

The ride back to Smolensk was made in silence. We clattered over the new pontoon bridge, and for the second time, entered the charnel house. It was the only way to reach the imperial headquarters, positioned on the hill overlooking the town. At least there was some chance of a breeze there. Down by the Dnieper, it was hotter than the inside of a baker's oven.

Keen not to be reacquainted with the awful things I had seen earlier, I barely looked where I was going. François was in sombre mood now too; he seemed content not to talk. Tonight, I decided, I would procure wine from the imperial quartermaster. If a man needed food or drink, it could be had, at a price. François and I could get blind drunk, and forget what we had seen today. I wanted oblivion more anything else, even if it was expensively bought and only lasted one night.

We were exiting the main gate when a troop of hussars came clattering towards us. My eyes went at once to the lead rider. It was Féraud.

He saw me in the same instant. 'Dupont!'

'Ignore him,' François urged. 'Ride straight past.'

I was touched by his concern. Despite the hundreds of francs he had taken in bets on me, he did not want to see me harmed. But I was not about to avoid Féraud again. We had not met since his visit to my sickbed, and I had been so busy, or tired, or caught up in violence, that he had not come to mind either. Meeting him again here, in this hellish abattoir, seemed inevitable, preordained. I decided that my death might as well be at Féraud's hands.

'Captain!' I called. 'A fine day for a duel, is it not?'

He looked surprised, but was swift to regain his composure. 'Indeed.'

'Let us get the thing over with. We can fight right now.'

A curt nod.

My eyes went off to the left, and the flat area between the wall and the ditch. Tell-tale stains marked the earth, but the French bodies that had lain there were gone, taken away for burial. 'Will that ground suffice?' I asked with a jerk of my chin.

'More than suffice,' came the answer.

Begging me not to proceed, to apologise to Féraud, saying that he would return all the bet monies, and cursing when I refused, François followed me off the road.

I had no idea what would happen if a senior officer came upon the scene, but I was beyond caring. A pistol ball from Féraud, a lance wielded by a Cossack, a stone in the fist of a peasant, it did not matter which way I left this world, and it might as well be now.

Féraud brought two men, one the friendly, gap-toothed corporal, the other an ordinary hussar. The former was to serve as his second, the latter to hold the horses' reins. It was against custom to have someone of lower social rank as a second, but it was not a point I was about to dispute. Two hundred yards from the gate, I dismounted. Féraud, who had also climbed from the saddle, was stroking his mount's neck and murmuring in its ear. Remembering that he had talked to it similarly outside the burning cottage, I wondered if he was quite the monster I imagined.

Leaving our horses also in the hussar's charge, I directed François, who had stopped protesting, to speak with the corporal. I did not give

Féraud the satisfaction of a sneer or snide comment, swiftly taking a pistol from its holster and walking away from him, wall to one side, ditch to the other.

François conferred with the corporal, who then had to speak with Féraud. He looked angry, but nodded agreement. The corporal returned to François.

'Due to the possibility of being interrupted, Captain Féraud has agreed to one shot each, and that first blood will be satisfactory,' François called out.

I nodded, thinking dully, he will make sure with his initial attempt.

It was also agreed – in case a senior officer appeared – to use our already loaded pistols, rather than following the custom of the seconds doing this for us.

The corporal walked out twenty paces, using the heel of his boot to scrape a line in the blood-soaked earth at each end. Féraud and I moved to our positions. François stood midway between, out of the line of fire. A handkerchief dangled from one hand. His face pinched, he glanced at me. 'Ready?'

'Yes,' I said loudly, standing side-on to my enemy.

'Captain Féraud?'

'I am.'

'Raise your weapons and cock.'

I lifted my arm. One metallic snick was echoed by a second. We stared at each other down our pistols. The muzzle end of Féraud's was a black hole that promised death, and beyond it was the cold mask of his face. I blinked in vain at the sweat stinging my eyes, and tried to ignore the unhappy thump-thump of my heart.

'You both know what to do, gentlemen,' said François. 'When I release my handkerchief, you may shoot.' He glanced at us both. 'Understand?'

'I do.' I was proud that my voice was calm.

'As do I,' said Féraud.

For the third time, I faced the duellist's sternest test. For the first time, I wanted to be struck by Féraud's bullet. Oblivion – death – would grant me blissful release. From the scorching wasteland that was Russia. From the unending journey. From perpetual hunger and thirst. From the depredations of savage Cossacks and peasants. From the cauldron of battle, in which men and horses were reduced en masse to lumps of glistening meat, or blackened, distorted shapes of what they had once been.

Perhaps fifteen seconds went by before François dropped his hand-kerchief. It fluttered from his hand, and my attention went solely to Féraud, and the end of his pistol. I fired immediately, but aimed slightly to his left. The ball shot past him and was gone. We looked at each other. He smiled.

'That was a deliberate miss,' I said. 'I have no wish to kill you, Féraud.'

Something flickered across his face – disbelief? – and then he regained his concentration. I tensed. His weapon belched smoke and fire, and then a smith's hammer struck me in the chest, and I was falling.

There was no oblivion, no discomfort, but my strength had evaporated. I lay on one side in the dust, staring stupidly at my pistol, lying just beyond my reach. A pulse throbbed in my ears. Shouts rang out, François's among them, and I wondered why there was no pain.

Then it hit, a searing blade that ran across me from armpit to armpit. I gasped in shock. Nothing had ever hurt so much. This, I decided, was what it felt like to die.

'Mathieu!' His face twisted with concern, François was kneeling, leaning down to look in my eyes. 'Do not move.'

'Sweet Christ, but it stings,' I hissed, thinking, what a stupid way to leave this world.

'Keep still,' he ordered, deftly unbuttoning my coat and shirt.

'Leave it,' I muttered. 'I am done.'

He began to laugh.

Confused, then angry that he should find my plight amusing, I found the strength to clutch one of his hands. 'What? Tell me!'

'You are the luckiest bastard in Smolensk,' he said, still laughing.

Féraud loomed over François, pistol still in hand. 'Well?'

'An inch to the right, and your bullet would have travelled straight through his chest. Instead, I think it glanced off a rib, and tore a nice line of flesh off his chest. It is a superficial wound, that's all.'

Féraud looked most unhappy. 'Is he able to stand? Can he shoot again?'

François got to his feet and squared up to Féraud. 'The agreement was first blood, Captain. Look! He is bleeding profusely. Your honour has been satisfied. Let that be the end of this nonsense!'

Féraud looked at François, and at me, then he nodded and stalked away.

Throw another insult at him, the little devil urged, but I had the wit not to listen.

That was the last conscious thought I had.

When I woke, night had fallen. I was in a tent, lying on a blanket, and the heat was intolerable. My chest, strapped up with bandages, felt as if it was on fire. Even the shallowest breath was pure, unadulterated agony. Despite this, I was glad to be alive. As my eyes grew accustomed to the dark, I tried to sit up. It was a foolish idea; I raised my torso perhaps three inches before the pain dragged me back down. Hissing with discomfort, I waited until my strength came back a little, and tried again. This time, I managed to get up on one elbow. I was alone, but the end flaps were thrown back, allowing me to see outside. There were other tents close by, fires, men walking to and fro, the noise of conversation and even laughter.

'François?' I called out.

My friend came hurrying into the tent. 'Mathieu! How do you feel?'

'As if an artillery wagon ran over me,' I said sourly.

'There are thousands of men worse off. Imagine waking to find one of your arms or legs had been amputated,' he said.

I winced, aware that I had been incredibly lucky. I indicated the cup in his hand. 'Is that wine?'

Without a word, he held it to my mouth so I could drink.

I drained every drop. 'That is good.'

'From the emperor's own stores. Cost me a pretty sum.'

'I hope there is more where that came from.'

'Half a dozen bottles.' He was grinning from ear to ear. 'The bets I took are providing a rich harvest. By the time it is all collected, you and I will be sharing upwards of a thousand francs.' François had wisely offered odds on various outcomes to the duel, including what had happened earlier.

'That is a considerable sum.'

It was difficult not to think that if I had wagered on my initial duel with Féraud, my winnings could have seen me come to an agreement with the owner of the gambling salon, thereby avoiding the possibility of being blackmailed by Bellamy. I sighed.

'What, you rogue? Are you thinking I should have taken more wagers?'

'Something like that,' I said, regretting that I could not tell him the truth.

'You could always challenge Féraud to another duel,' said François, with the ponderousness of the drunk.

'No.' My brush with death had made me reappreciate the sweetness of life. 'Where is this wine you talked about?'

As we got drunk together, we avoided talking about the campaign. That could wait until the morrow.

CHAPTER XVIII

Borodino, 7 September 1812

Restless, I came to. Today would be the day, I thought, the day Napoleon had been wanting, *longing for*, since the crossing of the Niemen. Suddenly, I was wide awake. I did not feel remotely rested. My pocket watch had read two a.m. when I retired. It was also still pitch black outside, but the creak of wheels and tramp of feet announced the mobilisation of the army. Realising that I had had perhaps an hour and a half's rest, and that it was not time yet to get up, I did my best to go back to sleep. My attempts were hindered by the noise outside, the heat and how it made my healing chest wound itch. François's stentorious breathing and the snores of the two other messengers who shared our tent did not help.

I began to brood on what had happened since Smolensk. Eighteen thousand French soldiers had been slain or injured, massive casualties for taking what was not an important objective. The horrors I had seen had not ended on the field either. Visiting a fellow messenger in a temporary hospital, I had seen similarly appalling conditions. With no bandages available, his wound had been wrapped up with tow. Other men's injuries had even been dressed with paper, torn out of books found in the town. Fortunately, my friend was recovering well; I wished the same could be said of the unfortunates who had been lying beside him.

On the twentieth of August had come good news; a Russian army commanded by Wittgenstein near Polotsk had been routed by the Marquis de Gouvion St Cyr, earning him a marshal's baton from Napoleon. Encouraged, the emperor had sent a letter to Tsar Alexander, declaring, 'We have burnt enough powder and shed enough blood. We must end this some time. But for Moscow to be occupied would be the equivalent to a girl losing her honour.' No reply had been received, as had been the case with his previous messages.

This had not stopped Napoleon – after fatuous talk of overwintering at Witepsk – from insisting that the Grande Armée continue its advance. In doing so, he ignored the counsel of almost all his senior commanders. I remember hearing one, Berthier maybe, muttering on the way out of a meeting: 'Well, so it's "Forwards, forwards, always forwards," is it? Hasn't he had enough yet? Won't he ever?'

It was concerning how many of Napoleon's close aides disagreed with him – Caulaincourt, as ever, was among them, yet he paid no heed. There was nothing that I, a lowly messenger, could do about it either. I concentrated on what I had some chance with: surviving.

The morale of the rank and filers was even lower than the senior officers, and it was no surprise. Their march since Smolensk had been even more arduous. The landscape was vastly different now, dreary and desolate, covered only by scrub and conifers, and areas of silver birch forest. Every village lay abandoned, and burnt to the ground. At night the entire horizon was aglow; the retreating Russians setting fire to all the settlements in our path.

There had been no rain for a month, and the dust on the broad, unpaved roads lay inches thick. Whirling gusts of wind raised such thick clouds that man and beast were coated alike; even the trees by the roadsides were obscured. Men tried to protect their eyes with little bits of windowpane, held in place by wraps of cloth. Others marched with their shakos under one arm and their head swathed in a handkerchief, only leaving an opening big enough to let themselves be led and to breathe through. Others made themselves leafy garlands.

It was impossible to tell one military unit from another, because all the uniforms were rendered the same white colour of the dust. On one occasion, I saw the emperor in his carriage – moving between the previous day's headquarters and the next – come up to a regiment of the line, which paused to salute him. Its soldiers were unable to give the customary cheer, 'Vive L'Empereur!' because their tongues were stuck to the roofs of their mouths.

I did not bat an eyelid now to see men, desperate with thirst, throwing themselves down on the road behind a horse, to drink urine from the wheel ruts. Fights broke out when a well was discovered, which got stirred up and fouled as a result. As for food, supplies were close to non-existent. This was in part due to the wagon train being left far behind the fast-marching army, and also because the damnable

Russians were torching the crops in the fields as they retreated. Flour boiled in water was the ordinary soldier's stew at night, or a soup of greasy water with fat, seasoned with gunpowder pretending to be salt. On the road constantly, rarely in the imperial headquarters for long, I grew used to both. I lost more weight, becoming ribby as a stray mongrel, and as hungry as one too. I took to gambling whenever and wherever I could: cards, dice, anything at all. It became normal to wager on whether a fly would land first on a dead horse's staring eyeball, or its lolling, swollen tongue.

The Cossacks were everywhere now, visible from dawn to dusk. They were lethal against the lone scavenger, cavalryman or messenger, and at ambushes they reigned supreme. Miraculously, I had delivered letters from Bellamy to them three times, and by loud shouting of fresh Russian phrases he had given me, avoided the kind of mistreatment I had received before. I had not been seen by any French forces either, something I lived in dread of. Féraud's suspicion at Witepsk, and his finding of my pistol, continued to haunt me.

Most of the Cossacks bore little resemblance to the first men I had met; they must have been an elite unit. Dressed in every thinkable fashion, the skirmishers sported a wild variety of headdresses. Lacking the least uniformity of appearance, dirty-looking and clad in rags, riding on nasty little thin horses with long necks, low heads, unkempt manes and guided only by a simple rein, and armed with a whip with a kind of nail at the end, they wheeled in confused and apparently enormous disorder, and to me, seemed like swarming insects.

I was brought back to the present by the sound of whistles, and the bark of orders. There would be no chance of a message-exchanging encounter with the Cossacks today, I thought. Instead I would run the risk of being shot from my saddle, or blown to pieces by a cannonball. Today a great battle would be fought, in and around the little village of Borodino, which lay on the new road between Smolensk and Moscow. Napoleon's greatest desire – and what I least wanted to see – was about to be granted.

Two days before, on the fifth of September, as the Grande Armée continued its dogged pursuit of the Russians, Murat had brought word that the enemy was digging in at last. The emperor had hurried through the foggy, drizzling rain to see for himself, and soon after, commanded that the army advance into position. Intelligence had come in that the Russians' commander Barclay had been replaced by the elderly, one-eyed Kutusov. Pleased, Napoleon had ordered two days' rest for the troops.

Some had had to fight, however, in an incredibly savage contest over a redoubt that lay in front of the main enemy line. The redoubt had changed hands several times, with the Russians only withdrawing at eleven that night. Their casualties were particularly high, at least seven thousand dead and wounded. The news had lifted the already improving mood throughout the Grande Armée. The prospect of a full-scale battle, so long denied, was something to be looked forward to, and this first defeat of the enemy presaged an even greater one.

It was hard not to be swept up by this feeling.

Then Napoleon had been struck down with a cold and a malaise of the belly – I had heard Caulaincourt talking with the emperor's physician, and heard the word 'bladder' mentioned – and was confined to his tent on the night of the fifth. Caulaincourt, meanwhile, dragged me with him on a night-time reconnaissance of the area, riding through the drizzle to visit bivouacs and the captured redoubt. We travelled up and down the line several times, so he could judge the enemy's situation with his own eyes. The Russian positions resembled a vast amphitheatre, lit by innumerable fires. The whole of their camp was one vast uninterrupted blaze of light. It was a stark comparison to that of the Grande Armée. Unable to procure wood, the French soldiers reposed in utter darkness, hearing no sounds but those of the wounded.

The whistles sounded again.

And so it begins, I thought, my stomach tightening.

François stirred. 'Time to get up,' he muttered. He said the same thing each morning.

I mumbled agreement, and wondered what the odds were of us both surviving to repeat the ritual again. Hastily, I buried the thought.

The other messengers, Pierre and Baptiste, were stirring.

'I hope the emperor is in better health than the past two days,' said Pierre, already pulling on his jacket. 'He has not been himself.'

'It is his bladder, I heard,' said Baptiste, coughing. 'He was in such pain yesterday that he had to dismount several times during his inspection of our lines.'

'I saw him with his head leant on a gun wheel for five minutes at least,' said François dourly. 'Just as well the fog prevented a battle.'

I stuck my head out of the tent. 'The sky is a little misty, but it looks to be clearing,' I said, nervously using the predawn light to read my watch. It said five o'clock.

'Unless the Russians have retreated again then, we shall have a fight,' said François. 'Best stir ourselves.'

Images of the slain and injured at Smolensk filled my mind. Today would be worse, much worse. I had seen the Russian guns, known by the troops as 'bone-crushers'. Napoleon's entire army was within range of these cannon. The death toll promised to be extraordinary, and that was before the musket volleys and bayonet charges. How I wished I was in Paris in that moment, or even London, instead of the middle of Russia, in the midst of a war.

And yet, I thought, François was joking about something with Baptiste. Pierre was munching on a crust of bread. Their faces betrayed a little fear, but none were complaining. I hardened my resolve. This was no time for self-pity. My task, delivering messages, was relatively safe in comparison to that facing the massed infantry and cavalry.

The four of us reached Napoleon's tent just as he emerged. He was moving slowly, but his pale face was determined. Caulaincourt was by his side, as ever, and Berthier was there also. Grooms had their horses waiting nearby.

'We have them at last! It's a trifle cold, but the sun's bright. It's the sun of Austerlitz!' exclaimed the emperor. 'March on! We'll break open the gates of Moscow.'

Caulaincourt held the stirrup so Napoleon could mount, and then moved to climb onto his own horse. We did the same, and rode after the emperor, past batteries of cannon and cheering artillerymen, to his command post in front of the ruined redoubt taken on the night of the fifth. A chair was brought for Napoleon; he turned it around and sat astride, with his arms resting on the back, and raising his telescope, keenly surveyed the scene.

We had a grand view of the battlefield, which was situated in picturesque rolling countryside between the new Smolensk road to our left, and the old road, to our right. About a mile distant was the village of Borodino and close by, a nice Byzantine church. The latter, rising from a gentle, tree-covered slope, had a pretty green copper-plated tower. Running across our position below the redoubt from left to right was a forking stream, and beyond it were copses of birch and pine, and areas of man-high hazel bushes and junipers. These hid some of the Russian troops from view, as did their newly thrown-up earthworks and arrowhead-shaped flèches, but for the most part, the enemy was in full sight. Packed into two massively deep, dense rows, the infantry were closely supported behind by thousands of cavalry. Bayonets and buttons glinted in the sun, and off the brass barrels of hundreds of guns that were arrayed all along the enemy front. They were especially prominent behind and around the earthen fortifications.

The French foot soldiers and cavalry were positioned in equal strength facing the Russians, except beyond Borodino. There Napoleon had judged the enemy right wing, massively over-strong and on the other side of a river, to be unworthy of an assault. The opposite could be said of the Russians' left wing, which petered out before the old Smolensk road a mile away on our right. Davout had sensed an opportunity the day before; I had witnessed him repeatedly urging the emperor to combine his corps and that of Poniatowski, their purpose to roll up the enemy's left. Give the order, Davout had sworn, and he would 'finish off the Russian army, the battle and the whole war!' Napoleon had refused, saying it would lose too much time, and take him away from his objective. Davout had stormed off, muttering.

Only time would tell if it had been a wise decision.

At a quarter to six, the words of Napoleon's address, issued to every officer, carried through the still air. 'Soldiers! Here is the battle you have so ardently desired. Now victory depends on you: we need one. Victory will give us any amount of supplies, good winter quarters and a prompt return to our native land. Fight as you did at Austerlitz, Friedland, Witepsk and Smolensk, and posterity will proudly remember your conduct on this great day. May it be said of each one of us: "He fought in the great battle under the walls of Moscow!"'

Cheers and rolling shouts of '*Vive l'Empereur!*' followed.

Despite myself, I felt my heart stir. It was extraordinary to stand looking at upwards of a quarter of a million men standing in clear sight of each other, moments before they fell on each other with murderous intent.

'Six o'clock it is to start?' I asked.

François gave me a look. 'You know as well as I do that that's the time.'

I glanced nervously at my watch. 'Ten minutes to six.'

'You need a distraction.' From his pocket, François produced a piece of cardboard. To my amazement, he unfolded it to reveal a homemade chessboard. 'Let's play. Five francs says I win.'

'Where did you get that?'

'I took it from an artillery officer in a game of écarté yesterday.' Carefully, he set up the cardboard pieces, each identified by an inked-on symbol. 'You're white. Move! We won't have long.'

Chess had been a favourite game of mine as a child, but I had not played in years. It had been something my father and I did on Sundays, after lunch. Surprisingly moved, I advanced a pawn. François did the same. We grew so engrossed that the first explosion – a gun firing from our lines on the right – came as a shock. A second later, another fired.

An exquisitely ominous silence followed.

I lifted my watch. 'Six exactly.'

François's reply was lost as the thunder of more than a thousand guns exploded all around us. The ground shook, the air vibrated. The uproar was so terrible that I imagined it was broadsides being discharged from warships rather than a land artillery engagement.

François indicated that he wanted to continue playing, but was unable to concentrate. I could not take my eyes from the scene. Thick clouds of smoke were curling upwards from the batteries; before long they had darkened the sun, which seemed to veil itself in a blood-red shroud. Down below our position, a horse came running, its rider thrown onto its crupper. An officer by his uniform, he was missing the top of his cranium.

Bile rose in my throat.

'Taken off by a Russian roundshot,' François shouted in my ear.

I leaned to the side and despite my empty stomach, was violently sick.

François handed me a cleanish handkerchief.

Nodding my thanks, I wiped my mouth.

'Want a nip?' He was offering me a hip flask.

I shook my head, no, then jumped as a roundshot thumped down in front of us, and came bouncing along the grass. Another followed.

François saw how tempted I was to reach out a foot and stop it. 'Don't go near the cursed thing! It still has the power to tear off your leg. I have seen it happen.'

I flinched at the toe-curling idea, just as three more roundshot flew overhead.

'They're not aiming at us.' Despite his confident tone, François's face was a littler paler than it had been. 'Typical Russians, aiming high.'

'Nobody told me about that,' I grumbled, hating the gnawing fear in my belly.

Wordlessly, François held out the flask.

I took it this time, downing a large slug of rough spirits that set me to coughing.

'That will put hair on your chest,' François said, smiling.

Watching to see how the first part of the battle unfolded, Napoleon did not send out any messengers for a little while. We had to remain where we were, however, and so it was that amid the thunder of the guns, with roundshot shooting over our heads, or again bouncing onto the grass nearby, François and I went back to our game of chess.

Of all the experiences I had had thus far, it was by far the most bizarre.

CHAPTER XIX

Three deafening hours passed, both sides' guns relentlessly pounding the other's lines. Time and again, the redoubts in front of our position were attacked and taken, and then seized again by the Russians. Napoleon threw in more and more men, Davout's corps joined by Ney's, Junot's and part of Murat's cavalry. Soon the struggle had grown titanic, more than forty thousand soldiers pitched against a similar number of Russians. As the two sides' muskets grew fouled with powder, they went at each other with bayonets and swords. I learned this from a blood-spattered messenger sent by Ney.

Through it all, the cannons on both sides, using canister shot fired at close range, wreaked the most brutal slaughter. I was not sent down to that particular cauldron of hell, for which I was pathetically grateful. Nor was François, but it was inevitable that we would be called on at some point. We continued to play chess with an unnatural focus, betting on each game to further the illusion that we were not at imminent risk of death.

I grew curious at various stages about Napoleon, and how he would direct this battle of battles. To my surprise, he did not stir from his chair, unless it was to walk a few steps to and fro, humming quietly, or to sit on the grass, and take from a waistcoat pocket some pills he had been prescribed against his cold. His face simultaneously expressed preoccupation and passivity. Now and again, he spoke with senior officers, and issued orders to be taken to various parts of the field. Not once did he mount his horse, however, the better to spy out the landscape.

It made no sense. From the emperor's position, all that could be seen was Ney's corps, and some of Davout's, and Murat's cavalry units. These units were directly in front of the redoubt upon which we stood. He could visualise the rest of the battlefield with his telescope, but with all the smoke and confusion, not well.

'Does he not usually ride up and down the line?' I asked.

'He does.' François did not look happy.

'Why is he not doing so today?'

'He is not himself.'

'But he might see where an advantage can be gained then, or where reinforcements are needed.'

An expressive Gallic shrug.

'The battle might be lost because of him!' And thousands of men die unnecessarily, I thought.

'It is not for us tell him that. Caulaincourt or Berthier, or Murat, they are the ones to advise the emperor.'

'Dupont!' Caulaincourt was calling.

Burying my misgivings, I tentatively made my way to Caulaincourt's side. 'Sir?'

'Take this to General Bonamy, commander of the 30th Regiment of the Line.' He handed me a folded letter, then noticed my confusion. 'The 30th is in Morand's division, which is attacking the Great Redoubt. You know where that is?'

According to reports, the fighting there was as vicious as that going on below our position. Throat convulsed with fear, I nodded.

'Bring back his answer as fast as you can.' Caulaincourt was already turning away.

Stuffing the message into an inside pocket, I went back to François. 'Well?'

'I am sent to the Great Redoubt.'

'Oh, mon Dieu.' François looked stricken. Given his usual jocularity, it hit hard.

'You can keep my winnings,' I said. He had still not collected them all. 'It has been good knowing you.' I stuck out my hand.

He took it fiercely. 'I will see you again!'

Again nodding, because I did not trust my voice, I put a foot in Liesje's stirrup and hauled myself up.

'Here.'

I stared down at the handkerchief in François's hand. 'I have one.'

'You might need another. Take it.'

He has taken leave of his senses, I thought, but accepted it, nonetheless. Without another word – there was no point in delaying – I turned Liesje's head to the west, and the Great Redoubt. I did not look back.

The first part of my ride was easy enough, away from the command post and along the ranks of the waiting Old Guard. Magnificent though they were in their dress uniforms and bearskin shakos, I noted many were barefoot, their shoes fallen to pieces on the long march to Borodino. They looked ready to fight, though, their faces eager and determined as they watched the fighting.

The same could not be said of the troops in the lower ground. Here what reserves that remained – precious few – were standing near those wounded who had thus far been carried off the field. The piercing screams and cries put me in mind of ten Bedlams. During my time in London, I had sometimes walked past the insane asylum. It had disturbed me then, but the magnitude of what I saw now was far worse.

The stream which the infantry had crossed to reach the Russians was running red. Everywhere there were wounded soldiers, lying, sitting, crouching. Their dress tunics or trousers were soaked in blood. They were missing whole limbs, or hands, or feet. They moaned piteously, and called for their mothers, and all the while, Russian cannonballs and canister rained down around them, sending more to eternity.

Some of the injured were unforgettable. One soldier sat quietly, holding his intestines in his lap, while a comrade with a shattered arm tried to offer him water from a canteen. Another, a huge Saxon, was being examined by a surgeon. He had a massive wound in his left buttock which revealed the entire length of the bare femur; incredibly, it wasn't bleeding. I was close enough to hear the Saxon cheerily declaring that he would cure quickly because of his good health and pure blood.

I averted my gaze, the living nightmare too much to take in. With the incessant cannonade ringing in my ears like a continuous peal of thunder, I rode on. I kept the Great Redoubt at a distance as far as was humanly possible, but in the end, I could put off my task no longer, and as I realised, my bowels would not be denied either. Only now did I understand why François had given me his handkerchief. Looping Liesje's reins around the feet of a dead infantryman – I could find nothing else, and wanted to prevent a repeat of my previous experience – I pulled down my trousers and got on with the business at hand. I was out in the open, and expected howls of derision from the soldiers close enough to see my mortification. I got none, however, just sympathetic looks, and a 'Plenty of us did the same, friend, before we advanced!' from a wounded grenadier.

Job done, I muttered an apology to the corpse whose feet I had used as a tether. 'Come on then,' I said to Liesje. 'The sooner we do this, the sooner we shall return.' *Or not*, cackled the little devil in my head.

We forded the stream. The ground beyond was churned up as if by the plough of an insane god. Every inch was scarred by the great furrows ripped by cannonballs, or indentations where they had bounced along the grass. On the previous bank, the wounded had outnumbered the dead; here the opposite applied. Freshly slain men and pieces of men – exposed entrails and severed limbs, even heads – lay in the ditches and folds. Scattered throughout were countless canister-shredded horses, most dead, some alive. I saw one, horribly disembowelled, nevertheless still standing. Others lay flat, sometimes lifting their heads to gaze mutely on their gaping wounds.

I studied the Great Redoubt. Earlier, its belching guns had made it look like an erupting volcano, I had heard another messenger say. Now I could see why. Gouts of orange-red were issuing all along the top of the earthwork, a rolling line of fire that went forward and back. There were twenty cannon at least, I decided. Clouds of dense smoke billowed and swirled in front of the redoubt, now revealing lines of French infantry – most with tell-tale gaps in their ranks – now obscuring everything from sight.

All was confusion and noise, blood and death, and into the midst of it I had to go. My bowels squeezed again, but I urged Liesje forward. Childishly, as if it would offer me any protection from the death whistling through the air, I leaned forward over her neck. The footing was too uncertain to urge Liesje into a canter or gallop. Marvelling at her willingness to advance into such clamour, with the thick, unpleasant smells of gunpowder and blood in her nostrils, I let her take me up the slope at a slow trot. We avoided the wolf pits, which were full of Russian dead, and on top of them French. Several times Liesje trod on bodies; there were so many, it was unavoidable. At length, one let out a piteous cry, which caused her to shy. With an effort, I brought her under control. 'Easy, girl, easy,' I said into her ear. She calmed, the wonderful creature.

Wondering why we had not been ripped apart, I realised that the guns directly in front of me had fallen silent. I could see French soldiers clambering in through the embrasures, and hear fierce cries as the Russian artillerymen within fought back. The attack was succeeding,

I thought excitedly. Liesje responded to my heels, and we reached the earthwork a few moments later. I could not take her within, so with a promise that I would be back soon, I stabbed a musket into the ground, bayonet first, and tethered her to that.

The noise of pistol and musket shots had replaced the guns, close by at least. Dry-mouthed at the prospect of joining a hand-to-hand struggle, I took both my pistols; my sword hung by my side. Peering through the embrasure, around the still-hot barrel of a 'bone crusher' cannon, I found no one close. Twenty paces away, however, scores of soldiers, each side recognisable by their blue or green uniforms, were fighting. The French were using bayonets, swords and pistols, while the Russian artillerymen had only ramrods and handspikes. The contest was one-sided, yet instead of running, the brave Russians stood and fought.

I climbed inside, cocked my pistols, and began my search. 'General Bonamy?' I shouted.

No one heard, or if they did, answered.

Skirting the dead, mostly Russian now, I walked forward, calling Bonamy's name. He would be at the front, I soon realised. That meant exiting the side of the massive earthwork, for the back was a solid line of sharpened stakes.

A Russian came at me, screaming, ramrod high above his head.

Without thinking, I shot him at point blank range.

His face disintegrated. He went down.

I was terrified now. Fire my second pistol, and I would have only my sword. François had had me practising with it, but I was no swordsman.

'General Bonamy?' I roared.

A man in front of me, a corporal, turned from the Russian he had just bayoneted in the chest. 'You are looking for the general?'

'Yes. I have a message from the emperor.'

He pointed. 'That way.'

Nodding my thanks, crouching low in the hope of not being hit – Russian troops further up the slope were firing over the back of the redoubt at us – I hurried out the open side, and worked my way around to the back. There I found General Bonamy, bleeding from more wounds than I could count, rallying what remained of his men. He was cursing, and waving the infantry to our left forward as well.

'Only the 13th Light have followed us, damn it! If I had five thousand men, I would completely smash the Russian centre. The battle would be won by ten o'clock!'

'Sir, I have a message from the emperor.' I proffered my letter.

He read it, before crumpling the paper into a ball and throwing it away. 'Hold the redoubt, he says! If I had enough men, I could, and more, but . . . cavalry!'

My eyes followed his outstretched arm. Thundering towards us was a line of white-uniformed Russian cuirassiers, magnificent in their high-crested helmets. Fear paralysed me. On open ground, scattered, and with their muskets fired, the French infantry stood no chance. I stood no chance.

'Retreat!' cried Bonamy. 'Back to the redoubt!' To me, he said, 'Are your pistols loaded?'

'One is, sir.'

'Make the shot count then,' he said grimly, walking backwards, face to the enemy. 'Come with me.'

In a sweeping line, sabres at the ready, the cuirassiers came galloping towards us. Their horses' hooves made the ground shake. It was indescribably, utterly terrifying. Nudging with my feet so I did not trip over a corpse, I retreated pace by pace. Soon, however, I could no longer take the tension. I raised my pistol and took aim at a cuirassier.

'Wait!' Bonamy ordered. 'They need to be far closer!'

We made it halfway to the redoubt before the Russians arrived. Shouting, blades flashing, they fell upon us. I shot my man in the chest from ten paces, punching him from the saddle. Bonamy ducked under the swing of another, and opened the cuirassier's thigh to the bone with a cut of his own. Screaming hideously, the Russian rode by.

'Grab the carbine!'

Too late, I heard Bonamy's suggestion. The horse of the man I had killed was already gone past, corpse lolling back in the saddle, carbine hanging by its strap.

Shoving my pistol into my belt beside the other, I drew my sword, but to my overwhelming relief, we reached the redoubt without having to face more cuirassiers. Crouched by the back wall of stakes, I took in the scene. The Russian cavalry had smashed apart what was left of Bonamy's men. Above them, marching down the hill at a steady pace, were massed ranks of green-uniformed infantry.

A sergeant came running in from the left. 'There are Russians coming along the slope, sir, hundreds of them – part of the defensive line, I think. Wouldn't surprise me if they was approaching from the right as well.'

Sighing, Bonamy wiped blood from his forehead with his sleeve. 'There is nothing we can do but pull back.' To the sergeant, he said, 'Everyone is to retreat, at once! Go!'

'What shall I tell the emperor, sir?' I asked, aware of how stupid my question was.

'Tell him that I took the redoubt, but without enough men to defend the position, was forced to withdraw.'

Something struck me hard in the upper left biceps. I stared dumbly at the spot, waiting for the blood and the agony, thinking, the surgeon will have to amputate.

Bonamy probed the hole in the arm of my coat, and with a laugh, produced a lump of lead. 'A spent musket ball – a souvenir!'

I took it, still amazed that it had not torn flesh and shattered bone.

He gave me a shove. 'Go. There is no point in you dying as well.'

'And you, sir?'

'I will remain until the last of my men has got out.'

In awe of Bonamy's bravery, I thanked him and ran to the front of the redoubt, and then exited through an embrasure. There were French soldiers leaping from the earthwork to either side, but sadly, not many. They charged down the slope, eager as I was to escape the Russian counterattack.

My heart soared then to see Liesje perhaps twenty paces away. I ran to her, and soon, we were skirting around the wolf pits and the corpses. I had a moment to consider Bonamy's orders. Without enough men to carry through with his attack had been pointless; so too had my mission. It was not a consoling thought, particularly as Russian musket balls were now whizzing past. Enemy infantry had reached the redoubt, I realised, in parts at least. Praying that having come this far, we would escape unscathed, I bent low, and urged Liesje on.

I had almost reached the bloodred stream when the guns in the redoubt began to thunder again. I clenched my buttocks, and prayed to be spared the indignity of soiling myself as I was blown to bloody pulp.

We crossed safely, covering perhaps another two hundred yards.

Then I was picked up by a giant's hand and sent tumbling through the air. I landed on the flat of my back and lay half-stunned, deafened, confused by what had happened. Slowly, I brought a hand up to my face. I could waggle the fingers. My other hand also worked. I felt down below my waist; my private parts were there, and my legs. I felt winded, but was not in screaming agony. Maybe Liesje stumbled, I thought, sitting up, my gaze searching for her.

She lay not far away, her beautiful head, neck and glorious mane untouched. The rest of her could only be described as a ruin of flesh and bone. A sob escaped me. She had been struck in the stomach by a shell, which, exploding, literally tore her apart. Unable to believe that I was unhurt, I studied my legs, arms, belly, felt around my back. I had not even a scratch. The odds of what had happened were incalculable: it seemed a miracle.

Tears running down my face, I went over and gave Liesje a final stroke, and then ran for my life.

At Napoleon's command post, I had an emotional reunion with François. 'I said you would come back.' His voice was thick as he pumped my hand. 'It takes more than Russian cannon to kill you!'

I could not answer him, images of poor Liesje filling my mind.

He forced a shot of terrible brandy down me, and then, the pepper and vitriol taste still smarting my throat, we went to find the emperor. François told me that the events at the Great Redoubt were being replicated elsewhere. The flèches in front of the emperor's position had now been taken and lost and retaken seven times. Each time the French were evicted, they reformed – under the fire of the enemy guns – and launched another assault. The carnage was indescribable, the dead piled as high as the earthworks. The most recent assault had seen Marshal Ney lead his men, accompanied by the dashing Murat, beyond the flèches and as far as the ruined village of Semeonovskoïë.

There was actually a messenger from Ney, an officer, waiting for the emperor's response as we drew near. Still on his skinny horse, whose flanks were heaving, he was begging for reinforcements.

'He wants me to send more men,' mused Napoleon, talking to himself. 'Says that he and Murat can make out the rear of the enemy army and the baggage train, can see clearly as far as Mojaisk. Victory will be mine, if only he is sent the Imperial Guard.'

François and I exchanged an excited look. The opportunity at the Great Redoubt was gone, but this one was not – yet.

'You can see better from over there, sire,' said the officer, pointing at a spot some two hundred yards distant along the redoubt. 'Marshal Ney says that he must act quickly. The Russians are beginning to regroup.'

Napoleon did not respond, or stir from his chair, still less climb onto his horse to go and look. Instead, impassive-faced, he dismissed the officer, who rode off, shaking his head in disbelief. The emperor listened to my report next, and made no comment. I was waved from his presence; only Caulaincourt gave me a nod of thanks.

Eleven o'clock went by, and still Napoleon vacillated. Finally, he ordered the artillery of the Young Guard forward to bombard the Russian positions beyond Semeonovskoïë, but with this well in train, as the Young Guard itself began to advance, he gave the command to halt. When General Lobau, the Guard's commander, surreptitiously had the guardsmen move a short distance towards the enemy, the emperor immediately sent orders to stop.

Around noon, Ney sent another messenger, his chief-of-staff this time, to plead with Napoleon to send in the Young Guard. He was still considering the request when news arrived that the Russians were consolidating their shattered units behind the stream at Semeonovskoïë. Napoleon hesitated again, declaring, 'Before I commit my reserves I must be able to see more clearly on my chess board.' The general went back to Ney disappointed; the Young Guard remained where it was.

For two further hours, Napoleon did not act, other than to order a response to the Russian cavalry incursion on the left flank. The rest of the Grande Armée remained where it was, giving the enemy's guns carte blanche to wreak death and destruction in the most terrible fashion. Murat's cavalry, packed together in the centre of the line, suffered horribly and unnecessarily. As more than one of us observed, there was no need for the cavalry to remain so close. Whether it was pride, or not wanting to lose face, they were never given permission to withdraw, and stayed within reach of the Russian artillery for the entire day.

At length Napoleon came to a decision. Two hundred guns were brought forward. For half an hour, they subjected the Great Redoubt to a brutal bombardment, and then a massed infantry and cavalry assault began. The cavalry were to feint an attack on the Russians protecting the flanks of the redoubt, but then charge in through its open sides. The clever tactic was successful, and by half past three, the Great Redoubt was in French hands again. This accomplished, it was discovered that the Russians had set up a second line of defence about half a mile further back. Try as it might, the cavalry could not break the enemy infantry dug in there. It was back to the Great Redoubt.

The positions of the two sides had not changed much on the left flank either. On the right, after a final push beyond the village of Utitsa, during which his men had faced Russian bayonets and even pikes, Poniatowski had also halted his troops. By five o'clock, after eleven hours of constant struggle, both sides, greatly weakened, were exhausted. Almost of its own volition, the fighting virtually ceased.

Using François's telescope, I estimated that perhaps one third of the original number of infantry remained in the line. The rest were wounded, dead, or engaged in carrying away the casualties, or rallying in the rear. The artillery, the terror of the day, now spoke only by sporadic shots, and even these sounded languid and muffled. The cavalry that had survived travelled at slow pace, at most making a tired trot.

Napoleon could have sent in the Guard at this point. Reports from the Great Redoubt suggested that the Russian line beyond it was weak. One hammer blow, some senior commanders said, and the battle could still be won. The emperor was having none of it. 'I will not have my Guard destroyed. When you are eight hundred leagues from France, you do not wreck your last reserve.'

Caulaincourt and Berthier agreed with him; so did Bessières, and even Murat.

It seemed the Russians had had enough too. By six in the evening, they were withdrawing.

The battle was over.

Tellingly, it had not delivered the victory Napoleon had wanted. A handful of enemy guns had been taken, but almost no prisoners. The Russian army had withdrawn in good order, taking most of its wounded. While their casualties were horrific – the next day, as the battlefield was explored, they were estimated to be in the region of fifty thousand killed and wounded – the losses suffered by the Grande Armée were also catastrophic. More than thirty thousand soldiers were dead or injured. Larrey and his surgeons worked through the night performing amputations – the pile of limbs outside the operating tent could not have been fitted in a large room – but try as they might, the majority of the casualties, still on the battlefield, went without any medical care whatsoever. It went without saying that most would succumb by the following day. The butcher's bill among the cavalry was particularly disastrous. Tens of thousands of carcasses lay on the field, bloody evidence. Many units had also lost between a third and half of their men. Part of me hoped that Féraud was among them, so I need not worry about him again.

Never had so many senior officers been killed or injured in a battle. Forty-nine generals, thirty-seven colonels and eighty-six aides-de-camp: the toll was extraordinary. I made enquiries about the heroic Bonamy, whom I had met at the Great Redoubt, and heard to my relief that he was still alive, although a prisoner of the Russians. He had apparently stopped himself from being slain by shouting that he was Murat, the King of Naples. Caulaincourt had lost his younger brother Auguste, cut down during the incredible cavalry charge on the Great Redoubt. The news hit hard; he was more downcast than I had ever seen him. Napoleon's words, that Auguste had been his best cavalry officer, brave and with a quick eye, and that by the end of the campaign, he would have replaced Murat, had been of scant comfort to poor Caulaincourt.

I counted myself lucky to have lost only Liesje.

CHAPTER XX

Near Moscow, 14 September 1812

Sent ahead by Caulaincourt with a message for Murat, I thought the road to the capital a masterpiece. Wide enough for ten vehicles, it had two rows of very tall, willow-like trees on either side; between those was a path for pedestrians. The hospitable shade gave welcome respite from the sun's fierce heat; in the winter, I imagined the trees served as a guide when snow filled up the frequent precipices.

Three months before, on the banks of the Niemen, I could never have imagined myself entering Moscow, yet it was only a few miles away, and if the cavalry reports were to be believed, lay ripe for the taking. This came as a surprise, because after Borodino, Kutusov's army had taken the road towards the city. Unsurprisingly, Napoleon took this to mean that a second, more decisive battle would take place before Moscow. Kutusov, he had told Caulaincourt, would offer combat once again before giving up the capital, but this time with a sword in one hand and peace proposals in the other. Having signed a treaty, the emperor intended to stay a week in Moscow, and then retire on Smolensk.

Now it seemed that he was to be robbed of his battle. Apart from some Cossacks, the enemy had pulled back entirely from the city limits. The inhabitants were fleeing as well. In my mind, this did not suggest that Kutusov would be suing for peace anytime soon – quite the opposite – and an empty Moscow was of no use to anyone. The sensible thing would be to withdraw, and as soon as possible. Whether that would happen was another thing entirely.

I rode through a forest pass, seeing half-finished enemy redoubts but not a sign of a Russian soldier. I passed footsore but happy groups of French infantry; word had reached them of the abandoning of the capital, and they were whistling and singing, something I had not heard since before Smolensk. They were also marching with energy, and every so often, a spontaneous cry of '*Vive l'Empereur!*' would go up.

Exiting the treeline, I reached the crest of a hill; the sight rolling away from it instantly caused me to rein in.

Two miles away lay a large city: Moscow. I pulled out my spyglass, which had been acquired for fifty francs from a soldier after Borodino. I had asked no questions, he had given no explanation for having an officer's piece of kit. Putting it to my eye, I studied with fascination the golden spires, the domes painted in bright colours, and topped with gilded crosses. The largest bell tower of many, with an enormous cross at its top, I decided had to be the Kremlin. There were palaces, mansions and more modest houses with red and black roofs. I saw parks too, green spaces inside the city, which bore no resemblance to English or French towns, and had a fantastical, wholly Oriental character. Most remarkable of all, perhaps, was the absence of a defensive wall. Only a shallow ditch fronted its suburbs.

Delighted, images of fine accommodation, food, drink and Jeanne filling my mind, imagining telling my mother about it one day, I rode down the slope. Nearer the city, I heard artillery, the hanging puffs of smoke close to and further off telling me that some Russians at least had remained to dispute the city's ownership. The cannonade was desultory, however, and no more than three or four shots had been exchanged when I reached Murat's position, straddling the road about half a mile from the city.

He was dressed as outlandishly as ever, in a short coatee of red sammet with slashed arms; a richly embroidered belt circled his waist. His boots were of red Morocco leather, and on his head he wore a big three-cornered hat, which he'd put on back to front. His long brown hair hung down in curls onto his shoulders. He was shouting at his artillerymen to cease shooting.

'There's an envoy coming, sir,' cried a man I recognised as Colonel Séruzier, a commander of the artillery attached to the vanguard.

Murat scowled, as ever displeased by the idea that a fight would end.

'A letter from the emperor, sir,' I said, drawing closer.

Eyes mostly on the party approaching from the enemy positions, he took it without acknowledgment, and did not open it. Beckoning Gourgaud, whom I had seen among his entourage, he demanded his pocket watch, which the fiery-tempered officer handed over unwillingly.

'Stay here!' Murat roared at his staff officers, and off he took, riding towards the Russians at a fast clip.

He was scared of nothing, I thought, part admiring, part judgemental. All it would take was one Cossack, one enemy cuirassier, who did not know who he was. A single pistol shot, and that would be the end of Murat. Not today, however. The party of Russians met him; both halted, and a conversation began. After only a moment, however, the Russians began to ride away. They went about fifty yards before Murat shouted after them; back they came. There was a little to and fro before an agreement of some kind was made; there was nodding among the Russians.

Next thing I knew, Murat was beckoning to me. I spurred my horse towards him. By the time I got there, he had dismounted, and was surrounded by a circle of admiring Cossacks, their lances inverted.

'Sir?' I asked.

Murat was feigning to ignore the Cossacks. 'Bring this news to the emperor: we are to pass through Moscow without halting and go as far as six miles along the Kasan road, our advance guard being preceded at a distance of two hundred yards by squadrons of Cossacks.'

'Shall I return with the emperor's response, sir?'

'There is no need. I have agreed to the terms.' Seeing my surprise, he said, 'I either did so, or the city would be set on fire.'

That explained the Russians riding away, and Murat calling out, I thought. 'I shall explain it to the emperor, sir. Will there be any reply to his letter?'

'Tell him I do not know.'

Nothing more was forthcoming, so I saluted and left him to it. When I looked back, Murat was handing Gourgaud's pocket watch to a Cossack officer. Giving such gifts to the enemy had been a habit of his for years, I had heard, but never until now witnessed. No wonder Gourgaud had been sour-faced: he knew precisely what Murat would do with his valued possession.

Napoleon's response to the news was to send Count Narbonne to Murat with the order to follow the Russians step by step, but as far as possible to circumvent the city, pressing the enemy as soon as they were outside the barriers. A deputation of the municipal authorities was also to be sent to meet the emperor.

I reached Moscow for the second time at noon, as part of the imperial party. To Napoleon's clear irritation, there was no sign of a Russian greeting party. Each instant, he kept sending out fresh orders, continually asking whether the deputation or any notables were on their way. Time passed, and no one appeared. He told Caulaincourt to write to his officials in Vilna and Paris, informing them that the Grande Armée had reached Moscow, and dated from the city.

Two hours passed, and still not a soul had presented themselves. The effect on the emperor was marked, bitter disappointment showing on his normally impassive face. Messengers sent by Murat, advancing after the last of the retreating Russians, brought word that the city appeared to have been abandoned by everyone but the dregs of society. At the Kremlin, a drunken mob armed with pitchforks, swords and a few muskets had charged Murat's cavalry. Three salvoes from his horse artillery had sent the rabble on their way. They were lowlifes and criminals, seemingly freed as long as they fought the invading French, but their resistance lasted all of ten minutes.

Napoleon ordered all the doors to be broken down with cannon if needs be, and at three in the afternoon, sent in the Guard. I went with its advance party of thirty men, my task to bring back news of what we found. It was thrilling, and if I admit it, terrifying, to ride in front of the compact columns of infantry, the band's music – *La victoire est à nous* – and the tramping of the soldiers carrying before us down the empty streets. The drums resounded in dull echoes off the walls of the single-storey timber houses. Every window was barred; every door was shut. Not a soul was in sight. Moscow, I thought dourly, seemed to be a huge corpse. It was the kingdom of silence, a fairy town, whose buildings and house had been built by enchantment for us alone.

It had not been entirely abandoned, though, and when a disorganised rabble came spilling onto the first crossroads, I decided that they were some of the criminals that Murat had had to deal with at the Kremlin. Poorly armed, most drunk, they took one look at us and fled.

We came to the stone bridge that led from the suburbs into the city proper. Hearing loud muttering as I reached the far end, I glanced over my shoulder to see a dripping figure clambering over the side of the bridge, obstructing the path of the following band and infantry. He was muffled up in a sheepskin cape, long grey hair fell down onto his shoulders and he carried a three-pronged fork, an agricultural implement. He looked like Neptune rising from the sea.

I have no idea if he was drunk, mad or both, but he did not move as the band drew close. More foolishly still, he thrust violently with his pitchfork at the drum-major, resplendent in smart uniform and lace. Snatching the wretch's weapon, the drum-major grabbed him by the shoulders; then giving a kick from behind, he launched him over the bridge into the water. The bandsmen never missed a note of their tune, but their delight was obvious. Aghast, I watched the greybeard struggling in the current. He came up twice, but then disappeared.

I turned away, my pleasure at our entrance souring like cream left in the sun. The city might seem peaceful, but death was never far away.

The majority of the houses now were also modest, single-storeyed timber affairs, but interspersed with them were superb stone palaces, many of extraordinary size. I peered into window after window, seeing no one. It was eerie, yet my thoughts were more fixed on the beds in these grand residences, and the food and drink that might be found within.

Murat's cavalry, which had entered before us, had been ordered not to dismount, on pain of death. The Guard had been commanded not to break ranks either. It was an instruction that was only ever going to be disobeyed, as the already open doors of some buildings revealed. Trying to prevent the Grande Armée's soldiers from pillaging an abandoned city, I decided, was like my mother's cook telling me as a boy not to eat the fresh-baked biscuits that had been set to cool on the work surface, and then leaving the kitchen.

My intuition was correct.

Carrying a message back to Napoleon later, I spied groups of French, Italian and German soldiers entering houses and palaces alike. From within, came cries of delight, and the sounds of cabinets and cupboards being smashed open. Tempted by my growling stomach – I had not had anything to eat since a crust of stale bread that morning – I decided that a short delay to my mission was of no import, and rode into the courtyard of a magnificent palace. Tying up my horse by the main door, which was ajar, I took both my pistols and entered.

I wandered from room to enormous room, all entirely empty of furniture, finding nothing until I reached the kitchens at the back. A bag of oats slung over my shoulder – good for porridge at least – I proceeded with my search. By the entrance to the cellar, I met several grenadiers of the Old Guard, bearded rascals with gold earrings and the look of proper vieux grognards. They were severely fuddled, telling me owlishly that there was so much wine within I was welcome to whatever I liked.

Tucking my pistols into my belt, I picked up a lighted candlestick from the floor, where one of the vieux grognards had set it, and entered. The floor was covered in empty bottles and spilt wine, far more than I judged the men outside could be responsible for. When I called out, I was told that that was how they had found it. 'The servants must have drunk all night before they left,' shouted one.

It was the logical conclusion, I decided, taking in the cellar's contents. In the centre of the sand-covered floor was an enormous, more than 400-bottle tun, still unbroached. Ten to one some excited soldiers took an axe to it, I thought. Most of it would be wasted. On either side of the tun, hundreds of bottles were laid out in neat rows in the sand. Stooping with the candlestick, I identified exquisite vintages: Bordeaux, Frontignan, malaga, dry madeira, as well as liqueurs and syrups.

Bread, cheese and meat would have served better, but I was not going to walk away emptyhanded. Fortunately, the cloth bag containing my oats was roomy enough to accommodate four bottles of wine. Loath to leave the Dionysian excess, I opened a fifth bottle and took it to drink as I rode. The vieux grognards bid me a solemn farewell; I could not help from wondering if they would be as amiable towards any Russians they encountered, particularly those of the female sex. Wherever Jeanne was, I hoped she was safe. I wanted to start looking for her, but with no idea where she might be, and with a message to deliver to the emperor, I had to hope that she would come to no harm.

I had almost finished the wine within half a mile of leaving the palace. It was rare for me to drink so fast, but the memory of the greybeard drowning in the river would not leave me. Nor would my sense of creeping doom, a feeling I had no reasonable explanation for, other than the inebriated vieux grognards and what men like them might start doing. Drowning my sorrows would not make my concerns go away, I knew that, but it would blot them out for a time. Thankfully, it worked. By the time I neared the city gate, I was in fine spirits, encased in the old, familiar wine-flush. I had even found the time – attracted by the noise and bizarre, carnival appearance – to pause by a group of soldiers lounging in the street on carpets, silken settees and satin cushions. In their midst blazed a bonfire of paintings and luxurious furniture. Barefoot, faces and hands blackened by the smoke, they were clad in the most bizarre dress, like Tartars, like Chinese, in Polish toques and Persian bonnets, there was even one clad as a pope. For whatever reason, the soldiers had taken not just clothing and alcohol from the houses they had ransacked, but musical instruments. Whether expert or novice, they were practising on pianos, flutes, violins and guitars, from which they were mostly extorting discordant notes.

The pleasant illusion was shattered by the sight of Féraud at the head of his hussars, riding in my direction. I had glimpsed him once a day or so after Borodino, his head wrapped in a bandage but to my relief, he had not seen me. This would be our first meeting since the duel outside the walls of Smolensk, when I had been wounded. I decided that he would be preoccupied, his mind set on Russian troublemakers, and finding accommodation for his men. I would ride by, head down, and he would not even notice.

I had reckoned without his gap-toothed corporal, who had also survived Borodino. Catching sight of me, he spoke to Féraud, who stared, and then with a leer of delight, spurred his horse forward.

I saluted him with my bottle. 'Welcome to Moscow, Captain.'

He sneered. 'You are drunk.'

'I am, and you are still alive.'

'I could say the same about you. Did you skulk at the rear for the whole of the battle at Borodino?'

Stung, because that would have been my preference had I been given the choice, my retort was hot. 'I was at the Great Redoubt when Bonamy took it! My favourite horse was killed under me.'

After a brief hesitation, he said, 'That is a sore blow.'

Surprised by his response, then thinking, he is a hussar, so animals are dear to him, I said, 'The only consolation was that she was killed instantly.'

'I had two horses die at Borodino.'

We stared at each other, bonded for a moment by our losses.

'Is that wine finished?'

I realised he was staring at the bottle in my hand. 'There is a little left.'

'Give it here.' Féraud was reaching out.

Stunned, I passed it over.

He raised it towards me. 'To our horses, poor dumb creatures. They do as we demand, loyal and faithful, and in return we see them die for it.' Tipping back the bottle, he took a long pull, then handed it back.

'To our horses,' I said, and drained the dregs.

'Until our next contest,' said Féraud, tipping a finger to his shako.

I nodded, thinking how bizarre it was to share a drink with a man with whom I had fought three duels, and with whom, it seemed, I was doomed to fight another.

CHAPTER XXI

We were up with the sun the following morning, the fifteenth of September. Napoleon was eager to enter Moscow. Sore-headed, dry-mouthed – François and I had finished all four bottles of wine before going to bed – I could not have cared less. What I wanted mattered not at all, and so, cursing that I had not had a soft mattress in a palace to sleep on as I had hoped, I roused myself into some state of wakefulness. François, who could hold his drink better, looked none the worse for wear, and laughed as I fumbled with the buttons of my shirt.

It was early – six, by my pocket watch – when we entered the city. One might have expected to see tradesmen and merchants, and servants sent out on errands, but again the streets were deserted. Caulaincourt, riding right behind the emperor, called me to his side. He spoke from the side of his mouth. 'Is this what it was like yesterday?'

'Yes, sir.'

'Such a gloomy silence.'

Miserable, my head fuzzy and thick, I was glad of the peace, and relieved when Caulaincourt sent me back to François.

During the whole of our long route, we did not meet a single soul. Napoleon gave away little emotion, but his restive gaze, forever moving from side to side, revealed his inner disquiet. He seemed pleased when the crenellated wall of the Kremlin came into sight. We entered one of the three massive gates, passing through several vaults separated by barriers, and into a grand courtyard. While Napoleon and Caulaincourt went up the Strelitz steps to the State Apartments, a few aides-de-camp following, the guard of soldiers and cavalry settled down to wait. François and I glanced at each other.

'I am parched,' he said.

'Wine would be better than water,' I grumbled. 'Hair of the dog and all that.'

'By rights, the tsar's cellar should be considerably better than the one you chanced upon yesterday. Shall we take a look?'

I needed no further persuasion. We wandered about the courtyard, trying door after door, investigating what lay on the other side of each. Finding the kitchens, and to my delight, a fine ham in a larder there, we paused for a brief repast. There were cheeses also, and dried fruits, and best of all, no one we had to share them with. We also drained a great silver ewer of water. I was feeling more human, and François declared he had never eaten finer ham. Reinvigorated, we soon discovered the entrance to the cellar at the back of the kitchen. On a table by the door were several candlesticks, left there as lights for the servants. We took one each.

The sound of our shoes echoed off the walls of the long, sloping passageway, which led to a series of vaulted chambers. The air was decidedly cool, making me grateful for my woollen coat. I half expected Russian soldiers to come charging out of the darkness with fixed bayonets, but my only adversaries were the cobwebs, which hung everywhere.

The first few rooms contained sacks of flour and other dried goods. There were barrels of pickled vegetables, and even a confectionery store with baskets of dragées, macaroons and grilled almonds. Our mouths full, enjoying the taste of foods we had not seen for months, our search continued. This time, I told François, it would not be four bottles. I had emptied a sack of flour; it would hold a dozen bottles, perhaps even fifteen.

'The wine will be in here somewhere,' I declared, raising my candlestick to peer into the next vault. My blood ran cold. There were small barrels within, stacked as high as a man. 'François,' I said.

He was at my side in an instant. 'Found it?'

'Is that what I think it is?'

'*Mon Dieu!*' He pulled my arm back, and darkness swallowed the barrels of gunpowder again.

'They were not put there by accident.'

'No, indeed. That policeman might not have been raving after all.'

We stared at each other. Both of us had heard about the policeman brought in late the previous night. Rambling, almost simpleton-like, he had sworn to Caulaincourt that the few small conflagrations seen thus far were not accidents caused by soldiers lighting campfires, but deliberate attempts at arson. Governor Rostopchin, he claimed, had given orders that Moscow should be burned to the ground, and more fires would soon be set.

'We had best raise the alarm,' I said, 'so they can be carried outside.'

Grim-faced, François nodded.

The thought went through my mind that if I were to run a line of powder up to the cellar's entrance and light it, I could rid the world of Napoleon. Bellamy would be ecstatic; I would be freed of all obligation to him. Despite the appeal, I had no wish to incapacitate François somehow, and then to blow dozens or even hundreds of men to smithereens along with the emperor, for that would surely be the result. Even if Napoleon alone could have been murdered, I did not have the stomach for it.

We had only gone a short distance when a tall figure bearing a candlestick appeared at the top of the passageway. It was none other than the ordnance officer Gaspard Gourgaud, who had ridden with us to find Junot at Valutina Gora, and whom Murat had deprived of a fine pocket watch. Hearing of our discovery – it was the concern about just such a possibility that had brought him to the cellar, not a base desire for wine – he insisted we show him.

He swiftly ascertained the amount of gunpowder to be in the region of three hundred kilograms. It was, he declared with a certain ghoulish satisfaction, enough to blow the central part of the Kremlin and all who were in it far up into the heavens.

Gourgaud looked so disappointed when I told him that we were on our way to tell Caulaincourt that I suggested he do it himself.

'You do not mind?' he asked.

'The important thing is that the emperor is safe,' I said. 'It does not matter who brings him the news.'

Gourgaud wrung my hand and François's, telling us we were fine men and true servants of the empire. He hurried off at once.

François was suppressing laughter. 'You did that so we can find the best wine, eh?'

'I don't know what you mean,' I said, leading the way to the next vault.

It was perhaps mid-afternoon when we, drunk as lords, simply lay down in the kitchen and fell asleep. There had been no summons from

Caulaincourt or the emperor, nor was there as we slumbered. The sound of breaking glass, close to my head, woke me. I opened a bleary eye to find a vieux grognard of the Old Guard, who had dropped one of my bottles, making off with several more. He ignored my croaked protest, and vanished. Mumbling a curse, my mouth furry and unpleasant-tasting, I sat up.

François lay a few feet away, still dead to the world. He had tackled a bottle of brandy, also from the cellar. Head fuzzy and sore, I thanked my stars that I had not.

I fumbled with my pocket watch. Almost nine o'clock, it read. I had been asleep for perhaps six or seven hours. I got to my feet, not quite trusting my balance, and drained the last of the water from another ewer. There was no more to be had, at least that I could find, so I went in search of a well. Somewhere as big as the Kremlin would have one.

As I emerged into the courtyard, a terrible explosion shattered the air. The noise was so loud and so sudden, I leaped in the air with fright. The sky to the east lit up bright yellow and orange; everyone was staring, not just me. The detonation did not end, but rumbled on and on. Rockets blasted up into the sky as well, I counted two, three, six, bright, streaming tails that soared up high before exploding in starbursts of yellow and gold.

The explosion might have been an accident – a careless soldier near a powder wagon – but our discovery in the cellar, and the immediate launching of the rockets after the explosion suggested the odds of that were vanishingly small. The Russians wanted Moscow to burn, and us with it. By the look of the skyline, which was growing brighter by the moment, their plan might succeed.

Ewer unfilled, I went to rouse François. 'Wake up!' I nudged him with my shoe.

He growled something incomprehensible and shifted position, but his eyes remained firmly shut.

I prodded him again, and then a little harder. 'François!'

'What? What in God's name – *what?*' A deep sleeper always, he was like a bear with a sore head when roused unwillingly.

'The city is burning.'

That brought him awake. 'Burning?'

'There was an almighty explosion a few minutes ago, and rockets straight after. There can be no question it is deliberate.'

Together we made our way to the terrace of the Kremlin, which provided a good vista over Moscow. Plenty of others had come to watch the spectacle as well, officers, aides-de-camp, ordinary soldiers. There was no sign of Napoleon, Caulaincourt, or any of the other more senior commanders yet.

A grim silence reigned as we stared at the site of the explosion. An enormous jet of flame stretched up into the sky. Balls of fire went up all around it, in greater or lesser trajectories, as if a mass of bombs and shells had been simultaneously detonated. The fires it was causing were, for the moment, confined to the eastern suburbs but the gusting wind, brisk in our faces, meant that that situation would soon change. The chance of the entire city being consumed seemed entirely possible. I for one would not have placed a single sou on it not happening.

François glanced at me. 'Your actress friend – she is here, isn't she?'

'She is.' Fear uncoiled in my belly at the thought of Jeanne. 'I could try to look for her, but the chance of finding and searching every theatre, in the dark . . .'

'You would have more chance of finding a needle in a haystack. Do not worry, Mathieu. She will have friends and co-workers. If the need arises, she will make her way to safety.'

He was right, I told myself, but it still felt cowardly to put her from my mind.

Our attention was caught by movement on the streets opposite the Kremlin, where the Chinese Quarter, known to the Russians as the Kitai Gorod, was situated. During the conflagration of the previous night, many of the shops had been emptied of their exotic commodities, which had simply been placed in the street and put under guard.

Now some inhabitants had come to see what could be pilfered. Outnumbered by some margin, the sentries soon resorted to brute force, using their musket butts and in one instance that I saw, the tip of a bayonet. It was like trying to stem the tide, however. For every looter driven back, another three swarmed in to snatch whatever was closest to hand: a bale of silk, boxes of tea, sets of porcelain.

'It will soon be like this all over the city.' François's tone was grim. 'Chaos and looting by Russians and soldiers of the Grande Armée alike.'

'We had best alert Caulaincourt,' I said.

At the entrance to the Master of Horse's quarters, we found his valet, a sniffy, rotund chap who had been with him since his days in St Petersburg. He had an idea of what was going on – so much light was streaming in through the windows, it could have been midday – and took little persuasion to wake his master.

We barged in behind the valet, ignoring his protests.

Caulaincourt was deeply asleep, but he came awake fast when he saw the three of us there. 'What is it?'

'The city is aflame, sir,' I said. 'There was a huge explosion, and then rockets were fired. After that, fires began springing up everywhere.'

Caulaincourt was on his feet already. 'Is the Grand Marshal awake?' This was Duroc.

'I do not know, sir,' said François.

'Go and rouse him.'

A few minutes later, Caulaincourt and Duroc were on the terrace, their brows furrowed, deep in conversation. It was shocking how much the fires had spread in the few minutes we had been gone; I said as much to Caulaincourt. Nonetheless, he and Duroc decided to let Napoleon sleep on. François carried a message to Marshal Mortier, commander of the Young Guard and the new military governor of Moscow, advising him to call his troops to arms. Caulaincourt took me with him on a reconnaissance mission, riding out to various quarters where different transport units attached to the imperial household were stationed.

A stiff wind was blowing from the two points of conflagration visible to us as we exited the Kremlin, and it was driving the flames towards the centre. The danger seemed no deterrent to those intent on pillaging, most of which appeared to be Napoleon's soldiers. Every direction I looked, locks were being forced and cellar doors bashed in. The streets were already littered with books, pieces of faïence, with furniture, with all kinds of clothing. The soldiers were not alone; the cantinières had followed them into the city. Laden down like beasts of burden, they were making off with firkins of liqueurs, sugar, coffee and rich furs.

I saw one harridan repulsing with her fist a grenadier who was trying to stop her from continuing into the city. He gave up and left her to it, and the next moment, she was blocking the path of a group of poor women and children with hardly any clothes on, presumably locals who had fled their house. Her savage gestures and the rolling pin she waved as a threat saw the tearful women begin to hand over whatever paltry valuables they had managed to save.

I had seen enough. Without asking permission from Caulaincourt, I turned my horse and spurred it towards the cantinière. 'Stand aside!' I roared.

She paid no heed.

I brought my mount to a halt in front of her and levelled one of my pistols at her head. 'Let those unfortunates go, or by all that is sacred, I will decorate the pavement with your brains.'

Her confidence vanished, and she stood aside to let the terrified women and children by. I waited to be sure they got away, and incredibly, the cantinière then managed to shed a few tears. The road to Moscow had been long and arduous, she whinged, and she was penniless and hungry.

'That does not give you the right to rob those who have lost everything,' I shouted. She cried and sobbed, and told me she was sorry, but it was all a pretence. I could not stay to watch over the wily creature, and well she knew it. I gave her a final warning, and rode after Caulaincourt. When I glanced back, the cantinière's beady eyes were on me; the witch even had the temerity to wave. I cursed her, and hoped that the group I had saved had got far enough away to escape her attentions for a second time.

Not two streets later, I came upon an even worse scene, soldiers robbing a group of sobbing women of their earrings and shawls. There were ten of them, all armed with muskets, and so I rode past, telling myself that the presence of children – there had been several – would prevent any worse crimes being perpetrated on the unfortunate women. I would not have wanted to gamble on it, however. A small consolation was managing to put out – beating with my gloved hands – a fire in the beard of an old man who had just hobbled out of a burning house.

The cause of the conflagrations was soon evident. I spied figures in the alleys and smaller lanes, slipping between the houses, clearly trying to stay out of sight. Wherever they had been, fires sprang up. Before long, I had seen bombs being dropped from church towers, from the tops of houses and into the streets. Caulaincourt ordered our escort to arrest the Russian incendiaries, and if they did not stop, to shoot them.

With at least two-thirds of the houses built from wood, the task of catching all the enemy incendiaries or preventing the conflagration

from spreading was doomed from the start. We returned to the Kremlin in low mood. Still Caulaincourt and Duroc did not wake Napoleon.
As I said to François, it did not really make much difference if the
emperor was awake or not. Even a man of his ability could not work
miracles. Waiting for the fires to reach us, my head aching, I brooded
about Jeanne, and whether I should have scoured the streets for her.

In the end, I simply curled up on the floor and went to sleep.

CHAPTER XXII

By noon the following day, a vast circle of fire had encircled the Kremlin. The wind was fanning the flames to a terrifying extent, carrying enormous sparks so far that they were falling like a fiery deluge hundreds of yards away, setting houses alight, so that the most intrepid could not stay there. The air was so hot, and the pinewood sparks so numerous, that all the trusses supporting the iron plates forming the roof of the Arsenal, a modern building nearby, were in danger of catching fire. The reason it and other parts of the Kremlin did not begin to burn was thanks to the men who had been positioned with brooms and buckets, their task to gather up the glowing fragments and moisten the beams.

Frightening as this was, more terrifying still was the presence in the Kremlin's courtyards of dozens of artillery wagons belonging to the Imperial Guard. Alerted by Caulaincourt, Napoleon went to see for himself.

The fire was attacking everywhere now. On the roofs of the stables, containing some of the emperor's horses, coachmen and grooms were using brooms and even their feet to knock down cinders. Two fire engines – intentionally dismantled by the Russians – had been made functional again, and were being manoeuvred into position to help. Parties of soldiers stood around the artillery wagons, ready to quench any sparks that fell upon them.

Windowpanes in the tower that linked the palace with the Arsenal were cracking beneath the heat. The iron roof of a burning church tumbled to the ground with a loud, sinister crash. Sparks floated down and set alight here, pieces of oakum, and there, a heap of tow used in the Russian artillery wagons. With flames licking high into the sky from buildings just a short distance from the Kremlin, it felt as if we were working beneath a vault of fire. It was impossible to stay more than a moment in any one spot; the bearskin on the Guardsmen's shakos was being badly singed. We were breathing nothing but smoke and even my lungs, which were strong, soon felt the strain.

The danger of a vast explosion in the Kremlin was immense, yet to my astonishment, Napoleon did not seem afraid. On the contrary, I felt the danger seemed to be keeping him there. His presence drove the Guard's gunners and infantrymen to insane acts of bravery; some were badly burned. In the end, Lariboisière, the officer in charge of the wagons, begged the emperor to leave the men to it before some of them were killed.

He agreed, but with clear reluctance, and retired to the state apartments. I followed. The air within was only fractionally less furnace-like, yet it was still a relief. Eugène was waiting for the emperor; so too were Marshals Bessières and Lefèbvre, and Berthier. All of them begged Napoleon to abandon the city before it was too late. He would not agree, in part because he thought this great catastrophe might be connected with some movement of the enemy – this in spite of Murat's frequent reports that the Russians were continuing to retreat along the Kazan road. Not until four in the afternoon, when Berthier pointed out that if the enemy attacked the corps outside Moscow, the emperor would have no means of communicating with them, did he relent.

By this point, more than seven hundred incendiaries had been arrested, and scores more shot on the streets as they were caught in the act. Interrogations ordered by Caulaincourt revealed that a few were policemen and soldiers, but the majority were criminals, freed from the prisons to take part in Governor Rostopchin's fiendish plan. Each man had been assigned a street, and had gone from house to house, setting them on fire. Anything that might have been useful: stores of food, warehouses, granaries, was to be torched. All the fire engines were to be disassembled or removed by their crews, which explained why only two had been in the Kremlin. Even if a sentry picket had been mounted on every corner, I thought, the incendiaries could still have worked their way through the back alleys, scaling walls and climbing through windows.

Rather than take the direct route out of the city, it was decided that it was safer for Napoleon and the imperial headquarters to travel a more circuitous path along the river and through the districts that had already been destroyed. At first all went well. The Moscow policeman charged with leading the emperor to safety proved reliable. The horses coped with the thick layer of hot ash underfoot, and the scarf everyone had wrapped around his nose and mouth sufficed to protect against the worst of the smoke. We turned up our collars against the cinders, and used handkerchiefs and gloves to cover our hands.

Emerging back onto one of the main avenues, we were forced to join the artillery wagons, which had departed after us, but had now caught up. Under normal circumstances, the only effect would have been the delay as we worked our way along the column. Now, though, all that was needed to blow to smithereens François and me, and the whole general staff, not to say the imperial staff and the emperor as well, was for one firebrand or smouldering roof-shingle to burn its way through the canvas covering a powder wagon. I clenched my jaw, and if I admit it, prayed, as we rode past the wagons. As for the odds of reaching the city gate unharmed, I did not even let myself consider them.

Welcome rain began to fall, lightly at first, but then in torrential downpours. My hope that it would extinguish the fires proved fanciful; as François wryly observed, it would take days and nights of precipitation to put out the flames destroying Moscow. I thought often of Jeanne, and guilt scourged me because I had not tried to look for her. I could not leave now, however. Caulaincourt began to send me, François and the other messengers back and forth to various points in the city, relaying the emperor's orders.

It was horrific; the whole city seemed to be on fire now. Thick sheaves of flame of various colours rose up on all sides to the heavens, blotting out the horizon, sending in every direction a blinding light and a burning heat. The flames were accompanied by a dreadful whistling and thunderous explosions resulting from the combustion of powders, salt-petre, resinous oils and alcohol contained in the houses and shops. Iron sheets came scything down from the collapsing roofs, threatening to decapitate me, while whole tin roofs and domes buckled, and exploded up into the air, odd-shaped metal missiles.

The unfortunate inhabitants gathered in crowds in the larger squares, terrified out of their wits. There at least they might be safe, I hoped, far enough away from the conflagration not to be burned alive. The scenes I witnessed at one of the overcrowded hospitals were etched into my memory forever. Hundreds of the patients had leaped in panic from the building's windows; now these soldiers lay untended, with broken limbs and reopened wounds, helplessly awaiting incineration by the approaching fires. I felt like the worst person alive riding past them, ignoring their cries for help.

Returning from one such mission, I reached Petrovskoië, half a dozen miles from Moscow, by seven in the evening. Behind me, clearly visible, the entire city appeared to be ablaze. Mesmerised, I watched it for some time. It could have been argued, I thought, to be the most beautiful fire in the world. Forming an immense pyramid, like the prayers of the faithful, it had its base on the ground and its summit in heaven. Tearing my eyes away from the majestic and imposing, yet horrible sight, I rode towards the imperial headquarters, set up in a summer palace.

An antique construction, surrounded by high brick walls, its severe appearance more resembled a state prison than a sovereign's residence. The heavy rain had reduced the approaches to a sea of mud, through which my tired horse picked its way with difficulty. I found the place more crowded than a Christmas market. There were no outbuildings, so the seven hundred staff of the two households – general and imperial – were jammed into the palace itself. As I found out, François and I were to share a stable with a dozen other messengers. We counted ourselves lucky.

It was three days before the fires died down sufficiently to allow a return to the city. Our return was no less gloomy than our departure. Four-fifths of Moscow was in ashes; in these areas, only stone or brick buildings remained, and even those were mere shells. The exception was the churches; set apart from surrounding structures, they had survived intact. They were taken over at once, serving as stables. One in a convent was converted into a slaughterhouse, and in the cathedral attached to the Kremlin, an enterprising cantinière set up her kitchen behind the high altar.

Outraged by the deliberate setting of the fires, Napoleon sent a letter to Tsar Alexander with the only Russian of importance that could be found, Ivan Yakovlev, brother of the tsar's minister to Jérôme Bonaparte's court at Cassel in Westphalia. The ragged old man came into the emperor's presence with several days' growth of beard, wearing a shabby riding coat, and a pair of odd, muddy shoes, the very opposite of a courtier. Whether he would succeed in his mission seemed most uncertain to me and François, and, I suspect, the entire court, but Napoleon sent him off with great exhortations.

While the emperor concerned himself with this attempted diplomacy, his soldiers' morale soared. For the first time since leaving Germany, supplies were abundant. Some grain stores had escaped the fire, as had laden-down barges at quays. The shops and great houses that remained were full of wines and liqueurs, delicacies like boxes of figs, as well as tea and coffee. After the months of hardship during the advance, these were most welcome, but I was happier that day to find stores of macaroni, salted meat and fish in a shop as I travelled to Murat's position with a message. Thousands of eager, hungry soldiers were swarming through into Moscow, so there was no chance of having all of it to myself – but I got in before the crowd, filled two burlap sacks and made good my escape without having to threaten anyone with my pistol.

Sad though it was to say, general drunkenness and ill-discipline now reigned supreme. Woe betide the man who did not surrender his booty to the rabble who demanded it – hence the need to carry a weapon. I had seen several brutal fights on the streets, all between soldiers of the Grande Armée; one had resulted in a fatality. I had no desire to experience the same.

Emerging from the shop, I spied figures peering out from the ruins of a house opposite. Locals, I thought, hungry like everyone else, but too scared to draw near until the French soldiers had left. I felt a pang of sympathy; the place would be picked cleaner than a skeleton by the time they got inside. If I donated some of what I had, however, François and I would go short. Not now, but in a week or two, when the weather had worsened further, and supplies and warm clothing would be most needed. Thinking of the cashmere shawls, fox furs and two massive black bearskins that François had already purchased – and agreed to share with me – I was even more grateful for his friendship than I had been before. Any chance of giving the civilians some of the contents of my sacks vanished. I averted my gaze and busied myself with tying them to my saddle horn.

'Mathieu?' It was a woman's voice, and a familiar one at that.

I turned my head. 'Jeanne?' I said in utter astonishment.

She crossed the street to my side. 'Mathieu! What are you doing here?'

'I am a messenger with the army.' I studied her face, which was thinner than I remembered. Smudges of soot marked her high cheekbones, but her lips were as kissable as they had ever been. 'It's a long story,' I added lamely.

A beautiful smile. 'I sent you several letters. You will not have received them, I am guessing?'

'No. I left Paris in May.' Quickly, I added, 'Otherwise I would have replied.'

The suggestion of a pout. 'So you did not come to Moscow to find me?' Her hand on my arm stopped my attempt to explain in its tracks. 'I jest with you.'

Relieved, I cast a look past her, to the companions who were watching us from the ruined house. 'Are those colleagues of yours from the theatre?'

'Yes. Can you help us? We have no real shelter, and have not eaten for two days.'

'I will move heaven and earth to see you all looked after,' I swore.

I immediately took the four – Jeanne, her friend Louise de Fusil, and two male actors – to Caulaincourt. I did not have the authority to requisition quarters for myself, let alone civilians. For my master, however, it was a simple matter of penning a short letter. Not an hour later, Jeanne and her friends were safely ensconced in an outbuilding of a palace belonging to one Prince Galitzin. Close to the Kremlin, it was far from grand, but it had four walls and a roof, which was more than most had. The lock on the door worked too, which relieved me. Not content with this alone, I bought a Russian musket and some powder and ball, which I gave to the older of Jeanne's male companions. A burly type from rural Burgundy, he was used to hunting boar. I told him to shoot anyone who tried to force their way in, and he did not argue. Theirs had been an ordeal, I had no doubt.

I insisted on sharing my macaroni and salted fish, which caused them to be even more grateful. I was glad when Jeanne caught my arm and asked me to stay a while. 'After all,' she said, 'we have not seen each other in months. I want to know how you have been, and since you did not receive my letters, you shall hear my tale.' She cocked her head at me. 'That is, if you are interested?'

'I can think of nothing I would like more,' I said, wishing I had also found some wine in the shop. There was a bench outside, miraculously unbroken or scavenged for firewood; we sat on that.

Her life had been going well, as it turned out. She had had a leading role in not just one play, but two, and supporting parts in others. French was the language spoken by the Russian nobility, and so French theatre was popular in Moscow. More roles had been in the offing; there had been the possibility of appearing on stage in St Petersburg as well. The plays had continued as news came of the battle at Borodino. Even the approach of the Grande Armée had not stopped the performances. The wholescale evacuation ordered by Governor Rostopchin had been a turning point, however. Suddenly, Jeanne explained, a divide had opened between the French expatriates and their Russian hosts. The previously welcoming atmosphere had turned glacial.

Petty though it was, I was relieved to hear no mention of suitors at any point. There must have been some – with her beauty, how could there not be? – but none had been important enough to talk about.

'Even if the city had not burned, we could not have stayed.'

I nodded. 'I am glad.'

She cocked her head at me that way she did. 'Why might that be?' she asked archly.

'Because if you did, I would never see you again.'

A smile. 'Well, as it seems we actors must also leave Moscow, that can be avoided.'

I could not contain myself. 'So you would like to see me again?'

'Perhaps.' She was smiling.

Grinning like an imbecile, I took her hand and kissed the back of it.

'Enough of me. Why are you here, Mathieu? You are no soldier.'

Even though I had no wish to join the army's ranks – especially after what I had seen since crossing the Niemen – I felt myself bridle.

'Men and their pride!' She tutted. 'I am not questioning your courage, Mathieu. You have plenty of that, as you proved in the Bois de Boulogne. And you must have been exposed to so much danger of recent months, yet here you still are.' I subsided, and she said, 'Come, tell me how my half-English spy came to serve Napoleon!'

It was ironic, I thought, how she had joked about my being a spy before, when I was not, and now here I was, an imperial messenger, involved in espionage. Even as I began to tell her of my misfortune in the Parisian gambling salon, a war broke out in my mind. I had been honest before, I thought, revealing my real identity to her, a trust she had not to my knowledge broken. It was one thing, however, to admit to being half-English in Paris, and another to reveal that I was an English spy in the Grande Armée.

'You lost fifteen hundred francs?'

I nodded, ashamed. 'I tend to lose control when there is wine involved. The proprietor of the salon knew that, curse him. He would appear at just the right moment, offering me more credit.'

'But you had no way of paying back such a sum.'

Fresh shame coloured my cheeks. 'I told him I was Monsieur Dupont's heir, that his business was eventually to be mine.'

'Mathieu! You did not promise him collateral in the tailor's shop?'

I could not look at her. 'I did,' I muttered.

Her face worked as she thought about it, and then she said, horrified, 'You became an imperial messenger so you could get away from your creditor, that I understand, but what about poor Monsieur Dupont?'

It was Bellamy who posed the real threat to Dupont, I wanted to say, not the gambling salon's proprietor. Without Dupont's countersignature, the document I had put my name to meant nothing. But to reveal this to Jeanne meant telling her about Bellamy's hold over me, and what I had been forced to do since the start of the campaign. Terrified that she would expose me, I kept silent.

The silence between us dragged on. A troop of cavalry clattered by, fortunately not Féraud and his hussars. Shouted orders carried from the Kremlin, the Imperial Guard at its drill. I tried to speak, and failed.

'I am grateful for the help you have given us, Mathieu.' She was standing, suddenly, and the warmth and sympathy that had been in her voice was gone.

'Jeanne, I—'

'It would be better if you did not visit.'

Miserable, I let her go inside. The door shut, the click of the lock a moment later an extra demonstration of the barrier that had sprung up between us.

If there were no more messages that needed to be delivered, I decided, I would drown my sorrows. Foodstuffs such as I had in my sacks were scarce; wine and spirits were not. It would be simple to drink myself into insensibility. I would not be alone. A hardened drinker, François would join in too.

Tomorrow, when you wake up, the little devil in my head jibed, *you will remember everything*. My attempts to drown him out only provided encouragement.

Jeanne never wants to see you again, he crowed.

I had no answer to that.

CHAPTER XXIII

Pride stinging, still fearful, I made no attempt to seek her out in the weeks that followed. It was not hard; we imperial messengers were busier than ever, carrying the emperor's letters to his commanders who were positioned outside the city. Every journey ran the risk of being attacked or killed by Cossacks, large groups of which now controlled the territory around Moscow.

When the messages were for Murat, the danger rose exponentially, because he was pursuing the enemy south-eastward, down the Ryazan road. It was magnificent countryside, covered in villages and châteaux of remarkable elegance, but it was not safe. Between the peasants, many of whom had armed themselves, and the marauding Cossacks, who were often hovering just a few hundred yards from the French camps, it was something of a miracle each time François or I made it through to Murat, and then returned unscathed. François had long since given up joking about it.

I was learning Russian – having taken up classes with a retired teacher I had met in the city – so could make myself known from the instant I encountered any Cossacks. This I had to do, unfortunately, because Bellamy's claws were still sunk in me. What use his messages were to the Russians, I had no idea, for a blind man could see what was going on with Murat's cavalry, and there had to be plenty of spies among the city's inhabitants. When I questioned Bellamy on this, however, he told me that I was to do what I was told, or Dupont would suffer the consequences in Paris. There was less conviction in his voice than before; I could not help but wonder if he was doing his job because he knew how to do nothing else.

My ability to get by in Russian afforded me something of an advantage over poor François with the Cossacks, but I could not admit it to him, let alone anyone else. The peasants were a different matter, however, because of their treatment at the hands of the Grande Armée. They had no interest in letters from Bellamy; my best hope if I met any was for a quick death. Thankfully, things improved in late September, when the danger was judged great enough to provide messengers with military escorts. This of course put an end to my being able to hand over Bellamy's letters. He left me alone from that point, for which I was immensely grateful.

The lack of contact with Jeanne did not mean I stopped thinking about her. Tortured by what had happened, my days spent in the saddle, in no mood to talk with my cavalry escorts, I brooded constantly. But no matter how I tried, I could not convince myself to tell her the truth. Several Russian agents had been executed since our arrival in Moscow; I did not wish to join them in Hell. Between my gnawing worries and the worsening weather – eleven days and nights of rain – and the dreadful conditions of the roads, and the wine I drank to blot out my unhappy existence, I grew hollow-cheeked and sunken-eyed.

My master Caulaincourt was also in a poor state. His obdurate refusal to agree with Napoleon about remaining in Moscow meant that he had been excluded from the emperor's company. He kept to his rooms, rarely emerging, and spending his time reading. The time spent alone meant that the grief of his brother's death at Borodino, held back until now, finally sank in. I was shocked by his appearance when I called to see him one day in late September. 'Happy are they who never saw that dire spectacle, that picture of destruction,' he said as we drank brandy together. Remembering the carnage, the thunder of the cannons, the smoke, and the shit-inducing fear I had felt all that brutal day, I was again grateful only to have lost my loyal Liesje.

The situation beyond the city walls was ever changing. Utilising the space granted by Murat's failure to skirt to the south of the city as Napoleon had ordered, Kutusov pulled his army back to protect the two most important Russian arms factories at Kaluga and Tula. Another major opportunity had been lost, Napoleon ranted one day, but he did not call Murat to task, nor admit that *he* had not followed through at the time to make sure the command had been obeyed. Instead, Murat was ordered to hold the plain to the south of the city, between Winkovo and the Russian fortified camp at Tarutino. Short of forage and food, it was not long before he began to suffer heavy casualties, men and horses both, from cold and hunger.

Meanwhile, a carnival air reigned in Moscow. It was as if each man stationed in the city had completely forgotten where we were, had put from his mind that winter would soon be upon us. Morale, and devotion to Napoleon had never been higher. While the unfortunate inhabitants scrabbled for food and fuel, the women often forced into prostitution, the soldiers of the Grande Armée held masked balls, staged impromptu concerts in the streets, and took sightseeing trips through the city. Every performance at the reopened theatres was filled to bursting point. When François somehow procured tickets for the play that Jeanne was starring in, I could not bring myself to go. Miserable, I faked a bad stomach, and let him take one of our comrades instead. I spent the evening thinking wistfully of my family, and England. Assuming a false identity was feasible, I told myself. The chance of clearing my name was remote, but not impossible. The thoughts were heartening.

By the beginning of October, Napoleon, who had been speaking of nothing but staying in Moscow for the next eight months, and of the sixty thousand Polish Cossacks who were to be sent by his ambassador in Warsaw, began to talk of burning the remnants of Moscow and then marching on St Petersburg. Caulaincourt was horrified by the idea, while Davout and Berthier explained at length to the emperor how arduous the journey would be, through vast areas of swamp, with Kutusov breathing down their necks – all while winter was about to begin. Only Eugène approved of this foolhardy idea. To everyone's relief, Napoleon did not mention it again.

Instead of organising a retreat whence we had come, however, he began to fixate on the notion of making peace. It was as if he could not remember Caulaincourt telling him what Alexander had said four years before, that he would never come to terms with an enemy until the last mile of Russian soil had been evacuated. To this end, General Lauriston was asked on the fourth of October to carry a message to the tsar suggesting just this eventuality. Like Caulaincourt, whom Napoleon had asked just two weeks before, Lauriston protested, saying that the Grande Armée needed to retreat, via Mojaisk.

'I like simple plans,' I heard the emperor say to him. 'And the less tortuous a path is the better I like it. But there's one path I won't set foot on again unless peace is signed. And that's the one I've come by. Take my letter to Murat's headquarters.'

'And then, sire?' Lauriston's tone was resigned.

'Seek an audience with Kutusov. Ask for safe conduct and bring the letter to Alexander.'

'Sire.'

'I want peace,' said Napoleon, appearing not to have noticed the even greater resignation in Lauriston's voice. 'I must have it. I want it at all costs, providing only our honour is saved.'

His hubris knew no bounds, I decided. I pictured the thousands of wounded soldiers in the city's hospitals, and bitterness coursed through my veins. Every day ... I corrected myself, every hour of delay decreased these unfortunates' chances of survival. I said as much to François that evening, in the midst of what had become our daily ritual. Chess first, before the alcohol we drank in vast quantities took effect, then cards – écarté and vingt-et-un for the most part – and lots of conversation.

He snorted. 'Never mind those poor wretches, Mathieu, what about your survival, and mine – have you considered that?'

Struck by his unusually serious manner, I stared at him, wondering if I too had been burying my head in the sand.

'The fur coats, hat, linings for our garments that Caulaincourt ordered us to buy – those are not for fun! Thanks to his four years in St Peterburg, he is one of the only men in the damned army to know what winter will really be like. That's why every horse under his command now has snow shoes, why he has had sledges built by the score, and thousands of hard biscuits baked.' François threw back a great slug of brandy. 'Mark my words, my friend. The road back to France will be worse than the one we took here – *far* worse.'

This was contrary to what most men were saying, indeed the polar opposite, because most had abandoned themselves to the moment. François tended to joke about everything; coming from him, this was chilling. Here I was, mooning over Jeanne and how she had spurned me, I thought, and in all likelihood I was going to perish in the frozen wilds of Russia or Lithuania, either of cold, or on the end of a Cossack lance.

'Cheer up,' said François.

Irritated now, I glowered. 'Why?'

'We are dead men already. Wasting the time left to us, worrying about our fate, is pointless. Enjoy what we have instead!'

'That has a certain warped logic,' I replied, thinking with a pang of my mother.

A sad, crooked smile. He poured us more brandy, larger measures than we were accustomed to, and raised his glass. It was fine crystal, taken from some palace, and probably cost more than either of us could afford in the real world. The brandy in it was premier quality. The elegant cut glass and expensive brandy encapsulated everything that was insane about the campaign, I decided, and our presence in Moscow.

A devil took me. 'What odds would you give of our reaching Paris?'

'I do not want to think about that.'

This coming from François, who loved to gamble as much as I, again drove home his conviction that we were doomed. 'Twenty to one? Worse?'

'Even if I wanted to accept the wager, which I do not, you are basing it on a false assumption.'

I looked at him, not understanding.

'That we will both live through this. Whatever the chance of one making it, Mathieu, there is far less chance that the two of us will.' He clinked his glass off mine. 'No more talk of such bets, eh?'

Nodding, I drank down the whole glass, thinking grimly, if François and I were destined to die, what possibility of survival did Jeanne have?

Another week went by. A long letter came from Murat, begging the emperor to be allowed to withdraw from Winkovo, where his situation was growing more precarious by the day. A large Russian army was assembling directly in front of his position, the musketry practice of new recruits was audible all day, and his men and especially his horses were steadily weakening from lack of food. The informal ceasefire with the Russians only applied to the front between the camps – at least that was how the enemy interpreted it – and fighting continued everywhere else. Not a day went by that Murat did not lose at least two hundred men. Not only that, he also wrote, the road back to Moscow passed through a long, deep defile with a stream at its bottom. There was only one crossing point, and if he were ambushed there, the results would be catastrophic.

Just as Napoleon had ridiculed Caulaincourt for his concerns about the weather, laughingly saying one sunny morning, 'So this is the terrible Russian winter he frightens the children with,' he mocked Murat, and told him to hold his position. A convoy of flour would be sent to him (it never was). Murat could scour the countryside for supplies, the emperor declared, despite being told that even brigade-strength foraging patrols would come back to camp almost empty-handed. At no point did he go to see for himself. According to François and anyone who had been with Napoleon for years, this was not the usual way he conducted himself. No one understood why, but the fire that had driven him to conquer Europe burned less brightly than it had in the days of Austerlitz and Eylau, Eckmühl and Wagram. The price that was being paid for this lack of focus was horrific.

I and every imperial messenger knew how bad the situation was for Murat at Winkovo, however. The cavalrymen were sleeping under straw at night, and then, breaking off the hoarfrost in the morning, feeding it to their cadaverous mounts. On a good day, they had barley or buckwheat to boil up into thin broth, or to grind into flour for bread. This latter task, however, was too much for some cavalrymen, so enfeebled were they. Candles were melted down and eaten; saltpetre from gunpowder was used as salt, although it caused such diarrhoea that most chose to live without this 'condiment'. On bad days, which were frequent, they had nothing to eat at all. On the countless journeys I made, I could count on one hand the number of times I was offered food or drink.

I could have told Napoleon; so could François and a hundred others. But if he would not listen to Murat, he was scarcely going to pay any heed to us. His priorities seemed to have gone astray also. While he spent every hour of the day at his desk, and much of every night, dictating orders to his overworked secretaries, he still somehow found two whole evenings to draw up new regulations for the Comédie Française. He also continued the daily parades in the Kremlin courtyard, handing out medals which were deserved, but of little use to men who had no bread to eat.

I do not think the emperor gave serious consideration to leaving until the snow that fell on the morning of the thirteenth of October. It was only a light dusting, melting under the warm sun, but its presence gave the lie to what everyone except Caulaincourt had been telling him, that the snow did not start in Moscow until mid-November.

Finally, detailed plans were made to move the wounded, more than twelve thousand of whom remained in the city. 'Too much time has already been wasted,' Napoleon declared. 'We must make haste to cope with the innumerable cares of so perilous a retreat.'

I rolled my eyes to hear his pronouncement, which should have been made weeks before, as it had for the casualties who had remained at Mojaisk and other locations to the west. To remain in Moscow as long as possible, though, seemed to have been Napoleon's heartfelt desire, even as he waited in vain for Alexander to sue for peace. I was reminded of a general I had heard recently talking to Caulaincourt. He had said quietly, 'In many a circumstance, to wish something and believe it are for the emperor one and the same thing.' I would have given it another name, I thought grimly: self-deception. And like it or no, we were all bound by Napoleon's wishes.

By the seventeenth, a general distribution was made to the army of leather, linen, bread and brandy. It was too little, too late, François said, especially for the low-rankers, who were throwing away everything that they could not use on the spot. On the eighteenth, morale dipped when the emperor suddenly abandoned his inspection of the daily Kremlin parade before he had seen even half of the assembled soldiers. His reason began to spread even as he retired to his quarters in Peter the Great's apartments.

'A surprise Russian attack has smashed apart not just Murat's cavalry, but Poniatowski's men too,' said François, who had heard it from a just-arrived messenger.

'And the casualties?' I asked, dreading the answer.

'Massive, by all accounts, including several generals. Dozens of guns have been lost. But for Murat, the mad bastard, the Russians would have cut the road to Moscow. He led two charges, despite being vastly outnumbered, and drove them back.'

We heard the effect this news had had on Napoleon before long. The departure of the Grande Armée, scheduled for the twentieth, was being brought forward to the next day.

Tomorrow, I thought with huge relief. Tomorrow we would quit this strange city. With the army in retreat, Bellamy, whom I had rarely seen, would hopefully have no cause to send me to the Russians with information. Even if he did want to, I would easily be able to avoid him as the various corps strung out along the road west. With luck, the same would apply to Féraud.

The first units set out at two in the morning on the nineteenth of October, with a constant stream following through the Kaluga Gate. By dawn, the sun promising another glorious day, the press was no better. Tens of thousands of men and hundreds of wagons would take all day and perhaps longer to quit the city, I decided. While the individual units assumed neat enough formations, everywhere else was chaos. It was not just the expatriate French who had decided to leave with the Grande Armée, but Germans, English and other nationalities. There were even Russians, who for whatever reason had thrown their lot in with the French.

I saw women, children, traders, hawkers of all kinds, and prostitutes. Hundreds of deserters, no longer wearing uniforms, were with them. There were servants, maids, sutlers and people of that sort. They were on foot, and in *kibitka* sledges and *droshkies*, Russian carriages, pulled by shaggy little cognats. Peasants pushed laden-down handcarts and barrows, while splendidly dressed ladies perched in elegant landaus. Literally thousands of these civilians had appeared, and they did not help the progress of the army column in any way. I searched for sight of Jeanne among them, but had no luck.

Beyond the gate – as an imperial messenger carrying dispatches, I had priority – the confusion was marginally better, but no less farcical. Thanks to the gold and silver items dangling from his crossbelts, every soldier clanked as he marched. Every back was bent under a knapsack packed to bursting point. Regimental baggage wagons were laden with non-regulation bundles, which explained the piles of discarded cannonballs and kegs of gunpowder I had spied in a quiet corner of the Kremlin. The horses pulling the artillery were in a pitiful state, barely able to perform what was expected of them. They would not last twenty miles, I thought, let alone the hundreds that lay between us and safety.

On a hilltop distance from the city, I reined in to take in the incredible sight. An immense caravan sprawled across the plain below, moving several vehicles abreast. Columns of horsemen and pedestrians spread out on either side, which, I thought, was all well and good when

214

there was space. But as soon as the road narrowed, passed through a defile or over a wooden bridge, or the ground became sandy or muddy, the entire procession would grind to a complete halt. The prospect of a Cossack attack would have upon this confusion was horrifying. François's warning came back to haunt me, and the odds of reaching Paris again, which I had considered at twenty to one, now seemed far too over-optimistic. I staved off my concerns with thoughts, however fanciful, of a return to England, and a successful life as the proprietor of an upmarket gambling salon.

Message delivered, I began to ride back towards Moscow, in search of Napoleon and his entourage. The sides of the road were already littered with discarded objects: framed pictures, candelabras and many books. Thinking there might be time to read in my blankets, I picked up volume after volume and leafed through them. There were editions of Voltaire, of Jean-Jacques Rousseau and Bouffon's *Natural History*, magnificently bound in red Morocco leather and gilded on their spines. The latter ran to more than thirty volumes. I kept one only, regretful I could not take more.

A mile down the road, my horse drew near to a number of light carts filled with exotically dressed men and women. They had stopped because one of their number had shed a wheel. I recognised Louise de Fusil at once, and then one of the actors who had been with Jeanne. A moment later, I was overjoyed to see her amid the group who was trying to lift up the side of the wagon. Several others waited with a large boulder, to balance the wheelless axle on.

'Unless you have a spare wheel, you are wasting your time,' I said loudly.

Louise de Fusil, who was directing the operation, threw me a glance. 'Why, monsieur?'

'There is no chance of finding a wheelwright in all this confusion, and if you wait too long here, thousands more people will get ahead of you. Just leave the wagon. Go.'

The group succeeded in balancing the axle on the boulder, but this, not flat enough at its base, simply tipped to one side. The wagon lurched downwards, the axle hitting the dirt with a dull thump. A couple of the men were lucky not to be injured as they scrambled back.

'Do not waste any more time,' I said, aiming my voice at the whole group. 'Load up the horse with what you need, and keep moving.'

Jeanne saw me now. She frowned. 'What are you doing here?'

'Carrying messages for the emperor, as usual. Lost wheel aside, are you well? Have you enough food and warm clothing?'

'I do not need your help, thank you.' She turned her back.

'Jeanne.'

She did not answer, but busied herself with beginning to unload the wheelless cart. Louise moved to aid her.

Jeanne would not take my assistance, I thought, but at least she and Louise were prepared to follow my advice. It was scant solace for my aching heart as I rode away.

CHAPTER XXIV

Borodino, 28 October 1812

I rode hunched, trying in vain to avoid the icy north wind. Furiously whirling snow into my face and eyes, coating my bearskin cloak white, it swept over me in a continuous, chilling wave. I was picking my way from Eugène's Corps' position, where I had carried a message the previous afternoon, towards the emperor's situation near the vanguard. To my right trudged a regiment of infantry, all semblance of order long vanished. The singing and good cheer of Moscow had been replaced by pinched cheeks and silence. The backpacks that had bulged with stolen riches now held essentials only. When a weakened man fell out of line – this happened with increasing frequency – one or two comrades would call out, encourage him not to give up. It was telling, though, how rare it was for anyone to actually aid the unfortunate concerned. Nine times out of ten, left, abandoned, he would sit down with a sigh, and watch his comrades – and his chance of survival – simply walk away.

I had learned to turn my head as I passed these wretches, and to block my ears to their piteous entreaties. There was little point in helping just one man, and I could not help them all. Every day of the nine since our departure from Moscow had been like this, and worse. I had seen burning villages light up the night, often with sleeping soldiers in the houses. Peasants rounded up and shot for the slightest of reasons. Foundered horses, still living, being cut up for meat. In the hospitals in Mojaisk, thousands of wounded men, emaciated and barely alive, their wounds undressed, surrounded by their own filth, their only food boiled cabbage stalks and raw horseflesh. Taking pity on their plight, the emperor had ordered them loaded into carts so they might be evacuated with the army.

Some would survive, I hoped, but if the story I had heard from François was anything to go by, they would have been better left for the Russians. Riding along a section of the column made up of wagons and caissons laden down with wounded, he had seen the drivers purposely driving over the roughest ground in order to rid themselves of the unfortunates with whom they had been saddled, and smile, as one would at a piece of luck, when a jolt would rid them of one, whom they knew would be crushed under a wheel if the horse did not step on him first. The plight of the wretches who survived this ordeal was little better, because the horses pulling their vehicles were commandeered by the artillery. François had wept to recount how he had ridden past these men, calling out in heart-rending tones that they too were Frenchmen, that they had been wounded fighting at our side, and begging tearfully not to be abandoned.

The withdrawal had not started out so badly, even taking into account the confusion of our departure. South we had travelled, not west. Napoleon had wanted to strike one more blow at the Russians, destroying the arms factory at Kaluga. The incredibly savage battle at Maloyaroslavets, a whole day and night of hand-to-hand-fighting, had put an end to that plan. The aftermath in the town the following day, the charred, calcinated remains of some of Eugène's Italians, had been as bad as Smolensk. Even the emperor had been shocked, and fortunate then, the next day, not to be captured during a surprise Russian attack.

The victory at Maloyaroslavets had been hollow, with Kutusov's army still blocking the route to Kaluga. Unusually, Napoleon had sought and taken the advice of his marshals, the decision meaning that for only the second time in his career, he was to retreat. Rather than aim for Smolensk via Medyn, however, a route that was three days shorter, he had opted to march north to Mojaisk, joining the road that the Grande Armée had used just two months earlier.

Mojaisk was an hour or more behind me now. Dread filled my belly, because that meant I was approaching Borodino. I shoved the thought away, and pulled my cloak tighter. 'Good boy,' I said to my horse, a shaggy little cognat I had ironically named Alexander. Tough and with seemingly endless supplies of energy, he existed on a fraction of the feed that Liesje had needed. Even though I could have taken him from his peasant owner without paying, as so many in the Grande Armée did, I had paid an exorbitant sum for him.

The ground, turned to a sea of mud by the torrential rain and now half-frozen, made for treacherous going, yet Alexander ploughed his way through, slow but sure. I patted his neck. Despite his steadiness, it would take much of the day to reach Napoleon. I thought of the letter inside my jacket, and frustration gnawed at me. The extended journey time between the various corps meant that orders were often irrelevant by the time they arrived. If the emperor noticed, he did not care, so my role and that of François continued to be ever-moving.

Time passed, and Alexander plodded on, avoiding the larger pieces of detritus cast away by the soldiers. I had long since given up looking at it. Fine porcelain, crystal glasses, books, even gold plates held no attraction, because they could not be eaten. A loaf of bread, though, or a hunk of cheese: my mouth watered at the thought. I was not alone in my hunger. It stalked through the ranks of the Grande Armée day and night. Constant vigilance was required in camps. To turn one's back risked losing saddlebags, which might contain food, or having the cookpot stolen from the tripod over the fire.

I reached under the bearskin to my pocket, and fumbled for the nub of pork knucklebone I had had from a kindly cantinière the night before. I had already sucked the marrow from it, the best part, but there were tags of gristle on one end to gnaw at. It would afford precious little nutrition, but was better than nothing, and served as a distraction from the cold.

I cast my gaze about. Although there had been no sign of any Cossacks, let alone Russian troops, for some days, I never let down my guard. Attention caught by some shapes on the horizon, I studied them closer. They were, I realised with horror, the former redoubts occupied by the Russians, now covered in snow. Shapeless hummocks now, they looked down on the vast solitude of the plain upon which the Grande Armée had formed. From the plain, so noisy and animated on that terrible day in September, came now only the relentless cawing of crows, immense flocks of which, I realised with disgust, were feeding on the still unburied corpses of the dead. I was used to the sight – they would rise, annoyed, from reddened patches of snow by the roadside as Alexander and I came near – but not in such numbers.

Closer I rode, unable to avoid the battlefield and the carrion crows. Soon Alexander was carrying me over the slain; to my left and right were thousands more. I did not want to look, but mesmerised by the horror, I could not stop myself. Many men as yet were hardly decomposed, and had kept what one might call a physiognomy. Almost all had their eyes fixedly open. Their beards had grown out of all measure for the epoch, and a bricklike and Prussian-blue colour, marbling their cheeks, gave them an abominably and messy aspect.

Close to the Great Redoubt, which rose like a pyramid in the midst of a desert, I remembered what I had lived through, and Liesje had not. Thankfully, snow covered the mounds of dead which still lay in front of the earthworks. I wiped away the tears that ran down my cheeks, before the wind had a chance to freeze them.

Seeing an object sticking up out the ground, something that was not a musket or a lance, I rode closer. It was a simple pine trunk, bearing a small noticeboard, on which was written in ink already half-effaced by the rain, these words: *Here lies General Montbrun. Passer-by, of whatever nation you may be, respect these ashes! They belong to the bravest soldier in the world. This feeble monument has been raised to him at the orders of his faithful friend the Marshal Ney.*

So many men had died here that day, I thought, so many brave men, and for what? The Grande Armée was marching back whence it had come, less than two months after the savage battle. Never had Napoleon's campaign seemed more pointless, and the situation was growing worse by the day. It would be a miracle if I survived. I thought sadly of my mother, sister, brother, and even my father, none of whom I would ever see again.

'Well, well,' said a familiar, mocking voice. 'If it isn't Dupont.'

To my surprise, Féraud was on foot. I glanced at the men with him, and seeing their hussar uniforms, realised they were among the many cavalry units whose horses were all dead. Rather than send the men back to France, as the valuable soldiers they were, Napoleon had ordered them to be equipped with muskets so they could fight as infantry.

'Féraud,' I said. 'You are still alive, I see.' I found myself pleased to see the gap-toothed corporal, even though he had also participated in the massacre of the French deserters.

Féraud glared. 'Are you not going to mock, call me a footslogger?'

'I am not. You must be mourning the loss of your horse. It was a noble creature.'

'It was.' The tiniest of nods.

Thinking he might let our feud go, I made to ride on.

'We have unfinished business still, you and I.'

'It does not have to be that way.' Nonetheless, I felt my left hand, which he could not see, move along the saddle towards one of my holstered pistols. Tempting though it was to shoot him down like a mad dog, yet again I shied away from the idea of murder. It was not as if I could get away with it; kill Féraud and the wrath of the corporal and Féraud's men would see me lying in the snow beside him.

'There has been enough slaughter here.' I waved a hand at a pile of nearby men, who were draped over and around each other in the emotionless embrace of death. 'Can we not put our disagreement behind us?'

'Will you apologise?'

'I have already done so,' I said, stung.

'Not in the courtyard of the imperial headquarters.'

Despite my best effort, my anger stirred. 'The only men who heard what I said to you are here, now. If anyone should hear me retract my words, it is they, not anyone else. You want a public humiliation – admit it!'

'Will you apologise or not? Wherever my hussars and I find ourselves encamped tonight will suffice.'

I pictured the scene. Scores, if not hundreds of men hunched around small fires, soldiers from every part of Napoleon's empire. Frenchmen, Italians, Croats, Poles, Germans, Dutch, even Spanish and Portuguese, none of whom knew me. I would probably never see any again either. Do it, I thought, and Féraud will have no reason to continue this ridiculous feud. I took a deep breath. 'Very well.'

His face was the picture of surprise. 'Really?'

'I said yes, didn't I?' Irritation had joined my anger. I added, 'There is a small chance I might be sent out again when I reach the imperial headquarters. In that case, I will find you again the following evening.'

He smirked, curse him, and I was sure he muttered the words 'stupid coward' to his corporal.

Just like that, the red mist descended. I had not the strength to resist it. 'What did you say?'

Now his expression was all innocence. 'I said nothing.'

'You called me a stupid coward!' My gaze moved to the corporal; his surprise told me everything I needed to know. 'Didn't you, Féraud? Have you forgotten that I faced you in the Bois de Boulogne, and again at Smolensk?'

He shrugged. 'Nonetheless, you were trying to weasel out of fighting me, just as you did at Vilna.'

'I am sick of this! Let us fight, here and now.' I leaped off my horse, and handed the reins to one of the startled hussars. I tugged out a pistol, my favourite of the pair, and turned to face Féraud. 'Well? Are *you* to play the coward now?'

That pricked him. 'Here is as good a place as any,' he snarled.

We found a little piece of flat ground. While Féraud and I glared at each other, several of the hussars gently moved aside corpses, muskets and pieces of discarded equipment. The corporal scraped two lines in the snow twenty paces apart. As we took up our positions, the whirling snow parted to reveal the nearest section of the column. It had come to a halt. Curiosity had trumped misery; men wanted to watch our duel.

I was dimly aware that this was further proof of how stupid our quarrel was, but still enraged, I was not about to back out. It was time to pluck the thorn from my flesh that was Féraud once and for all.

There was no preamble, other than to agree we would take as many shots as necessary to end the duel. Like me, Féraud also wanted to end the vendetta. We faced one another. He was looking in the direction of the march; I, whence we had come.

The corporal, standing between us and a little to the side, had fished out a grubby handkerchief. He held it up. 'Cock your weapons, and take aim, sirs,' he said.

I drew back the curved metal that held the flint, and levelled my pistol at Féraud. This duel was different from the previous ones. My hand was steady, my aim sure. The reason why was clear. My mind was full of the horrors of the previous few months. During that time, I had killed men in cold blood and during a battle. Now Féraud had to die, or he would plague me forever.

For the fourth time, I stared at the black, death-giving end of his pistol. At last fear uncoiled in my belly, but my resolve did not waver even a fraction.

'Ready, sirs?' The corporal's voice seemed far away.

'Yes,' I said loudly.

'I am,' said Féraud.

'When the handkerchief falls, you may shoot.'

This time I welcomed the greatest test of the duellist. Breath in, breath out. On the edge of my vision, the little square of off-white that

222

was the corporal's kerchief. Down the length of my pistol, and twenty paces further, Féraud's weapon, his hard eyes, his side-on shape. I would shoot for his chest, I decided. He was an arrogant bastard, but an honourable one. He deserved a quick death.

Beneath my boots, I felt a tremor in the frozen ground. Hooves, I thought.

My attention shifted; my eyes searched the terrain behind Féraud. Nothing. Back to him they went, quickly. He had not reacted in any way. I focused on him again, took first pressure on the trigger.

The handkerchief dropped. I had time to think that but for its grubbiness, it would have been impossible to see against the snow.

Féraud's lips peeled back.

I tightened my grip on the trigger.

Behind my opponent, the shape of a Cossack materialised out of the white. In he thundered on a mean, raw-boned little horse with an unkempt mane, his lance aimed squarely at Féraud's back.

I did not think. 'Féraud! Down!'

He heard, and threw himself forwards onto his face.

The Cossack filled the space where he had been. I pulled the trigger. Smoke and flame. The pistol kicked in my hand, and the Cossack was driven from his saddle, lance falling from slack fingers.

Another Cossack appeared out of nowhere, and made for the corporal, who grabbed for his sword.

There would be more. I sprinted for Féraud. Alone, we had no chance, but together, we might make it back to the column.

He was on his feet already. Calmly, he shot the Cossack threatening his corporal. 'Take his horse!' he shouted.

I snatched up the lance belonging to the man I had killed. It was a crude long pole with a sort of nail at its point, but it was better than nothing.

Two more Cossacks galloped in. Féraud waited until they were close, fifteen paces away, and then threw his pistol. It spun through the air and hit the man in the face. Yelping with pain, he hauled his cognat around and rode away. I levelled my lance at the Cossack coming at me. My bowels lurched; facing a charging cavalryman on foot, even with a weapon, was ball-clenchingly terrifying.

Crack. Crack, crack. Musket balls whistled through the falling snow. The soldiers in the column had seen what was happening, and were raining down protective fire. We were at the limit of musket range, but horses were large targets.

The Cossack whirled about and rode away. His dozen comrades, who would have ridden in on us and finished the job, also turned tail.

Ragged cheering carried from the column.

'Get over here!' shouted Féraud at his corporal; he had failed to catch the Cossack's mount. We would be better three together than men apart.

Féraud and I stared at each other. 'The duel?' I asked. 'Do you wish to continue?'

His moustache twitched, and then, remarkably, he began to laugh.

I could not help but join in. The corporal looked at us as if we were mad.

'What kind of a creature would I be, Dupont, to shoot the man who had saved my life?'

'It would be a curious decision,' I agreed.

'And we have enough enemies in the Russians.' He stuck out his hand.

We shook. His grip was firm, and his gaze, meeting mine, was level. Féraud, I decided, was a man I could trust.

It was a good feeling.

'Sir.' The corporal's voice was uneasy. 'We had best get back. The Cossacks are circling.'

I looked, and saw that he was right. Féraud laughed uproariously at my next comment that it would be stupid to die on the end of a lance. Quickly, I retrieved Alexander, who had shied away a little distance, and we made our way back to the column.

CHAPTER XXV

I woke on the morning of the eighth of November, snug and warm in my cashmere shawls and bearskin. On either side, packed as tight as meat in one of the new-fangled cans I had heard about, were François and another comrade, both snoring like lords. There was a wall to my right, and a couple of feet above me, through the warm fug of our exhaled breath, the part-collapsed roof of a cottage came angling down to the dirt floor. This situation now counted as luxury accommodation; most men continued to sleep outdoors, often with no cover other than their greatcoats.

I had spent several nights in the last seven doing the same. They had been hellish experiences, hunched in front of fires that were difficult to keep alight, and which barely warmed us at all. Sometimes there had been nothing to eat, at others a couple of biscuits made from groats and straw, baked in the ashes, or a few mouthfuls of watery pottage made from cabbage stalks and tallow candle stumps, with a pinch of salty gunpowder added to give it flavour.

The lack of shelter had been brutal, the biting wind able to find me even under my bearskin. Frozen on one side, scorched on the other, suffocated by the gusting smoke, alarmed by the roar of the wind as it tore through the trees of the dense woods nearby, I had suffered as never before. And yet I had been fortunate, because I lived to tell the tale. Every day there had been several in the company who had frozen to death where they sat, and since the steep drop in temperature two nights before, the numbers of casualties had soared. Each morning, hundreds upon hundreds of soldiers simply never woke up again.

The suffering of the poor horses, emaciated from lack of food, sliding all over the ice on their iron shoes, was also tremendous. During the first real overnight freeze a couple of nights before, during which two feet of snow had fallen, thousands died, many still in the traces of their wagons. Any cavalry regiments still with mounts had simply ceased to exist. Only the sturdiest French horses remained, and of course tough little cognats like Alexander, who were used to the harsh conditions.

The catastrophic losses meant that most of the guns, carriages and wagons had had to be abandoned. The bitter truth of this very advice, given to Napoleon by Caulaincourt and other senior officers before the departure from Moscow, was now all too evident. On the roadsides, the stiff-angled, half-butchered horse carcasses had been joined by innumerable carriages and gun caissons, carts, kibitkas and droshkies. The noise of explosions, as powder wagons were blown up, was common.

Eleven days had passed since my bizarre encounter with Féraud on the grisly battlefield at Borodino. I had not met him since; nor had I seen Jeanne. There was little chance of meeting either in the straggling confusion that the army had become, but my job as an imperial messenger had also changed. The emperor had finally recognised the futility of dispatching orders to distant parts of the column. In the treacherous conditions – snow, ice, frozen mud, Cossacks, the westward-moving mob that jammed the road – messengers were almost guaranteed to fail to reach their destination. Survival was also far from guaranteed, whether the death came from Cossacks or one of our own. As food and means of transport grew ever scarcer, robbery and murder had become daily occurrences.

I wriggled my toes, grateful that they were warm, and that I could still feel them. This time before we had to get up was to be relished. I considered the last few days, when François and I and our comrades had been used to carry orders short distances. For the most part, however, we were useless hangers-on, spectators to the unfolding disaster that was the Grande Armée's retreat.

Inevitably, thoughts of Jeanne surfaced. Where was she, I wondered, worry tickling me. According to Louise de Fusil, whom I had seen several days before in an officer's carriage, the group of actors and actresses which she and Jeanne had been a part of had been separated during the fighting around Gzhatsk on the second of November. Louise had no idea where Jeanne was now. Powerless, I tried to put her from my mind, but I could not. Too many of the stiff, frozen corpses I had seen recently had been civilians.

I had to act, I decided. I could not save myself and not at least try to find her. François might offer to come with me, the great heart, but

I would not let him. My life was my own to throw away; I would not have his on my conscience.

By mid-afternoon, I had covered perhaps eight miles. It was reasonable progress, but there had been no sign of Jeanne amid the tide of miserable humanity that was slowly making its way west. I could have continued, but finding shelter before darkness fell was critical. As luck would have it, I encountered a group of Polish lancers, one of whom recognised me. A lieutenant, he said I had brought their commander a message near Smolensk, back in August. I was happy to agree, although I could not remember. When I mentioned needing a place to sleep, the hospitable lieutenant insisted that I join him and his men.

We rode away from the road – there had been reports of a village some two miles away – and finding the hamlet, surrounded it. Nervous, for I was sure the lancers were about to engage in a massacre, I watched in amazement as the lieutenant made a deal with the fearful peasants. No harm would be done to a soul, he declared in acceptable Russian; in return, the lancers asked only for shelter and a little food.

Grateful, almost ecstatic that they were not to suffer the same fate as so many others, the peasants welcomed us into their homes, and made room in the barns for the horses. Famished as I was, the greasy mutton stew given us that night was the finest meal I could remember eating in many days. Fed hay that was only a little mouldy, Alexander was well content also.

Sad to leave the Polish lancers the next morning as we rejoined the road, I nonetheless continued on my journey. 'She must be a wonderful woman,' the lieutenant called after me; I had related my tale over a capful of his fiery aquavit the night before. 'She is!' I shouted back, praying that I managed to find Jeanne, first alive, and then unharmed.

On I rode, through the half-frozen mud, past abandoned wagons, overturned guns and the carcasses of more unfortunate horses. The sinister activities of the clouds of carrion crows which shadowed the Grande Armée were areas of messy, reddened snow from which protruded the hideous remains of half-eaten corpses, but there were too many even for the birds to consume. My queasiness returned; I brought up the mouthful of water I had drunk a short time before.

Several miles later, however, my belly, which had had nothing since the previous night's stew, had recovered enough to register its hunger. François had given me some figs, as well as a pistol, powder and ball. I ate two of the fruit, but saved the rest. There was no guarantee when I would next find food.

To my surprise, I came upon a natural break in the raggletaggle column; the last stragglers told me the reason was an artillery caisson behind them, which had broken a narrow plank bridge over a stream. The water was not deep; some people were fording it, but anyone with a vehicle – and unprepared to abandon it – was stranded on the far bank. Engineers were coming to repair the bridge, apparently, but no one knew how long they would be.

Deciding that I would ride across, and bizarrely optimistic that Jeanne would be among the crowds waiting for the engineers, I let Alexander pick his way along the welcomely empty road. The only figure coming towards me was a carabinier, for some reason marching alone. Relaxing a little, I fell to imagining Jeanne's reaction to seeing me. I decided that coming back to find her would surely count for more than what she thought I had done to Dupont. *Or it might not*, the little devil taunted. In that case, I thought, I would tell her the truth. In this world where death beckoned at every turn, the risk of revealing what Bellamy had forced me to do seemed almost inconsequential.

I sensed a flicker of movement at the corner of my vision. My head turned. There were Cossacks in the woods to my left, and to my horror, also amid the trees to my right. The air filled with their bloodcurdling war cry, which for all the world sounded like 'Hurrah!' I glanced behind me, and decided the people I had spoken to were further than the stream, visible about a quarter of a mile away. I jabbed Alexander with my heels, something I had never done. Startled, he jinked, and I did it again. 'Move!' I shouted. 'Move!'

Three Cossacks emerged from the cover on the left. I saw them gallop towards the carabinier, who had a bandage encasing his entire head. To my shame, I felt relief not to be their target. It was not as if my intervention would make any difference to his fate. Drawing a pistol, and cocking it with difficulty with my gloved hand, I kept Alexander aimed towards the stream. The Cossacks on the right were still shadowing me, choosing their moment to block my path. I wondered what the odds were of fighting through, but shoved the idea away.

228

An awful cry of pain.

I could not help myself. I looked back. A Cossack had thrust his lance into the carabinier, and as I watched, one of his comrades did the same. Poor bastard, I thought, and rode on. To my surprise, a fierce battle cry then ripped the air.

'*Vive l'Empereur!*' cried the carabinier. '*Vive l'Empereur!*' He had drawn his sword, and using it as a staff, had regained his feet. Blade held high, he continued to roar his defiance at the Cossacks.

My heart stirred at the sight, and I pulled on the reins. 'Whoa, Alexander. We have some business before we ford the stream.' Turning, I judged the distance to the carabinier and his enemies about two hundred paces. Effective pistol range was a fifth of that, probably less. By the time we got that close, it would be too late, but I had to help the courageous wretch. 'Hold on,' I shouted. 'Hold on!'

I prayed for him as we trotted closer. I roared and shouted every insult I could think of in Russian, calling the Cossacks cowardly bitch's gets, yellow-livered spawn of the Devil, murderers of innocent women and children, hoping my rage would put them off. All the while, the carabinier, leaning like a man on a canted ship's deck, kept swinging and slashing at the circling riders. Any time they got near, he would scream and spit, actually spit at them.

At fifty paces, I fired at the nearest Cossack. I missed, but he heard the loud crack, and noticeably flinched. Shoving that pistol into its holster, I drew my second, and somehow managed to cock it with my teeth. The freezing metal tore away sections of my lips.

'*Vive l'Empereur!*' I roared, my voice cracking. Alexander pulled on the reins, eager to play his part. At thirty paces, I pulled the trigger. Misfire. Rage filled me. I had no time to draw and cock François's weapon, so I jammed the useless pistol back into the holster and drew my sword instead.

It might as well have been a stick – I was useless with a blade – but the Cossacks did not know that.

With fierce hurrahs, waving their lances in the air, they rode away.

'You took your time,' said the carabinier. 'In fact, you nearly didn't come at all.'

I flushed. He had seen me ride past. 'I'm sorry.'

He laughed, a real belly laugh, and said, 'You came, though. That is all that matters. I am grateful.'

'How badly are you hurt?' There was blood on his greatcoat, over where his hip would be, and one of his trouser legs was sodden red. Icicles hung from his beard; his face was smoke-blackened, and burnt in places.

'They are pricks only, I think. If there is one small mercy about the Cossacks, it is that they use those stupid lances with nails at the end.' He gestured behind me. 'I think we have more to worry about over there.'

Six Cossacks had ridden out of the trees on the right, deciding it was their turn with us. Their hurrahs carried, sinister and menacing.

'We will never make it to the stream,' I said, thinking, if I am to die now, at least it will be alongside a brave man.

'That is true.' He had sat down in the snow and was loading his musket as if we had all the time in the world.

I chuckled, and did the same with my pistol. There was even time to empty out the pan of the one that had misfired, and clumsily refill it.

The carabinier gave me an appraising look. 'Three pistols and a musket? Maybe we have a chance.'

That was when another five Cossacks joined the half dozen. A great hurrah went up.

'Why do they cheer so?' I snarled. 'Hurrah?'

'Someone told me it means "death" in their language,' said the carabinier.

'That seems apt,' I said in disgust. 'This cursed country, eh? Oh to be in France again!' Or England, I thought. I would have more chance of survival there.

'I could not agree more.'

Once more I resigned myself to death.

A drum roll.

My heart leaped.

In the distance, where the bridge was, a little line of infantry had appeared. Only ten or twelve men, but they were advancing towards us, a beating drum their accompaniment. They had seen our plight.

A volley rang out, aimed at the enemy riders. The muskets were firing at the extreme limit of their range, but it was enough discouragement. Shouting a few insults, the Cossacks vanished into the trees.

'God does not want us to die now, my friend,' said the carabinier, crossing himself.

I grinned at him like a fool. 'It seems not.'

The brown-haired carabinier's name was Théophile Louvel, and he was from the far west of Brittany. A career soldier, he had served under Napoleon since the heady days in Italy, more than fifteen years before. Slightly rotund, something that was serving him in good stead, he told me, what with the lack of food, he had been injured in the head during the defence of an abbey at Kolotskoïe some days before. Left with the seriously wounded, he had soon realised that to stay behind was to die.

'You've heard what the Russians do to their prisoners?' he asked.

I nodded. Mutilation, being buried alive or used as target practice, the list went on.

'Aye, well, I wasn't wanting that, so I decided to follow my unit, catch up to them if I could.'

'And the broken bridge?'

A snort. 'I wasn't going to freeze my balls off waiting for the engineers. I scrambled across easily enough.'

I smiled. Théophile was a man after my own heart. He had let me examine his wounds, and not complained at all. He had been correct about the Cossacks' lances; his multiple layers of clothing had also protected him. His hip wound was only a scratch. The one on his leg was the more serious, a deep laceration that would bleed with each step. I had bound it up with half of my spare scarf, and now I insisted he travel on Alexander.

'I cannot take your horse.'

'You're not taking him,' I snapped. 'You are riding him, while I lead. Get up.'

He did not demur, instead accepting my help to mount.

'This is the wrong direction,' he said as I took the reins and began to walk toward the stream and the shattered bridge.

'That is the only condition of accompanying me.'

'Are you crazy?'

'You saw the route I was travelling. Nothing has changed.'

'What is the point of taking a message that way? You will never make it back to the emperor.' I had told him I was a messenger.

'I am not carrying any letters.'

'You are entirely mad then.'

I did not answer.

'A comrade or a woman then . . .' He studied my face. 'Aha! It is for a woman that you are throwing away your life, and mine.'

I gave him a look. 'Get off Alexander right now, if you wish. Make your own way west.'

He glowered; we both knew he could not walk far or fast enough. Rather than dismount, he let out a long, theatrical sigh. 'So what is her name, Monsieur Dupont, this paragon of beauty?'

'Jeanne. Jeanne Drouin. You might know her as the actress Mademoiselle Préville.'

'No! I saw her several times in Moscow. She is magnificent!'

'She is.' I thought of kissing her, and how good it had felt.

'Is that where you met?'

'I knew her in Paris.'

A disbelieving look. 'And you joined the Grande Armée to follow her?'

'In a manner of speaking.' Decent though Louvel seemed, I was not about to tell him my life history, and certainly nothing about Bellamy.

'And you and she were . . .?' One eyebrow rose.

'We were close, but . . . we did not part on good terms in Moscow.'

Louvel whistled. 'Two paramours who quarrelled, and were separated by war. Quite the love story!'

'All I need to do is find her now.'

'We shall find her together, God willing.'

But we did not. Not on the other side of the stream, nor in the five miles after. We spent that night huddled in the ruins of a peasant's cottage, lucky to find a group of men who still recognised authority – my imperial messenger's satchel enough proof that I was on the emperor's business. They had no food to share, but the shelter of the walls, the little fire they had, and my bearskin kept me and Louvel alive overnight. The heat radiating from Alexander, brought inside so he was not stolen, helped also.

My first choice, the small house nearby still with its roof, proved no better than our own accommodation. The officers within, who had refused us entry, were unable to prevent freezing soldiers outside from tearing off every last roof slat to use as firewood. As a result, their night was more miserable than our own.

The next dawn was even colder; it seemed that the partial melt of the day before had been a freak occurrence. The mud, fresh-churned into deep new ruts by the wagons, was again hard as stone, and doubly treacherous with it. A simple misstep for man or beast could result in a bad sprain, or even broken bones. The entire column of men and vehicles was also moving in the opposite direction to our own, which meant that the slopes they descended were the ones we had to climb, each now coated by a lethal, shining layer of ice.

Exhaustion threatened with the ascents, because our footholds had to be stamped out before taking another, and the injured Louvel was incapable of doing this. Considering the pain he must have been in, he did well just to follow in my steps, holding onto Alexander's tail for balance. Our speed that of snails, falling twenty times on every slope, we persevered. The descents were a little easier, although undignified. I learned to sit on my arse, and slide down the ice, using my bootheels as brakes. Louvel did the same, but a lot more slowly, while Alexander, stoic and stolid, his reins at their maximum length, walked down behind the pair of us.

Those who had succumbed lay everywhere: frozen and dead by the sides of the road, and often in the middle of it too; but at the bottom of the slopes, to my dismay, they were alive. Soldiers, horseless cavalrymen, artillerymen, civilians, deserters, drummer boys, no one was immune. French, Polish, German, Italian, Dutch, Spanish, Croat, Russian, they all fell victim to the brutal conditions. Many pleaded for help, or cried from the pain of their broken limbs, but it was surprising how many just lay there, eyes dull, the only signs of life the plumes of breath leaving their open mouths.

I tried to look at no one, save those who were women, to check that each unfortunate was not Jeanne, but to try to take in the vastness of the horror risked losing my wits.

A couple of hours into our journey, Louvel declared it too dangerous to continue. Great bands of Cossacks were on both sides of the road, and bold enough to charge in now and again, probing for weaknesses in the raggletaggle lines of soldiers and civilians. It was ridiculous, I said to Louvel, how much fear they could cause given how easily they fled if men stood up to them.

'The French soldier is easily demoralised,' he replied. 'Four cavalrymen on his flank terrify him more than a thousand in front. If we continue, Dupont, death is the only certainty. We must turn back, and aim for Smolensk. Place your trust in God; He will protect Mademoiselle Préville.'

This approach was far too vague, far too trusting, but as the daylight leached from the sky and the temperature began to plummet, I had to concede defeat.

If I had thought to find warmth and safety in Smolensk three days later, I was sorely mistaken. The fire-blackened remains of the city were covered in snow, the domes of the venerable cathedral rising majestically amid heaps of ruins. Most of the Grande Armée had reached it before us. Any supplies were long gone, taken first by the Imperial Guard and bands of stragglers and deserters, the latter creeping through holes in the walls at night to raid the stores, and secondly by the arriving soldiers to whom the foodstuffs rightfully belonged.

With the city gates shut by those within, most of the army had been forced to sleep outside. Miserable bivouacs set in deep snow, sometimes in the ruins or courtyards of burnt-out houses, or amid heaps of Russian dead from the battle in August, marked where they had set up camp. With barely any food, and the only fuel the debris of weapons, caissons, guncarriages, it was small wonder that large numbers perished in the intense cold. The survivors resembled thousands of ghosts, enraged by hunger, and a man risked his life going among them alone or unarmed.

Deaths among the civilian hangers-on, who were entitled to nothing from the army stores, had been even more catastrophic. I spent half a day wandering around Smolensk, turning over corpses, staring into waxen, frozen faces, and calling in vain for Jeanne among the living. I asked everyone I encountered, describing her as best I could. The ones who claimed to have seen her I did not believe, not least because they promised she was just a short distance away, and demanded food before they took me there.

'She is dead,' Louvel told me sadly. 'Best forget her, and concentrate on surviving yourself.'

Maddened, obsessed, I did not listen. Rather than follow Napoleon and the imperial household, who had already departed Smolensk, I had asked permission to stay with Marshal Ney, who was again to take up the rearguard. I would act as a messenger for Ney's corps, I told Caulaincourt before he left. Preoccupied by his workload, and, I suspect, thinking like Louvel that I sought a woman, he had granted my request without question.

François, with whom there had been a brief reunion, told me that I was insane. I replied with a vacant smile, and said I would see him in Paris. Having both heard the rumour that casualties had reached thirty thousand since leaving Moscow – one third of the Grande Armée – we knew it for a lie. The real figure had to be higher. There was no benefit in saying so, however, so we embraced sadly, and parted.

My quest was almost hopeless, even I knew that. A large number of the civilians with the army, including the actress Louise de Fusil, had departed with the emperor. There was no way of knowing if Jeanne was with them. It was better, I told Louvel, to stay behind and keep up my search, than return to Moscow and find that she was not with the vanguard.

Even if that means losing your life? he demanded.

I nodded.

'Forgive me, but I will not be accompanying you.'

'I would not expect you to.' He had found a handful of his unit.

He kissed me on each cheek, solemnly, and wringing my hand, wished me Godspeed.

I had known Louvel for less than a week, but there were tears in my eyes as I watched him hobble away.

CHAPTER XXVI

Laid low by a fever that evening – a result, perhaps of the ordeal I had been through with Louvel – I was fortunate enough to be carried, insensible, into one of Smolensk's churches. I had vague memories of seeing an altar, candles burning, and lines of wounded, before I slipped away.

Waking I knew not how long later, my ears ringing with shouts, I struggled back to consciousness. Hunger racked my frame; my mouth was dry, clothing damp with sweat. I was lying on a thin blanket, a fold of which had been laid on top of me. I managed to get up on an elbow. On either side, filling the entire church, were scores of wounded and dying men. The air, rippling with their soft moans and gasps, reeked; an unpleasant combination of unwashed bodies and putrefaction. Of surgeons or orderlies, there was no sign.

The shouting continued; it was outside on the street, officers issuing orders. I could hear the tramp of feet, and the creak of wagons. The city was being abandoned. There could be no other conclusion, and the unfortunates in the makeshift hospital – I among them – were being left behind.

I got to my stockinged feet, wincing at the icy cold emanating from the flagstones. My boots were nowhere to be seen, and my bearskin had also been taken. My heart sank. To go out without a cloak or shoes was one of the quickest paths to frostbite, gangrene and death.

Affixed to a nearby pillar was a handwritten notice. Curious, I walked towards it. As I passed, a soldier lifted an arm in supplication. 'Water,' he croaked. 'Please.'

I clasped his hand, which was fever-hot, then laid it on his chest. The smell rising from the stump of his left leg was horrendous. 'I will get some if I can.'

He smiled and closed his eyes.

The sheet of paper on the pillar was in three languages, French, Polish and Russian. The men within this building were soldiers, casualties of war, it said, begging that they should be treated with compassion. It was signed by Dr Larrey, Napoleon's chief surgeon.

The notice would make no difference. Anyone still here when the Russians arrived would receive either a swift death, or one from neglect. I had no intention of staying to find out which it would be. First, I needed footwear. Without that, I might as well lie back down among the wounded and wait for the end. An image of Alexander came to mind, and forgetting that I was in a church, I spat a savage curse. It was not just my boots that had been stolen; Alexander would also be gone.

I was without cloak, shoes, weapons or a horse, in a city that was being abandoned to the advancing Russians. The complete hopelessness of my situation sank in. So did the realisation that I had no chance of survival, let alone seeing my family again. I staggered to the altar, weeping, and fell on my knees. Head propped against the stone, I gave into despair, sobbing like a baby. My breaths juddered in and out, my ribcage heaved. Soon my nose was blocked; snot ran down my chin unchecked, hanging in strings that reached halfway to the floor.

'M-mother.' The voice was so weak and distorted I only heard it because my crying had eased. 'Mother . . .'

I looked. A young soldier lay near me on his back. If he had had a blanket, it had been stolen. Missing a leg like the thirsty man, he had also lost an arm; whatever had done that to him had in addition ripped away a good part of his face. Charpee dressings covered his limb wounds, but there was nothing covering the red, oozing ruin that had been his right cheek. The jawbone, half his teeth and the side of his tongue were all exposed.

I palmed away the snot, self-conscious, and crept over to him.

He sensed me coming; his head turned.

Bile surged up my throat. The canister shot, for it must have been something like that, had shredded both of his eyeballs. It was a miracle he was still alive.

'Mo-therrr.' The word came out slowly. He was near the end.

Thinking of my own mother, I gave his hand a gentle squeeze, and whispered, 'I am here.'

The corners of his mouth twitched. 'Mo . . .' he began, but the rest of the word never came. A rattling gasp left his lips, and he was still.

I cried again then, not for myself, but for the poor boy – he could not have been more than sixteen – who had died wanting only his mother's comfort.

I muttered a prayer, the best I could do, and got up. My chances of living were vanishingly slim, but I was not ready to join the boy, or even those who yet breathed in the church. Remembering the man who had asked for water, I scooped some from the font, and carrying it in my cupped hands, went to find him. He was dead. I had no time for more grief. Drinking the water myself, I returned to the font and quenched my thirst. God would forgive me, I decided.

Next, I went up and down the lines of casualties. Few were conscious, which was a relief. I hoped their sleep became a permanent one, and before the Russians entered the church. To the ones who realised I was there, I whispered words of comfort; I fetched water for two, and said that I hoped food would be coming soon. It was not a complete lie.

Not a single one of the wounded had a decent pair of shoes or boots, which was unsurprising. The surgeons and orderlies would have stripped them of such valuable items before leaving. I found a fox fur lined cap, though, and unwrapped a blood-encrusted silk scarf from around the chest of a corpse. I stripped several more of their clothing, donning three pairs of trousers – one of blue broadcloth – and four shirts. I tore up another dead man's trousers into lengths of fabric that I could wrap around my hands in place of gloves. My left foot, wrapped like my right in more lengths of fabric, I shoved into a large boot that was missing a heel; on my other foot went a shoe with no laces. These were woefully inadequate for the conditions that awaited me outside, but were better than nothing.

I selected a musket from the stack in the porch of the church, and rummaged among the cartridge pouches there for ball and powder. I also took a bayonet, but there were no pistols, sadly. Mine had no doubt gone with whoever had taken Alexander. I judged by the powder in the pan that the musket was loaded, but I wanted to leave nothing to chance. I cocked it, aimed at the ceiling and pulled the trigger. Fire and smoke belched, and the ball smacked into a wooden rafter far above. Carefully, I reloaded it, and then, fox fur cap jammed on, bloody scarf wrapped around my face, blanket part-cloaking the rest of my body, I heaved open the door. A blast of frozen air struck with the force of a physical blow.

God help me, I thought.

The sight that met me outside was truly horrible, and almost made me forget the cold. Hearing their comrades leaving, the strongest of the injured had managed to leave the church before I had come to. Weakened, emaciated, they had not gone far. They lay in the ice and snow, mostly dead. Not all had succumbed, though. Noticing my approach, a hussar with a belly wound pleaded that I should take him with me. 'Do not leave me for those Russian animals,' he cried. 'I beg you, please!'

I did not have the stomach to put a bullet in his head. Muttering an apology – which felt vile, because I was passing a death sentence – I stepped around him.

Already my toes were tingling, and losing sensation. I had to find footwear, I decided, before I left Smolensk. Venture onto the open road as I was, and I would suffer severe frostbite. That would guarantee my death.

I scouted in vain along the main street, and soon began to think that I would also die here. Quite by chance my gaze fell on an alleyway to my right, and a little way within, a shape slumped against the wall of a house. There were boots on the ends of his legs, and so I hurried towards him.

By his fine uniform, the man was a general. To my surprise, he was alive, his chest rising and falling faintly. He was missing an arm, so must have been in the hospital, I decided. All senior officers had been evacuated, however – I had seen none among the wounded – which made me think he must somehow have been missed when the surgeons were leaving. He had followed, and unable to keep up, had crept into the alley for shelter.

I hesitated, torn. If I took his boots, which looked to be my size, he had no way of walking out of Smolensk, other than taking my pathetic footwear. Ruthlessness came to the fore. He was going nowhere. I stooped and tugged at his right boot, glancing all the while at his face, and hoping he would not wake. His chin lifted a little, and he made an incomprehensible sound, but the boot came off cleanly. Joy filled me – not only was the boot lined with fur, but he was wearing a long cotton sock. I peeled that off as well. When I laid his foot on the cold ice, his eyelids fluttered.

'What are you doing?' he mumbled.

I said nothing, concentrating on removing the other boot and sock.

'Stop.'

I pretended not to hear.

A whisper. 'Can you not leave me to die in peace?'

'Mon géneral,' I said, 'I would be quite happy to, but another will take your boots if I do not, and I prefer it to be me.'

His head sank down on his chest. Even as I sat alongside him, stripped off my boot and shoe and donned my new replacements, he said not another word. I stood, and picked up my musket.

'Shoot me.' He had rallied the last of his energy, and was looking into my face.

I managed to meet his gaze. 'I cannot, sir.'

'You would steal my boots and socks, yet you will not end my suffering?'

I walked away, his pleas filling my ears.

My degradation continued. A short time later, inside another makeshift church-hospital, I found a colonel in a fine fur cloak. Half propped up against a pillar, he had a terrible sabre cut that had sliced off one ear, and carrying down, smashed his clavicle and cut deep into his chest. It was a miracle he was still alive, but the faint clouds that left his nostrils every so often proved he had not yet departed this world. I made no attempt at conversation, simply undoing the buttons at the neck, and beginning to ease it out from behind him.

'Peste, I'm not dead yet.'

I jumped. Leaning over him as I was, the words had been whispered almost into my ear. Stricken by my conscience, which was still smarting from my encounter with the general, I stood up. 'My apologies, sir. I will wait.'

His lips twitched into the semblance of a smile.

Rather than stand by his side, I began to search for supplies and clothing. To my delight, this hospital had been less well emptied, perhaps because the surgeons and orderlies had departed in a panic. I replaced the innermost of my trousers with a woollen pair taken from a still-warm corpse. The crusted blood around the groin did not dismay me at all. To this I added a bearskin shako that had somehow rolled into a corner and not been seen, a flannel shirt, then a sheepskin waistcoat, and treasure of treasures, a pair of mitts made of the same material. Returning to the colonel, I was relieved to find that he had expired.

Suddenly feeling like a grave-robber, I asked for his forgiveness, and God's, as I took the cloak. I laid him down flat, crossed his arms across his chest, and closed his eyes. It was a pathetic attempt to restore normalcy to the macabre situation.

I had no food, but buoyed up by the flask of brandy that I had also found, and not wanting to fall any further behind the army, I made my way to the town's front gate. Again I had to run the gauntlet of the wounded and incapacitated. Blocking my ears to their entreaties, I set out on the road west.

I did not look back.

A day passed. I had had several near escapes, hiding amid the trees as Cossacks rode by, and spent a night alone, teeth chattering, in a half-collapsed cottage. I was still alive, however, and making better speed than most of the rabble that continued to struggle westward. Reaching a nameless village – I found out later it was called Korytnia – I walked through slush that stank of brandy. Apparently there had been so much of it in the smashed-up shops that the vanguard had poured onto the ground that which they could not drink. Shaking my head at the waste, I continued west. The sound of cannon fire directly in my path filled me with dread, but I did not stop. It was one thing to spend a night on my own off the road, quite another to strike out into the wilderness cross country. If the Cossacks did not get me, the cold and hunger would.

The press of people grew greater and greater, until at last I was forced to a halt. Fear was writ large on every face; many of the women were weeping. A baby bawled its distress; there seemed no one to soothe it. I picked my way through the throng, glad I had no pack for someone to cut off me. Ever alert, I regularly slapped away hands that came sliding in under my cloak, searching for something, anything to steal. In my right hand, I gripped my bayonet, ready to fight if needs be. It did not come to that, for which I was glad. It was one thing to walk away from a dying man, to take his boots or cloak, and quite another to stick a comrade in the guts, even if he was trying to steal from me.

241

Reaching a group of twenty soldiers, still together, and with a sergeant, I enquired, 'What's going on?'

'The Russians have blocked the road just before Krasny, a little town. Eighty thousand of them, there are,' said the sergeant. 'This is the third time in three days the bastards have done it. First it was to Eugène, then Davout, now us. Each time our men somehow fight their way through, they just block it again, set up their cannon in a line and . . .' He gave an expressive shrug.

'Are you part of Ney's rearguard then?'

He gave me a look of surprise.

'I was ill, left behind in the hospital in Smolensk.' Quickly, I told him the most recent part of my story.

He whistled. 'You did well to come this far on your own.'

'A shame he won't be going any further,' said one of his men sourly.

I glanced at the sergeant. 'What does he mean?'

'Did you not hear me? There are eighty thousand Russians facing us. That didn't stop Ney of course. He sent in two charges, one after another, straight frontal assaults. Both broke.'

'They advanced against a line of cannon?'

A proud nod. 'They almost succeeded too, in spite of the canister shot, and the Russian cavalry charges. If the rumours are true, whole regiments were cut down, eagles lost, you can imagine. The road to France is cut off for us. I am just glad to be here, not near the front.'

It sounded like Borodino all over again, and for once, I was grateful that my stomach was empty. 'What now?'

'Surrender, I suppose.' The sergeant's tone was weary. 'What else can we do against such numbers?'

'Have you not heard how the Russians treat their prisoners?' I asked.

'Not all the tales can be true.'

'I am not about to stay and find out.' I eased out to the side of the column, and, picking a path between the horse carcasses and dead men, continued on towards the firing. I looked back after about fifty paces. The sergeant was staring after me, his expression resigned. I beckoned, but he did not move. Each to their own, I thought. It was better to try and fail than simply give up, as he was doing.

As I neared the fighting, the cannon fell silent, but the evidence of Ney's failed charges became all too clear. Some quarter of a mile away, in front of the line of Russian guns, lay a ravine. It was filled with corpses, two, three, four deep. Any visible snow was a horrible red, and the air rang with wretched cries for help, and the screams of those whose pain was unbearable. I did not let my gaze linger; the carnage was too awful. Instead I worked a path towards Ney, who was standing in the midst of his officers. A short figure in a sable cloak, curly hair straying from under his bearskin shako, he was clearly furious.

'That bastard has abandoned us; he sacrificed us in order to save himself; what can we do?'

He meant Napoleon of course. No one answered.

'What will become of us?' Ney cried. 'Everything is fucked!'

Again no one volunteered a reply. The senior officers around him looked downcast, beaten. Seeing their mood, remembering the resignation of the sergeant and his men, my own spirits began to fall. Perhaps we *were* all doomed.

I did not know Ney then as I came to know him in the hours that followed, however. His face expressed neither nor disquietude. After a few moments' silence, he spoke. This time, his voice was resolute, determined. All eyes were fixed on him.

'We're in a bad way, but there must be another way to Orsha.' This was the town on the Dnieper some miles to the west.

'What are you going to do, sir?' asked one of his officers.

'Cross the Dnieper. The road runs parallel to it here, does it not?'

'I think so, sir,' said one of the generals.

'We'll find the river then.'

'And if the river isn't frozen, sir?'

Ney stuck out his chin. 'It will be.'

'Well, the best of luck to us, sir!' The officer seemed a little more confident.

I found my voice. 'I found shelter away from the road yesterday afternoon, sir, and I saw the Dnieper in the distance. It did look as if it was running in roughly the same direction as the road.' I prayed I had been right.

Ney's keen eyes fell on mine. 'Good. That is good! We shall retreat a couple of miles, so the Russians cannot see us, and pretend to make camp. Once night has fallen, we shall strike out for the river. Cross that, and we can march unhindered along the northern bank, and rejoin the emperor at Orsha.'

Heads began to nod, as they always do when the decisive act with assurance. It felt as if the abyss had retreated, just a little.

'Are you an officer? If so, where are your men?' Ney was talking to me.

'I am an imperial messenger, sir. Caulaincourt attached me to your staff at Smolensk' – I saw no reason to explain why – 'but I was laid low by fever the same day. I woke in the main hospital there when your corps had almost left.'

He barked a surprised laugh. 'You escaped from Smolensk?'

'I did, sir. I have been following the army for almost two days.'

'On your own?'

'Yes, sir.'

He strode forward, and clapping me on the shoulder, declared, 'This is the type of man that makes the Grande Armée what it is!'

His officers nodded and muttered their appreciation, and uneasy with the recognition, remembering how I had come by my cloak and boots, I flushed. 'I was only doing my duty, sir, and following on as best I could.'

'That is what we are all doing, my lad.' Ney's eyes were bright with purpose. 'Stay close by me from now on. We shall be reunited with the emperor, by God, see if we are not!'

An hour or so after darkness had fallen, Ney pronounced that enough fires had been lit to give the impression we had settled down for the night. A Polish officer, sent to reconnoitre, had returned with good news. There was a ford over the Dnieper on the other side of the woods that flanked the northern side of the road.

Perhaps two of the six thousand men Ney had had at the beginning of the day remained. There was no way of calculating the quantity of civilians and stragglers, but they far outnumbered the soldiers. It was a shocking change; as far as Smolensk, the number of combatants had exceeded those of the disbanded; now it was the other way around.

I was one of those given the miserable task of announcing our plan to this raggletaggle mob. They were to follow if they wished, or stay to treat with the Russians in the morning. To the inevitable questions and pleas, would they be protected, would the soldiers help traverse the dangerous cross country route, I gave no answer.

Mostly, my silence was met with resignation, but sometimes feelings boiled over into anger. The two grenadiers sent to accompany me repeatedly had to shove people back with their muskets. Once, they even levelled their weapons and cocked them, the muzzle ends almost touching the foreheads of the pathetic unfortunates who were effectively being abandoned to their fate. The cold metal and the hard faces of the grenadiers was enough threat. I kept my head down, unable to meet the accusing gaze of those who still possessed some spirit. My section of the civilian camp dealt with, I made to go. The sooner I got away from these living dead, I decided, the sooner I could put their fate from my mind. A good slug of the brandy I still had would help.

'Mathieu?'

It could not be, I thought. I turned, searching the desperate, pinched faces. 'Who is that?'

'Mathieu, it is I.' There she was, a shadow of her former self, her head covered by a pair of men's breeches; under a scorched silk shawl, there were several blankets wrapped around her slender body.

'Jeanne?' I could not believe my eyes.

'Mathieu!' She broke free of the mob, and stumbled towards me.

The grenadiers barred her way with crossed muskets.

'Let her past!' I ordered.

She fell into my arms, sobbing. I held her close; she was shrunk to skin and bone. 'It is all right,' I whispered. 'I am here.'

Sensing weakness, the nearest civilians began to push forward. It would not take much for the pair of grenadiers to be overwhelmed. 'Back away, facing them,' I ordered. To the mob, I shouted, 'Anyone who comes too close will be shot!'

I eased Jeanne away from my chest, and slipped an arm around her waist so I could support her. 'Your friends?' I asked.

A little shake of her head, no.

So many deaths, I thought. 'Come,' I whispered in her ear. 'I will take you to Marshal Ney.'

CHAPTER XXVII

U pon recognising Jeanne as a famous actress, Ney had insisted on giving her a cloak lined with satin and marten fur, from his own stock. She already had a pair of fur-lined boots, better than most soldiers' footwear. The only reason they had not been stolen, she revealed to Ney, was because they had been made for a child. 'Never have I been so grateful for having tiny feet,' she said, smiling. Charmed, Ney also gave her a pair of fur mitts. 'Take care of that woman,' he ordered. I muttered that I would not let her out of my sight.

By nine that night, we had reached a hamlet close to the Dnieper by the name of Danikowa. Bivouacs were set up, and fires set. Food was prepared and Jeanne further restored by a goblet of good wine and a bowl of boeuf à la mode – the cynical name given to the spiced horse-meat stew served by Ney's manservant. She was, she said, ready for our next ordeal. My own spirits revived by both stew and my reunion with Jeanne, I felt a new man. Being presented with a pair of pistols by one of Ney's aides-de-camp – the colonel who had owned them having succumbed to his wounds – capped it all.

Most of us were on foot, the vast majority of the horses having perished, but there were still a few beasts alive. Some were pulling the half-dozen guns left, which I thought absurd, but Ney was insistent. The rest were hauling supplies, the wounded, and women and children who were too weak to walk.

It was the first time in some days I had been with the soldiers themselves. Before Smolensk, there had been some retention of discipline and appearance. Now they resembled bizarre circus acts. Most had icicles in their beards; every last one had the smoke-blackened visage of a wild-living gypsy, but it was their clothing that drew the eye. Some were covered with a moujik's caftan, or a plump kitchen wench's short fur-lined dress. Others wore rich merchants' coats and almost all had on the fur-lined pink, blue, lilac or white satin mantles of the kind Russian commoners make into articles of luxury.

Spirits were remarkably high, in spite of the darkness and the bitter cold. Before moving out, Ney had gone among the soldiers, his face betraying neither indecision nor anxiety. His self-confidence, on a par with his courage, was infectious. Nobody dared to question him, instead placing their trust, and lives, in his care. I resolved to do the same, and, following his orders, stayed close to his group at the front.

Inevitably, we got lost and disoriented soon after setting out into the dark and the cold, even with the help of the lame peasant from Danikowa who had been coerced into guiding us. The wavering light cast by Ney's bodyguards' torches illuminated little more than twenty or thirty paces in front. Undeterred, Ney kept us moving forward, often taking the lead with the lame peasant. Finding a gully, he clambered into it, and stamping up and down, declared that it had to be a stream. The peasant agreed with vigorous nods of his head. Soldiers were called forward, pickaxes produced from a wagon; not long after, the snow removed and ice exposed, they had hacked down to running water.

'See that?' Ney was pointing. 'The stream runs that way, and it must lead to the Dnieper. 'Follow it, and we shall find the river.' He glanced at the peasant, and one of his Polish officers rattled off a question, telling Ney a moment later, 'He says that we are on the right path, sir. The section of the Dnieper we want is not far.'

'See?' I whispered to Jeanne. 'He will guide us through this.'

She gave me a tremulous smile.

Reaching the steep riverbank, Ney called a halt for what remained of the night. Despite his earlier declaration that the Dnieper would be frozen, some parts were not. It was crucial to be able to see clearly so as to find those points where the ice was thick enough to bear the weight of men and horses. Dawn would succour us, he said, immediately taking the opportunity to lie down and rest.

Jeanne and I did the same, lying close as we had in Paris, what seemed a lifetime before. This time, however, we clung to each other for warmth, not in passionate embrace. Our rest was short. At midnight, the sentries posted at the edge of the village came hurrying in. Squadrons of Cossacks were close by, and advancing in our direction.

'There is nothing for it,' Ney said. 'We have to cross now.'

Having scrambled down to the river on our backsides, I saw him and the lame peasant make it safely across, together with several of his aides-de-camp. At once I set out, walking gingerly over the ice with Jeanne a few paces behind, following my exact path. Like Ney, I used a musket butt to test its thickness. My stomach lurched with each ominous groan it gave; despite my own fear, I kept telling Jeanne that we would be all right. I reached the far side shaking like a leaf, only to find a steep twelve foot climb to the bank. Ney was up there, gesticulating that we should ascend. I steadied my nerves, and hugged Jeanne. 'Not much further,' I whispered. On hands and knees, reaching out to her now and again if she slipped, we somehow worked our way to the top.

Pausing to catch my breath, I looked out over the river. Despite Ney's order that each unit was to make its way across in turn, disorder and confusion reigned. Every man was trying to get down first; there were even a few cavalrymen among them. Incredibly, these last traversed without incident, although the sharp cracking sounds carrying to me seemed an ominous portent. Soon, inevitably, the ice had given way.

Horses went down first, submerged to their shoulders, their thrashing contributing to more ice breaking. Their riders, hanging on to their mounts, pleaded with comrades still on the ice for help – aid that could not be given without risking one's own death. One by one, the cavalrymen went under. Their horses, being stronger, continued to swim about, but were completely unable to climb out of the freezing water. Their doom would come, just more slowly.

A wagon with wounded men on it appeared at the top of the slope on the far bank, and I could witness no more.

'Let us away from here,' I said to Jeanne.

She did not move, her eyes fixed on the dreadful spectacle. 'Look,' she said.

A sharp bark echoed over the noise of men's cries and splashing water.

'There. A dog.'

I peered. On a small, broken away piece of ice, perhaps ten or fifteen feet from this bank, I spied a small, four-legged shape.

'The poor creature is trapped.'

'It is terrible,' I said. 'Come. We must go.'

'I stroked that dog earlier. It belonged to a grenadier who had seen my play in Moscow.'

I smiled, and patted her hand. 'It will not suffer for long.'

'The grenadier said that he could die happy, having seen me perform. It was as if he knew what would happen at the river. He said that his dog enjoyed the show too – he smuggled her in under his coat, and she sat in his lap all evening.' Jeanne tugged at my arm. 'The grenadier must have drowned, but it is too cruel that his dog will also die. Please, Mathieu.'

I wanted to say that it was just a dog, but the plea in her eyes was more than I could stand. Silently, I shuffled to the edge of the slope, and without a backward glance, went down on my rear, using my heels as brakes. The ice at what would be the water's edge looked solid enough, but further out, where the dog was, I could see cracks galore. Fear surged within me. Unwillingly, my gaze rose to Jeanne; she smiled and called out something encouraging. Go up there without at least trying to save the poor mutt, crowed the little devil, and you can kiss goodbye to whatever hope of romance you are clinging onto.

With a savage muttered curse, I laid flat on my front, and began to worm my way over the ice. To my good fortune, there were no soldiers trying to cross straight in front of me; at least I would not be trampled underfoot, or kicked into the water. My breath clouded in front of my face. Cold seeped through my clothing; despite my mitts, my fingers tingled with every handhold. Eager to reach the dog, I moved too fast. Crack. A line moved in the ice, out from my chest and off to the right. I froze, scarcely able to breathe for the fear. The ice beneath me did not shift; I was not tipped into the death-offering water. An inch at a time, I crept towards the dog.

'Here, boy,' I called out. I tried to whistle. 'I'm coming.'

I reached the dog, or at least came as near as I could. Perhaps three feet separated me from the piece of ice it was on, which had cracked away from the rest and now sat in open water, for all the world like the yolk of an egg in the midst of the white. Fear consumed me at the thought of entering the water. I would drown long before I rescued the dog. My reach was not long enough to catch hold of the unfortunate creature either. I decided I would have to return to Jeanne emptyhanded; better to suffer her disappointment than sink into the icy depths.

I began to shuffle around, preparing to work my way back to the bank, and fate intervened. A group of soldiers walked out onto the

frozen river too close together; the ice cracked, tipping them, screaming, into the water, and everything shifted and moved. The section the
dog was on came towards me, propelled by the current. Terrified, it
crouched down.

'That's it,' I said, reaching out. 'Good boy.'

Closer the ice came, the dog not moving.

'Good dog. Good dog.' I took off my right mitt with my teeth, and
set it to one side. Then I shifted forward, easing as much of my body
out over the water as I dared, stretching out my hand. 'Easy, boy.'

I reached over the back of his head and took it by the scruff. To
my surprise, it relaxed in my grip rather than struggle. Taking a deep
breath, I heaved it up and towards me, and edged back onto the safety
of thicker ice. The dog was small, and had a thick coat, but mercifully,
he was dry. I managed to turn myself around, still lying down, and
holding it in the crook of one arm, worked my way back to the river's
edge. My ears rang with the cries of drowning men all the way back,
and I wept with guilt and sorrow. I had lost my mitt too.

'I knew you would do it!' Jeanne cried as we reached her. She kissed
me full on the mouth, and then busied herself wrapping the dog in a
blanket. It was time to leave, I decided – Ney was already gone, and
more and more men were scrambling up to our position and leaving. If
we fell too far behind, our deaths were certain.

'How is he?' I asked.

'In shock, I think.'

'Give him here.' Gently rubbing his paws for a time, talking to him
all the while, I wrapped the dog in one of my blankets and then, with
Jeanne's help, fashioned a kind of sling around my chest; it was not
dissimilar to the way peasant women carried newborns. I ripped off a
section to use as a makeshift mitt, and hoped it would be enough to
prevent frostbite.

Eyes shining, Jeanne kissed me again. 'You are a good man, Mathieu.'

Inside, I was wondering if I had delayed us too long, if Ney could
really work the miracle that was needed for us to reach Orsha. Nor was
it as if our ordeal would end there; hundreds of miles still lay between
us and safety. I mentioned none of my worries.

Reaching Ney again, we continued through the snow for an hour or
more, happening upon a village of sleeping Cossacks. We took them
captive, and found the place well stocked with provisions. We fell on

the food like wild beasts. Our hunger momentarily sated, Ney allowed us a few hours of sleep before we set out again, leaving the tied-up prisoners behind. Dawn broke, crisp and clear. It was not long before the Cossacks' comrades found us, and with light field-pieces mounted on sleigh runners, began to rain down volleys of shells. Some dismounted and began firing their carbines at us. They were poor shots for the most part, but at one point, a sergeant who was walking close by fell screaming to the snow.

A swift glance told me he was beyond help, his left leg shattered by a ball. In a field hospital, he might have survived, but in this wilderness, in these brutal conditions, under fire by the enemy, there was no hope. I passed by, hardening my heart.

'Comrade!'

I paid no heed, and ignored Jeanne, who kept twisting around.

'Here's a man done for, take my pack,' he called out.

I thought of the dog, who kept slipping from my blanket wrapping, and turned.

Blood was pooling around the sergeant's leg; the wound must have been agonising, yet he had taken off his black and white hide pack. He half-threw it towards me. 'It will be more useful to you,' he said coldly.

I took it with muttered thanks, and unable to meet his eye, walked away. Jeanne gave me a horrified glance. 'He needs his leg amputated,' I said. 'I cannot do that, and even if I could, I could not carry him.' The little devil in my head asked how many such men I had ignored since Moscow. The same fate would have been mine long since if I had tried, but the realisation did not ease my guilt.

Jeanne must have known the same. She nodded miserably, and together we continued.

A thick stand of trees gave us cover from the Russian field pieces; the Cossacks on their horses could not penetrate it either. At one point, a senior Russian officer came quite close to shout to us: 'Surrender, surrender – all resistance is useless.' A general whose name I did not know roared back, 'Frenchmen fight but don't surrender.' We howled appreciation of that, and our musket volleys repulsed any attempts to reach our position for the rest of the afternoon. As night fell, Ney led us off again. 'Those who get through this will need to have their balls tied on with iron wire,' he shouted.

His words raised a faint but defiant cheer. After that, energy spent, no one spoke.

Late that night, unsure of our bearings, Ney sent out a Polish officer to reconnoitre. He returned in the early hours of the twentieth of November, fresh from an encounter with Prince Eugène's pickets on the outskirts of Orsha, no less. Borne up by this uplifting news, Ney himself rode to the front. On foot with Jeanne, I did not witness the joyful reunion between Ney and Eugène, but every man who saw it said they fell into each other's arms, weeping.

At Orsha, it seemed that our suffering might ease. Word soon spread that there were plentiful supplies of food and weapons, and even some fresh detachments of troops from France. These men's shock was noticeable as the haggard survivors stumbled into the town. Caulaincourt's surprise was no less great when I arrived at the imperial headquarters, which was in a requisitioned merchant's house in the centre.

'Dupont, you are alive!' His face lit up.

'Sir.' I was grinning like a fool.

'I heard the happy news that Ney had reached us, but with so few men, I thought you . . .'

'It was not my time, sir,' I said, still amazed at my good fortune.

'Who is this?' He was looking at Jeanne, who had come with me. His brow wrinkled. 'Your face is familiar, madame.'

'I am but a poor actress, sir.'

Quickly, I explained.

Caulaincourt stooped to kiss her hand, and declared that Mademoiselle Préville should have everything she needed that was within his power to grant. As soon became plain, this meant she would be granted not just a bed for the night, but a seat in one of the carriages attached to the imperial party. Fewer and fewer horses remained alive to pull such vehicles, but of those that were, a good number belonged to Napoleon. With a deep bow to Jeanne, and telling me to report for duty within the hour, Caulaincourt took his leave.

'You must also come in the carriage.' Jeanne had tears in her eyes.

'I cannot.' I shrugged, as if it did not matter. 'I am a messenger, nothing more.'

'That is not fair!'

'Fair has nothing to do with it.'

'I will not go without you! I will walk to Paris, if needs be.'

'No.'

She flinched, and although I regretted the harshness with which I had spoken, I spoke with even more force. 'You will sit in that carriage each day, and not leave it unless you are told it is safe to do so – do you understand?'

Her mouth opened to protest.

'Jeanne!'

She bent her head, nodding, and her tears fell onto the carpet, filthy with mud and chunks of half-melted snow.

I walked out before I too began to weep.

Within a few steps, I realised the dog was still slung from my chest. He had not fitted in the backpack, which I had soon discarded. I almost went back. With Jeanne, he would have an excellent chance of survival; with me, the likelihood was poor to highly improbable. I did not turn around, however. The thought of the march west alone without Jeanne was bad enough, but to deprive myself also of the dog, a friendly little type, was more than I could bear.

My gloom changed to joy as I collided with a man entering the door. It was François, beard and moustache festooned with hoarfrost and icicles, haggard, thinner than I had ever seen him, but still François. He recognised me in the same instant. Speechless, we pumped each other's hand as if we were the last men on earth.

François stared into my face. 'I never thought to see you again, Mathieu, yet here you are!'

'I could say the same about you! Your pistols are gone, I am afraid, and your bearskin.'

A dismissive *tch*. 'I care nothing for them. You did not trade the skin for the dog?' He winked.

I chuckled. 'No. They were stolen in the hospital at Smolensk. I have a new pair – you can choose one.'

He waved a hand. 'I long since replaced mine. Hospital? I can see we have much to talk about. Tell me, have you eaten?'

'Nothing really for the last two days.' At the mention of food, I was suddenly aware of being ravenous.

'Come with me.'

He linked his arm conspiratorially with mine, and led me to a house down a side alley. The short distance was not enough to prevent me noticing his bad limp, but I had no chance to ask him about it. For two gold coins, François told me, he had secured the entire property apart from an upstairs room; the owners, an old couple with no children, had retired there until the Grande Armée left Orsha. The house was filled with messengers, thirty or more, lying or sitting with their backs to the walls, busily running the seams of their inside-out garments over candle flames. The sight made me scratch my own lice bites, which were myriad, and a source of torment each night.

I recognised many of the men. All looked exhausted; their faces were wind-chapped and fire-scorched, and several were also wounded. I got cheery responses to my greetings, though; everyone's spirits had been lifted by reaching Orsha safely, and the arrival of a comrade long thought dead was always welcome.

When François produced a small loaf of bread and a hunk of ham – they had been guarded by a friend – I gaped. The bottle of wine that came out next brought tears to my eyes. Men shuffled aside so we could sit in a corner. I began to ask François about what had happened to him, but he refused to listen until I had eaten. He also made light of the poor condition of his footwear, the remnants of a pair of boots around which he had wrapped lengths of cloth, tied in place with strips of leather. Tomorrow was another day, said François, and he would find the perfect pair of shoes during the march. I told him about the first signs of frostbite, and that he had to rub the sensation back, painful though it was, and not warm it rapidly at a fire.

'Later,' said François, a curious expression on his face. 'They are not that bad.'

Exhausted and overwrought from my trials, I did not think to question him further. I set the dog on the floor beside me, and fed it little pieces of bread and ham; the poor creature sat there, its eyes fixed on what remained. Touched, and thankful for its company, I gave it more than I would ever have given a dog before.

François watched me, amused. 'Quite attached to him, eh?'

I nodded, realising that he had only been with me for two days or so. It felt like an eternity.

Shoving the cork into the bottle with a thin surgeon's probe, François took a long pull. With a loud smack of his lips, he passed it over.

I rolled the wine around my mouth, relishing the dark, earthy flavour, and deciding it was the best thing I had ever drunk. 'Where did you steal it?' I asked.

François's face was baby innocent.

'You bought it from someone while he was asleep,' I said, mock accusingly. Theft was so much the norm now that the witticism was heard throughout the army. It was not just when men were sleeping either. A cooking pot left unattended on a fire would vanish; saddlebags were lifted from the backs of horses. I had heard a captain of hussars complain how his mount's reins had been cut and it taken from right behind him.

'He was sleeping, true, but it was forever.'

I raised the bottle in salutation. 'Whoever he was, he had good taste. I want to know how you fared since we were parted.'

His story was similar to my own. Snow. Cold. A horse dying. Hunger. Attacks by the Cossacks. He made light of it, as was his way. 'Did you find Jeanne?'

'I did.'

He gasped. 'Alive?'

'I gave her into Caulaincourt's care just before we met.'

'It sounds like a miracle. Tell me!'

There was rapt attention as I recounted my tale. Meeting Louvel near the shattered bridge, failing to find Jeanne, and returning to Smolensk only to fall ill. How I had followed in Ney's wake, catching up at Krasny, and then, by chance, been reunited with Jeanne. I told how we had circumvented the Russian blockade by crossing the Dnieper at night. 'That is where I got this fellow,' I said, stroking the soft fur behind the dog's head. 'His paws are a little frostbitten, but with luck he will heal up all right.'

'What's his name?'

'With everything that's been going on, I haven't had time to think of one.'

Suggestions rained in. Napoleon. The Emperor. Coco. Gustave. Wolf. Garçon – boy. Alexander, said one man, to boos and hisses.

'I know,' said François, who had remained silent until this point.

My curiosity was pricked. 'What?'

'Marshal Ney.'

'That is perfect,' I said, laughing. Pouring a few drops of wine onto a forefinger, I made the sign of the cross on the dog's forehead. 'I hereby christen you Marshal Ney.'

He licked my finger clean as if in appreciation.

'May he bring you the same good fortune as the marshal did over the last few days,' said François.

What went unsaid was that I – and everyone else – would need a huge amount of luck once we left the safety of Orsha. It was sixty miles to the crossing over the Berezina river at Borisov, and more than thirty after that to the city of Minsk, a vital storage depot.

'That test is for another day,' I said. 'Let us be thankful instead that we are here, alive.'

'I can drink to that.' One of the older messengers had a silver flask in his hand. He held it up. 'To comradeship.'

We all muttered the same, and the flask slowly did the rounds.

CHAPTER XXVIII

We left Orsha at first light. No one wanted to leave the warmth of the houses; sergeants and officers had to drive men onto the street with threats and curses. There were not enough horses for more than the most urgent communications, which meant that most messengers had to walk, just like the rest of the Grande Armée. Five hundred sick and injured men were to be left behind for lack of horses, as well as twenty-five unserviceable cannon, and by Napoleon's direct order, the entire quantity of pontoon bridges, timber and tools.

François and I stuck together, and I carried Marshal Ney in his new, better-fashioned sling. One of the emperor's surgeons had quickly examined him the night before at my request; if his paws were to heal, Marshal Ney should not walk for at least a month. It was no less than I expected, and in fact served me well. He was not that heavy, and the heat of his body kept my chest comfortable. I took François at his word that he did not need to see the surgeon about *his* feet.

Our pace was slow. Each man moved with his head bowed, hands dug deep into his clothes and his eyes fixed on the ground, silently and sullenly following the unfortunate who walked ahead of him. Any conversation was curt and brief. Distinctive sounds carried. The plaintive screech of the few remaining wagons' wheels on the hardened snow, the sound of horses being struck and the sharp but frequent curses of the drivers when they found themselves on an icy incline which they could not climb. From above came the croaking of the swarms of crows, of northern rooks and other carrion birds which followed the Grande Armée; alongside there were snarls and growls from the packs of stray dogs which tracked our path. Both were grim reminders that all of us were possible future prey.

As it had been since Smolensk, the road was covered in abandoned caissons, carriages and guns that nobody had even thought of blowing up, burning or spiking. Here and there were dying horses, weapons, effects of every type; broken-open trunks and disembowelled bags marked the way taken by those who had preceded us. By the roadside were trees at the foot of which people had attempted to build fires and, around these trunks, transformed into funerary monuments, the bodies of those who had expired while trying to warm themselves.

Our entire route was lined with dead bodies, stiff, rimed white. Some were showing their naked toes through their torn shoes or boots, first purple, then frozen dark blue or brown, and finally black. Not long before, the sight would have revolted me; now, I felt complete dispassion. I saw the men who sat down by the roadside with their backs to trees or heaps of rocks, and did nothing to help, watching with detachment how they at first seemed merely drowsy, but then became agitated, and made futile attempts to get up. Their struggles were convulsive, eyes haggard and glazed, mouths fringed with froth, their intelligence visibly extinct.

I walked by every last one. I had to.

Of far more interest and importance was finding shelter and fuel before nightfall. Orsha had been an oasis in the midst of a desert; only God knew when we would have the same luxury again. I was also worried about François's limp, but each time I asked, he insisted he was fine. The sight of what appeared to be a lane leading off the road to the left made up my mind. More than an hour of daylight remained, by my reckoning, earlier than most tended to seek a roof for the night. A quick conference with the other messengers proved that they were of the same mind; to locate shelter was more important than travelling another mile or two. Breaking away from the column, weapons at the ready, we followed the lane for perhaps half a mile. In the clearing at its end was a decent-sized wooden cottage and several outbuildings, including a large barn. All lay abandoned, the inhabitants presumably having fled our advance with their livestock.

'This is perfect,' said François.

'And the risk of being attacked by Cossacks?' I asked.

He glanced about. 'Reasonable, but worth it, I would say.'

'It's not as if the rest of the buildings will remain empty for long. That should keep us from being Cossacked,' said one of our companions. 'Men began to follow us the moment we left the road.'

He was right. A dozen figures were already in sight along the track. More would surely follow. Setting François and another man to walk up and down in front of the cottage doorway, keeping warm, and their muskets obvious – clear warning that it had been taken – the rest of us set about breaking up the wooden livestock pens for fuel. Before we were done, scores of men had arrived, forcing several more of our companions to guard the cottage. The barn and outbuildings were rapidly filling up.

The numbers present meant we should be safe from the Cossacks, I decided, and between the fuel and the fifteen of us packed into the cottage, there would be enough warmth overnight. If anyone demanded entry, we would reveal ourselves to be imperial messengers, and hope that enough discipline remained to ensure this saw us unmolested.

Because François and I had led the way to the little farm, we took the places closest to the merrily crackling stove. Naturally, Marshal Ney stayed with us. Straw taken from inside the barn served as our mattresses; after the day's walk, our conditions felt the height of luxury.

Soon the blackened cooking pot that François had miraculously obtained since our parting was perched on the stove, first melting fistfuls of snow, then boiling up a gruel from some buckwheat he had also 'chanced upon'. Once the lumps of horse meat in it had cooked, we would have a tasty stew to share. After that, it had been decided, our companions could use the pot.

I lay back, dozy with tiredness, one hand stroking Marshal Ney.

'Lucky we have some meat tonight, eh?'

I did not open my eyes. 'Eh?'

'Else we would only have had Spartan broth!'

'What's that?'

'Here's the recipe: melt some snow – and you'll need plenty to get only a little water.'

'I know that,' I said with feeling.

'Put in some flour. Then, for lack of salt, some gunpowder. Serve up hot and only eat when you're really hungry.'

All too familiar with this grim dish, we both laughed; so did any of the others who had heard.

François was more like his old self as he cooked, cheerily talking about our return to Paris, and how getting drunk would be our priority.

We would spend a week together in a gambling salon, he declared, and with our winnings set up our own establishment. When I mentioned having no money, and opining that he could not have much either, he winked and tapped his midriff. 'You need not worry in that regard,' he said in an undertone. I burned to question him further, but there were too many ears who might hear.

The prospect of funds, and with them, the ability to raise more, lifted my spirits; I could see us, dressed in the latest fashion, a fine pair of dandies. If I worked hard and kept away from the drink, I fantasised, François and I would both become men of means. Jeanne would agree to marry me; we would have plenty of children, and live a long, happy and prosperous life.

Before long, however, I remembered Bellamy, and my mood soured. It was as if François had read my mind.

'Sad to say, one customer we will not have in our salon is your friend Carnot.'

'Who?'

'You know, that friend of yours with the combover. I met him in Vilna.'

Bellamy, I thought in shock. 'Is he dead then?'

'Deader than dead. I saw him perhaps a week since. Froze to death sitting by a fire from the look of it.' François shook his head in regret. 'I didn't think to say before, sorry. There have been so many casualties.'

I made a pretence of being sad, but inside I was exultant. Of course one of Bellamy's colleagues might try to blackmail me if I made it back to Paris, but his death was a good start.

The Spartan broth ready, we took turns with the one spoon in our possession. Famished, neither of us took the time to blow on the hot liquid, and burned ourselves more than once. Marshal Ney's intent gaze stayed throughout on the spoon, moving from pot to my mouth or François's and back again. Soft-hearted, François gave him perhaps a third of his lumps of meat; I probably fed him half of mine. As I allowed Marshal Ney to lick the pot clean, our eyes met.

'What are we doing?' François asked, smiling.

'Caring for my dog. At least we can do that,' I said, thinking ashamedly of all the men I had walked past, of all the cries and pleas for help I had ignored.

There was no need to explain. François knew what I meant.

'Are you done?' One of our companions was hovering impatiently.

We shifted to one side so that he could cook food for himself and several others.

'I had best warm these feet,' said François, fiddling with the ties around one boot. Silently, he unwound strip after strip of filthy linen and leather, revealing an enormous missing section in the sole. 'Just need to get them warm.'

I remembered his limp, his protestations, and cold fear filled me. 'You can't do it at the stove!' I cried.

'Eh?'

'Don't you remember what I told you?'

He tutted. 'Nobody else does that.'

'The Polish do,' I retorted, my concern coming out as anger, 'and they know these winters far better than us.'

François swivelled on his arse so that his legs were pointed away from the stove, and with a grunt of effort, pulled off the right boot. At once the front section of the sock in which his foot was encased sagged. I watched, aghast, as he peeled it off. Three toes had come away cleanly; they tumbled out of his sock onto the dirt floor. There was no bleeding, and no apparent pain. Worse, the rest of his foot was the tell-tale white I had come to know and dread.

Realisation flooded in; the curious expression François had given me when I had told him how to treat frostbite; his declaration that he had seen the surgeon; his brushing off of my queries about his limp. I wanted to scream, shout, rage. Instead I bit the inside of my cheek until I could taste blood.

'So much for that foot,' said François, his tone light, even humorous. 'Let us see how the other one has fared.'

I stared as he undid the leather and linen wrappings. The left foot was, if anything, worse than the right. François felt his big toe, pinching and prodding it, and then, before I could protest, tore the whole thing off with a single twist. Again there was no blood. I gasped, but not even a murmur of discomfort passed his lips.

His gaze met mine. Incredibly, he shrugged, as if to say, what can a man do?

'Why didn't you say anything last night?' I demanded.

'The damage had already been done.' Calmly, he explained how, ignorant of the correct treatment, he had held his feet to the fire for two nights before we had met. 'What could the surgeon have done at Orsha, save what I did just now?'

Not much, I thought, but I did not say it out loud. François was right, and his fatalism made it even harder to accept. Guilt battered me. 'If only we had met before, I could have told you—'

'It is not your fault, Mathieu, and besides, I am not done yet! I can still walk.' They were fighting words, but his outlook had suddenly become precarious. Toes were vital for balance; from this point on, he would be able to walk only with assistance. And that, I thought grimly, was before the Cossacks and other dangers were taken into account.

'I will stay by you,' I swore. 'We shall make it to Paris together.'

Both of us knew my words for falsehood, but at times the truth is more than a man can bear. *Either he will perish*, the little devil chipped in, *or he will die* and *you will also, trying to save him*. There was another horrible possibility too, that I would survive after he had gone, only to succumb later. *Leave him here*, the devil advised. *That is your only chance of survival*. Sickening though it was even to consider, this made sense. The odds of making it through with François as he was were incalculable. I shoved the thought ruthlessly away.

François was now smiling, which made me feel even worse. 'As thanks for your assistance, I will buy the drinks for the first *week* we are in Paris,' he said. 'How's that for a start?'

Guilt-scourged because of my uncharitable thoughts, I could only nod mute acceptance. We spoke no more. Our dreadful situation made silence preferable.

Also exhausted, the others in the hut talked little once their meal, such as it was, had been consumed. I recall a brief conversation about who should stay awake on sentry duty; enough men offered for me not to have to. Thankful, wrapped up in my furs and blankets, with Marshal Ney a warm mass at my midriff, and François alongside, I lay down, closed my eyes and hoped for dreamless rest.

It was not to be, initially at least, because of the lice in my clothing. Because we had a stove rather than an open fire, there had been no way of running the seams of our garments over flame, as was the custom. And so I writhed and scratched, scratched and writhed, as everyone else did. My weariness was such, however, that I eventually fell asleep. Rather than calm, I plunged at once into dreadful scenes in which François and I were attacked by Cossacks, or others when I abandoned him, walking away as he sat disconsolate on the frozen snow, ignoring his piteous entreaties. Waking from one such with a cry, the room black as pitch, I was reassured by Marshal Ney licking my hand.

François had heard too. 'It is all right, Mathieu,' he whispered. ''Twas a nightmare, that is all.'

Grateful as a wakeful child soothed by a parent, I soon fell back to sleep. Even the lice could not keep me awake.

The next thing I was aware of was the cold on my cheeks, the only part of my face that was exposed. Opening my eyes, I saw my breath smoke before me in the dim light. There had been no movement nearby that I could remember; I decided that the stove had gone out a little while before. Fully clothed, encased in my blankets and furs, Marshal Ney lying close, I remained comfortable, if not warm. I lay there for a short time, not wanting to get up and face the day, nor the harsh reality that François's pace, even with my aid, would be painfully slow. I dreaded to think how our companions would react to his predicament, and did not let myself contemplate what would happen if any Cossacks appeared.

The little devil was ready and waiting. *Leave him here*, it crowed. *None of the others – not a single one – will slow down for you and him, hobbling at snail's pace. Even if you do reach the road, he will be exhausted.*

Then I will carry him, I shot back, or find him room on a wagon.

Mocking laughter filled my head.

I will not leave him! I shouted silently.

Then you will die.

I do not know how long I struggled with the misery, the certainty, of that knowledge rolling around my head. Eventually, though, with men stirring and coughing, and the lice driving me insane, the inevitable could be put off no longer. Ignoring the little devil, determined that I would stay with François as long as was humanly possible, I sat up, murmuring to Marshal Ney that it would soon be time to leave.

Utter shock filled me.

The straw where François had lain, not two feet away, was empty. Tellingly, terrifyingly, his cloak and furs were still there.

My eyes searched the cottage's interior. 'François? Where are you, François!'

The desperation in my voice turned heads. None were my friend's; all registered surprise and concern.

263

'Has anyone seen François?' I demanded.

'He is not there by the stove?' called a voice from the far end of the room. 'God above, I could have had his place.'

No one laughed. Men stood up, as did I.

I made for the door, stepping over my companions. 'Anyone who was on sentry duty – did you see him?' My gaze moved around accusingly. No one would meet my eye, and the bitter realisation sank in that one man, if not more, had slept through his duty.

At the door, my suspicions were confirmed. It was not barred from within, which meant that someone had gone outside, and not returned. Somehow stifling my tears, for they would only freeze on my cheeks, telling Marshal Ney to stay inside, I pushed the door open. The vicious blast of freezing air that entered took my breath away. I could not see François immediately outside.

'Put on something first, man, lest you suffer the same fate!' One of the messengers by the stove handed first my cloak and bearskin shako to the next man, and as they moved towards me, he did the same with the rest of my things.

Recognising the wisdom in his words, the truth in them battering me, I let the door close. A few moments later, the filthy trousers that served as my scarf were wrapped around my head, with the bearskin shako perched on top, and the cloak around my shoulders. I even had my mitt and its homemade fellow – my comrades were not prepared to steal from me yet – and with these on, I again opened the door.

I stepped outside, praying that I would see a set of footprints leading off towards the road, that perhaps this was one of Francois's silly jokes. If not, that he had set off hours earlier to increase his chances of reaching it before the rest of us.

Instead I saw a trail that led off to the left, away from the cottage and the barn, the marks left by a pair of boots, and perhaps thirty paces away, at the treeline, a shape sitting with its back against a tall pine. My throat closed with grief, and I stumbled the short distance on tottering legs, hoping against hope that it was not François, or if it was, that he could somehow still be alive.

It was François, though, and of course he was dead, frozen solid, his skin a pale, whitish-blue colour. A sob escaped me. Fully aware that he could not march, and would cause my death as well as his own, he had done the noble thing and sacrificed himself.

I wanted to believe François was smiling because it was in his nature to be happy, but I had seen too many men die of recent days. For reasons beyond me, it was part of dying for the lips to curve upwards, much as men's eyeballs rolled up in their heads.

'Is it François?' The voice came from the cottage.

'Yes.' I had no more words. I stared down at my friend, with whom I had endured so much, the sour knowledge filling my head that I could not even bury him. Even if I had had the strength to hack a grave from the iron-hard ground, it would take hours, by which time my companions and the soldiers in the barn would be long gone, leaving me alone and at the mercy of the weather and the marauding Cossacks. I could not negate François's sacrifice. I would not.

This was a preferable solution to the dilemma that had faced us, I thought bitterly, but that did not stop me feeling like the worst kind of friend. I took off his mitts – he would have wanted me to have them – then touched his frost-rimed shoulder, and muttered goodbye. I was about to walk away when I remembered how he had told me not to worry the night before. Asking for his forgiveness, I slipped a hand under his shirt, down to the waistline of his trousers. Feeling a thick belt, my heart skipped a beat. I knelt, avoiding François's fixed glassy expression, and with a little effort, undid the money belt and pulled it free. I did not look within, but by the weight judged it to contain a decent quantity of gold coins. Where they had come from, I had no idea, but I was not about to look this gift horse in the mouth. There might even be enough to honour my debts.

Thanking François, grateful that far from the road, he would not be used by the wagon drivers, like so many other corpses, to plug the many ditches and ruts, I secreted the belt under my cloak. Then I made my way back towards the cottage. Inside, where it was warmer, I would find a quiet corner to don my newfound wealth, and also be sure to retrieve François's cooking pot, an item of massive value. I cursed myself for not having taken it outside with me.

To my intense relief, it was returned, albeit shamefacedly, by the man who had been next nearest to the fire. I do not think he missed the way I meaningfully lifted my musket toward him. Of course he could use the pot that night, I told him. It was not a lie, I thought, if we happened to be in the same place.

There was little conversation as we readied ourselves to depart. Once, there would have been questions about why François had acted as he had. Not now. There was little sympathy either. I did not bear any grudge against my companions. They were doing it to survive; anyone who allowed himself to be affected by the deplorable scenes of which he was a witness condemned himself to death – as I would have done, had François not taken matters into his hands. Shame scourged me even as I felt relief that he was dead, but he had given me a chance.

The only way to honour his sacrifice, I decided, was to live.

CHAPTER XXIX

Despondent, unable to prevent myself from grieving François's death, I soon fell behind my fellow messengers. Eager to reach the road and the safety in numbers granted there, their eyes constantly studying the trees for Cossacks, they made little attempt to encourage me to keep up. Two asked for the cooking pot, but ready for just such an eventuality, I cocked and levelled my musket at one then the other, declaring that the first man to take a step in my direction would die. Quailing before my intent, neither prepared to take the initiative and with it, certain death, they cursed and walked away. Although the risk of being left alone was great, I judged the odds of being robbed by my own even more likely, and so I stopped and let my comrades depart. Only one looked back – I could not see who it was, and at that moment, I did not care. When they were several hundred paces ahead, I set out once more, using the breaks in the frozen snow that their feet had made.

The cold was brutal. Breath hurting in my chest despite the scarf wrapped around my mouth, using my musket as a staff, I struggled on. My belly was rumbling its protest, mouth dry with thirst, but I had neither food nor water. A short distance from the road – I could see it, could see the army column, such as it was – my strength failed me. François was gone; I forgot why he had sacrificed himself. Jeanne was safe. My family in England might as well have been on the moon, the hope of clearing my name an impossible fantasy. I had nothing to live for. Letting fall the musket, I dropped to my knees and laid down slowly on my side so that Marshal Ney was unhurt. I eased him out of the sling.

'Go on,' I said. 'It's not far. Follow the soldiers. Someone will look after you.'

He stood there, looking at me in confusion.

'Go!' I waved a hand, made as if to strike him. I refused to admit to myself that alone, he was likely to end up frozen stiff. If not that, stewing in a pot, or as I had seen more than once, skewered on a cuirassier's sword and roasted over a fire.

He stepped back, his posture cowed.

With nothing left to give, I closed my eyes. This was where I would meet my end, I thought dully, alone, in the middle of nowhere, in a country I did not know or care about. It did not matter. Like François, like so many thousands of others, my race was run, my adventure ended.

Exhaustion, physical, mental, overcame me, and I slept.

I was cold. So cold. That made no sense, I thought. Hell was burning hot, its fires undimming. Not all of me was chilled to the bone, I realised, feeling a ball of warmth at my midriff. I moved a hand down, and felt a familiar shape. It was Marshal Ney, the faithful creature. He had not heeded my command. I stroked him, and felt his tail wag. I lay there, coming awake, facing the fact that if I did not move, Marshal Ney would also freeze.

I would have much preferred to remain where I was, my suffering almost over, but the thought of his death was too much for my conscience. Sitting up, opening my eyes, I found myself in a white world. In front of me, around, above, was a whirling curtain of snow. Great, fat flakes, the like of which I had never seen, fell from the heavens in thousands, millions, uncountable numbers. Peering into the blizzard, the objects that stood out were the great pines, funerary trees, with their funereal verdure, and the gigantic immobility of their black trunks and huge sadness. The all-encompassing, falling snow made me feel as if I were enveloped in an immense winding sheet.

Panic took hold. The mere fact that I was alive meant that my slumber had been brief, but the footprints of my comrades were gone, buried under the fresh fallen snow. Walk in the wrong direction, back the way I had come, for example, and Marshal Ney and I would die. I did not care to consider the odds. A noise – the creak of wagon wheels – reached me. Hurriedly placing Marshal Ney in his sling and retrieving my musket, I stood up – with great difficulty, thanks to the stiffness of my clothing – and set out towards the sound, soon plunging to my knees in the snow.

'Hello?' I called. 'Is anyone there?'

The whiteness swallowed my voice. No answer came.

Stroking Marshal Ney for reassurance, I plodded on, walking through an atmosphere of ice. Wondering why my cloak felt as it were made of lead, I took hold of it with my free hand, and pulled around a section that lay on my back. It was frozen solid. I had seen the same happen to the cloaks of men who had slept without shelter, and died. I shed the garment and did my best to break off as much as I could.

I partly succeeded, and did feel warmer for it. There was less I could do with my inner layers. Swinging the cloak around my shoulders again and fumbling the clasp closed, I set out again. Within twenty paces, I tripped over a large hummock. Breaking my fall with a hand, thereby protecting Marshal Ney, I barked both knees against the snow-covered obstacle. Assuming it was an elongated slab of rock, for it had seemed that hard, I scraped away some snow. Instead, it was the carcass of a horse. Once, I would have been revolted. Now I felt only hunger.

I moved at once to the hindquarters, but men had been there before me. Great chunks of flesh were missing. Plainly, the poor brute had served as a mobile meat larder while still alive, the intense cold preventing it from feeling pain as starving soldiers hacked and cut at its rump. It had succumbed not from blood loss – there was none visible that I could see – but more probably from thirst. This was now a common cause of death, because every puddle, stream and brook had been ice-bound for days now.

I did not care. All I wanted was food. Something, anything to eat. I had no bayonet or even a pocket knife, so tore at the frozen muscle with my fingers. My only success was to make my nails bleed. Laying my head on the carcass, I tried to weep, but I could not even do that. The cold seeping into my skull soon threatened to curdle my wits, so I sat up. I noticed that around the horse's head, the snow was a shade darker. Brushing away the top layers, I found solid red snow all the way down to its throat. Something, perhaps one of the many stray dogs that shadowed the army, had worried at the neck before it died and froze.

I scooped up a handful and put it in my mouth. Soon I was swallowing the stuff without waiting for it to melt. Marshal Ney stuck his head out of the sling, and I offered him a bit. He wolfed it down, so I took turns, some for him, some for me. The amount of blood in the snow was tiny, of course, and before long my entire insides were unpleasantly cold.

Heartened even if my stomach was not full, pleased by the sight of another horse-sized hummock close by, because that meant the road was not far, I clambered to my feet. Step by step, using my musket as a staff, feeling weary as an ancient, I trudged fifty and then a hundred steps. The snow-covered bumps and mounds became more numerous, some clearly identifiable by their contorted shapes as human. A man sat against the trunk of a pine tree, his lips peeled back in a mirthless grin, and another knelt, held up by the death grip on his earth-planted musket. Thankfully, most of the dead had been buried by the snow, so I did not have to consider the brutality of their exit from this life.

Energy fading, my progress grew slower and slower. Reaching what I thought was the road, I became confused. Frozen, ridged ruts ran from left to right; corpses and bits of equipment and detritus lay scattered about, but of soldiers, indeed living humans of any kind, there was no sign. It was too much. Despairing, deciding that somehow the entire army had passed by, leaving me at the very rear, I stroked Marshal Ney, and said, 'This is it, boy. This is the end.'

François had died for nothing. Never had I felt so alone, so helpless.

The best choice was to blow out my own brains, I decided, but I could not leave Marshal Ney on his own.

He whined.

Thinking he was sensing my purpose, I said, 'I'm sorry. There is no other way. I am not leaving you to starve, to freeze, or to be eaten by a filthy Cossack.'

'Who's there?' It was a woman's voice, and she had spoken in French.

Startled, I peered into the murk. 'Who is asking?'

'I am!'

I stared in astonishment at the plump woman who came marching towards me, snow and ice crunching beneath her boots. A sharp pair of eyes was all that was visible from inside the grimy shawl that encased her head; above, ludicrously, perched a peasant's bearskin cap. Wrapped in numerous layers of clothing, the outermost of which was a soldier's greatcoat, she had a musket in her mitt-wrapped hands, and it was aimed at me.

'I am an imperial messenger. Dupont is my name.'

The round, black end of the barrel remained pointed at my heart. 'Planning to rob me, were you? Take my cooking pot?'

'No. I have a pot of my own.'

'What do you want then?'

'I want nothing,' I said wearily. 'Walk on by.'

'You going to follow me then, is that your plan?'

'No.' I added in a mutter. A memory tickled. I recognised her voice, but from where, I could not remember.

'If you come creeping after me, I *will* shoot you dead.'

'I will save you the effort,' I muttered.

'About to shoot yourself, eh? Don't let me stop you.' Her eyes went to Marshal Ney.

'You will not eat him!' I shouted.

'What do you care, you shortly going to be dead and all?'

The situation was altogether too bizarre. 'Wait,' I said. 'Please, I mean you no harm. I have been lost, alone for hours, perhaps longer. Tell me – are we at the back of the column? Is there anyone after you?'

She stared at me, and her eyes softened a little. 'There's plenty of poor bastards behind us still.'

As if to prove her correct, half a dozen men, soldiers once, but no longer, appeared. From what was visible of their uniforms, they were each from a different unit. Not a single one had a musket; only two had backpacks. All but two had their feet wrapped in linen and the bark of trees, tied with bits of string.

They shuffled past without even glancing in our direction.

'That all you be wanting?'

'Yes, I – thank you.'

The muzzle of her weapon moved towards Marshal Ney, and I scooped him up. 'No!'

'I could shoot you, do you a service, like, and kill him after.' Again the musket was aimed at me.

'No! He belongs to a lady friend of mine, and is much loved – I am looking after him.' Suddenly, I wanted François's sacrifice not to have been in vain. I wanted to live, and to save Marshal Ney, even to see Jeanne once more.

'I have no time for this.' She shifted the weight of her backpack, and made to walk past. 'Do whatever you damn like.'

'Wait!' Finally, I had remembered. She was the cantinière I had met on the road, what seemed a lifetime before. 'You gave me some stew some months ago. I stopped to ask directions of the soldiers you were feeding, and you saw me look at your pot over the fire. "You'll have a bite," you said. It was kind.' I thought it politic not to mention the violent diarrhoea.

'Am I s'posed to remember that? I've done the same a thousand times.'

'You have a long scar on the inside of your left arm,' I said, remembering. 'I saw it when you handed me the bowl.'

She glanced at me, her expression less hostile. 'I don't recall you, but as I said, I fed many messengers.'

'No matter,' I said, just pleased by the thaw in her attitude. 'I will come with you,' I said. 'That is, if you agree?'

'I thought you was committing suicide?'

'I have to look after the dog,' I muttered, aware of how ridiculous I sounded.

'I ain't sharing no food!'

'I would not ask you to.'

'You'll get no favours from me neither!'

'I will not ask for any,' I said stiffly. 'We might help each other.'

'People ain't doing that no more. It's every man for himself, and every woman.' A jerk of her head. 'Come on then, Dupont. Walk, if you don't want to freeze.'

Her name was Catherine-Victorie Petit, she told me. As I suspected, she was a cantinière, and had abandoned her wagon before Smolensk. Her husband was dead, one of the thousands who had fallen at Borodino.

'I am sorry.'

'I don't need no sympathy!' Her fierceness had returned.

'I think I saw you and your husband once in Paris,' I said, another memory surfacing.

She stared. 'Where?'

'Outside the Gaîté. You were telling your husband off for drinking all his pay in three days.'

'That was him all right, to be sure.' She laughed, and her fierceness eased again. 'Your woman alive?'

'I think so. I hope so. I left her in Orsha, in the care of Marshal Ney.' At the name, I felt a tail wag inside the sling

'He's a tough one. God willing, she will make it through with him.'

I nodded, offering up a silent prayer that that was the case.

'Any children?'

'No, fortunately.' Because she had none with her, I did not dare ask the same question.

'Just you and the dog then?'

'Yes. Marshal Ney, he's called.'

Another wag.

An amused snort. 'I like that.'

'How many days to Borisov?' I asked, dreading the answer.

'That depends on how many miles a day you can walk. I heard an officer say this morning that it was fifty-odd.'

'And only thirty after that to Minsk.'

'If we can avoid being Cossacked, and not freeze to death, it isn't that far, eh?' She cackled.

She plans to do it, I thought, feeling some of my determination return. If a woman can do it, I can too. And so can Marshal Ney.

Four days later, cold, footsore but still alive, we neared Borisov at last. It was about an hour after darkness had fallen. According to an artillery officer we encountered, it was the twenty-fifth of November.

Over the course of our journey, we had – with others – fought off several attacks by Cossacks, by this point sarcastically named after their hurrahs, 'les hourrassiers'. I had searched the faces of the women I had seen, living and dead, never recognising Jeanne. I hoped that that meant she was still alive. We had dined on raw and half-cooked horsemeat, sometimes with gunpowder, sometimes not. Diarrhoea was sometimes the result, which allowed me to forgive Catherine for the stew she had given me in the summer. More often than not, however, we had eaten nothing at all. Our stomachs had not been entirely empty. Enriched by the discovery of a chest of tea on the second day, we had drunk the stuff at every opportunity.

In addition to Marshal Ney, I was carrying a Polish lancer's portmanteau, found in the snow; inside it nestled two pairs of shoes and boots for each of us, as well as a pistol. The former came from an overturned wagon full of footwear, the latter from the saddle holster of a dead cavalry horse. I had procured powder and ball from the body of the pistol's owner.

Each night, we had spread blankets on the snow and huddled together under our furs, Catherine and I as close as man and wife, and Marshal Ney snuggled in between. I had no more intention of getting amorous than I had of becoming the Tsar of Russia, but that did not stop her waving a wicked-looking *bistourie* in my face. If my hand touched any part of her, she warned, she would slice my balls off. It was a considerable relief that my earnest assurance was accepted. We took turns staying awake as much as our weariness allowed, so that no one stole our furs, or anything else.

Our luck continued in this regard. It was perhaps too much to hope it would do so at Borisov.

The first intimation was the traffic coming to a complete standstill before the town was even in sight. A few people had lit torches, and by their light it was possible to see that only confusion reigned. The faint hope I had had of the army here remaining as a viable force vanished. I saw a rabble, and in it only broken men, shells of the soldiers who had so proudly marched into Russia five short months before. There were only a small number of officers visible, and even fewer discernible units.

My former admiration for Napoleon had been replaced with disgust. He was solely responsible for the enormous catastrophe. Since the commencement of the invasion, and apart from the deaths of hundreds of thousands of men, nothing had been achieved. The emperor's hands were bathed in blood, and unless we could cross the Berezina soon, thousands more lives – by which I meant everyone in the queue and in Borisov – would be added to the dreadful tally.

Promising Catherine I would be back soon, I worked my way into the throng. The artillery officer I had spoken to earlier was a short way in front, cursing and ordering the civilians in a kibitka out of his path. They protested loudly there was nowhere to go, if the rabble in front of them would not move. The men in question, a ragtag group of soldiers in furs, women's dresses and bonnets, roared that no one was getting past unless they wanted a fight.

I made it to the artillery officer's side. 'What's the hold-up? Has the bridge been closed?'

A surprised look. 'You don't know?'

A tendril of fear. 'I have no idea what you are talking about.'

'The Russians fired the bridge two days ago, maybe three.'

'The river will be frozen, though. Surely we can make it over that way?'

'Should be solid ice in this weather, eh?'

I was dumbstruck. The Berezina was not a big waterway to my knowledge, but flowing, bridgeless, it could as well have been the Rhine. I was no swimmer. I should have slain myself four days ago, I thought, the bitterness coursing.

The artillery officer wasn't finished. 'There is no point crossing here anyway. Minsk has also fallen.'

I stared at him.

The bridge, gone. The river, unfrozen. Shelter in Minsk, and a hundred days' of supplies and food, gone. Despairing, I teetered on the same precipice I had faced before meeting Catherine. Summoning up the dregs of my self-control, telling myself that I *would* see my mother again, I demanded of the artillery officer, 'Why are you trying to get past then? Borisov is tiny, or so they say.'

'And it is a shithole of the first degree. Three hundred houses, and every last one bursting at the seams with imperial staff and soldiers of the Imperial Guard.'

'Has the emperor given orders to construct a new bridge?'

'There are too many Russian guns on the far bank. Even if the engineers succeeded, the casualties during the crossing would be horrendous.'

The officer's desire to get past made no sense. I lowered my voice. 'If you aren't trying to enter Borisov, where *are* you going?'

'It will be public knowledge soon anyway,' he said with a shrug. 'A brigade of Corbineau's cavalry found a better place to cross the Berezina upstream. Studzienka, it's called, and barely a Russian in sight on the opposite bank. The turn for it is only a quarter of a mile further down the road.'

'And the engineers?'

'Oudinot sent hundreds of them up there yesterday. They are already working on two, even three pontoon bridges. Thank God the chief of engineers didn't burn all of his tools and equipment, eh?'

That particular order of Napoleon's I had not heard.

In a whisper, the officer added, 'The emperor is bound for the site this evening.'

Hope stirred in my breast. In spite of his arrogance, Napoleon had a way of achieving the impossible, and in his presence, men were often driven to superhuman efforts. 'How far is Studzienka?'

'Eight miles, I heard.'

Nodding my thanks, I made my way back towards Catherine. His news had rallied my spirits. We could make it that far.

The little devil in my head cackled, and demanded to know what would happen on the other side of the Berezina. With the weather likely to worsen, and other Russian armies to the west, the question was horribly pertinent. It was more than two hundred miles to the relative safety of Vilna, and another fifty after that to the River Niemen, the limit of Russian territory.

Again, I stared into the abyss.

It was probably the smell of the horsemeat being roasted over a small fire by the roadside that grabbed his attention, but Marshal Ney chose this moment to stick his head out of the sling and look up at me.

My heart squeezed. 'Hungry, boy?' I asked, and felt his tail move.

'Mathieu!'

A short distance away, Catherine was beckoning. There was even a smile on her face.

There were reasons not to despair, I decided, two of them at least. Remembering François, and what he had done, I added a third to the list.

CHAPTER XXX

I stamped my feet up and down as I walked, trying, hoping to get them warm. Catherine gave me a dunt with her musket butt, a habit she found amusing, but which I, unsurprisingly, did not.

'Toes numb?' she asked.

'No, thank God,' I said, staring up at the eastern sky. Clear, still full of stars, it was paling ever so slightly. Dawn was not far off.

'Good.'

'You?'

'My bunions are aching, but that is normal enough.'

After this long, we both knew that the danger was greatest if one stopped. Keep moving, walking, and the blood continued to flow.

It had been a long, bitterly cold walk. My first thought had been to sleep on the side of the road, setting out in the morning. Catherine had agreed, but when the jam had inexplicably cleared at about ten in the night, it had seemed better to continue our journey. When it became clear that the majority were taking the track for Studzienka, any thoughts of camping vanished. I was unsurprised that the artillery officer's news had spread like wildfire. Scores of men must have heard about the engineers who had been sent north by Oudinot.

There would be a fight to cross the Berezina, I said to Catherine, and quite possibly not just with the Russians. It was better to reach the still-in-construction bridges sooner rather than later. Following wagons and a long line of stragglers, we had walked along a track that was hardly distinguishable in the starlight. Already there were shapes lying on either side, poor souls that had expired or were in the process of doing so. Inured to the suffering, deaf to the pitiful supplications from those yet living, I kept my gaze fixed on the route ahead. A mile or so along, a fork presented our first dilemma. Left, I had said, because it follows the river. Right, Catherine had argued, because that was the way most people seemed to be taking.

She was more certain.

We went right.

In the end, although both routes went to Studzienka, her choice proved a better one. After a climb to the hamlet of Staroï-Borisov, we had found soldiers slaughtering cattle outside a set of great barns. Perhaps even more miraculously, the soldiers had been from the same line regiment Catherine had travelled into Russia with, the Twenty-First. Welcomed to the fireside, with meat to spare, we had stayed an hour to warm ourselves and devour hunks of half-scorched, half-raw beef. Marshal Ney had eaten well also.

News and gossip went back and forth across the fire; cut off from the vanguard for days, I listened with intent. It was soon clear that our decision not to try and enter the town had been wise. The place was littered with corpses, overturned wagons and debris from the fighting of two days prior, and the streets were packed with women, children and unarmed men – deserters – all in the conviction that the bridge would be repaired and that the crossing would be made at Borisov.

'Better to freeze here than be trampled to death there,' I muttered to Catherine. She pretended not to have heard, a practical solution to the foolish mention of our predicament. There was every chance still that we could succumb to the bitter cold. As to prove the point, a soldier by the fire had then claimed to have heard the emperor's surgeon Larrey – in possession of a lapel thermometer – declare that the temperature several nights before had reached minus twenty-five degrees on the Réaumur scale. To resigned, muted laughter, more than one man had declared it had to be that cold right now.

Unsurprisingly, leaving the fire and its warmth had been pure torture. Driven by my desire to find a spot close to where the bridges would be, I had ignored our new-found companions' advice to stay until it was light. The frozen grass crunching beneath my boots, I walked back towards the track. Catherine joined me, not a protest or complaint passing her lips then or for the rest of our ordeal. As she had opined before, no one would listen anyway. I did not let myself think about what I would do if she fell and could not get up, nor if the roles were reversed.

'There it is.'

At her mumble, my eyes moved to the line of the Berezina.

It ran from behind me along my left side, its almost straight course disappearing off into the silvery murk of fog and cloud. It was not wide, perhaps seventy feet, the same as the Rue Royale in Paris. Just as at Borisov, it was not completely icebound. Thanks to the flood waters, the flat and marshy right bank had doubled its width, and if the half-frozen marshes were added, the obstacle in our path was even more problematic.

Thousands of troops, and hundreds of wagons and carriages had already assembled close to the river. More arrived every minute, and they would not stop coming. Our wait could be long indeed.

My fears swelled. The army's position was unheard of. If Napoleon got away with it, he was the devil himself.

With an effort, I steeled my nerve. Now was not the time to give in to despair. As distraction, I pictured my parents' house on a summer's evening. It helped, although I could not truly imagine being warm.

In a fold of ground encasing the river, and invisible from the other side, I spied six unloaded wagons, and two carts full of what looked like coal. Scores of men were busy there. It was preparatory work: tending a pair of forges, sawing lengths of timber, hammering nails into place.

'They are building bridges,' I said excitedly.

'And see there. Is that not the emperor?'

She was right, I thought.

On the path that shadowed the river came two files of cavalry followed by half a dozen carriages, and after, long columns of infantry. Napoleon had come to evaluate the situation, and where he was, Caulaincourt might be as well. There was small chance of my being allowed to cross the bridges before the rabble, but I might be able to persuade Caulaincourt to let Catherine do so, with Marshal Ney. That would be one weight off my mind. The Master of Horse would know where Marshal Ney the general was, and from him I might discover Jeanne's location. Fresh worry spiked me thinking of her.

She was safe and well, I told myself, perhaps with the staff of the imperial headquarters. She might even be one of those disembarking from the carriages.

'Come on,' I said to Catherine. 'Let us see if I can win you passage over the river.'

'A cantinière go before the troops? Pigs might fly,' she said, but followed willingly enough.

My effort came to an abrupt halt a hundred paces before Napoleon's position. Elite gendarmes mounted on emaciated horses had thrown out a protective cordon; I was told in no uncertain fashion that without the right paperwork, I could go nowhere near the emperor. My protests that I was an imperial messenger were met with a demand for the communication I carried. To this I had no reply, and the officious gendarme, who was wearing a miraculously spotless uniform, blocked my path. Defeated, my position not helped by Catherine's presence, I took us off to one side, right to the water's edge.

'That did not work then.'

I gave her a sour glance. 'I shall try again, when I see Caulaincourt.'

'Do you really think he will help?'

'I do not know,' I said, frustrated, 'but it is worth a try.'

She did not argue.

The cordon of gendarmes was closer to the emperor here; I could see Napoleon, busily chewing on a chop. He was wearing a fur, and instead of his customary headgear, a green velvet cap, lined with furs, that came down over his eyes. Berthier was there too, and Oudinot.

Their attention was not on the four Russian guns on the opposite bank; thanks to a barrage from Oudinot's cannon, they had just been forced to withdraw, but rather on the Dutch pontoneers who were gathering on the section of riverbank that lay between us and Napoleon. Hundreds, there must have been, stripping down to their underclothes. Perhaps two dozen heavy trestles of varying height stood there; these would form the piles upon which the bridge sat.

'*Sacré Coeur*, are those men going into the water?' Catherine's voice was a whisper.

'The bridge will not build itself.'

'They will die!'

'Some of them, probably,' I said. 'But the Russians are coming, and if there is no way to cross . . .'

I had no need to finish the sentence.

*

Several hours passed. Catherine had gone off into what was fast becoming a vast, sprawling encampment. Nothing was free anymore, so I had given her two gold coins. If she had the good fortune to find food, or a fire to warm ourselves by, she would return to find me at the same spot.

I remained by the river, hoping to speak to Caulaincourt and in the meantime watching the construction of both bridges. The position of the second, for the artillery and wagons, was close to my own. Inside the new cordon formed by the gendarmes, overlooked for whatever reason, I had not been moved on. Of Caulaincourt there was no sign, so I stayed where I was, also keeping an eye out for Catherine.

The pontoneers' efforts were heroic in the extreme. Often in the freezing water up to their necks, avoiding where possible the large ice floes, they manhandled trestle after trestle into place. The effort required to fix them in the riverbed was clear, because each one took an age, and the price paid was heavy. Now and again, a cry would go up as, overcome by the cold, a pontoneer would go under. Carried away by the current, not a single one re-emerged, yet their comrades' energy wasn't the less for seeing them come to this end. On and on they pressed, and gradually, the bridge grew in length.

The emperor was now quite close to me. His back against a trestle, arms crossed inside his overcoat, Napoleon watched with the intentness of a cat by a mousehole. 'It's taking a very long time, General. A very long time,' I heard him say to Eblé, who commanded the Dutch pontoneers.

Eblé's response was self-assured. 'You can see, sire, how deep the water is for my men, and the ice is holding up their work. I've no food or brandy to warm them with.'

'That'll do,' replied the emperor, staring at the ground. But a few moments later, he began complaining again. He seemed to have forgotten what Eblé had said.

A group of about sixty lancers was sent across the river to scout out the Russians' positions. Columns of the enemy had been visible, marching south on the road to Borisov, but it was unclear if this was a feint designed to confuse. The lancers were followed by a hundred chasseurs, most with a voltigeur clinging to their horse's crupper. It was not long before word was sent back to our side of the Berezina. I was close enough to see the emperor as he was listening to the messenger, take hold of the man's earlobe and pinch it.

The sight heartened me, because it meant that the news was good. A few minutes later, hearing two staff officers talking, my hunch was proved correct. The Russians had retreated – inexplicably – and the Cossacks who remained had been driven off. The opposite bank was ours, said the one. For the moment, his comrade shot back, receiving a sour grimace by way of reply.

By eleven that morning, word came to Napoleon that the first bridge was complete. Leaving the half-constructed second at once, he walked off.

My eyes trailed the emperor.

The structure of a sloping sawhorse, suspended like a trestle on shallow-sunk piles, the bridge was covered by long stringers, planks fashioned from the dismantled timber houses in Studzienka. Across the planks were only bridge-ties, which were not fastened down. Nothing about it looked particularly solid; in ordinary circumstances, I would have been reluctant to use it. Now I cheered '*Vive l'Empereur!*' with everyone else as a column of troops, led by Oudinot himself, walked slowly across. Cavalry followed in single file, each dismounted rider and reins-led horse some distance from the next.

I dared to think of survival, and a reunion with Guillaume in Paris, but wary of disappointment, did not let my hopes rise any further.

It was at this point that my chance to speak with Caulaincourt came. Recognising his characteristic walk as he passed the cordon, aiming in Napoleon's direction, I took to my heels and, holding onto Marshal Ney so that he did not fall out of the sling, ran. I say ran, but I was so weak from deprivation that it was more of a shambling lope. I called to him several times, but my voice was lost amid the noise of shouted commands and the tramp of feet, and from the other side, the carbine shots that showed not every Cossack had fled.

At last, however, he heard. No trace of recognition was in his face, however, as he turned.

Realising that I was no different to any other wild-eyed, filthy creature, and similarly accoutred in layers of mismatched clothing, I shouted, 'It is I, sir, Dupont, your messenger!'

'Who?'

I reached him, my chest heaving. 'It's Dupont, sir. We last met in Orsha. I was with Mademoiselle Préville – you helped her.'

He sighed, and rubbed at the reddened tip of his long nose. 'Of course, I know you, Dupont. It is good you are alive. I had heard about your comrade François, and when you did not return with the others, assumed the worst.'

'I am still here, sir.'

'That is well. You have the dog also.' Since I had stopped, he had stuck his head out of the sling.

I grinned. 'Marshal Ney, he is called.'

A chuckle. 'If you are here wanting to carry messages, do not concern yourself – you have no horse anyway. Just get over the river when the time comes. I shall see you on the other side, God willing.' He made to leave.

'A question, sir, if I may?'

A preoccupied nod. 'Yes?'

'Jeanne Préville, sir, is she still with the imperial headquarters?'

A frown. 'She is not.'

Panic seized me. 'She is not dead, sir?'

'I hope not.' Seeing my confusion, he continued, 'There was a woman at Borisov, a cantinière, giving birth by the side of the road. Mademoiselle Préville wanted to help.' Caulaincourt's expression grew pained. 'I offered what assistance was possible; even if I could have had the woman placed in one of the carriages, she was in no condition to be moved.'

'Jeanne stayed with her?' I could picture the scene.

'She would have it no other way.'

Horror rushed in, and with it, guilt, to think I had been so close to Jeanne and passed her by.

'Take heart, Dupont,' said Caulaincourt. 'She is a strong-willed woman. If anyone can get through, it is her. Now, I must go.'

I caught his arm. 'Sir, there is one more thing.'

'What?'

I poured out my tale. 'Catherine, sir, she is a fine woman. She lost her husband, at Borodino and a child too, during the retreat from Moscow' – this last part I was making up, but I needed it to sound as worthy as possible – 'I do not ask for myself of course, but I wondered if it might be feasible . . .' I hesitated, then gambled '. . . if you had a word with the gendarmes, sir, she could pass through the cordon and cross the river now.'

A slightly pained look. 'At Orsha, Dupont, I was glad to help, but things are different here. Combatants have priority, you can understand that. Let her go over when it is dark. No one will stop her. The troops are to recommence crossing at dawn.' With a preoccupied smile, Caulaincourt left me.

I watched him go, hopelessness, fear and anger fighting one another for control. Jeanne, who I had hoped was safe and well, who in her carriage would have been among the first to venture over the second bridge, had been missing since Borisov. By now, she could well be dead, just another frozen corpse among the multitude. Catherine *could* cross the river tonight, but in the pitch black and freezing cold, it was hard to see how she would do so alone. For alone she would be, I decided. I could not go with her. I corrected myself. While a chance remained that Jeanne was still alive, I was unprepared to accompany Catherine.

I did not like to think of the kind of man that that made me.

It was perhaps half past three and growing dark when I met up with Catherine again. She was in fine humour, and did not immediately notice my black mood.

'Here!' She held out something, an indeterminate yellow-white blob.

'What is it?'

'Honey, you fool. D'you want it or not?'

I took the lump of honeycomb, for that is what it was, and bit off a chunk. Wax or not, it tasted divine, the sweetness like nothing I had tasted in weeks. Even here, happiness was still possible, I decided. 'Where did you find honey in a hellhole like this?'

'Walk, and I will tell you.' I obeyed, and she said, 'Judging by your manner, you had no luck in winning us passage?'

As women do, she had read my mind despite my effort to reveal nothing. 'You can cross when it is dark.'

Again her response was razor sharp. 'And you?'

'I – I have to stay.' I explained about Jeanne. Dreading Catherine's reaction, guilt filling me, I went on hurriedly, 'That does not mean *you* have to remain. It might be better to go at nightfall, when there is no crowding on the bridge.'

A derisive laugh. 'I am not insane! There is hardly a civilian on the other side, and God knows how many thousand Russians are in the vicinity. Oudinot's position is far from secure.'

To my surprise, there was no accusation of abandonment, that I was obliged to accompany her to the far bank. Somehow that made me feel worse. Awkward, wanting to fill the silence, I asked, 'You found a fire?'

'I did,' she said proudly. 'It ain't too far either.'

That was an unexpected relief. I was glad she knew where to go, because the terrain was covered as far as the eye could see with cannon, ammunition wagons and all kinds of vehicles. Fires burned everywhere, with a variegated mass of people crowded together around each one, a ring of gaunt, smoke-blackened faces, ice-encrusted beards, hollow cheeks, sunken eyes. Their numbers were impossible to know accurately, but it was in the tens of thousands. Seldom among any of the miserable specimens did I see anything reminiscent of a complete uniform. At least half the men were unarmed. Perhaps a quarter looked capable of fighting.

The Grande Armée, the finest spectacle in all of Europe five months before, was no more, even as its greatest test drew nigh.

The Russians were closing in from almost every direction.

I shoved that grim thought away.

It turned out that soon after Catherine had left me, she had chanced upon a group of soldiers gathered around a tree, at the top of which was a large beehive. Declaring that they might as well die of a fall as perish from hunger, two men had clambered perhaps thirty feet up into the branches and from there, with the aid of a pair of rods, smashed the hive open. 'They threw it down bit by bit,' said Catherine, chuckling. 'Their comrades threw themselves on it like famished dogs. It was easy enough for me to grab a few pieces. They cursed me, but there was only so much they could cram into their mouths.'

'You are a miracle worker,' I said, relishing my last mouthful. 'Is there any more?'

A snort. 'I used your money, though.'

'What did you get?'

'With one gold coin, a bottle of rum.'

I laughed with excitement. 'And the other?'

'Two big loaves of rye bread.'

As the wind strengthened, and the snow fell furiously, I decided that tomorrow was another day. I would do my best to find Jeanne: more than that I could not do.

In the meantime, there were worse things than food, drink and a fire.

CHAPTER XXXI

I was woken by Catherine kicking me in the shins. 'Stir yourself!'

Resentful, for I was reasonably warm, I peered out from under the bearskin. 'Why?'

'Nine o'clock it is, or so I heard an officer say. Don't you want to find your lady friend?'

Realising that I had slept for more than fifteen hours, I sat up. The twenty-seventh day of November, it was sunny and clear, and far milder than I would have expected after the previous day's bitterly cold wind. 'Nine o'clock?'

'That's what I said.'

'When did you get up?' I had not even felt her move from under the bearskin.

'A little while after the soldiers and artillery started crossing at six. I couldn't sleep with the noise. I went to see if I could cross, but the gendarmes aren't letting any non-combatants over. I shoved my musket in one's face, and told him I would fight the Russians, but he would not budge an inch, the jumped-up little prick. I'm surprised my shouting didn't wake you up.'

'I didn't hear a thing.' She had been gone for hours, I thought. It was a miracle that the bearskin was still on me, that someone hadn't stolen it and run. The reason soon became clear. Our companions on either side were also still wrapped in their blankets; it was their presence that had helped deter thieves.

'Sleep like the dead, you do,' said Catherine drily. 'You didn't even stir when the artillery bridge gave way in the middle of the night. There was a fearful commotion.'

It was alarming news. The bridge had done so once already, at eight the previous evening. 'Has it been fixed?' I hated how my voice quavered.

'It has, some time since. Those Dutch pontoneers are bloody heroes.'

I did not ask if there were many left alive.

'So there is no way across at the moment?'

A scowl. 'There is, if one keeps trying. The gendarmes' cordon is porous. "Only combatants to pass!" they shout, but no one pays any heed. Enough people are pushing forward; the gendarmes cannot stop them all.'

'Why don't you go then?' I was also tempted, but my pride would not let me leave without a proper search for Jeanne.

'They are shoving and fighting just to get onto the bridge. I do not wish to be crushed or trampled!' A sigh. 'It's almost worse on the thing. The press is terrible; I have seen more than a dozen people fall into the water.'

It was a dreadful image, and drove home the improbability of getting Jeanne, and a woman freshly delivered of a child, not to mention the infant, over the Berezina unharmed. The odds of success were fantastical. The little devil was quick to chip in. *Get yourself and the dog across*, it advised. *The cantinière too, if you must. Jeanne is dead, you know that. So is the woman she tried to help, and the babe. Save your own life, while you can.*

Summoning up the last of my stubbornness, I told the devil to go to Hell. In all likelihood, I decided, I would be joining it soon, thinking with black amusement that at least it would be warm there.

'What are you going to do?' challenged Catherine.

'Look for Jeanne.' I fished about under the bearskin and found the half rye loaf remaining to me. It was half-frozen, but I did not care. Marshal Ney seemed happy enough with his portion too.

'I will help.'

'You don't have to.'

A shrug. 'Better than sitting about doing nothing, isn't it?'

I stood up and before she could react, planted a smacking kiss on her cheek.

'Get off me!' Then, 'What was that for?'

'You are a good woman, Catherine.'

'Go on with you.' Despite her growl, she was pleased.

'Two of us can work through the camp twice as fast.'

'If Jeanne is here, we now stand a chance of finding her.'

I could not stop the little devil joining in. *And if you do not find her?*

288

We will cross the bridge at the first opportunity, I shot back.

The response was instant. *It might be too late.*

Then I will see you in Hell, I thought savagely. With Marshal Ney and Catherine.

That silenced it, for a time at least.

'I will go this way, and you go that,' Catherine ordered. 'Meet back here by two o'clock. That will give us an hour to try and cross before it starts to get dark.'

I nodded agreement.

'Her stage name is Mademoiselle Préville?' I had told her this before.

'Yes.'

'And her real one?'

'Jeanne Drouin.'

'Mademoiselle Préville!' Catherine's bellow would have woken the dead. 'I am looking for Mademoiselle Préville! Or Jeanne Drouin!' Off she stalked, musket in hand, without a backward glance.

'Come on, boy,' I said to Marshal Ney. 'We can't let her steal all the glory.'

It took more than three hours, but in the event, it was I who found Jeanne. My voice reduced to a dry croak from calling her name, I had paused to suck on a mouthful of clean snow to try and soothe my itching throat. My eyes roving without success over the unfortunates in the vicinity, I actually heard Jeanne speak behind me.

Thinking I was imagining it, I paid no heed.

'Let her alone! She has a baby, can you not see?' It was definitely Jeanne.

My musket was coming up even as I turned.

Perhaps twenty steps away and facing me, Jeanne stood in front of a fur-wrapped shape on the ground. Between us, the subject of her attention, was a scrawny shape in filthy rags. There was a knife in his right hand.

'The bitch is almost dead,' said the would-be thief. 'She don't need the fur. I do. Move aside.'

'I will not!' Jeanne was scared, but she did not budge.

'I'll gut you.'

'Not before my musket ball blows a hole in your back.' I cocked my weapon.

He whirled.

'Go on, piss off.'

With a peg-toothed snarl, he vanished into the crowd.

I swung the muzzle of my musket left to right, in case there had been accomplices.

'He was on his own,' said Jeanne, her face alight. 'Thank you, Mathieu.'

I strode forward, and because of my musket, drew her into a one-armed embrace. She sagged against my chest, for a moment drained of energy. 'I cannot believe you are alive,' I murmured.

She poked me. 'I can look after myself!'

'Unless I am mistaken, you needed help just now.'

Her face fell. 'I left my pistol beside Aimée just now. It was stupid.'

'No matter.'

'I am glad to see Marshal Ney.' She gave him a pat; his tail moved inside the sling.

I peered past her. The woman under the furs, Aimée, I assumed, was asleep. I indicated the little bump beside her. 'Her baby?'

'Yes. A little boy – Jean-Baptiste, he is called.'

I had seen the sadness in Jeanne's smile. 'Is he well? Healthy?'

A tiny shake of her head, the suggestion of a tear. 'The birth was difficult. He is sickly. Weak.'

I did not like this at all. 'And the mother?'

'She bled a little after the birth, but it stopped. I am not sure when it started again, probably during the journey from Borisov, I suppose. I had found her a space on a carriage, but the track was so bumpy . . .'

'And the bleeding continues?'

Jeanne's gaze met mine.

'The carriage she came on?'

'It has shed a wheel.'

Not that it mattered, I thought. Civilian vehicles were not being allowed onto the bridges. 'Can she walk?' I whispered.

No answer.

'Jeanne—'

'I will not abandon her! She has no one, except the baby.' Determination blazed from Jeanne's eyes.

'Very well,' I said. 'We shall have to find her a place in the back of a military wagon.'

The tiniest trace of hope in her careworn face. 'Can you do that, Mathieu?'

'I will do my best.'

'Thank you.' She squeezed my hand.

'Jeanne?' The voice was faint.

She knelt by Aimée. 'I am here.'

'It is past time for Jean-Baptiste's feed.'

'I will help you.'

I watched as Jeanne moved aside the fur and picked up a tiny, swaddled shape. My heart warmed; despite the indescribable horror all around us, life could go on. Then I noticed Jeanne's expression, which was stricken. She was lifting the baby up, placing her ear against its mouth. *No*, I thought. No.

'Let me hold him,' said Aimée, unaware.

'Soon.'

Mother's intuition. 'What's wrong?'

I crossed to Jeanne, asked a question with my eyes. She shook her head.

'My boy! Give me my boy!'

'A moment, Aimée,' said Jeanne, doing her best to sound reassuring.

I slipped a forefinger under the swaddling clothes onto the baby's chest and waited. A full minute passed, counting in my head, with no heartbeat. *He is gone*, I mouthed to Jeanne.

'Jean-Baptiste!'

Heads were turning, people looking, but I did not care. The world had shrunk to a mother who was about to discover that her newborn was dead.

'*Nooooo!*' It was a terrible, throat-tearing scream.

Tears welled. I could not look at Jeanne, still less Aimée.

Of all the deaths I had witnessed since the Niemen, this was the most tragic, the most poignant. The hundreds of thousands of men and women who had died had committed some sins at least. Jean-Baptiste, not even a week old, was entirely innocent, guilty of no wrongdoing.

He had died, nonetheless.

I could hear Jeanne trying to soothe Aimée, her voice calm and gentle. Aimée was crying, great wracking sobs that tore at my heart. It was too hard to listen; telling Jeanne that I was going to find a space on a wagon, I walked away.

'Mathieu?'

I turned. Jeanne was staring at me. 'Yes?'

'You will come back?'

A fresh dart of pain struck, that she could even think such a thing. 'I swear it on my life, Jeanne.'

A wan smile.

There was almost no chance of finding someone who would agree to carry Aimée, but I had to try. And when I failed, I had to return, and help in whatever way was possible. At that, the little devil's laughter reached new heights. I had no reply, other than to ignore him. I would do my best, until the end, and that would have to do.

An hour later, and ill fortune was my only companion. I had been refused by the soldiers in charge of any military vehicles I approached, and as I had thought, no civilian carriages were being permitted to cross the river. Despite this, the jam around the approach to the second bridge was horrendous. Pulled by horses that were more dead than alive was the greatest variety of vehicles I had seen since the departure from Moscow. It was incredible that so many had come this far, but their journey would end here. As the gendarmes barring the way kept shouting, only caissons, gun carriages and military wagons could cross.

Their declarations did not stop the desperate.

An elderly man in a fine astrakhan coat had somehow manoeuvred his cognat-drawn kibitka right up to the bridge. 'Let me by!' he demanded, waving his whip as he might have done at a servant. It was a foolish move. Without warning, the nearest gendarme raised his sword. He struck the old man's shoulder with the flat of the blade, hard enough to knock him from his seat. 'Away!' shouted the gendarme. 'Get away, if you do not want worse!' Cowed, the man retreated, but his kibitka remained, blocking the entrance to the bridge.

It took four gendarmes a little while to turn the cognats and move the vehicle out of the way. In that time, several dozen people had scrambled onto the bridge. The gendarmes shouted and threatened in vain, but they could not give pursuit, lest those in the surrounding crowd charged forward.

Even without a space in a wagon, I decided, it *was* possible for a strong, uninjured person to get onto the bridge. I could do it; so could Jeanne, and without question, Catherine. Aimée was a different matter.

Frail and overcome with grief, she had no more chance of fighting through the mob than I had of singlehandedly defeating the Russian army.

I refused to give up, and began to work my way along the queue of wagons and gun carriages. At each, I tried a new ploy, the sick mother who had a baby, who was too weak to walk. This elicited some sympathy, but few men were prepared to help, in the main, I think, because so many others were in a similar plight. Every vehicle had a crowd around it; the air rang with pleas and entreaties, offers of physical favours from women, and coin from men. When, desperate, I offered ten gold coins to a kind-faced artilleryman, I was faced not just with demands for the money, but for the woman and babe to get into the wagon immediately.

Defeated, I realised that I should have brought Jeanne and Aimée to the bridge. There was a hidden blessing to this. It was not yet two o'clock, the time I had arranged to meet Catherine. If I had found a place for Aimée, the temptation to cross at once would have been hard to resist. I had not, so I began to make my way to where I had left the two women.

My mood was bleak. We were all going to die here in this icebound, frozen wasteland, if not from the cold, then at the hands of the Russians. I wondered about going back and trying to give Marshal Ney into the care of one of the artillerymen, but I could not do it. He was too dear to me.

I stroked his head. It was a habit I had fallen into on the walk to Borisov, something comforting to us both. 'We will make it,' I told him. Wag, wag went his tail.

He did not know that I felt like the greatest liar in the world.

CHAPTER XXXII

I found Jeanne hunched in her blankets beside Aimée. Even at a distance I sensed all was not well. She was not moving or speaking, and Aimée was quite still. Closer, I saw the all too familiar waxen sheen of her skin.

A sudden heavy impact on the back of my head. Stars bursting across my vision, agony lancing my brain, I dropped, stunned. Cold snow bathed the side of my face; in my dazed state, it was comforting.

From somewhere far off came a woman's screams.

Jeanne, I thought fuzzily.

Now there were pleas for help.

With a superhuman effort, I pulled in my arms and pushed myself up off the snow. A man in rags was fighting with Jeanne, slashing a knife at her with one hand, and trying to tear away her blankets with the other. She, pale-faced, dodged back and forth out of the way of his blade, and determinedly refused to relinquish her grip.

Dull-brained as I was, it was clear she would soon be stabbed. Move, I told myself. Move, or she is dead.

Musket serving as staff, I somehow clambered to my knees, and then my feet. With what seemed like infinitesimal slowness, struggling for focus, I brought the musket up and managed to cock it. I aimed it at Jeanne's assailant, but with them weaving back and forth, I had as much chance of hitting her.

She screamed.

I stared. Blood was welling from a cut on her cheek.

I took several steps towards them, the muzzle wobbling. Neither of them saw. Jeanne was weakening, but somehow still had hold of her blanket, all that stood between her and freezing to death.

Close in, I brought the end of the musket up against the man's right side – Jeanne was to his left – and pulled the trigger.

He went down roaring. There was little to see on his back, but crimson immediately began to flood out around his body, colouring the snow.

Jeanne threw me a look of utter relief, and collapsed beside Aimée. Her frame jerked; she was in tears.

Not knowing what to say, my head a sea of pain, I rested a trembling hand on her shoulder.

'She is gone.' Jeanne spoke in a whisper.

Aimée, I thought. 'Long ago?'

'It was soon after she realised Jean-Baptiste had died. She just . . . gave up.'

'God rest her soul,' I said, not remotely surprised. A small part of me was sorry, but mostly I felt overwhelming relief. Aimée, unknowing, had aided our cause. I did not say so, but instead let Jeanne grieve, and, keeping an eye out for other attackers, slowly reloaded my musket.

Time passed. My headache eased a fraction; fortunately I had been struck a glancing blow, the man who had done it in a weakened state. As for him, he died whimpering. I paid no heed. I heard men yell that Napoleon was crossing the river. He should stay until the very last, I thought bitterly, and suffer with his men, as they have for him. It would never happen of course. To survive, an empire needed its emperor. It was perhaps surprising that Napoleon had stayed this long.

The news of his departure saw an immediate and noticeable dip in the mood in the encampment. I fought a nagging dread myself. With the emperor gone, the chaos at the bridges would worsen fast. If we did not cross today, I thought, no, as soon as possible, we might never reach the opposite bank.

'We had best leave.'

Startled, I glanced at Jeanne.

'I would like to dig them a grave—' she faltered.

'The ground is hard-frozen. It would take us a day at least.'

'The Russians will be here by then.'

'If not before,' I said, trying not to feel terrified. It was surprising that there had been no shooting from the direction of Borisov yet.

'Give me a moment.' Jeanne placed Jean-Baptiste on Aimée's chest, and with difficulty, wrapped her arms about him. Kissing them both, she stood. Her gaze was haunted, but incredibly, she was dry-eyed. 'I am ready.'

'We must find Catherine.' Jeanne's surprise made me realise there had not been enough time to tell her about the tough cantinière. 'You will like her,' I said, praying that Catherine would be at the appointed meeting place. If she was not, we could wait, but from what I could see, my concern about crossing was already being borne out. The entire area around each bridge was a seething, heaving-to-and-fro mass of humanity. Even as I watched, two people fell off the infantry bridge, into the Berezina.

My sense of urgency redoubled. Order was never going to be restored. Every moment of delay risked disaster.

To my immense relief, Catherine was exactly where we had agreed.

'This is Jeanne?' she asked, abrupt as ever.

I nodded, wincing at the waves of fresh pain this caused. 'Jeanne, meet Catherine.'

Catherine gave me a meaningful look. 'Just the two of you?'

'Yes,' I said, picturing Jean-Baptiste cradled in Aimée's arms.

'I am sorry,' she said to Jeanne.

The two clasped hands, the small gesture meaning more than any words.

When I declared that the press was too bad at the artillery bridge, there was no objection, so I led the way to the infantry one. Worryingly, it was a good deal lower in the water than it had been; near the far bank, there was water lapping over the planking. This new danger – the possibility that the bridge might collapse under us – made my guts lurch, but there was no other option. It was this, or wait. Freeze in the cold, or let the Russians kill us.

I chose our approach with care. Arrive anywhere but directly before it, and we risked being pushed off the bank and into the river. From the cries and protests, this was already happening. The gendarmes were still trying to block the passage to non-combatants, but they were so few in number that their presence scarcely mattered.

My musket slung over one shoulder and portmanteau hanging off my back, I went at the front of our little line. Then came Jeanne. Catherine took up the rear.

'Do not stop for anything,' I ordered. 'Hold onto each other at all costs.'

Catherine nodded.

Jeanne tried to speak, but I cut across her. 'If it comes to it, you save yourself. Understand?'

At last, tears in her eyes. 'Yes, Mathieu.'

I drove into the back of the throng with every ounce of my strength, using my elbows to open a path. I paid no heed to those around me, blocked my ears to the clamouring voices. When a paunchy, bearded man furiously objected to my standing on his foot, I drove a fist into his midriff. Winded, his mouth a shocked 'O', he would have fallen but for the density of the crowd. What became of him I never found out, because a sudden great movement all but picked me up. Twenty, thirty paces I must have been carried forward. Panicking, I called out to Jeanne and Catherine, and was greatly relieved to hear their voices close behind.

Just as my hopes rose – I was within fifteen paces of the bridge – there came a great heave from the left. Packed tightly by those around me, my feet left the ground, and I was carried off to the right. I struggled and fought, but arms trapped by my sides, was completely powerless to prevent what was happening. I prayed that Marshal Ney was not being crushed in his sling.

'Jeanne! Catherine!'

'Here!' Catherine was behind and to my left. 'Jeanne is with me!'

At least they were close, I thought.

Heave. This time the surge came from the back. I was driven forward, in the direction of the river. Raw panic tore at me.

'No!' A woman's voice, terrified, from in front of my position. 'Please!'

There was a horrible cracking sound – ice – and then splashes, and more screams and cries. Heave. Again I was pushed, again towards the riverbank. 'Get your feet down. Try to get a grip,' I urged the people on either side, but they, terrified out of their wits, either did not hear or paid no attention.

Time slowed. I was being moved inexorably to the water's edge. Taller than most, I had a good view of my impending fate. The Berezina, which had part-frozen in the night, was flowing again. Its surface was dotted with ice floes, some small, others large as ammunition wagons. Less beautiful were the bobbing heads of those who had fallen or been pushed in, and who were attempting to swim to the opposite side. Even as I watched, one, two dipped under the surface. They did not reappear.

Closer, there were men and women in the icy shallows, drenched, distraught, heads turning this way and that. They were calling for their companions, or seemingly paralysed, unsure what to do. Their dilemma was tragic, heart-breaking: whether to try to regain this bank or make for the far one.

I felt fresh despair.

Heave. I was propelled forward again, and the next instant, felt the squelch of semi-frozen mud under my boots. I tensed, but as the next heave came, was unable to prevent myself falling off the bank and into the Berezina. Shouts, roars of pain filled my ears; I was driven to my knees. The shock of the cold water in my boots, all up my legs, was tremendous. I barely managed not to be sent down onto my face, where I would surely have drowned. Somehow I got up, having the wits to retreat further into the river where there was more room. Marshal Ney seemed unharmed, and dry, which was something.

'Jeanne! Catherine!' I bellowed, thinking, I will never see them again.

'Here!'

Incredibly, there they were, not twenty feet away, both wet and scared-looking, but alive. With my musket held like a club, I waded my way to them. Numbness was already creeping up my legs.

'What can we do?' Jeanne asked, her voice small. 'I am no swimmer.'

I glanced at Catherine, and saw my resignation mirrored in her eyes.

'Mathieu?'

There was no way out of our predicament other than an icy, watery death, so I did not answer.

'My God, look.' Catherine's voice, raw with shock.

My gaze followed hers to the bridge. So many people were crossing that those on either side of the rickety structure risked falling off at every step. Desperate to avoid this fate, the majority had turned to face the river. Using their heels as brakes, gripping onto whoever they could behind, they inched along, their expressions utterly terrified. They prayed. Wept. Begged those at their backs not to push.

It made no difference to the fate of some.

A young woman fell from the bridge, taking with her a girl of perhaps ten. A cloaked soldier who tried to grab the girl toppled in after. His was the only head that came to the surface. Mesmerised with horror, I saw him start swimming towards the opposite bank. Perhaps a third of the way across, he vanished without trace.

Splash. Agonisingly close to the far side, a man with a crutch fell into the freezing water.

Sickened, I turned away.

'Even if we get onto the bridge . . .' Jeanne's voice faltered.

I had no words of comfort. We were going to die, I thought. Here. Now.

'Back! Back! Out of my way!' A smacking sound followed, and a scream of pain.

The awful sounds were not much different to the others filling the air, but for some reason my attention was dragged back to their source. Near the bridge I spied two figures, as filthy and ill-dressed as any; they were using the flats of their sword blades to clear a path out of the river. Judging from the cries of pain, they seemed full-willing to break bones and crack pates. The nearest man's head turned, studying the mob for a better route. To my complete shock, it was Féraud. No discernible trace of his hussar uniform remained, but it was Féraud.

From the depths of despair, utter determination. 'If you want to live, come with me!' I said to the two women. 'Féraud!' I shouted, striding towards him. 'FÉRAUD!'

He heard, and paused in what he was doing. A few paces out, he recognised me. 'Ah, Dupont.' His voice was as casual as if our encounter was on a Parisian street. 'I had not thought to meet again.'

'Nor I you,' I said, smiling back at his companion, who was no less than the gap-toothed corporal. I gestured at Jeanne and Catherine. 'There are two women with me. One is the actress Mademoiselle Préville – she was starring in the *Pied de Mouton* the evening we met.'

'How could I forget?' Féraud made a deep bow. 'Mademoiselle.'

'The other is a cantinière who saved my life.' But for Catherine, I thought, I would have killed myself that day.

Féraud inclined his chin courteously at Catherine. Then he said, 'Follow, if you will. Stay close.'

Even as we muttered our thanks, he and the corporal set to again, literally beating a passage through the crowd. I was a pace to the rear, leaving barely enough room for them to swing. Jeanne and Catherine were at my back.

The two hussars applied themselves to their task with focused, brutal dedication. It did not matter who was in their path: men, women, soldiers, civilians, wounded or whole. Up and down went their sabres, each dull slap accompanied by a cry or oomph of pain and surprise. The crowd parted before them, almost as miraculously as the Red Sea in front of Moses.

Up the bank we went, beside the pilings laid by the pontoneers. Not long after, we were on level ground, and I saw Féraud's purpose. He and the corporal executed a sharp right turn, and began to clear our way to the bridge, which was close by. Delaying our advance a fraction, they brought us into position just in front of a horse-drawn ammunition wagon. The pushing and shoving grew terrible at this point; even the fear of the hussars' sabres could not stop people from trying to get to safety.

Driven almost to my knees, it took all my strength – and Jeanne and Catherine's help – to stand again. We were going to fail, I thought with an almost detached interest. The bridge might as well have been a thousand miles away.

'Go on!' Féraud had managed to place his back against the crowd, so that we might pass in front of him. The corporal was doing the same. 'Go!'

Sudden hope ignited in my heart. I urged Jeanne forward. She squeezed through and under the necks of the lead horses, onto the bridge. Catherine made to protest, but I seized her arm and with brute strength, heaved her past myself *and* Féraud.

'Now you,' I said, even as he was driven hard up against me by the people behind.

'Not this time.'

I sensed his purpose, and tried to drag him with me, but he and the corporal had linked arms.

Our eyes met.

'This repays my debt,' said Féraud.

I could not shift them. He knew it. The corporal, grinning, knew it. I knew it too.

'I will see you both on the other side,' I said, hoping against hope. 'Go!'

I scrambled forward, gripping the nearest horse's harness so as not to fall into the river. Ten breathless steps, and I was in front of it, joining

Jeanne and Catherine. Marshal Ney licked my hand, as if to tell me he was also unhurt. The press was terrible, but we were moving forward, over the bridge, and thanks be to God, we were right in the middle of the crowd, with a wagon behind us. Copying Féraud and the corporal, we linked arms, and step by slow step, began to cross the Berezina.

From the depths of despair, a flash of pure joy. I would see Paris again, I decided, and so would Marshal Ney. I would be reunited with Guillaume. More than that, I would return to England's shores, there to see my family. They were what mattered to me.

My last glimpse of Féraud came a few moments later, when we were carried a little to the right, and I could see past the wagon. He was right at the edge of the crowd, struggling, fighting to stay on the bridge, and the corporal was swearing blue murder, threatening the people pushing in on them. Abruptly, Féraud vanished from sight, and I heard the corporal cry out. The splash that followed chilled my blood, but trapped amid the throng, able only to keep moving forward, I was powerless to help.

I kept glancing back as the far bank drew closer, but the wagon and the multitude behind me meant that the corporal and Féraud, if he was still on the bridge, had been lost to sight.

A fist clenched at my heart.

'Those two brave men saved us,' said Catherine. 'But for them . . .'

'I know.' My voice cracked.

'Who were they?' Jeanne asked.

'Friends.' I added hoarsely, 'Like both of you.'

AUTHOR'S NOTE

I called this novel *1812* from the start, but an editorial conversation in September 2022 concluded that a different title might grab new readers' attention. I think that *Napoleon's Spy* is pretty catchy; hopefully, it garnered lots of new readers. If that's you – welcome! I know, I know, technically Mathieu Carrey was not a spy for Napoleon, but *against* him. Forgive me for that, along with any other errors that you might find. I am optimistic these will not be too plentiful because as is my habit, I sought the opinion of academics before the book went to print. Thank you, Dr Zack White and Dr Alexander Mika-beridze, both of whom were extremely generous with their time and comments.

Moving to the Napoleonic period was simultaneously an absolute joy and an impossible nightmare. Used to Roman texts which describe entire wars in a few lines, and medieval ones that are little better, I was faced with enough first-hand accounts to take up years of reading. The text that inspired me to write this novel – Adam Zamoyski's extraordinary *1812: Napoleon's Fatal March on Moscow* – provided a rich and vivid overarching sense of the whole affair, but it was Paul Britten Austin's unsurpassable 1200-page tome *1812: Napoleon's Invasion of Russia* that became my constant companion during 2022. Written over a twenty-five year period, it draws together in linear fashion more than one hundred and fifty first-hand accounts of the campaign. It would have been a privilege to thank Mr Austin for a text that made writing this novel easy, but sadly he died in 2005. *Dis manibus*. Another real favourite was *Men of Steel* by Michael Crumplin FRCS, an unputdownable text about the treatment of injuries and wounds in the Napoleonic wars. Sharp-eyed readers may notice several homages to the author Ronald Welch and his wonderful novel *Escape to France*.

The seam of historical information is so rich that this book almost feels like a work of non-fiction with a few fictional characters thrown in! Almost every incident, as well as a lot of the conversations, is taken directly from sources. Even still, only a fraction of the research made it into this book. Unable to include all the real characters who could experience the campaign as themselves, I plundered their stories with abandon. I hope that their shades look with kindness on this book, recognising that I hold them in deep respect.

An incomplete list of texts and novels in my library includes: *Napoleon's Hussars* by Emir Bukhari and Angus McBride; *The Campaigns of Napoleon* by David Chandler; *The Georgian Art of Gambling* by Claire Cock-Starkey; *The Note-Books of Captain Coignet, Soldier of the Empire, 1799–1816*; *The Exploits of Brigadier Gerard* by Sir Arthur Conan Doyle; *With Napoleon in Russia: The Memoirs of General de Caulaincourt, Duke of Vicenza*; *The Memoirs of Baron de Marbot* by Jean-Baptiste de Marbot; *Borodino and the War of 1812* by Christopher Duffy; *Swords Around a Throne* by John R. Elting; *Honour and the Sword: The Culture of Duelling* by Joseph Farrell; *The War of Wars* by Robert Harvey; *The Theatre Industry in Nineteenth-Century France* by F.W.J. Hemmings; *Voices of the People in Nineteenth-Century France* by David Hopkin; *The French Cavalry: 1792–1815* by David Johnson; *Russia Against Napoleon* by Dominic Lieven; *Clothing the Poor in Nineteenth-Century England* by Vivienne Richmond; *Secret Service: British Agents in France, 1792–1815* by Elizabeth Sparrow; *War and Peace* by Leo Tolstoy; *Behind Closed Doors: At Home in Georgian England* by Amanda Vickery; *The Diary of a Napoleonic Foot Soldier* by Jakob Walter; and last but not least, *Napoleon* by Adam Zamoyski.

Read all my published novels and wanting more? Seek out my Kickstarter-funded digital novellas *The March* (a follow-on from *The Forgotten Legion*), and *Eagle in the Wilderness*, *Eagles in the East* and *Io, Saturnalia* (all feature Centurion Tullus of the *Eagles of Rome* trilogy). There is a stand-alone novella out there too – *Centurion of the First*, set on Hadrian's Wall in second century AD Britain. Don't own an e-reader? Simply download the free Kindle app from Amazon and read the stories on a phone, tablet or computer. [If you are not of a mind to read e-books, most of these stories are available in print and in an audiobook, *Sands of the Arena*. Order it in your local bookshop or online.]

Enjoy cycling? Google Ride and Seek (rideandseek.com); this company runs epic cycling trips (Hannibal, Napoleon, Marco Polo) that I am involved with as an historical guide.

I am a long-term supporter of the charities Combat Stress, which helps British veterans with PTSD, and Medecins Sans Frontieres (MSF), responsible for sending medical staff into disaster and war zones worldwide. I have walked Hadrian's Wall in full Roman armour twice to raise money for these causes. In 2014 I marched with two author friends from Capua to the Colosseum in Rome. A documentary about it, 'The Romani Walk' is on YouTube, and narrated by Sir Ian McKellen – Gandalf! Watch it at: tinyurl.com/h4n8h6g.

I also fundraise for Park in the Past (parkinthepast.org.uk), a community-interest company which is building a Roman marching fort near Chester in north-west England. As of autumn 2022, the partly constructed fort is open to the public.

Thanks to everyone who has contributed to the causes over the years. To continue the fundraising, I auction minor characters in my books. In *The Emperor's Spy* the characters acquired in this manner are Catherine, based on my loyal reader and fan Krystal Holmgren, who has also starred in *King* and two of my novella-length Kickstarter novellas, and François, aka Bruce Phillips, gentleman reader, previously encountered in *The Falling Sword, Crusader* and Kickstarter novellas. A third character, Louvel, is based on Jonathan Lowe, another star reader.

Big thanks to my wonderful editors Sam Eades and Lucy Brem, and to the whole team at Orion! You are all fab. *Dziękuję*, Magdalena Madej-Reputakowska and everyone at Znak in Poland.

Which brings me to you, my incredible readers. Your emails, and comments/messages on Facebook, Twitter and Instagram are an important part of my life, never more so than over the last couple of years. I often give away signed books and goodies and auction for charity via these media. A short review or just a rating of this book (left on Amazon, Goodreads, Waterstones.com or iTunes!) would be a real help. Historical fiction is still a shrinking market, sadly, so a moment of your time helps a great deal. *Gratias tibi ago!*

Lastly, I want to thank my children Ferdia and Pippa, who are very cool young people.

There is one other thank you as well. Always.

Ways to get in touch:

Email: ben@benkane.net

Facebook: facebook.com/benkanebooks

Twitter: @BenKaneAuthor

Instagram: benkanewrites

My website: benkane.net

Soundcloud (podcasts): soundcloud.com/user-803260618

YouTube (short documentary-style videos): tinyurl.com/y7chqhgo

CREDITS

Orion Fiction would like to thank everyone at Orion who worked on the publication of *Napoleon's Spy* in the UK. And so would Ben!

Editorial
Sam Eades
Lucy Brem
Sahil Javed

Copyeditor
Sally Partington

Proofreader
Linda Joyce

Audio
Paul Stark
Jake Alderson

Contracts
Dan Herron
Ellie Bowker
Alyx Hurst

Design
Tomás Almeida
Joanna Ridley

Editorial Management
Charlie Panayiotou
Jane Hughes
Bartley Shaw

Production
Ameenah Khan

Publicity
Frankie Banks

Marketing
Katie Moss

Sales
Jen Wilson
Esther Waters
Victoria Laws
Toluwalope Ayo-Ajala
Rachael Hum
Anna Egelstaff
Sinead White
Georgina Cutler

Finance
Nick Gibson
Jasdip Nandra
Sue Baker

Operations
Jo Jacobs
Dan Stevens

Read on for an exclusive extract of STORMCROW,
the first gripping and epic Irish Viking adventure
from *Sunday Times* bestseller Ben Kane

COMING MAY 2024

PROLOGUE

Mesmerised, I stared at the dark shape on the sand.

Just ordered by my mother to see what the previous night's storm might have sent ashore, I had disgruntledly spooned down the last of my barley porridge, thrown on my cloak and left the longhouse. There would be sea wrack, I had decided, lots of it, hard to work through for flotsam and jetsam. There would be dog whelks too, on the rocks. If my luck was in, there might be timber. Every so often, ship's cargo washed up; that too would be cause for celebration.

What I had not anticipated this gusty spring morning was a corpse.

The man lay on his back some fifty paces away, where the receding tide had left him. I wove a path in his direction, staying on the drier patches of sand, all the while my attention returning to the body. What flesh I could see was wrinkled and pale, the effects of time in the water. Bearded, fully clothed in tunic and leggings, he looked to be a Norseman, like my father Thorgil.

It could not be my father, however, because I had seen him already, sooty-faced, hard at work in his forge. It could not be my father, because he wore a silver arm ring, and there was a scabbarded sword attached to his belt. Only the wealthy afforded such jewellery and weapons.

Fascinated, for I was not allowed to handle the few swords that my father made, I went closer. I was only a little scared. Death, of animals and people, was an everyday occurrence. Not every newborn lamb survived; every autumn, we slaughtered a pig. People died too, like Rodrek the thrall, taken by a fever two years before, or our nearest neighbour, Old Inga, whom I had found dead in bed some months since. This corpse was very different. Half the top of its head was missing, sliced off by the look of it. This man had not drowned, I thought, but been slain.

Alarmed, my gaze went seaward. The water was choppy, white horses capping the waves to the horizon, but of longships there was not a sign. Relief filled me. It was not raiding season, yet stranger things had happened. I wondered uneasily if anyone would come looking for this dead man. It was unlikely, I decided. His comrades would have no idea that his body had ended up on the strand at Linn Duachaill.

Krrruk. A flutter of black wings, and a raven landed a dozen steps away. It cocked a beady eye at me, and hopped towards the corpse.

The sudden cold I felt had nothing to do with the wind.

Ravens were sacred to the god Oðin. Two of them he had, Huginn and Muninn, Thought and Memory. Flying hither and thither over the world, they returned each evening to perch on his shoulders, bringing news.

Only now did I notice the absence of gulls. Expert scavengers, they should have been here in numbers, feasting on the dead man's flesh. There were none. 'Because Oðin's bird is here,' I whispered.

If my mother had heard me, she would have boxed my ears. Irish and a devout Christian, she reviled the Norse gods. My father, though, still held faith with the beliefs of his ancestors. I did too, finding little to admire in the Christ worshippers' turn-the-other-cheek behaviour.

Krrruk. The raven hopped onto the dead man's belly. To my amazement, it did not make for his face, but the hilt of the sword. Mine, the gesture said. That was very plain, even to my thirteen-year-old eyes.

'Finn!'

We had few neighbours; the voice could not have been that of many people, but I would have known Vekel's voice anywhere. The same age as me, near enough, he was the only other boy in the immediate area. Tall, gangling, womanish, he was my best friend.

'Finn!'

'What?' I did not turn my head, but watched the raven. In between pecks at the yellow-white hilt, it appeared to be studying me. I was not sure where the courage came from to stare back, but I did.

'Did he drown?'

'No. Someone took off the top of his head.'

'And now Oðin's raven is on him? Finn, come away!' There was an unusual nervousness in Vekel's voice.

I saw the sword first, I thought stubbornly, and took a step towards the corpse.

'Finn! *Finn!*'

I hesitated. I had always been fierce tempered, and loved rough and tumble horseplay. When the chance came to battle another boy, I took it every time. Fighting came naturally to me, I did not know why. I had regular dreams of being a warrior, a painter of the wolf's tooth. In all likelihood, though, I would train as a smith like my father. Vekel was very different. Living with his grandmother, both parents dead, he was, most agreed, destined for a seiðr life, an existence entwined with magic. It wasn't just his feminine behaviour; he liked darkness, tales of Ragnarök, anything to do with the spirit world. When his uncle died, he had crept unseen from his bed and sat out all night by the grave, so, he proudly revealed afterwards, he could better commune with the shade.

The mere thought loosened my bowels. Why then, I wondered, did I not feel the same fear about possibly depriving a god's chosen bird of its prize?

Two more steps. Now I eyed the sword with naked greed. It was magnificent. The hilt seemed to be ivory, and the silver-chased scabbard ran down to an elaborately carved chape. I wanted it, more than anything in my life before.

Another step.

The raven let out a croak, and stayed where it was.

'Finn! Are you mad?'

'I saw the sword first,' I told the raven.

'What did you say?' Vekel shouted.

The bird's head cocked this way and that. Its beak clacked.

A raven could not carry a sword away, I thought. Maybe Oðin himself would come to claim it, but I doubted that. Sightings of gods were rare as hen's teeth. After the raven had eaten its fill, it would fly off, and whoever next came upon the body would take the princely blade. It might as well be mine, I decided.

Another two steps, within touching distance of corpse and bird.

Incredibly, the raven did not move.

'Let me have the sword,' I said, the words rising unbidden to my lips, 'and I swear to serve Oðin the length of my days.'

Time slowed. Vekel's cries and questions dimmed in my ears. My focus narrowed. All I saw was the raven's glossy black head, beak slightly agape. Its flint-black eyes bored into me.

My mouth dried. A pulse beat in my throat.

'Is this truly your oath?' the raven seemed to ask.

'Strike me down if I lie.' My voice, not quite broken, cracked on the last word. 'From this moment, I am Oðin's servant.'

Krrruk. Krrruk. The raven hopped off the corpse, as if to let me approach. Its head bobbed up and down; it did not fly away.

Something made me glance over my shoulder. Vekel was watching from a short distance away, and his mouth was hanging open. That reaction, from my magic-loving friend, was a spur to the last of my indecision.

'With your permission,' I said gravely to the raven, and reached down to slip off the dead man's baldric.

A little while later, I was walking the strand. The baldric was not adjustable, so the sword, by my side, reached almost to my left foot. I did not care. A quick look had revealed the blade to be every bit as magnificent as the scabbard. I felt like a giant. I did not know how long my euphoria would last, however. I suspected that upon my return my father would take the sword from me. Therefore, I decided, my search of the beach would be slow.

Vekel had not challenged the raven as I had. After a wary look at the corpse , he had come with me. He wanted every last detail. There wasn't much to it, I told him, laying out my story. Repeating the oath to Oðin, however, the magnitude of what I had done drove home.

'You did what?' Vekel's expression was a picture.

'In return for the sword, I dedicated myself to Oðin.' My cheeks were warming; said aloud now, it sounded childish. Stupid.

Vekel walked on in silence.

I glanced sidelong at my friend, expecting him to chide, or even make fun of me, but he was deep in thought. I concentrated on looking for timber, or anything of value that the tide might have delivered. I could not resist a peek over my shoulder either. The raven was gone. Gulls were quarrelling over the corpse. More circled overhead. The air of mystery had vanished.

'Of course!'

'What?' To myself, I said, do not let him tell me that Oðin will curse me unless I put the sword back.

'It's so obvious I didn't see it at first.' Vekel's thin face had lit up.

'Tell me!'

'The raven knew you were going to be there.'

'It did?'

He buffeted me with an arm. 'Oðin told him!'

All I could do was stare.

'Oðin wanted you to have the sword, so he sent the raven,' Vekel said. 'Huginn, it will have been.'

How he ascertained the god's purpose, I had no idea, still less how he knew which raven it had been. But Vekel's words held the ring of conviction, and I believed them. My father would too. My friend's manner, his behaviour, meant that many people regarded him as spirit-touched. I think it helped that there was no goði in the area, no one else associated with seiðr. Few would have the conviction to deny what Vekel said.

My hopes of keeping the blade soared.

'Look.' Vekel's arm pointed into the freshening breeze.

Great banks of cloud, black and thunderous, had gathered far out to sea.

'Another storm is coming,' I said.

'Oðin again. He has interceded with Thor to mark the occasion.'

I gave him an uneasy smile. It was incredible enough for a god to give me a sword; quite another for two deities to be involved.

'There can be only one name for you now.' Vekel's expression was solemn.

I dared not speak my mind: Sword-stealer. Corpse-thief.

'Stormcrow.'

PART ONE
AD 994

CHAPTER ONE

No one ever came looking for the corpse or his sword, and over the next four years, many things happened. The first and most significant occurrence was my mother's death in labour, birthing a third child she, narrow-hipped, should never have borne. It was a kindness that the babe, a girl, did not live out the day of its arrival in this world. The family shrank, leaving me, my younger sister Ashild, and my father. Ashild, strong-willed and capable, took over the running of the house. It was as well, for my father's heart had been broken. Despite his Norse background and my mother's Irish one, they had made a good match, and largely been content with one another.

During this time I grew, mostly upwards, but I also filled out. By seventeen, I was stocky, broad-chested and the same height as my father, who was about two fingersbreadth taller than most. I was cocky with it, not least because daily work in the smithy and on the land had seen me muscled like an ox. I was able to use an axe and shield, thanks to my father. He had long given up war, but as a young man sailed with the Dyflin Norse, his kin, raiding down the coastline and around to the kingdom of Mumhan. He rarely spoke of it, and was at first reluctant for me to learn weaponcraft. 'Better to be a smith,' he would growl. 'It's safer.' I ground him down, though, with a mixture of flattery, begging, and when it came to it, beer.

He was too busy to train me as much as I wanted, or as I suspected, had wanted me to smith, not make war for a living. War is not pretty, he would sometimes say in his cups. Better to have soot stain your hands than blood. Imagining myself a hero in one of the sagas, I paid no heed. Long after our sessions ended, I would practice the moves he taught me outside our longhouse. A training partner would have been good, but the only boys of my own age in the settlement were a neighbour's son Berghard, dim-witted since being kicked in the head by a bull, and Vekel. The latter had an aversion to weapons. It was rare indeed that I could persuade him to pick up axe and shield and stand against me.

Despite my dreams, I was no battle-ready warrior, but at least my father had not taken the sword from me, as I had first worried. I think he might have, but Vekel's account of how I had found it changed his mind. He would not teach me how to use it. Better learn from a master, or not at all, he said, adding, especially when the blade came from a god. It was hard logic, but I accepted it. I lived in hope that Vekel had been correct about the raven, and that because of it, my time would come one day. Whether it was because of these hopes, or just an innate wanderlust, I had long been eager to spread my wings and leave Linn Duachaill.

Few people except Vekel called me 'Stormcrow', but everyone had heard the story of the sword. The tale had grown with the years. There had been two ravens, one of which had guided me to it, while the other had picked up and offered part of the baldric to me. Thunder had rumbled overhead when I took hold of the weapon. Enjoying the untruths, I made no effort to dispel them.

Soon after that momentous day, Vekel went to live with a goði who had passed through Linn Duachaill from time to time. He came back after three years, a changed person. Where he had been different, he was now strange. His femininity was even more pronounced; he wore eyeliner, women's necklaces and a silver bracelet from which hung tiny silver chairs; he spoke in a high, lilting tone. Few said a mocking word or joked about his appearance. One look at his iron staff, the mark of a seer, was enough to terrify most.

I regarded him with a degree of wariness, but he was still my friend. After all, I had known him since we were snot-nosed brats. Whether it was stealing fresh-baked bread, digging trap trenches in the sand to catch fish when the tide went out, gorging on blackberries and apples, we had done it together. True, there were times we did not share – such as when he wanted to sit near graves to commune with the dead, or when I was off chasing girls – but that did not stop us being closer than kin. I had missed him sorely when he was gone, and now he had returned, his oddness was not going to stand between us. Vekel did not admit to any regrets, but even he could not hide the pleasure in his eyes the first time we met. He sought me out each day as well, gladdening my heart further.

One bright morning, I was preparing to go and check on our cattle. In winter we kept them close to home, where it was easy to see when one sickened, or wolves were after the calves, but in summertime we grazed the kine a good distance away. Many days could pass without seeing them. I had been putting off the task, as if it would somehow get done regardless, but in the end, I had to go. The slave minding the cattle could not booley them on his own.

I took the blanket from my bed, which, with Ashild's and my father's, were situated at one end of the longhouse. Our home was one of the few structures still occupied in Linn Duachaill. The Norse had largely abandoned the settlement half a century before, decamping to Dyflin, but some families had stayed. My father's had been one of them. Some might have found it strange to live in what felt at times like a ghost village, but it was all I had ever known. Empty longhouses held no fear for me.

'How many nights will you be gone?' Ashild was busy at the fire, stirring something in a pot. Smoke trickled up to the vent hole in the thatch overhead.

'One, maybe two.' I rolled up the blanket and tied it with leather thongs. 'Have you food for me?'

'When have I ever let you go unfed, brother?'

'In truth, I cannot remember.' At times I had to remind myself that Ashild was only fifteen, because she had the carriage and assuredness of a woman ten years older. Only a little shorter than I, she had dark red hair like my own, keeping hers concealed under a linen cap.

She held out a cloth-wrapped bundle. 'You should have enough bread and cheese there, if you are not too greedy.'

'I cannot help it if I am always hungry.' I hefted the bundle, pleased by its weight.

'Leave some for the herdsman.' This was our only slave, whose job it was mind the cattle at pasture.

'Is there enough for me too?' Vekel had entered unseen.

'I do not have to feed you also.' Ashild's sense of humour was acerbic.

'Don't be like that,' he said, slipping an arm around her waist. 'You know how much I love your cooking.'

'Get away.' She escaped his grasp, but there was a smile on her face.

I raised the bundle. 'There is extra in here, for you, I assume.' It was common knowledge that Vekel's grandmother's cooking and baking was famously bad.

Vekel darted in and began kissing her cheeks. 'You are wondrous, Ashild.'

A snort. 'Should I be scared that a goði wants to kiss me?'

'Very,' he said, planting one more. 'I will put a spell on Cormac and steal you for my own.' Cormac, a stolid young farmer who lived nearby, was Ashild's betrothed.

'You will do no such thing.' Ashild had broken free and her forefinger was wagging in Vekel's face. 'Don't even think about it!'

'Come on,' I said to a grinning Vekel. 'We have a decent walk in front of us.'

He blew one last kiss at Ashild and joined me at the door. I paused there, whistling to Madra and Niall, my two cattle dogs, and checking I had everything ready. Food, blanket, light cloak, bow and quiver, hunting spear. A roll of old leather tied at both ends with some iron-mongery to barter with. Also hanging from my belt, crossways, my seax. An all-purpose knife, it had been made by my father. After the sword, it was my most treasured possession.

'I will pray for you. That all the cattle are safe, that you both come to no harm,' called Ashild.

Vekel made a rude noise under his breath, muttering something about the White Christ being as useful as Sleipnir, Oðin's eight-legged horse, on a steep icy slope. I also cared little for the Christian god, but there was no need for upset so I thanked her, and promised that yes, I would say a prayer for our mother at the church of Mainistir Bhuithe, a small monastery we would pass.

'I am not setting foot inside the place,' Vekel warned.

'There's not much chance of that, looking the way you do.' Although we were only going to booley cattle, Vekel had dressed as if about to perform a sacred ritual. His dress was blue, his eyeliner black. A trace of red had been added to his thin lips, round his neck hung a woman's glass bead necklace. On his belt was a leather skin-bag, inside which would the talismans needful for the practising of seiðr. Hairy calf-skin shoes adorned his feet, the laces of which ended in copper lattens. I thought he entirely looked the part.

He linked his arm with mine, as if we were a courting couple about to take a stroll. 'I shall wait outside and scare off anyone planning to enter the church.'

'No. You can buy honey while I'm praying.' The monastery's bee farm was famous.

Bickering the way old friends can, we went to the forge. My father's dog, a huge wolfhound appropriately named Cú, was sprawled, shaggy grey-haired, at the entrance. He paid my dogs no attention, but his tail thumped the ground at me.

My father looked up from his anvil, where he was beating out a rim for a wagon wheel. 'On your way?'

'Aye.'

'Don't forget a drop of mead.' The monastery's produce was tastier than his own homebrewed ale, and stronger with it.

'I won't.' My attention went past him, seeing the sword on his workbench. It normally lived in the longhouse, under my bed. 'You remembered,' I said, pleased.

A grunt. 'I'll take a look at it when I'm done with this rim.'

Despite the oiled wool inside the sheath, the sword's immersion in the sea had seen some salt damage. I had scrubbed it clean with sand, but tiny pits remained. I had had to oil it well ever since. I checked it regularly for rust spots too, and had mentioned this the previous evening. My father must have fetched it when I went for my daily walk along the strand; that had been a habit come rain or shine since finding the blade.

'Thank you,' I said, wondering if I might finally persuade him to instruct me in its use. If I would ever become a renowned warrior.

The sun shone as we set out. I waved at the few neighbours who were about; they responded, but cast wary looks at Vekel. He saw me scowl.

'They're scared, I know, but they come to me regardless. If they're sick, or going out in a boat to fish, or worried about the harvest.' A knowing chuckle. 'Or like yesterday, when they want to curse someone.'

'Who was that?' I demanded. Linn Duachaill and the land around had a population of a couple of hundred, no more. I knew everyone, to see at least.

A long-nailed finger touched his nose. 'That is between me and the spirits.' When I tutted, he said, 'If I told you, the seiðr would not work.'

I spent the first portion of our journey wondering who in the settlement hated someone enough have a curse laid on them. I asked Vekel twice more, but he ignored me, humming to himself, and calling Madra and Niall to have their ears rubbed.

'I do like that your father's dog is called "Hound", and one of yours is called "Dog",' he said eventually.

It was impossible to stay annoyed with Vekel for long. I chuckled.

'It's risky calling the one "Niall", don't you think?'

The Uí Néills were the supreme rulers of Midhe, the area we lived in. We owed allegiance to a smaller king, but also to the head of the Uí Néills. The men of the clan were known as 'the sons of Niall', after the dynasty's progenitor, and thanks to their overbearing attitude, universally disliked.

'What are the chances of an Uí Néill ever hearing me call the dog?' I countered.

'Someone else might tell them.'

'He's four years old and it hasn't happened yet,' I replied with the confidence of youth.

We made good time, bright sunshine gilding the green, rolling landscape. There was little forest, it having been cut down so the ground could be cultivated. At farm after farm, dogs barked challenges, but rarely came close. The dwelling houses were small, one-room thatched affairs, surrounded by fields of oats and barley and hurdle-fenced areas for cattle. There were also raths, circular earthen banks with a single gate, and animal enclosures within. The name was deceptive, because none of these fortlike structures had enough men for defence. The raths' primary purpose was to keep livestock safe from night-time raids by wolves.

Half the morning's walk from Linn Duachaill, we came upon Mainistir Bhuithe. Set in in a hollow, the monastery had been founded centuries before by Saint Buite. Its main street and twenty-odd buildings, and after that, the round tower, church and cloister buildings, meant it was the largest settlement I knew.

Five or six spear casts from the first houses, I called in Madra and Niall and looped a rope around both their necks. Otherwise they were wont to chase hens or scavenge from the tanner's premises, both of which might elicit a violent response.

By rights we should have booleyed the cattle first and visited the monastery later, but I was tired and thirsty. A sup of ale or mead, or both, was too appealing to pass up. Unsurprisingly, Vekel agreed. We beat an eager path to the brewery, situated among the monastery buildings. No one paid me any heed, a youth in yellow tunic and dun breeks with a couple of dogs. Vekel was a different matter. His outlandish array, not to mention the outrageous swagger of his hips, positively demanded attention.

People crossed themselves as we went by, and at least one housewife retreated into her house and slammed the door. A greybeard dropped his walking stick and almost fell over, so frightened was he. When I stopped at the bakery to buy a loaf – Ashild's supplies would not last us, for we both ate like horses – the serving girl would barely look at me, let alone Vekel. He, loving the effect, kept asking her questions. I told him to let her alone, and he just laughed. 'You will have a babe ere the winter,' he declared, leaving her open-jawed behind us.

'How did you know that?' I hissed. I would not have guessed in a hundred years.

'Seiðr.'

I dunted him with an elbow. 'What else?'

He leaned in close. 'Now and again, she rubbed her stomach gently–'

'–in the manner of a woman who's carrying a child,' I said, finishing.

'Just so.'

I shook my head, wondering how much of Vekel's seiðr was related to his acuity of vision.

The monk in charge of the brewery didn't bat an eyelid at either of us. In the main, I suspect it was because he was drunk. This was his usual state; whether he had been like it before, or had acquired a taste for his own produce after taking the job, I had no idea. Red-nosed, whiskerier than monks were supposed to be, his brown robe stain-spattered from neck to ankle, he was an amiable sort.

'There you are,' he announced from behind the taproom's rough wooden counter. It was as if he'd been expecting us, but was also suitable greeting when you didn't know, or couldn't remember, someone's name.

'Greetings, brother,' I said respectfully. Thanks to my mother, I was fluent in Irish.

Vekel inclined his head.

'The blessings of God upon you both.' Vekel arched an eyebrow; unabashed, the monk continued, 'You are both thirsty on a warm day like this.'

'Parched,' I said. 'Beer for both of us.'

The monk dipped a wooden tankard into a barrel, then a second. Liquid spilled as he unceremoniously plonked them down on the counter. 'Come far?'

There weren't many other customers, but I sensed all of their attention.

I had nothing to hide. Downing half the beer, I belched and said, 'Linn Duachaill.'

'Any news?'

'Nothing much.' I drank off the rest of the beer. 'Another, if you will.'

Vekel placed his tankard beside mine. 'And for me. It's good.' Like most people at Linn Duachaill, he also spoke Irish.

The monk gave us refills, and without being asked, produced a wooden bowl of water for Madra and Niall.

'My father's fond of your mead,' I said. 'If you could set aside a small barrel, I'll call in for it on the way back from booleying the cattle.'

He blinked. 'Ah, yes – the smith from Linn Duachaill! Thorgil, was it?'

'That's right.'

A brown-pegged smile. 'He likes a drop or two.'

'He does.' Sadness tugged at me. Since my mother's death, my father took himself here on occasion. According to our neighbour Ingolf, also fond of a tipple, my father would drink until he fell down, sleeping on the floor and starting afresh the following day.

'Another?' The monk reached for my tankard.

My appetite soured, I said, 'No. Maybe later, when I come for the mead.'

Vekel was put out not to have a third – he liked his beer – but did not argue when I chided him about our primary task. 'Trying to move kine when pissed is never a good idea. We'll be back before you know it.'

'Very well.' He clicked his tongue. 'Madra, Niall, time to earn your crust.'

The dogs leaped up. Rather than pet either, my eye went to a short man further along the counter. Clad in farmers' clothes like everyone else, he had a sharp, stoat-like face.

'Niall, is that your dog's name?' he asked.

My heart lurched. I wanted to slap Vekel. Of all the places to say his name out loud, this was the worst. Caught flat-footed, I struggled for an answer.

Vekel, bless him, leaped in. 'The beer, it's already affecting me. Njal, he is called. Njal. My friend here is half a Norseman, see.'

Stoat Face didn't look as if he believed it, but the warning rattle of Vekel's bracelets and the meaningful way he lifted his staff made sure that he didn't say so. With his gaze heavy on our backs, we walked out of the taproom, the red-nosed monk telling us to return soon.

'I'm sorry,' Vekel said the instant we were alone. 'I'm so stupid – and after what I said earlier!'

'It's of no matter,' I said lightly, telling myself nothing would come of it.

The cattle were grazing the slopes of a nearby hill, common land that overlooked the Bóinne River. As always, I searched along the distant bank for the sacred and mysterious site of Sí an Bhrú. I knew the spot where it lay, although it was not visible until one was much closer. The massive circular mound had been built untold centuries before, by whom no one knew. Christians and pagans alike revered it, however. As Vekel said, a man would have be a corpse not to feel the seiðr there. He said we should visit it at Samhain, the night when the dead walked the land, and I told him to go on his own. 'A frost giant could not drag me there at that time,' I swore, and meant it.

I knew our shaggy, brown, black and red beasts from other stock by the cut in their right ears. The herdsman, a slave, was with them. We greeted each other warmly. He had belonged to the family since before I was born, and my father treated him well, which was why he could be off minding the cattle on his own. Wolves roamed the area, but there were stone enclosures where he could take the cattle at night.

With his and the dogs' help we cut the twenty-four beasts out, and set off for the fresher pasture, common land some distance to the east. It was still bright by the time we were done. It was good to stand and watch them graze.

'This will do until after the harvest, maybe,' I said. The slave grinned and bobbed his head as I shared my food with him.

'I am for the monastery. To be more exact, the taproom.' Vekel set off without a backward glance.

'We need to be careful,' I warned. 'Especially if Stoat Face is about.'

'I'll soon scare the living daylights out of him.' Vekel his staff forward.

'It might not be the best idea to do that near the monastery.' I did not want to spell it out further. Goðis and vitkis, sorcerers, were feared and respected, but they were also loathed by many. It wasn't unknown for a whipped-up mob to lynch or murder a goði.

'All right,' Vekel said. 'If he is still there, we shall find a quiet spot outside the settlement to sleep. But if not, I see no reason not to pass an enjoyable evening in each other's company.'

'I'll drink to that!' I raised an imaginary tankard, and laughing, he did the same.

THE LIONHEART SERIES

MADE IN BATTLE. FORGED IN WAR.

'A rip-roaring epic, filled with arrows and spattered with blood'
Paul Finch

'Deeply authoritative'
Simon Scarrow

THE
CLASH OF EMPIRES
SERIES

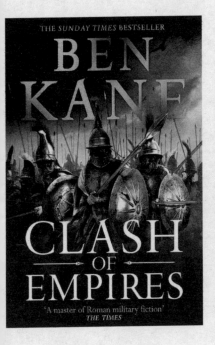

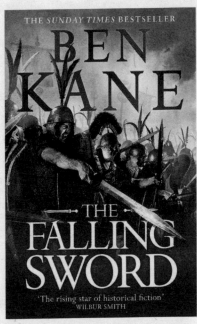

Can Greece resist the might of Rome?

The final showdown between two great civilisations begins . . .

'A triumph!'
Harry Sidebottom

'Fans of battle-heavy historical fiction will, justly, adore Clash of Empires'
The Times

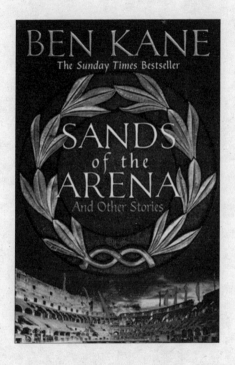